Praise for *The Book of Dirt*

'An immense work of love and anger,
a book Bram Presser was born to write.'

JOAN LONDON

'Working in the wake of writers like Modiano and Safran Foer, Presser brilliantly shows how fresh facts can derail old truths, how fiction can amplify memory. A smart and tender meditation on who we become when we attempt to survive survival.'

MIREILLE JUCHAU

'*The Book of Dirt* is a grandson's tender act of devotion, the product of a quest to rescue family voices from the silence, to bear witness, drawing on legend, journey and history, and shaped by extraordinary storytelling.'

ARNOLD ZABLE

'A beautiful literary mind.'

A.S. PATRIĆ

'In *The Book of Dirt* the fractured lines of memory create a gripping story of survival and love.'

LEAH KAMINSKY

'An impressive and captivating story of remembrance, a journey into the past for the sake of deciphering our present.'

DAŠA DRNDIĆ

Bram Presser was born in Melbourne in 1976. His stories have appeared in *Best Australian Stories*, *Award Winning Australian Writing*, *The Sleepers Almanac* and *Higher Arc*. *The Book of Dirt* is his first novel.

brampresser.com

BRAM PRESSER

TEXT PUBLISHING MELBOURNE AUSTRALIA

textpublishing.com.au

The Text Publishing Company
Swann House
22 William Street
Melbourne Victoria 3000
Australia

Published by The Text Publishing Company 2017
Reprinted 2017, 2018

Cover design by W. H. Chong
Page design by Jessica Horrocks
Maps by Simon Barnard
Typeset by J&M Typesetting

Printed in Australia by Griffin Press, an Accredited ISO AS/NZS 14001:2004 Environmental Management System printer.

The publishers gratefully acknowledge permission from Penguin Random House UK to reproduce the front cover image of *The Trial* by Franz Kafka (1953) on p.61

National Library of Australia Cataloguing-in-Publication entry
Creator: Presser, Bram, author.
Title: The book of dirt / by Bram Presser.
ISBN: 9781925240269 (paperback)
ISBN: 9781922253071 (ebook)
Subjects: Jews—Europe—Biography—Fiction.
Jewish families—Biography—Fiction.
Holocaust survivors—Europe—Biography—Fiction.
Holocaust, Jewish (1939-1945)—Fiction.
Biographical fiction.

This book is printed on paper certified against the Forest Stewardship Council® Standards. Griffin Press holds FSC chain-of-custody certification SGS-COC-005088. FSC promotes environmentally responsible, socially beneficial and economically viable management of the world's forests.

For Debbie and Dari

We're constantly correcting, and correcting ourselves, most rigorously because we recognise at every moment that we did it all wrong (wrote it, thought it, made it all wrong), acted all wrong, how we acted all wrong, that everything to this point in time is a falsification, so we correct this falsification, and then we again correct the correction of this falsification, and we correct the result of the correction of a correction and so forth…

Thomas Bernhard, *Correction*

Contents

CAST OF CHARACTERS

BISKUPSKÁ STREET

Jakub Rand—a teacher, my grandfather

Rabbi Aharon Rand—his father

Gusta Randová—his mother

Růženka Randová—his sister

Hermann Rand—his brother

Shmuel Rand—his brother

BISKUPCOVA STREET

Františka Roubíčková—a milliner

Ludvík Roubíček—her husband

Daša (Dagmar) Roubíčková—their daughter, my grandmother

Irena Roubíčková—their daughter

Marcela Roubíčková—their daughter

Hana Roubíčková—their daughter

Papa Roubíček—Ludvík's father

Mama Roubíčková—Ludvík's mother

Emílie—Františka's sister

Jiří B—a businessman

Ottla B—his wife

Bohuš B—their son

Žofie Sláviková—a shopkeeper

Štěpánka Tičková—a tattletale

Jáchym Nemec—a busybody

Marie Moravcová—a Red Cross volunteer

Alois Moravec—her husband

Ata Moravec—their son

WORKERS OF THE PRAGUE JEWISH COMMUNITY

Jiří Langer—a teacher and writer

Otto Muneles—an undertaker, head of the Jewish Burial Society (*Chevra Kadisha*)

Georg Glanzberg—a teacher, Jakub's friend

Professor Leopold Glanzberg—his father

Berta Glanzbergová—his mother

Tobias Jakobovits—Jewish community librarian, school principal and wartime Specialist Head of the Central Jewish Museum

Dr Emil Kafka—head of the Jewish Religious Council of Prague

Gonda Redlich—a youth leader

Fredy Hirsch—a youth leader

STUDENTS OF THE JÁCHYMOVA JEWISH SCHOOL

Arnošt Flusser

Hana Ginzová

František Brichta

Kurt Herschmann

Kurt Diamant

Markéta Fischerová

Frederick Fantl

Marta Kleinová

OTHER CHARACTERS

Pan Durák—a businessman

Paní Duráková—his wife

Anděl Richter—a canny restaurateur

Gisela Diamontová—a seamstress

Otakar Svoboda—a school photographer

Avram Becher—an art dealer

Yitzik Berenhauer—an artist

Magda—a block warden in Theresienstadt

Benjamin Murmelstein—the last camp elder in Theresienstadt

Isaac Leo Seeligman—a scholar

Rabbi František Gottschal—a scholar

Josef Eckstein—a scholar

Franz Weiss—a carpenter and labourer

Michal—a prisoner in Birkenau

Arno Böhm—a criminal and camp elder in Birkenau

Büntrock—a Kapo in Birkenau

Tadeusz—a Kapo in Birkenau

PRESENT DAY CHARACTERS

Ludvík K—Hana's son, my mother's cousin

Uncle Pavel—Irena's husband, my great-uncle

Věra Obler—a survivor and archivist at Beit Terezín

Ruti—an archivist at Yad Vashem

Maria—a resident of the town of Terezín

Ze'ev Shek—survivor, founder of Beit Terezin, diplomat

Alisa Shek—survivor, archivist

Within a few generations almost all
of us will have been forgotten. Those who
are not will have no bearing on how we are
remembered, who we once were. We will not
be there to protest, to correct. In the end we
might exist only as a prop in someone else's
story: a plot device, a *golem*.

In the Beginning an Exodus

In the region of T, not far from the city of U, there once stood a village that had been in Poland, then Hungary, then Subcarpathian Ruthenia, then Czechoslovakia, then Slovakia, then Hungary again, then the Union of Soviet Socialist Republics, then the Ukraine and now cannot be found on any map. This village, satellite to a satellite, changed hands like a crumbling heirloom, each time losing a part of its essence, until one day it ceased to exist. Even its name is forgotten, for nobody is left to lament it. In its place now there might be a field, or forest, although no animal would dare roam there. Or perhaps God, in His infinite wisdom, erased that tract of land, so the world might be smaller and less full of sorrow.

In the beginning, God etched a natural border along the outskirts of what would become this village: a wide river that flowed gently for most of the year, until *Elul* and *Tishrei*, as its people would know those months, when it raged with what they took to be righteous anger. For centuries the river served to keep the village-folk to themselves. They did not look across the water, nor did they wonder what lay beyond the trees on the opposite bank. God had given them their land and it was enough. But the natural order was destroyed when the king, drunk on hubris, commanded his stonemasons to cross the river so that his empire might expand. The most skilled men in the land came from the forest with their horses and carts and tools and set about their work.

The village-folk watched on in awe, thanking the God of Abraham, Isaac and Jacob for the creation unfolding before them. When the bridge was finished, the village-folk sent out a party to see what lay on the other side. The three men walked across the cobbled deck and through the line of trees that had once marked the end of their world, only to find another village.

In time, the two villages—one predominantly Jewish, the other predominantly Jew-fearing—came to share a common market, crucial to both for their survival. Depending on where the greater power lay—royal families, landed gentry or municipal councils—the market shifted from one side of the bridge to the other, so that the lowest monthly tithes could be paid when the collectors rode in to take what by rights was not theirs. And so it was that the village-folk would hesitantly welcome the traders from the other side of the bridge, and at other times those traders would begrudgingly welcome the village-folk, and they would put their differences aside, if only for the morning.

'It is because God sighed on our village,' said Mottel D, who would later choke on poisonous gas, the jagged fingernails of those desperate to climb over him digging into his back, but who is, for now, a teacher of schoolchildren. He was pointing at the sagging thatched roof of the *shtibl* where older men went to pray when called by the *shammas.* The children giggled, savouring the thought that God might take time out of His busy schedule to check on their insignificant home. How could He not be moved, Mottel wondered, by the devotion of these people in their simple clothes, who spent as much time praising Him as they did trying to feed their families?

Mottel liked to tell stories and the children liked to listen. 'Beware the bridge,' he would say when the border shifted to the other shore. 'Under it lies a *dybbuk,* who would just as soon eat you as one of Reb Shlomo's sweet buns.' Many in the village believed in the *dybbuk* under the bridge and blamed it for the misfortunes that befell them. Crop failures. Stillbirths.

Disappearances. Those who doubted came to believe when Lazar V, who was only trying to take his wares to the market on the other side, was swept over the railing in a freak storm, never to be seen again. Which is why each year for *tashlich*, as the village-folk went to cast their sins into the water, they would make sure to do so downstream lest the *dybbuk* find in their time of melancholy and repentance a reason to rejoice.

Across the bridge, it was the same. 'They hide there and will snatch you and use your blood to bake their bread,' said Karel T, who would later stand guard on a concentration camp watchtower, but for now was also a teacher of schoolchildren. He had read a case in which there was incontrovertible proof that a young Christian child had been killed and her blood used for their dirty ritual. And what a great shame it was that their esteemed President, Tomáš Garrigue Masaryk, had besmirched his reputation defending these heathen murderers. Sure, thought Karel, it was fine to trade with them, and for the most part they kept to themselves, but it was still best to warn the children not to go near the bridge alone because no matter how nice they might seem at the market, you never really could trust a Jew.

Back in the Jewish village, the women gathered around the well to listen to the wet nurse Barbora D, who would later die standing over a ditch, staring down at her shrivelled breasts, embarrassed, counting the bodies of the children she had suckled, but who was, for now, the source of all gossip. She was welcome in most homes on this side of the river and knew their secrets. 'They say *dybbuk*, but I know better.' Barbora had not forgotten a certain child brought into this world, a boy, who was not right and who, according to his parents, failed to come home one day. Nor did she fail to notice that at *tashlich* these parents would stand at the very end of the line, upstream from the bridge, and empty their pockets, which contained, unlike the crumbs that fell from the pockets of most other people, large chunks of bread and, if Barbora was not mistaken, meat and sweets.

'Let's see what horrors our people have caused this week,' said Jakub R, the rabbi's son, who will die peacefully, hours after sucking on a wet ball of cotton, but who is now making mischief. He opened the paper and showed the article to his brother Hermann, of unknown fate, pointing at the smudged ink. It was unusual for boys on this side of the bridge to read the papers brought in on the back of Mikuláš K's cart. They were expected to devote their time to studying the *Torah* in *cheder* or learning a trade, not wasting it on the frivolities of an irrelevant world. As Reb Shimon T, the blacksmith who would die covered in blood and shit in the back of a cattle train, liked to say, 'A horse doesn't shoe itself.' However, young Jakub was different. Each fortnight, when the pedlar passed through the market, Jakub would secretly buy a copy of the city newspaper with the few coins his mother had given him to buy bread and cheese for lunch because, he reasoned, an empty stomach might grumble but an empty head will most certainly scream. Then he would gather his brother and two friends and read the paper to them on the lower riverbank, by the bridge. 'Knowledge is their *dybbuk*,' he would often say.

Of the outsiders who regularly passed through the village, Mikuláš K was the best known and the least liked. Destined one day to swing from the gallows for treason, although it is not altogether clear against whom, he would arrive in the village each time from the north-west, walking beside his poor donkey as it dragged an overloaded cart, on which one or the other wheel was broken. He would demand a drink from the first villager he encountered, as if he had walked all the way from B, or another city. Among the village-folk it was rumoured that he was rich, that he stocked his cart with odds and ends from the backs of trucks that had dumped their loads in the forest. His books, often missing pages, or not matching the titles printed on their jackets, were always sold for a premium, as were his other assorted wares. He knew the wants of his customers, and brought for each what he was sure he could sell and nothing more. Pity the poor donkey, who would carry a greater weight on departure, for coins weigh more than paper and tin, particularly when the pedlar demanded so many for each worthless item.

Mikuláš K appeared to hate these Jews. He would rush across the bridge the moment he had done his business. But he liked Jakub R; the boy would meet him on the other side, away from the prying eyes of the village-folk. He liked bringing the latest newspaper, in which the Jews were invariably cast in a bad light, and selling it to the boy for so great a profit. Most of all he liked that Jakub was always grateful, never questioning the discrepancy between the price printed on the paper's masthead and the one he was charged.

Jakub knew that the paper could only have been popular among the city's rabble. But from it he gained perspective on his place in the world. He also learned that he had friends out there, friends in high places, like this man Masaryk, who had risked his career to help Jakub's people.

'That Jakub is trouble,' whispered Old Chava Z, who would not live to see what was to come but instead die in the drowning agony of consumption.

'Of course he is,' said Marta B. 'He is friends with the *dybbuk*.' She smiled crookedly, much as she would again when, only a few years later, she was packed into the back of a truck, where she felt the air slip away amid a symphony of crunching gravel and wretched sobs.

'And to think, our poor rabbi…' Old Chava Z trailed off into a wet cough, then nodded thoughtfully. 'With a son like that, studying in *cheder* to take his father's position…What will become of our children?'

Old Chava Z was right. She foresaw the disaster, although it did not come to pass in the way that she anticipated. When the children died in hails of bullets, or in gas chambers, or were thrown into furnaces to burn alive, Jakub R was nowhere to be found. For on the night the holy judge from the *Beth Din* was to arrive so he could sit his final rabbinical examinations, Jakub had packed his bags and fled the village along its only road, in the direction from which he often saw Mikuláš K approaching.

And so it was that he left behind those ever-changing borders, the river, the bridge, the *dybbuk*, his family and the hundred or so condemned souls whose paths were many but whose final destination was the same dark one.

One

THIS IS A BOOK of memories, some my own, some acquired and some, I suppose, imagined.

It begins with a warning: almost everyone you care about in this book is dead.

Some disappeared up chimneys in plumes of smoke that, it will later be said, frightened away the birds. Some were shot like lame dogs, without so much as a thought, let alone a care. Some starved. Some froze. Some succumbed to disease. Some threw themselves at electric fences in the desperate hope of a quick end. Some died on the battlefield, believing to their last breath in the sacred cause. Some managed to live on, escaping to distant lands where they built new lives while being chased across daybreak by ghosts until death caught up to take the pain away.

Only the scantest of details remain that might offer clues as to when or where most of these people died. Train schedules. Ship manifests. Names of places where we know some of them must have perished. Auschwitz. Treblinka. Dachau. There are, however, no dates. No graves.

Truth be told, I know little about the fates of the people in this book except this:

In the early hours of 12 December 1996, while I slept soundly at home, my grandfather, Dr Jan Randa, died at Cabrini Hospital in his adopted hometown of Melbourne, Australia. He had survived my grandmother by less than eight weeks.

This is their story.

My grandfather was born in 1911 in a village at the foot of the Carpathian Mountains. In the local parish register he is listed as Yaakov, son of Rabbi Aharon and Gusta Rand, the first of many names by which he would come to be known. As a boy, Yaakov was schooled in the rituals of the Jewish faith. He grew out his *payes*, donned *tzitzis* and would often hide beneath the billowing folds of his father's *tallis*, listening to the swirling chorus of prayers and lamentations that tumbled from the old man's lips. At nineteen, Yaakov turned his back on his family and fled the village for Prague. There, he immediately changed his name to Jakub and was soon accepted to Charles University in the Old City, where he attained a doctorate in law. It was an impressive feat for this country boy. Then, a fortnight after he graduated, the Nazis occupied the country and banned Jews from practising in the legal profession. His career was over before it had started. And so he was forced into the line of work that would come to save his life: he taught Jewish children. He taught them in Prague. He taught them in Theresienstadt. And he taught them in Auschwitz. It's how he survived. When the war was over, and he came to Australia, it's what he continued to do. He was a teacher and a survivor.

For as long as he was with us, we knew this, or something like it, to be true. We had created this version of his life for ourselves and, when he died, committed it to the kiln of memory.

To doubt is improper. That is the thing with survival: it cannot be challenged. It cannot be subjected to interrogation. And so we did not ask how a boy with no secular education, no Latin, no formal qualifications, could be accepted into Prague's most prestigious university. We did not seek details of his time in the camps. We did not question the likelihood of a school for children operating in the shadows of the crematoria. Above all, we did not dare contemplate the depths to which he might have sunk in order to survive. Every survivor is a saint. Every survivor is a hero. No survivor is merely human.

At his *shloshim*, the service to mark the thirtieth day after his death, I recounted a famous rabbinical tale that I thought best summed up my grandfather.

> *Somewhere in Eastern Europe, sometime in the late 1940s, a young student, fiery and rebellious, confronts his teacher. 'Reb Yosef,' he says, 'you teach us of God and the goodness of our people. But I have lost my faith. Not in God, no. I have lost faith in my fellow man. Gone are the days of the* tzaddikim, *the righteous men. Pardon my impertinence, Reb Yosef. I mean you no disrespect. But everywhere I look there are ordinary people, unremarkable people. And beyond them, there are only frauds. I need to find a* tzaddik. *I need the guidance of a righteous man. If one cannot be found, then I see no reason to still believe.'*
>
> *The rabbi looked at his student and could see that he was wise. 'Young Reb Yitzchok,' he replied. 'I am afraid you have been looking in the wrong place. To whom did you turn? The man who prayed the loudest in synagogue? The man who stuffed wads of notes into the charity box? Me, your teacher? I am not a* tzaddik. *None of us is. You want to know where to find the* tzaddik, *the man of pure, honourable faith? Don't look to the sky, don't search a man's eyes. Look instead at his forearm. Yes, go into synagogue tomorrow morning and look under the straps of every man's* tefillin. *If, by chance, you spot a black mark, a tattoo, numbers, then there is your* tzaddik. *There is your righteous man. For this poor soul has been to hell, has faced death while God turned away, and yet he still believes. This, young Reb Yitzchok, is the only kind of man who can still be called a* tzaddik.*'*

'That righteous man,' I went on to say, 'was my grandfather.'

I was wrong.

Like many survivors, my grandfather renounced his covenant with God immediately after the war. He had survived. Most of his family had not. He didn't waste time looking for an explanation. He didn't feel abandoned, as so many others had described it. He didn't even question how a loving God could have allowed the Holocaust to happen. His was a practical renunciation. His beliefs were sacrificed on an altar of pragmatism. On returning to Prague, he changed his name to Jan Randa—less Jewish, less Germanic—and started work as a legal clerk, supplementing his income by serving as secretary to the Chief Rabbi, Gustav Sicher.

Jan Randa continued to love the Jewish traditions, the language and, most of all, the literature, but felt he owed nothing to an abstract deity perpetuated to give meaning to things he could not explain. Anyway, he had married my grandmother, first in a civil ceremony and then later, when her childhood conversion from Catholicism could be proved, at the Altneu Synagogue. By the second wedding, she was already pregnant. No sooner had their daughter been born, and Jan Randa's legal practice begun, than she fell pregnant again. A few months after the birth of the baby, this one a son, he got word that he was wanted for questioning. His political agitation in the fledgling communist state had fallen on 'interested' ears. There was talk of labour camps, re-education. Or worse. The young family had to get out before the borders closed. He would not make the same mistake twice.

In his work for Rabbi Sicher, my grandfather corresponded with a man in Melbourne about the certification of kosher Czech pickles. In one letter he floated the idea of setting up home in that distant land and received an enthusiastic response. He was, however, unable to secure exit permits. Seeing no other option, he gathered the family and, under cover of night, paddled across the river into Germany on top of a mattress. From there he purchased four third-class tickets on the SS *Sebastiano Caboto* bound for Australia.

They arrived on 29 October 1949 and, along with several other families, were lodged by the local Jewish welfare agency in the south-eastern suburbs of Melbourne. Jan, now Jack, found work on the production line of the Ford Motor Company factory. He thought of returning to university so that he could practise law in his new homeland, but he had neither the time nor the money to do so. Within a year of starting at Ford, a chassis fell on Jack's chest and crushed his lungs. He was hospitalised for weeks. No longer fit for manual labour, he was forced to look for another job. He tracked down the pickle importer and was told of Mount Scopus College, a new Jewish school that had opened not far from where Jack and his family lived. With a heart weighed down by broken dreams, he typed up a résumé that included all his previous teaching experience and walked to the school. He was employed on the spot. From that day on, he was known as Dr Randa, Australia's foremost expert on Hebrew grammar. Or, as some liked to call him, the *Dikduk Doc*.

My grandparents kept a traditional Jewish home, although it was by no means religious. For them, the Passover *Seder* was a story of human triumph. *Yom Kippur*, the Day of Atonement, was a time to reflect on the wrongs they had done to others. Every other holiday was just another excuse for family and friends to gather and sing and feast. Jan Randa had no need for God. But that changed when I was born. God, who might perhaps exist after all, had called his bluff.

I was a sickly child from the outset: prone to infections, pallid, lethargic. The diagnosis was over a year in coming: *Patent Ductus Arteriosus. Ventricular Septal Defect.*

'A very slim chance of survival.' My mother repeated the doctor's words.

'His heart?' my grandfather said.

'Yes.'

'I'm sorry.' My grandfather mashed his fist into his palm and lowered his head. He ran to his study, closed the door and refused to come out. My parents were stunned. My grandmother went to the study door and knocked. He did not answer. She knocked again, then banged with her fists. Still nothing. Turning the knob, she pressed her shoulder against the wood and pushed. The door did not budge. He had wedged the daybed up against it. From inside, she could hear the clacking of his typewriter and the turbulent strains of Smetana's *Má Vlast.* With one last smack for good measure, and a curse from the old country, she stormed off to the TV room. He did not emerge until the next morning. While she was still sleeping, he left the house and went to synagogue. He had, it seems, resolved to make a deal. Donning his *tefillin*, those weathered phylacteries, he gazed skywards. 'God of my childhood. God of my father. You challenged me and lost. Now I challenge you. Prove you exist,' he implored. 'Save the boy!' If his survival had severed the tie between them, mine would fuse it back together.

After the operation, the surgeon made his way to the waiting room. My mother was asleep, clutching my father's arm. He nudged her awake. The surgeon smiled. Good news.

The following morning, 7 August 1978, as rain tapped out a redemptive backbeat on the roof, Jan Randa locked himself in his study and, for the first time since the war, prayed *shacharit.*

He tried his best to make sure we didn't inherit his trauma, although he struggled to navigate the diverging streams of memory and freedom that distance brought with it. When I was approaching thirteen, the age of *bar mitzvah*, he sat me down in front of the old TV in the back room of his house and made me watch Claude Lanzmann's documentary, *Shoah*, in its six-hour entirety. I wasn't to ask questions. I wasn't to look at him. Just watch and absorb. After the famous moment when the railway engineer, Henryk Gawkowski, runs his fingers across his throat, I turned to my grandfather and looked at the number on his forearm. *A-1821.* 'No,' he said and jabbed at the screen. 'Watch.'

Three years earlier, at my brother's *bar mitzvah* party, he had tried a more direct approach. Late in the evening, he took to the podium and started to speak. 'In periodic nightmares I relive this experience and awake in a cold sweat with the confusion as to what is reality and what is dream.' His words jarred in the revelry. He spoke of his best friend who should have survived in his place. 'To this very moment I have not even mentioned this to anybody. Why now? Because deep in my heart I have often wondered about my reality, since there is no rational explanation for my being alive. Why me? Why not Glanzberg?'

And then he spoke of his mother in Birkenau.

> *I remember it was June 1944. I would come out every evening to meet her. One day, towards the end of the month, I came to the meeting place and waited. She came out, but this time had tears streaming down her face, for I must have looked like death. I looked down. In my mother's hand was her daily ration which she laid out before me. I grabbed without asking and wolfed it down in one go, with a burning in my eyes. I felt like a starved animal. The next week we were called out for selections. I was chosen. My mother was not. For the last forty-six years, every night in my prayers, I have begged her for forgiveness. How could I take that one little piece of bread that meant life or death? I often see her in my nightmares, there, in the distance, and I ask, 'How could I?'*

I have watched the video over and over. His forty-five minutes were edited down to less than five. Seeing the audience wriggle uncomfortably, some going outside to smoke, others talking among themselves, I know that we weren't ready to hear it. And now that we are, we can't.

He gave up on us after only one try.

My grandfather cheated death so many times that, until the last clump of dirt was tossed over his grave, I genuinely believed he was the Messiah. He survived Auschwitz. He survived the secret police. He survived an industrial accident, prostate cancer and a botched heart bypass. In the end, my grandfather died because he chose to die. As long as my grandmother was alive he had something to live for, but once she was gone he simply gave up. She had always been his insurance policy against further tragedy after he had watched almost everyone he loved get wiped out in the Holocaust.

A vivacious young woman, Daša—my grandmother—must have represented everything he could have hoped for in his future. She had come through the camps but was still young enough to build a life away from them. Her Aryan looks, a life-saving gift from her mother, would protect him and his children from further tides of prejudice. His children would not be stopped on the street, hit or spat upon. They would not know what he had known. I am told that he was certain from the beginning that she was the girl for him. Daša, on the other hand, took some convincing. When she was in hospital towards the end of her life, I sat down and asked why she chose him.

'He was not a wolf,' she said. 'And I saw the way he treated his mother. Any man who treats his mother like that...I could see he will make a good husband.'

This is what she didn't tell me: my grandfather was not her first choice. There was another man. He wasn't Jewish; she didn't care. After my grandmother died, I was given a photo of them that her youngest sister, Hana, had kept. It could almost be a stock photo, the sort you see behind the glass in a frame when you first buy it, a suggestion of what you might put in its place. Daša looks to be around twenty. Beside her is a dapper young man in a heavy grey trench coat. The two are walking along Národní Street, near the National Theatre. He is tall and holds himself with pride. She is smiling, a young girl in love.

Soon after the photo was taken, the man broke off their romance to take up with a non-Jewish society type. Daša was heartbroken. She saw in that man what her soon-to-be husband saw in her—a future far removed from the horrors she had just survived. She hid away at her mother's apartment in the Žižkov district of Prague. Every few days my grandfather would visit and try to coax her from her torpor. He brought flowers, jewellery, little cakes, none of which he could really afford. It soon became ritual, a way to escape the silence of an empty house. He had no one. Only her. But she was not interested. Each time he knocked on their door, her mother and three younger sisters would welcome him with affection and a tinge of pity. I suspect one or two of the girls fancied him for themselves.

My grandfather would not be swayed. He met his love in Theresienstadt and took an instant shine to her. He knew she would grow to be a beautiful woman, but at the time she was too young, only a teenager. Nothing could come of it. But I imagine he fantasised about her, dreamed of the two of them, free and well fed in the open fields, surrounded by three—no, five—children. Far from the teeming ghetto where sewage slopped over the ditches and brown-uniformed soldiers hit you in the head with the butts of their rifles.

My grandmother had no such dreams. When she returned to Prague in 1945, she tried to distance herself from anything that might remind her of the camps. That included my grandfather. She was irritated by his presence. Why must he come, wrapped in memories of barbed wire, dysentery and Zyklon B, to vie for her hand? She had found love. Until it abandoned her. Then, one particular memory resurfaced: my grandfather, standing with his mother at the platform in Theresienstadt. She was there too, watching their quiet farewell.

Any man who treats his mother like that...I could see he will make a good husband.

They married in 1947 when Daša was twenty-one and Jan was thirty-five. He saw those fourteen years as a guarantee that he would die before her. For many years, things went according to his plan. He was always sick, often in hospital. She, on the other hand, stayed healthy while smoking two packets of cigarettes a day. In her sixty-eighth year, she went to the doctor complaining of stomach pains. She was diagnosed with stomach ulcers and told to stick to a bland diet. The pain continued. By the time they opened her up to have a look, it was too late. They removed the cancer, and her stomach for good measure, which bought her six months. As she grew frail, she boasted that she would soon be skinny enough for the catwalks of Milan.

Twenty-second September 1996. The eve of *Yom Kippur*. While my brother and I raced to get to the hospital to be with her in her final moments, my father was trying to get Jan to come. He refused. He must have known he was about to witness one last tragedy. She was already dead when he was wheeled in. He began talking to her, clutching her still-warm hand. When she didn't answer, he looked up at us. 'Is she gone?' he whispered. My mother nodded and put her arm around his shoulder. '*Baruch dayan ha'emet*,' he said. *Blessed is the true judge*. And with that Jan Randa sank into his wheelchair, into himself, and resolved to die.

It wasn't much at first, a light cough. Then we got a call from a nurse at his aged-care home that he had been admitted to hospital. He could barely breathe and had been refusing to eat for days. His stubborn march towards the grave lasted less than a week. I tried to keep him hydrated, wetting a cotton bud and sticking it in his mouth. Then he died.

I kept only one thing of his, a 1953 Penguin edition of *The Trial*, by Franz Kafka. He had left it face down beside his typewriter. I often hold it and think of him.

For nearly ten years our collective memory of who he once had been rested undisturbed. He was the kindly, learned man we loved and revered. *A man of worth, a teacher of generations.* Photos found their way into frames on our dressers and walls. In our old family home, he was a greater presence in death than he had been in life. The peaked cap, the tortoiseshell glasses, the pipe. When we visited his grave we found comfort in the ever-growing pile of stones that his former students had left as marks of respect.

Then he appeared again, except it wasn't him. Resurrected in 2005, in black ink on the pages of the *Australian Jewish News*, this man with my grandfather's face, my grandfather's name, had a different story.

DR JACOB RANDA AND THE BOOKS
OF THE EXTINCT RACE

It was called Hitler's Gift To The Jews. Theresienstadt, a concentration camp like no other, a self-governing Jewish town, only one hour's train ride from Prague. Behind its fortress walls was gathered the entire Jewish population of Czechoslovakia, struggling to survive in terrible conditions, busily passing the days until they were sent on a train to their deaths in the East. Many stories have been written about this unique town but one has remained untold until today: that of our very own Dr Jacob Randa.

Born in Brno and raised in Prague, Dr Randa came of age just as the Nazis conquered his homeland. Like all Jews he felt the German noose constrict around his neck; forced to wear a yellow star, excluded from normal life, he was rendered an exile in his own city. In late 1942, he received his summons and, along with his mother and brother, was transported to Theresienstadt.

Soon after Dr Randa arrived in the camp, he found his name on a list of one hundred scholars, rabbis and academics summoned to the camp's German headquarters for special questioning. They waited outside in a large group and were called one by one to a cramped office in the back of the building where a German officer, wearing a crisp uniform and with a monocle screwed into his eye, sat at a desk. The officer stated his name and rank—he was an SS Obersturmführer—and explained that he had been a professor of Jewish studies in a German university before the war. He then subjected Dr Randa to a most peculiar examination, asking him to look over a pile of Jewish books and explain their significance. Dr Randa did so, noting all the while that the books were stamped with the names of libraries across the Occupied lands: *Amsterdam, Warsaw, Budapest, Vienna.*

When the officer's inquisition was over, he excused the young man and had him escorted from the room by an SS guard. Dr Randa was sternly forbidden from discussing what had happened in the office until day's end. That night, one hundred scholars crammed into the camp library to compare their experiences. Some had been curtly dismissed almost immediately after having entered. Some, like Dr Randa, were grilled for what felt like an eternity. A strange game was afoot, and Dr Randa sensed that it had a sinister edge. He didn't have to wait long to find out.

The following day, the Jews who had been interviewed were divided into two groups and loaded into trucks. The first truck disappeared into the Czech countryside, while the other truck, carrying Dr Randa and about forty others, headed in the direction of Prague. Only when they stopped did Dr Randa realise where he had been taken: the grand, gothic entrance to the Prague Museum. The scholars were unloaded and made to wait in a large hall from where, once again, they were summoned one by one into an adjoining room. Stepping inside, Dr Randa saw the same SS Obersturmführer waiting for him, a large collection of books spread out on his desk. 'Sort these into groups however you feel is appropriate,' the officer commanded him.

When Dr Randa had finished, the SS Obersturmführer looked over the desk and nodded with approval. 'Very good.

You will remain here and be issued with special privileges that even the elder of Theresienstadt cannot imagine. You will be joined soon by three others and your work will begin.' Before dismissing him, the officer sat back down and said gravely, 'Don't get any ideas. You are still a prisoner.'

Dr Randa was shown to a cold room in the basement of the museum in which two bunk beds had been erected. The SS guard gave him his pass and told him he no longer needed to wear the yellow star. 'You may travel between here, the bathroom, the kitchen and your office. Everywhere else is off limits.'

The next morning he awoke to find three others in the room: Dr Eppstein was an antiques dealer, Dr Muneles, a museum curator, was an expert in Jewish calligraphy and illuminated manuscripts, and Dr Murmelstein, a former rabbi from Vienna, was a celebrated authority on Jewish ritual artefacts. They were the only men who remained of the hundred who had first been summoned. They had been selected, by order of the Führer himself, to put together a special catalogue of Jewish life and culture that would be turned into a grand display when the war was over. It would be called The Museum of the Extinct Race.

Each morning for the next two years, the men were separated, taken to a room filled with their respective type of artefacts, and forced to sort through the Nazi plunder. They met at night to discuss their progress. For the most part it was dull, laborious work but occasionally they would come across a book, a curio, a *Torah* scroll of immense beauty, a true treasure. They would describe it to one another with the wide-eyed wonder of cultural archaeologists. Eppstein even found his father-in-law's Chanukah candelabra. He recognised the inscription. That night, as he told the others of his family, he broke down in tears for what he had lost.

One after the other, Dr Randa's colleagues disappeared —first Eppstein, then Muneles and, finally, Murmelstein— until only he was left in the museum. By then the building had become as much a prison as Theresienstadt. He had never even had the opportunity to look out the window and see the streets of his beloved city of Prague. His solitude didn't last long. The work was deemed complete and he was deported to Auschwitz.

There is no documentary evidence, nothing about how it was set up or who was involved. It is all hearsay. And yet the Museum of the Extinct Race has become the central pillar of the collective Czech memory. *Hitler planned a museum to commemorate his greatest achievement: the total annihilation of European Jewry.*

It is what sets the Czech wartime experience apart from all the others—a ghoulish spectre from an alternative past, haunting the Jewish imagination. Just as this Dr Jacob Randa, who might have been my grandfather, now haunts mine.

His former students approached me in the street, wanting to talk, wanting to ask if I had known. I was forced to wear the story like an old coat, all the while digging through its pockets for clues, anything that might have given me cause to doubt.

There is one clue, from when I was ten years old, that I return to again and again.

The garden bed lay at the far end of my grandmother's backyard orchard, behind the fig tree. Like all the other beds, it was framed with dry wooden planks, but the dirt inside was unturned, untended. When I asked my grandmother why it had been left alone, while everything around it flourished, she either pretended not to hear me or said, 'That one isn't mine.'

At first I just heard him. A soft, melodious humming. I was old enough to know that the tune had its roots in another country, another world. There was also the occasional word, breathed rather than spoken. I sneaked past the fig tree and there he was, sitting in that lonely garden bed, his back to me, legs crossed. He was running his finger through the soil as if to plough it, but in a circular motion. I stood silent. There sat a man, always so impeccably clean, often to the point of vanity, now in scruffy clothes, covered in dirt. This was not the grandfather I knew.

His humming grew louder and, I thought, more joyous. It rose to a crescendo, but then descended to the doleful tone I had first heard. He rubbed out the tracks his fingers had made and fell silent. I ducked behind one of the trees, but I needn't have bothered. He didn't look up, simply resumed his singing, words this time, in what must once have been a beautiful voice. I recognised some of the words from the beginning of every Jewish prayer, blessing God, king of the world.

I leaned forward, trying to decipher the rest of the prayer. Without warning, he thrust his hand into the ground, pulled out a clump of dirt and, holding it to the sky, cried out. I stumbled backwards, fell over the mess of broken branches at my feet. My grandfather spun around and looked at me, tears streaming down his face. I will never forget that look of fear and sadness. As if I'd just tripped over his soul.

How many lives does the Lord bestow upon one man?

If I had only known Yaakov, son of Rabbi Aharon and Gusta Rand, who fled his village at the foot of the Carpathian Mountains in search of a greater life/

it would have been enough.

If I had only known Jakub Rand, who found his calling in the grand academic halls of Prague, only to have his dreams snuffed out by the malevolent course of history/

it would have been enough.

If I had only known Dr Jacob Randa, hand-picked by a monocle-wearing Nazi professor to curate an exhibition on the liturgical texts of an extinct race/

it would have been enough.

If I had only known A-1821, sickly, emaciated prisoner in a place with no birds, teaching children while the furnaces were being stoked to receive their withering bodies/

it would have been enough.

If I had only known Jan Randa, survivor, hapless suitor and, eventually, husband to a reluctant bride with whom he would father two children/

it would have been enough.

If I had only known Jack, labourer in a new land who, after almost dying in an accident on the factory floor, found a path back to the world of teaching thanks to a letter about kosher pickles/

it would have been enough.

If I had only known the Dikduk Doc, grammar maven and revered teacher to four generations of Jewish children in Australia/

it would have been enough.

If I had only known Grandpa, avowed non-believer, who was prepared to challenge God to save his youngest grandson/

it would have been enough.

If I had only known that nameless, faceless man sitting in a five-by-five plot of dirt, humming and thrusting his fist to the sky/

it would have been enough.

I knew them all, and yet I didn't know my grandfather at all.

Arrivals

I

František Roubíčková peered into the empty biscuit tin and cursed her husband. *Damn him! Damn his religion, damn his gambling but, most of all, damn the goodness in his heart*, for that was the root of her own weakness. He knew it, took advantage. Once again he was off on one of his special 'sales trips', leaving her and their three little girls almost destitute. But who ever heard of a salesman returning with less money than when he left? It wasn't as if she needed him. Soon her hats would be prized throughout Žižkov. Already what she earned she used for the family. She bought the food, the clothes, the household goods. Anything left over she would hide away. In a drawer, in a shoebox, between the mattresses. Even in little Daša's jewellery box, the one that refused to sing. *Damn him!* He found them all. And so, like it was a game, František Roubíčková had taken to using the old biscuit tin. They never spoke about it, for it would be an admission that she, too, was keeping secrets. Whatever pittance he earned he gave to his girls. And he honestly believed that it was only a matter of time before luck would find him. 'We don't live like royalty now,' he once said, 'but one day we will. Mark my words, there will be a plaque on the street bearing the name Ludvík Roubíček.'

'Trinkets!' she said, exasperated. He would be back on Thursday, carrying useless baubles wrapped in scraps of butcher's paper, as if he was Saint Nicholas himself. That, to him, made everything all right. What should it matter that he had left with enough money to buy a chicken, unplucked mind you—they could never afford the luxury of Pan Hašek's fine plucked birds—and came back with only enough to buy some potatoes and an onion? Could he not, just once, find his way back to his employer without stumbling over a card table? 'You'll see,' he told the last man, the one who threatened to have him thrown in jail and his family tossed onto the street, 'I'll make you more than you can possibly hope to get from this junk you have me hawking. Luck is on my side.' The other one, fist clenched, had said—Ludvík was laughing when he told Františka, and perhaps a little drunk—'Luck? Young man, you are lucky your girls aren't on the street right now selling the only thing your family has left to sell!'

Františka Roubíčková was determined not to cry this time. She had made the ultimate sacrifice, she had taken on his religion against her better judgment. 'He is a nice boy, true,' her mother had said. 'But they are trouble. They hunger for money, you know?' She had never thought that her mother meant it literally, that he would actually devour money, her money, before she could turn it into anything useful. Look how she lived, in a cramped apartment, with all of *them*, while her sisters were frolicking in the country, in their summer homes, because they had all married well above their stations, to prosperous butchers and bakers. They sent her photos with inscriptions on the back. 'We miss you!' and 'Our love to the girls, bring them here to play.' The girls. Daša, her oldest. Then Irena and little Marcela. With another child on the way, maybe this time a son. Ludvík was determined to have a boy to carry on the family name. He was the only child of an only child. He had no cousins. When he died, the very essence of Roubíček as it had existed in him would be extinguished. Maybe it's a good thing, she thought. At least the girls will be able to hide behind their new names. They could undo her mistake, marry fine young men of the gentry. Get out of Žižkov.

And yet, all the same, she knew that when Ludvík came back on Thursday evening she would take him into her arms, and eventually into her bed. Every return played out in the same fashion. She wouldn't ask him about the details, the money. She wouldn't ask how many of Pan Whoever-it-was-this-week's wares he'd managed to sell. They would put the girls to sleep, tuck them in, sing them lullabies, and then make their way to the other side of the gauze curtain. He would make a big show of putting some notes in the moneybox they kept in the chest of drawers, notes that had already been in his pocket when he left, only fewer. He would say that she had grown even more beautiful in his absence. Then he would climb into bed and they would wriggle towards one another and, as if she had forgotten every one of the curses that she had uttered over the past few days, she would hold him close and they would make love in silence. As he ran his finger over her belly in the afterglow, they would choke back their laughter, remembering that life was just getting started, because when little Roubíček arrived it would all be different. Good fortune would finally come their way. They would move out of Žižkov, where Ludvík knew she hated living, and spend more time with her family. No longer would he spend his days hustling for these charlatans. He would work on his own terms, while everyone in Prague sang the praises of Františka Roubíčková, the most celebrated milliner in all of Bohemia.

Daša stood at the door, her lip twitching as she watched Františka. Their eyes met for a second and the girl looked away. From the other room, the sound of Marcela crying. Daša disappeared back into the dimly lit hallway.

Serious little Daša. What was a mother to make of her? Soon she would be old enough to work, maybe at Žofie Sláviková's grocery store down the street, although Františka would prefer she concentrated on her schooling. Already at nine the girl showed a quick mind, was wise beyond her years and possessed a formidable will. She seemed happy within herself, popular with her peers. Now Ludvík's mother, Mama Roubíčková, was insisting that she move schools, to begin a Jewish education. How dare she! When her son had married outside the faith, Mama Roubíčková had mourned him as if he had died, and for three years continued to act as if he were dead just to spite them. Never mind that her own husband sneaked over most afternoons to give the young couple whatever treats he could gather without the old bat noticing. 'Frantishku,' he would whisper, this fine and pious Jew, 'I brought you a ham. Let us eat it in the garden together, our little secret.' Fine and pious, indeed.

Six years ago, when it became known that a second child was on the way, Papa Roubíček had summoned her to his office at the factory. 'Please sit down,' he said, taking her woollen cardigan and ushering her to the leather armchair.

'I am tired of this business,' he said. 'Two years and Mama Roubíčková has yet to see little Daša. Now another one. She pretends not to care but it weighs on her mind. A husband knows these things. She misses her son, but she longs for a daughter even more. She wants to undo what was done, to take back her *shiva*. You have a good soul, Frantishku. Perhaps even a Jewish soul.' Papa Roubíček let out a great sigh and placed his hand on her knee. 'I don't believe in it either, but to her it is everything. Save a mother from her torment. Take our faith, your husband's faith.' His voice softened and he looked at Františka ruefully. 'Please.'

That she did so should have been enough. Now Mama Roubíčková was at it again. 'I won't ask anything more of you, I promise,' she said as the two fussed over the stove one afternoon. 'It is easy to forget, with your painted eggs and festive trees, but these girls are Jews. I know you try, and perhaps I am to blame for raising a son like Ludya, but they should be with their own kind. Learning the traditions. Here they will know nothing of our God.'

'But Mama.' The word clung to Františka's throat. 'She is happy. Her teachers are happy with her progress. Her friends—'

'She is a child. She will find happiness again.'

'But to interrupt her—'

'Papa Roubíček and I...We want to help. Them, yes, but also you. I won't force it. We are not the kind to make demands. But it is something to consider, no?'

Františka clenched her fist around the wooden spoon and continued to stir. Again she would relent. Maybe not today or tomorrow. But eventually. This she already knew.

2

Jakub R didn't know whether he saw or smelled or heard the city first. But here it was, towering above him. He was an ant, no, something smaller, a louse. All about he saw city people doing what he could only surmise were city things. They looked like another species. He would not fit in, even with his *payes* tucked behind his ears and *tzitsis* shoved under his belt, half-bunched into his underpants. They would see through him. Why had he even bothered to shave his beard on the ride from B? Their city eyes could grow whiskers on his face as soon as cocoon him like a moth in a tattered *tallis*.

Jakub's first step onto the platform of his great city dreamscape was tempered by the soot spewing from the train's stack. It was in his chest now, clutching at his lungs, squeezing out what little air was left. Prague, seat of culture and learning, home to President Tomáš Garrigue Masaryk, to everything Jakub had longed for, already despised him. Dirt. That was what struck him most. He looked through the gaping hole above, a wooden halo that canonised the station. A series of blackened statues gazed down solemnly, as if to say: 'Welcome and beware. Beyond this place there is nobody to watch over you.' Was this the message that Josef Fanta had intended when he designed the magnificent railway station as a monument to his beloved Emperor Franz Josef I? The declaration of Czechoslovakian independence in 1918—only twelve years ago—saw the city's ever-pumping heart renamed after the first President's friend and ideological ally, Woodrow Wilson, but Herr Fanta's imperial vision could not be ignored, no matter how hard Masaryk tried.

A shove, and our new arrival found himself surging forward. He glanced down the platform, towards the stairs that ascended like Jacob's ladder to the main concourse. Three gypsies were huddled at the bottom, their jangling tunes dancing into the pockets of the milling crowds. People stopped to watch. Others spat on the floor as they rushed past. Jakub tried to look into their mouths, to count their teeth. What was the saying about gypsy teeth? Something about omens. His mother used to mutter it under her breath every time a band of them neared the village. He searched the crowd for other gypsies who might take advantage of a distracted traveller. Nothing. But could they not appear and disappear at will? Jakub clutched his bag to his chest and felt a pang of guilt. It was exactly what the people across the bridge would do when they saw a Jew.

Jakub resisted the invitation of the two archangels beckoning him to the streets of Prague, and approached a man in what he took to be a uniform.

- *Sir, I am lost.*

- *You must go north-west.*

- *I'm sorry, I don't understand.*

- *I cannot help you, other than to say head north-west when you exit the station but not so far as the river. I am told you will find those like you in that direction.*

- *Like me?*

- *Yes, people of your kind. But I suggest you buy yourself a new hat and, if fortune permits, a matching coat.*

- *A coat? In this weather?*

- *It is not for the weather, but for the journey.*

- *The journey?*

- *I must be going now. Head north-west, I say. If you reach a bridge then you have gone too far.*

- *But how will I know when I get there?*

- *You can't miss it, wherever it is.*

The man disappeared into the crowd.

Jakub dropped his bag on the ground, sat on it and stared at the exit. All of a sudden he noticed a stall with a row of hats hanging from the awning. It almost certainly hadn't been there before. He leapt to his feet, scooped up the bag and rushed across the hall.

- A hat for the nice young man, if I am not mistaken. And I am very rarely mistaken.

- Well, yes, perhaps, but for now I am only browsing.

- Oh, but, sir, time is of the essence if you wish to reach your destination before sundown.

- My destination?

- Why, the northern part of west or the western part of north, however you wish to say it.

- How did you…?

- I can see it in your face. Everyone like you heads that way.

- Yes, but—

- Sir, might I save you time and recommend this fine hat, lined with fur for the ultimate in comfort.

- It is a fine hat.

- And I hope I am not being presumptuous in suggesting this coat that matches so perfectly. It will keep you free from the dirt…

- I suppose I could—

- Here, let me help you, young man, and, yes…see how it fits you. Your very own tailor could not have done better.

- I am sorry, but I don't think I can afford both.

- Oh, but, sir, look at you, suddenly a fine city gentleman, sure to be quite the ladies' man.

- I will take the hat.

- And the coat, you must, to be grey with the city. There's no telling what predator might see fortune in a country boy.

- Very well, but I only have—

- I'll take it.

And with that, Jakub R, in a new long coat and gentleman's chapeau, ventured into the city.

3

The baby, little Hana, slept on her mother's naked breast, and with her slept the dreams of her father. It had been a girl after all, and the name Roubíček, *his* Roubíček, would not live on. Now Ludvík had four of these miraculous blessings, four hearts hollowed out by disappointment, unable to dream like other children—the sort of dreams that might one day come true. He could not hold down a job for more than a few months. He owed God knows what to only God knows who. Some nights he could not even look up from the table.

When the midwife appeared in the entry hall to tell him of the new arrival, there was a resounding *Mazal tov!* His neighbours slapped his back, shook his hand, before disappearing behind their doors. *Mazal tov*? Another mouth for her hats to feed? Not that he disliked bread dumplings, but occasionally he would have liked some duck fat smeared across them. Or *zeli*, cabbage, with caraway seeds.

That night Ludvík would be expected to show his miserable face at the local inn and shout everyone rounds of drinks until they could no longer stand. That is what a father does to mark such an occasion. Doubly so if the child is a girl, for his friends could not get drunk at a *shalom zacher* or *bris*. The first time, with Daša, it was only the finest spirits for everyone—Becherovka and *slivovice*. For Irena it was a red wine from the Vinařská region, cheaper but still respectable. By the time Marcela arrived he was struggling, but the minute he stepped into the inn and saw those faces, waiting, longing, he called out, 'Pilsner for everyone, it is another girl!' and was met with a rowdy cheer. But what is left when one cannot even afford beer? Perhaps this time they will shout him rounds in commiseration. After all, they must know that nobody suffers like he who fathers only daughters. They bring you heartache from the start. Your initial disappointment is swept away by their beauty, and you worry about their every move. And when they leave the house, when they no longer need you, the tragedy is even greater.

Oh, to be his neighbour Jiří B. Fortune had smiled upon him, bestowing but one child, a boy whose birth name was a distant memory but whom everyone lovingly called Bohuš. Ludvík and Františka had been married only two months when they arrived in Žižkov. Jiří B came from across the road to introduce himself and invite them to his newborn son's *bris*. It was Františka's first taste of a Jewish celebration and she almost fainted. The speck of blood. The pathetic little wail. 'Please,' she had whispered to Ludvík at the feast that followed, 'let us have only girls.'

When Daša was born, Jiří B was the first at their door, holding flowers and a bottle of wine. Little Bohuš, almost two, was clutching at his hand, making a game of jumping up and snatching petals. 'So let me see my future daughter-in-law,' Jiří roared and pulled Ludvík into an embrace. That night at the inn, while the whole neighbourhood toasted the latest arrival, Ludvík confided to Jiří that he desperately wanted a son. 'And you aren't willing to wait another few years to have mine?' the other joked. The mirth grew with each new daughter: 'Well, now little Bohuš has a choice.'

Time was like salt in Ludvík's wound; he stood by, helpless, forced to watch the fruit of his dream grow on another's tree. At school Bohuš excelled; in the streets he was everyone's favourite. An amiable boy, unafraid to engage with the world around him. His parents didn't boast like most Jewish parents. They didn't need to exaggerate. News about Bohuš had a habit of just wafting out like the fine aroma of a royal banquet. There was no doubt about it. Bohuš was destined to be *someone*. And now, separated only by a quiet street, there were four girls for the boy to pass over.

Ludvík leaned across his wife and looked down at the baby. 'So this is her, then?'

'Yes,' she said, trying to shield little Hana from her father's disappointment, 'this is her.'

4

Indeed it was a fine coat because Jakub R did not feel too hot as the sun beat down on him in the Old Town Square. He paused for a moment at the statue of Jan Hus and watched the city bow before the great philosopher's bronzed feet. The surrounding spires cast spectacled shadows across Hus's brow, their rims as thick as railings. The resemblance was uncanny. Look closely, it could be Tomáš Garrigue Masaryk himself, ready to defend the Czechoslovak state from the invading hordes.

Jakub spun around in a daze as a column of marionettes danced past, heads bowed low. Faceless patrons at cafés swayed gaily to the fine melodies of the buskers who skipped from corner to corner. And to think that everything he knew had once fitted into a town the size of this square. Jakub wanted to take off his hat in deference to the great Masaryk, but he feared that the marionettes, the priests, the café patrons, the buskers, the kings in their surrounding castles would all stop their endeavours to point at him and laugh.

Jakub reached into his bag for the few coins that remained from the journey, walked to a food stall and found his way to the back of the queue.

Please, you first. Jakub let people through, afraid of this thing, whatever it was, that God did not condone.

How many would you like, sir? He was face to face with the saleswoman. The smell, baked goods and, well, something else. Jakub held up a single finger.

We who have seen such things in every corner store know the ingredients: yeast, flour, sugar, oil, duck fat, minced pork and spices. And we know the flavour. But Jakub R, the rabbi's son, would never find the words to describe the taste of that bun, the bun that saved him from hunger, but which also might have damned him forever in God's eyes.

Jakub leaned against the statue of Jan Hus and ate. Colour washed over the square, its denizens rising to a standing ovation. In the windows of the nearest buildings, he saw people smiling, waving. One woman, her breasts pressed against the glass, was signalling to him with her right arm. *Go,* she mouthed. *Go.* He tipped the last morsels on the ground and watched the pigeons descend to feast. One of the flock, instead of filling its belly, perched on the statue beside him and whispered in his ear: 'You are almost there.'

Pařížská Street extended from the walkway in the town square. Jakub felt his bag lighten, his strength returning with each new street name that appeared in its metal bracket. Jáchymova. Kostečná. Josefovská. He found himself on a deserted corner, the wind whistling, not a soul about. He had never felt more alive. Down a set of uneven stone steps, an open door. Flashes of movement from behind. Whispers. On the doorframe he spotted a familiar wooden box, a *mezuzah*. He huffed into his hand, and quickly sucked the breath back up through his nostrils.

In the street, or from behind the door, laughter.

Soon it would be dark.

5

The day she moved into the basement apartment at 13 Biskupcova Street, Františka Roubíčková was so full of joy that anyone encountering her might have thought she had just taken up residence in Vyšehrad Castle itself. It was as if she had forgotten her childhood home altogether—the large country cottage in the region of Miličín, with its adjoining fields beneath rolling hills—for the four rooms she now proudly called her own seemed infinitely more grand. Ludvík had promised her a good life, a city life, and, while she had faith in her new husband, she never dared hope for such an apartment with its own kitchen, a separate dining room, a spacious bedroom and even its own bathroom. *I expected to share a closet with the neighbours*, she boasted to her sister Emílie in the first letter back to her family. *Ludvík has even bought me a table to set up my sewing station. Emí, I have a studio. A studio! You must come on the next train.*

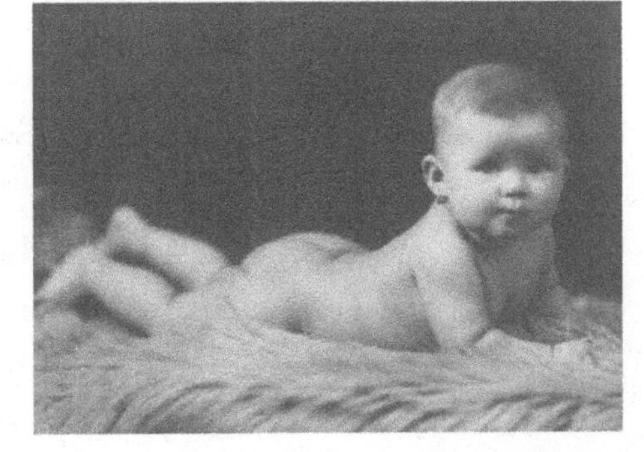

The arrival of little Daša served only to compound her elation. The baby slept through the rattle of her machine, and did not stir when Františka flew into a fury over a broken thread. 'Tell me what to do, little muse,' she said to the child, and instantly the storm would pass. Three years later, when Irena was born, Ludvík hung a gauze curtain across a third of the bedroom so the children could have some space of their own. 'You won't mind if we reduce your studio by a few feet,' Ludvík said, more a statement than a question. 'This way we will have a lounge too, to spend time as a family.' Františka liked the idea of looking up from her machine to see the girls playing in this lounge. *Surely only the most pampered women in Žižkov have a lounge!* He also surprised her with an ornate dresser, made of oak, with blackened handles on its drawers. 'For your supplies,' he said as he placed it next to her table.

Little Marcela arrived three and a half years later and, again, Ludvík took it upon himself to modify Františka's studio. 'This is a good thing,' he said as he dragged the table and chest to the back corner of what they both now thought of as the girls' room. 'By day this whole area will be yours. You can draw the curtain if you don't wish to be disturbed. Daša is old enough to watch over the little ones. She'll call you if there's any trouble.'

'And at night?' asked Františka.

'At night you should rest.'

Františka didn't have the strength to protest. She pulled the crib nearer her station and returned to work.

Františka Roubíčková no longer boasted to her sisters, and would have stopped inviting them over had she not needed help with the girls. One day, while Marcela slept on Emílie's lap and the other two played on the patch of grass in the courtyard, Františka held up a needle only to realise that her entire kingdom fitted neatly within its eye.

Now Hana's broken wooden crib stood blocking access to Františka's corner. 'You will still have room,' Ludvík had tried to comfort her when she told him there was to be another. 'How much space can you possibly need to make your hats?' What would he know? The end product might be compact, but to get to that point one must spread out. Lining board from here, a feather from there, felt from somewhere else.

On top of the dresser, its lacquer now chipped and faded, was the enduring symbol of her life's failure. A hat, unfinished, grey, with a red bow. A hat for the rabbi's wife, intended to be worn on *Rosh Hashanah*. 'You will make one, simple but elegant,' the woman had instructed. 'You know I depend on you.' Depend indeed. Františka Roubíčková knew that the rabbi's wife referred to her as 'that darling, unfortunate *shikse*' behind her back. She was a charity case, to be pitied. When Ludvík first brought her to the rabbi's house for lessons before conversion, the wife clucked and crowed, as if this exotic girl with the golden hair was manna from heaven. Like Moses's people wandering in the desert, suddenly gifted this strange white substance, the rabbi's wife could make of her whatever she wanted.

When they were alone, at the start of her first lesson, the woman had raised an eyebrow and said: 'So...Ludvík Roubíček? Of all our people, why him?'

She was expecting it. Ludvík had warned that he was not held in high esteem. 'He is a good man,' Františka had replied. 'A kind man.'

Not like the rest of you. That is what Františka wanted to say. She had grown up believing all sorts of terrible things about the people she had committed to join. They featured in the ghost stories she was told as a child—as sorcerers, murderers, cannibals. What a shock when she learned that Ludvík, the boy she had met on a country path in the nearby town of Sudoměřice, the town of all her fondest childhood memories, was one of them. He didn't seem capable of any of that. He had disarmed her, lulled her into loving him, and convinced her to be his wife. Their first years together were perfect and Ludvík paid his faith no heed; he enjoyed her rituals, her traditions. He didn't seem to care that his mother would not speak to them, that she had not even tried to see her granddaughter. 'She lives in the past,' he said. 'It is her loss.' Later, when she told him of his father's plea, she was shocked by his response: he was quiet, and then muttered, 'I am all they have.'

Persuading the *Beth Din* to allow her to undertake the conversion process proved difficult. These Jews were not fond of proselytising, they were not missionaries. 'No,' one of the older rabbis said, not two minutes after she entered the room. 'Don't worry,' said Ludvík, 'they always try to discourage you. You won't even be considered before they have refused you three times.' He was right, it was not until their fourth appearance that the same rabbi asked her why she wanted to join such an accursed nation. 'We have great traditions to offer you,' he said, 'but also suffering and persecution. That is the lot your children will inherit.' Františka gasped. 'We cannot permit a conversion simply because you married a Jew. You must believe. We must find in you and your child a Jewish *neshamah*, a soul that was misplaced at birth and that wishes to be reunited with its true corporeal vessel. So tell me, young lady, what is it that you believe?'

Františka turned to her husband, who met her pleading glance for a moment then looked away. He was sweating. It all came down to this. 'Rabbi, sir…I do not know enough to believe.' She was dismissed, and Ludvík followed her out to the anteroom. What would become of them, she wondered, now that the court was certain to deny her application?

'You will learn with my wife,' said the young rabbi who came to deliver the verdict. 'And you,' turning to Ludvík, 'you must learn with me. This process will be as difficult, perhaps more difficult, for you than it is for her. And whether or not she will pass will depend as much on your observance as hers.' He gestured for them to stand, then ushered them towards the door. 'Wait a few days,' he said. 'I will call for you. That is all.' Overcome with gratitude, Františka went to grasp his hand but he pulled away. The door slammed, and from behind it several others.

The following Sabbath, Papa Roubíček attended synagogue—reluctantly and very much at his wife's insistence—for the first time in three years. When he was called to the *Torah* he blessed the young couple in their absence and pledged a contribution, so that God might look favourably on the conversion process and, perhaps, see fit to hurry it along.

Františka Roubíčková knew they had secrets, terrible secrets, but nothing prepared her for what she was learning from the rabbi's wife. It was an entire world, hidden from view. Six hundred and thirteen commandments. A way of life that made sense only if you had faith. The dietary laws of *kashrut*. The laws of *niddah*, family purity. The Sabbath. 'It is beyond me,' she said one evening. 'Before your mother interfered you didn't care, and now I am supposed to live like the matriarch Sarah herself?' Ludvík only laughed. He had thought much the same thing. 'You think I could live like that? Let's discuss what we've learned and draw up a ledger. Some rules we will follow. Others, well...They cannot know everything that goes on in our house.' Ludvík pulled out a small leather-bound book, opened it to the first page, and drew a line down the middle. 'On the left, the things you cannot abide. On the right, concessions we make for God.'

'I shan't give up my favourite foods.'

'I shan't hand my underwear to a rabbi for inspection every month.'

'Only once will I dip in their dirty rainwater but after that, never!'

'If there is a show at the theatre on the Sabbath that I particularly wish to see, we will go.'

'If there is a dress I love, or a suit for you, I shan't care if it mixes wool and linen.'

'The children will know their cousins, their family, my family.'

'Christmas trees. Our children will have Christmas trees.'

'We shall have one bed. We will not be separated. Ever.'

Each class brought new rules to put in the book, in one column or the other. But mostly the one. To correct the disparity, Ludvík took to writing the few rules they could follow in grand, exaggerated letters and the rest in the most compact script he could manage. 'There,' he said, holding it out before her. 'Perfectly even.'

'And what of the witchcraft?' she said one night as he lay beside her, waiting for sleep. 'I listen to her and wonder what she doesn't tell me.'

'There are stories, yes,' he said. 'But good stories. Stories that give strength. One day I will tell our children. It is what I can give them of this faith.'

'Please,' she said and nestled into her pillow. The gauze curtain fluttered beside them. 'Just one. Tell me.'

'I know this to be true because my grandfather told it to me. As did his to him. And so forth right up to the very man who witnessed it.' Františka rolled closer to her husband. 'Once there was a great rabbi who watched over his congregation, the people of our lands. They called him the Maharal, though his name was Rabbi Judah Löew, a great sage and mystic like none we have known before or since. For the most part, his was a time of peace, of prosperity. And then...you know our history. The Maharal could see it, could sense the change. And so he made a man, like Adam, from the mud of the riverbank and gave him the task of protecting his people. This *golem* was both manservant and warrior, simpleton and sleuth. He did his master's bidding by day and, come night, he would appear before the Maharal and, with a whisper and a gust of breath from the sage's lips, be put to sleep.

'It so happened that on *Purim*—or maybe it was *Walpurgisnacht*—there was a great celebration and the Maharal drank until he fell by the side of the road. A loyal student ran to his house and summoned the *golem*, who came quickly and carried his master home. The great rabbi slept as his creation lay him in bed. Having never experienced the night, the *golem* ran outside and into the heart of the city. Startled by the flaming lamps, the masks, the painted faces, and the strange and awful sounds of revelry, he took fright and began to rampage. He tore down fences, chased animals from their pens, set fires. The people began to—'

'Ludya,' Františka said as she clutched her pillow.

Ludvík looked down and saw that she was trembling. He had been lost in the story, and had perhaps embellished too much. 'I was just trying to say—'

She lifted her hand to his mouth and placed a finger across his lips. '*Shhh*...Promise me this.' She waited to feel the movement of a nod. 'You will never tell it to the children. Never.'

'So, you make hats?' the rabbi's wife asked one day. Františka smiled. 'Ludvík made me a studio.' 'Well,' the other continued, 'it is a fine profession, millinery. I am always in need of new hats. You can't possibly know the demands on a woman like me. They say one can judge the health of a community by the appearance of its *rebbetzin*. She must be plump, but not fat, elegantly dressed but not ostentatious.' The woman adjusted herself on the seat, upright, confident. 'When this is over, when you have returned to your people, our people, I will look after you. We will look after each other, you and I. Yes, you will make my hats. And I will pay you, though one can only afford so much on a rabbi's stipend. But everyone will see me wearing your hats and they, too, will want one. I assure you, dear, you won't be able to keep up with demand.'

The hat on Františka Roubíčková's dresser lay as a scornful reminder of her initial trust. The rabbi's wife had kept her promise to wear only her hats. And she paid, yes, it's true, but Františka dared not protest the few coins she was given. 'I'd give you more but I have a congregation to feed,' the rabbi's wife would say. And each time Františka stepped into the synagogue she would see her hats, the ones she had made for the rabbi's wife, on other women. For the rabbi's wife gave them away as charity. 'Is it right that those who can't afford should covet their *rebbetzin*'s hat? It is a *mitzvah* you are doing, little Roubíčková. A good deed. And, moreover, you are helping me to do a *mitzvah* that otherwise I could never do.'

So there was the hat, the one she had not been able to finish before going into labour. There was her career, or what was left of it. There were her children, and her husband, gone again on one of his trips. She was alone.

It was like the day she became one of *them*. The *mikveh*, the ritual bath, two weeks after Irena was born. The rabbi's wife led her through the halls of the synagogue, out the back door to the windowless structure against the fence. She was holding a towel and a prayer book. The day was cold and Františka was shivering, clutching the baby against her chest to keep it warm. 'Once you have been submerged, you will come out a Jew. I need only report it to my husband, to the *Beth Din*, and we will welcome you as one of our own.' Františka handed over her sleeping daughter and removed her clothes, disconcerted by the other woman's refusal to avert her gaze. She lowered herself into the pool, the water stinging every inch of her body. Františka repeated the words after the rabbi's wife.

'Now, hold yourself under.'

Darkness. Only her hair remained on the surface. How long was she in the water? Forever. Františka, daughter of humble farm owners, would be left behind, frozen in place. Rushes of warmth. Roaring, a storm of voices calling her Jewish name. *Rachel.* Ancestors welcoming her back. So this is the *neshamah*, the Jewish soul? Františka shot up from the *mikveh*, icy water dripping from her skin. The hair on her arms was standing on end. Through a film of water she saw the rabbi's wife standing there, grinning. 'Get out, dear girl. You will catch your death.'

And so she emerged, this dripping, trembling rag doll. A Jew.

6

From the bottom of the stairs, a voice. 'Ah, you're here. May I take your hat and coat?'

Jakub R clumsily removed the coat and raised his hand to the brim of his hat. The old man held out a cloth *kippah* and smiled at Jakub. 'I thought you'd got lost but I'm glad you're here. The rabbi asked me to welcome you. I am the *shammas.*' A flourish of the arm. 'Please.'

The *shammas* led Jakub through a stone archway to the central hall. Two rows of wooden pews lined the walls on either side. At one end, a simple ark with a faded velvet curtain pulled across its opening. Beside it, a large, ornate throne carved from oak. On the other end, cases filled with leather-bound books. Everything faced towards a podium enclosed in wrought-iron latticework. There, where the rabbi usually stood, where the *Torah* was unfurled three times a week, where God's words were sung back to Him with joy and reverence, Jakub saw his father: a phantom, a warning. Then he was gone.

'You know,' the *shammas* said, 'this is not Avraham's tent. We don't welcome every traveller. Unless there are services, this door is closed. But our dear rabbi forbade me to lock up before you arrived. When will he be back? Who knows? Time means nothing while we wait for the Messiah. Let me tell you a story to calm your nerves. For every arrival there is a new story to tell and this one is yours. So listen already.'

On the balcony of a sanatorium for the criminally insane, a prisoner sits strapped to a rickety wheelchair. He peers into a telescope at a distant hill upon which there stands a tower that reaches to the sky and beyond. It is a tower of pure onyx, no visible entrance, no discernible purpose. The prisoner is convinced that it is the axis pole around which the world rotates.

One day, when he is admiring the perfect blackness, the prisoner is startled by a shock of colour in the corner of his eye. He swings the telescope, trying to centre it in his view. He gasps. It is a young girl, completely unlike anyone else he has ever seen. She does not face him. Instead, she slides her hands up and down and across the tower's smooth surface as if she is searching for something. He watches her in awe for eight days as she traverses the width of the tower before disappearing over the other side. For three weeks his view returns to black. Then, just when the prisoner has consigned her to memory, she appears. 'Kaja!' he calls out, as if he has always known her name, but she does not answer. She just faces the tower and begins her search anew.

And so it continues: eight days on his side of the tower, three weeks on the other. Month after month. Year after year. The prisoner comes to count his sentence by her presence—never mind that his sentence is indefinite—and readies his telescope on the twenty-second day for her arrival, waiting to see how she has grown. Without fail Kaja is there. Older. More beautiful. It is a routine from which he does not tire, for that is the nature of love and madness.

In his twelfth year of watching, on a day that Kaja is over the other side, the prisoner looks into his telescope and sees an open door at the base of the tower. He is aghast. Could this be the answer? The thing for which his beloved has been searching? The prisoner scans the area around the door until his gaze lands on a crumpled, impish man tilling the earth. All day this man continues to toil. Then, as the sun begins to set, he gathers his things, hobbles back to the tower and closes the door behind him.

Kaja passes by. Another time. Then another. The prisoner watches with glee as a beautiful vegetable garden sprouts at the foot of the tower, but Kaja does not turn around. She cannot see the life that is rising from the earth behind her. She continues to run her hands against the smooth black surface, searching, searching.

In time, the garden becomes a forest, its vines and branches tangled across the wall, obscuring the prisoner's view of the tower. When Kaja appears, he can see her only in glimpses: a snatch of hair, a patch of blouse. He is quite unprepared for the pink of her face. She has turned around. The prisoner watches as Kaja approaches the thicket with caution. She glances about, as if suspecting a trap. Then she picks at some of the vegetables, rubs them against her dirty skirt, and eats them. She darts back to the tower and resumes her search, slamming her fists against the blackness.

Years pass. Kaja is now an old woman. The prisoner, too, is approaching his end. The garden is dying, its branches dry and broken. Still the prisoner watches and waits. Until the day that Kaja begins to dig. She scratches frantically, not in the garden, or the earth around it, but into the tower itself. The prisoner stares as her hands turn calloused and bloody. He notices that, slowly but surely, she makes an indent into the smooth tower wall. The hole is lined with her blood.

The digging continues for a year. The garden is all but gone. The prisoner is ravaged by illness; every breath is an effort. Still he watches longingly as Kaja digs away with her broken hands, burrowing deeper and deeper, until one day she has made a hole big enough to climb inside. She nestles into the grotto and turns to look directly at the prisoner. Then she lies down and dies. After seven days, he sees the crumpled, impish man come out of the tower, brick up the hole, smooth over his handiwork with thick black sludge, and hurry back to the door.

Not long after, the prisoner succumbs to consumption. He is given a pauper's funeral, which no one attends. The little man in the tower is never seen again.

Jakub sat motionless on the stone bench. From beyond the archway he could hear murmurs, greetings. Men began to file into the synagogue and take their seats for the morning service. 'I'm afraid the rabbi has taken ill,' said the *shammas*. 'Come back another time if you must, but for now take this.' He passed Jakub a scrap of paper with a few scribbled words: *Dr J. Langer, The Jewish School. 3 Jáchymova Street*. 'It is not far. He is expecting you.'

7

25.VIII

My dearest Emí,

How is it that almost a month has passed and yet I still feel like I am with you in Sudoměřice? Every morning I wake up in a daze, hoping to run outside and jump in the lake like we did as children. I so miss you when we are apart! Last night I dreamed that I was on the stairs, where the bees gather near the attic. A whole swarm had blocked out the sun and I was sure I would fall back down. I called out to you but you didn't come. I woke with a start—I could still hear them. Would you believe it was the light bulb near my head? I must have fallen asleep without turning it off.

As always, returning to the city has taken some adjustment, but we have settled back into our life. Little Hanička is growing fat in time for the winter. Marcela has been parading around town in the dress you gave her, stopping strangers in the street and telling them what a wonderful aunt she has in the country. So, too, with Irena, who accompanies me to the store and asks why they don't sell honey from her Babička's town.

Last week we celebrated Daša's eleventh birthday. It was a quiet affair, but joyous nonetheless. She was particularly enamoured of your present and is convinced that you sewed it yourself. Only Auntie Emí can sew like this, she insists. (Should I be insulted?)

When the birthday meal was over, I sat her down and tried to impress upon her the importance of the next twelve months. In a fortnight she will begin her middle schooling at a Jewish academy in Josefov. I want to tell her that it is not my doing, that I am sorry for dragging her into this with me. I try my best not to turn her against her father or grandparents, and so I explain what I can of the choice she will have to make when, next year, she attains the age of bat mitzvah. *She can cast it all away, escape the confines of this spiritual prison. If that's what she decides, which, secretly, is my heart's desire, it will be as if she were never Jewish at all. If, on the other hand, she chooses to embrace it, then she, too, must find her way with God.*

I dread what sort of impression the horrible things I learned will have on her delicate mind. So I must remind her of her mother's heritage.

Send me pinecones and tinsel. Have the carpenters of Miličín carve us a glorious angel. This year we will have the grandest tree in all of Žižkov.

You asked about Ludvík, why he did not come with us this time. I am grateful that you did not push further when I said he stayed in the city for work. I know how you feel about him. But it was the truth, Emí. So here it is at last, what I couldn't tell you in Sudoměřice: we are getting a car! I can scarcely contain myself. That is why he stayed, to work and make the payments. Can you believe it? He has changed! Not like the other times. This time he really has! It is like the life he always promised. We also had a little help from Mama Roubíčková—she was so glad we decided to enrol the girls in the Jewish school that she offered to help get them there in style. You should have seen her crowing when I told her. 'No grandchild of mine will arrive like a gypsy!' Papa Roubíček helped us with the calculations. It can be paid off in less than a year, he said.

Could you ever have imagined your sister being driven around in her very own car? Ludvík and I spent many afternoons perusing the garages of Prague. What fun we had! Eventually we settled on the Škoda 420 in deep cherry red. The standard, not the sports model. You will see it soon enough. I can't wait to watch your face, and Mama's and Agnes's, even Maria's, when we arrive for our visit. They will think it's the queen herself who has come!

As I write this I have the last payment beside me. You don't want to know how much. Ludvík hardly sleeps as the time draws near. Next week he will return from work after lunch so that he can take the money to the garage and return with our chariot. I promise to send a picture as soon as possible with the car and the girls and Ludvík and…Finally, a happy family, a portrait that you can hang in the house so that Mother can look at it and know that it all works out in the end.

I smother you all with kisses.

Ever your loving sister,
Františka

Every car turning into Biskupcova Street was met with yelps of excitement.

'Is that the one, Mama?'

'Is that Papa?'

Františka Roubíčková had to hold them back, to stop them from running onto the road. 'No,' she said, laughing. 'Compared to Papa's car, that is an old pushcart.' Or 'That one is green, Irča. Papa's car is red.' The girls cheered as the cars passed, some of the drivers waving back or tooting their horns in good humour. Františka blushed as the occasional hat was tipped in her direction. If she was not mistaken, one man even pulled the cigarette from his mouth and winked. Fancy that. Such a perfect picture they must have made at the doorway, this young family in their finest summer dresses.

Looking down the length of their street to the intersection with Mladoňovicova, as Daša and Irena raced back and forth, as Marcela weaved between the trees along the kerb, feeling Hana's tiny hands clutching her ankles, it occurred to Františka that for the first time since her second child was born, she was truly content.

It did not concern her when Ludvík failed to appear at the appointed hour. Purchases like that took time; there were contracts to sign, registration forms to complete. She imagined Ludvík sitting in the salesman's cluttered office when it was all over, the two of them puffing on cigars and raising tumblers of whisky in celebration. It would take a while for him to steady himself, to settle his nerves. Looking out towards Mladoňovicova, Františka gasped, thinking she had spotted him. But it was the wrong model. She let out a sigh and hoped that nobody would notice the dawning of her doubt.

The delay only fuelled the girls' excitement; their energy was boundless. They had no expectations of their father; he was a ghost, a chimera. It was something they gleaned from the outset, something they saw replicated in other houses. If he was present at all, a father was the lingering musk of tobacco smoke, the odd cough, the melting cubes of ice in a glass on the kitchen bench. He was the snap of a belt, an ever-looming threat. His approval, a hug, a kiss; these were treasured. The boiled sweets, the toys, the moments of joy, when the family was together. Like now. This summer. This street. This family.

Another gasp. At last, the car. A Skoda 420. Red. It was exactly as Františka remembered. The colour of the richest Moravian wine. A shiny silver grill, with its crossbar of lights, the new Roubíček coat of arms. The whole street had frozen: the children, the neighbours. A few people had their hands to their foreheads, to shield their eyes from the sun, to make certain this apparition wasn't a play of shadows. The girls clung to their mother.

Františka could barely make him out through the cloud of cigarette smoke in the cabin. Just as he had once promised, Ludvík Roubíček was now the very height of modern sophistication. The horn sounded once, twice, a regal call to attention. Františka stepped forward, pushing the girls in front. The car slowed to a crawl, veered towards the kerb. Another step. Františka readied herself for the moment, pictured herself as the princess in the stories she read to their children at night. Close enough now that she could hear the whir of spinning tyres. Františka looked around, smiled and took one last step onto the road.

The girls screamed as the car came to a sudden stop, its horn bleating like a wounded sow. From inside, an explosion of curses, clearer as the window rolled down. 'Are you crazy, lady? Get off the road.' Smoke spewed out, revealing the driver, face crooked with rage, shaking his fist. 'I should call the police. How could you involve your children in this farce? For shame!' The elegant gentleman—blond, with a waxed moustache, in other words nothing like her husband—continued to rant, but Františka could not hear a word. The two younger girls were crying, huddled against the door to number thirteen, removing themselves from the damaged creature on the road.

The neighbours. Children. Passers-by. They were all watching, aghast. Her shoe was off, the heel wedged into the rusted grate beneath the concrete lip of the gutter. She refused to scream, refused to cry. Let them have their moment of mirth, of condemnation. Františka took a deep breath and cautiously touched her foot to the ground. It would require ice, a tight compress. Biskupcova Street swirled around her. Another breath, this time for composure. Curse them all. She put her hand on the car's bonnet and reached down to remove the other shoe. Pain was her ally; it slowed her every move. A pull. Nothing. Just as sure as the other was ensnared in the drain, this shoe seemed nailed to her foot. Again she straightened, tugged at the hem of her dress. To return home, those few steps, to collect the girls and continue with their day as if none of this had happened. She would come back for her shoe later, once the sun had set, on the street, on her, on Ludvík.

There was no apology, no contrition. Just the stench of cheap spirits.

'Don't,' he said, steadying himself against the wall.

'We waited—'

'It was my mother's dream, Františka, not ours.'

She stood her ground, would not let him pass.

'For God's sake, woman, let them go like everyone else. I will speak with Jiří tomorrow, have the boy escort them. Now I must sleep.'

8

Black scuffs streaked the linoleum. From beyond the stairwell, he could hear laughter echoing through the halls. Jakub R could smell the children, their food, their dirt, the rich scent of their new leather shoes. He reached into his pocket, pulled out the envelope and glanced at the words. Yes, this was definitely the place. Where it had all led. Jáchymova Street. Number three.

Jakub climbed the stairs to the second floor. Someone was pulling on his arm, dragging him through a door; he could not see who. Piles of books reached to the roof. The watermarks on their spine hinted at far-off lands. He was in a metropolis, a city of paper skyscrapers. Jakub R turned to look at his escort but his face was obscured in shadow. 'Remember this place,' said the man. Was it a man? The voice gave no clue. 'It will one day save your life.' Jakub was pushed through the endless alleys of books until they reached the door. He spun around one last time, but there was nothing. A janitor's closet, a storeroom. His escort was gone.

Jakub continued down the corridor until he reached a door with a plaque that read 'Staff Only'. He pushed the door open. Two men sat at a fold-up table, their bodies hunched over a chessboard, a canopy for the opposing armies beneath them. The man playing black glanced up at Jakub. 'Ah, just in time, Herr Doctor,' he said, lifting himself out of the chair. 'We can leave the good Doctor Glanzberg here to play on his own. He will find himself a more satisfactory adversary, no doubt.' The man walked over to Jakub R, patting down wisps of hair on his skull with sweaty palms. 'Jiří Langer,' he said. 'Head teacher, lamentably inadequate player of chess.' Jakub took Langer's hand. 'Jakub R. I'm new here. From—' 'Yes, I am well aware,' Langer interrupted. 'Your reputation precedes you. Welcome. It's good to have a young man such as yourself here at Jáchymova.'

As Langer explained the day-to-day workings of the Jewish school, Jakub R looked at Doctor Glanzberg, who continued playing as if his opponent had never left. He bit his nails, squinted, every imaginable sign of concentration. He looked about the same age as Jakub, but he had the slimness and pallor of a man who spent his life in deep thought. His suit was dark, tailored and yet somehow ill-fitting. There was something oddly familiar about his face. Jakub knew that look of general desperation and anguish. Of genius, challenged. His severe widow's peak swept upwards and to the right, as if escaping in panic.

'These are your most important instruments,' concluded Langer, as he handed Jakub R a thick stick of chalk, a cloth and a long wooden ruler. 'And also your weapons. Your first class will be on Sunday. I am sorry we cannot offer you more, but prove yourself and we'll see. I have told the children about you. The new teacher from the country. They are excited. I am sure you will not disappoint them.'

'Checkmate!' Glanzberg stood up, scraping his chair. 'Looks like you've won, Doctor Langer.'

Langer turned to Jakub R with glee. 'You see. He claws back victory for me. I am a far better player when I am not at the table. Do you play, Doctor?'

Jakub R shook his head. No. His father had not approved of it.

'Never mind. A month at this school and Doctor Glanzberg here will have you playing like a professional. He has gambits even the greatest champions haven't thought of.'

9

The tram came to a halt at Náměstí Republiky. Daša had been to this part of the city before, helping her mother buy materials for her hats, but today she was lost in a sea of shoulders and satchels. Bohuš grabbed Irena's arm, dragging her off the tram. 'Hurry up!' he said, snatching her bag. 'We'll be late.' The three of them made their way into the town square, up Pařížská Street to Jáchymova Street, towards the sound of the school bell.

They descend like locusts, hundreds of children pouring into the cobbled stretch that runs between two of the Old City's grandest parades. Paní Klarfeldová leans her ample body against the school's pale peach brick cladding, trying to move out of harm's way. She waves the solid brass bell above her head as the seemingly endless column hurtles past.

Here we lose sight of Daša, Irena and the boy. They have been swallowed by the crowd of children.

Wait. There they are.

Irena, still holding on to Bohuš. Daša two steps behind. Or is it? I can no longer see her. The Jewish school on Jáchymova Street is wedged between identical buildings. Irena is grasping at her bag. No, we have lost her too. The whole image is fading. Where is Daša? Bohuš? Now I see nothing, can be sure of nothing.

Sometime later, a photograph will be sent home to her mother:

10

The staffroom fills with teachers. They drop their books on the central table, some in triumph, others in defeat. Most huddle around the new arrival. In this chaos of shaking hands, questions and answers, it seems I have also lost sight of Jakub R. Can this be? This whole story, for nothing? Wait. There! The corner of his head. A pant leg. Shoes not yet polished, scratched and dusty from his travels.

Lunch will come and go and Jakub R will roam the halls, preparing to teach the Hebrew language, or religious studies, or history. But for now, I pull back. The staffroom, the corridor, the stairs, the door, the pale facade of the school, Jáchymova Street itself, Pařízká, the Old City, Prague…

Two

If only I could know him now, when it is too late/
that would be enough.

I KEPT ONLY ONE thing of his...

It is a book that is a man that is a life. A book like many others, mass-produced, published in 1953 and purchased soon afterwards in Melbourne for two schillings by a Czechoslovakian refugee who must have been pleased and surprised to discover it had found its way to these distant shores. Unabridged. In a new world. Maybe it was the first English book he purchased, a tool with which he would try to master this new language, his last. Czech, Latin, Hebrew, German, Yiddish, Polish, French, Russian and now, to confuse things once again, this mocking tongue, or a dialect thereof, that relied on linguistic contortions. A subversive language, English.

It was a flag on a shelf of almost identical flags. Orange, white, and orange again. Two words on the spine would have caught his attention. The name of an author he had long admired, who was here in this foreign land, clinging to

the raft of substandard translation. My grandfather must have pulled the book from the shelf and looked at the cover. What to make of the impudent bird gazing up in bewilderment, perhaps at the jumble of letters that might fall on its head? Or was it looking forward, stupefied by the tattoo it could see above the hand that held it? *A-1821.*

Now, forty years later, the spine is no longer intact: glue, marrow, sparkling on its lower third. The whole book is rotten, the former feasting ground of some creature. A beetle, perhaps.

I have cradled it countless times. It has kept me company through this lonely journey. And yet I only found the courage to take it down from the shelf ten years ago, long after my grandfather had given up on life, after that comfortable mirage that was his past had dissolved. Since then it has found a new home wherever I go. *Fiction*, it says on the cover. But is it fiction? To me it signifies death, but this book is his life. All the words he never said, the experiences he could not speak about. I hid it away for years, but now it sits beside me as I type, as I try to understand the bridge it formed between us.

I open it a fraction, and close it again. There is a cut on the top right-hand corner of the cover and behind it the raggedy-eared pages. All over there are specks of mould consuming it from within. In this book, he is here again. One of the many faces drifting away with time. *Someone must have been telling lies about Jan Randa.* But who?

He was not the type to draw attention to himself, preferring instead that his story be subsumed into the greater whole, audible only as a minute fraction of the testimonial cacophony. Perhaps it was a function of survivor's guilt, a common enough response, but in his case compounded by the knowledge that he had not fully shared in his people's suffering. While his family and friends were being shot or gassed or starved to death, he was tucked away in a museum, sitting at a desk, living in relative comfort. By rights he should have died first. He was the weakest, the least cut out for survival. And yet he had survived, *like a dog. As if the shame of it would outlive him.* So, as much as he could, he kept it to himself, allowing fantasies to swirl in the minds of those who knew him.

But the nightmares had a way of sneaking out, just like his screams, which kept my mother awake throughout her childhood. My grandfather didn't like to talk about the war, but every whisper, every confession left a trace. The fanciful nature of the article that appeared in the *Jewish News* made sense in the context of its telling. The journalist hadn't sat down and interviewed my grandfather, but he did sit next to him in Caulfield Synagogue every Sabbath for over thirty years. He probably didn't realise that the ramblings of his friend would amount to anything until the last piece of the puzzle had slipped out in conversation. Only then did he know he had an important story. But he had to go back and reconstruct it from scratch, filling in details he couldn't fully remember. My grandfather wasn't someone who invited questions. He controlled the flow of information. So this man did the best he could with the little knowledge of Theresienstadt he had, making the mistake of using well-known names, which he thought added credibility to his article, but which in fact did the opposite.

While there might not have been an Eppstein, Muneles or Murmelstein involved in whatever it was my grandfather was doing in this Museum of the Extinct Race, there were others. One of them must have talked. And what of the mantra that has, for seventy years, congealed in our throats with its phlegm of indignant admiration:

They were the exemplars of order.

They kept meticulous records.

It is to them I must turn.

Nobody could have foreseen the important role the Red Cross International Tracing Service (ITS) would come to play in documenting the Holocaust. It was, as originally conceived in 1943, a way for Jews outside the Nazi net to find displaced or missing family members. In its early days, it moved from London to Versailles to Frankfurt am Main, before finally settling in the German town of Bad Arolsen. Easily accessible to the Allied victors, it became the main storage location for all original Nazi documents, of which there were legion. When it became apparent that the war was lost, the Nazis tried to burn the evidence, but not even their best accelerated efforts could make a dint in the mountains of paper. Whatever the Allies recovered they sent to be stored in the vast underground hangars of the ITS, which now comprises some 26,000 linear metres of original documents as well as 225,000 metres of microfilm and over 100,000 microfiches.

For fifty years the International Red Cross sat on this incredible resource, claiming that any disclosure would breach German privacy laws. It was an ill-conceived argument. Most of the enquiries came from survivors desperate to learn what became of their loved ones or who were attempting to piece back together their own trajectory through the war years. For those seeking solace or some sort of resolution, it must have been excruciating to know that the documents existed but that the gatekeepers had no intention of granting them access. In January 2000, all eleven governments that are party to the ITS endorsed the Stockholm International Forum Declaration, which demanded the opening of the archive. Again the Red Cross sat on its hands, resisting countless attempts by international Holocaust remembrance centres to get copies of the files into their own archives or, more importantly, online. The United States Holocaust Memorial Museum issued a scathing press release in March 2006, accusing the ITS and its governing body of persistent recalcitrance. Three months later the ITS board voted to open the archives, albeit mainly for research purposes, and relinquished its administration to Yad Vashem, Israel's Holocaust museum. Two more years passed before the records were made available to the general public.

I would finally be able to learn what information the Nazis had on my grandfather, sixty-three years after the war had ended.

For all the promise of the road leading into Yad Vashem—spectacular train tracks re-imagined as the Red Sea split skywards—the museum's research centre was a surprisingly small, cramped room tucked away in its administrative wing. A few outdated computers sat on communal desks. At one, a visibly frustrated fellow traveller was biting the nails of one hand while speedily tapping the keyboard with the other. I dumped my backpack on a nearby chair and settled in, trying to make sense of the clunky search system. I clicked on the most obvious icon, the *Yad Vashem Shoah Names Database* and typed in 'Jakub Rand'.

They all jumped out at me at once, an explosion of Jakub Rands, as if I had released their souls from the dusty white box that whirred innocuously beside me. Jacob Rand, a merchant, born in 1908 to Moshe and Chaya in Gorlice in Poland, and who perished in Bełżec at the age of thirty-four. No. Yaakov Rand from Łódź in Poland, born in 1937, killed when he was only five, most probably during the liquidation of the Warsaw ghetto. No. Yaakov Rand, another child, this one from Drohobycz in Poland, who was murdered the year before he would attain *bar mitzvah*. Two children who would never grow into their names, never have the chance to become anyone's grandfather, let alone mine. Yaakov Rand, born 1872 in Lutowiska, Poland. A married teacher, details about whose ultimate fate are unknown, other than that he did not survive. A teacher, closer. But dead, so no. Yakov Rand, again a Hebrew teacher from Turka. Yes, finally. Turka. Born in 1880, married to Sara Meier and killed on 15 November 1942. So no. Yaakov Rand, from Carpathian Ruthenia (again, yes), date of birth unknown, killed at age eleven at place unknown (and again, no). Jakob Rand, another teacher, also married to a Sara, killed at Auschwitz in 1944. So many Rands, dead. Jakub. Dead. Jacob. Dead. Yaakov. Dead. All of them. Dead. The Holocaust had done away with many people who shared his name, but nobody on this list could have been my grandfather.

I headed to the counter, where a woman was sorting papers. I explained that I wished to have my Dr Jakub Rand, teacher and lawyer, added to the museum's database. 'Do you know where he perished?' she asked, without looking up. I launched into a garbled account of his survival, making sure to slip in the remarkable role that had been foisted upon him as literary curator of Hitler's Museum of the Extinct Race. 'I'm surprised you don't have him on your lists,' I said. 'I suspect he contacted you sometime back in the eighties.' She cut the papers like a deck of cards and placed the top pile across the rest. 'And I'm surprised,' she said with a smirk, 'that you expected to find him listed among the dead.' She shook her head and continued,

'Young man, you were searching the wrong database. You want the Tracing Service.'

The woman stepped out from behind the counter. 'I'm Ruti,' she said. 'Come this way.' Ruti escorted me back to the benches, humming under her breath. She looked to be in her late forties, a typical first-generation *kibbutznik* who had left the fields at the first opportunity and settled into the tedium of city life. 'People come here expecting us to give full reports about their lost family members,' she said. 'But for the most part, the victims only existed as index cards. What did the Nazis care about particulars? These weren't people. They were vermin to be exterminated.'

I tried to disguise my disappointment. 'But if he was a Privileged Jew, if he had been used for a special project, surely there would be documents. They might not have kept detailed records of every Jew, but in his case—'

'You might think that. Yet we only know of this Museum of the Extinct Race from survivors, not the perpetrators. We cannot be sure exactly of the grand design. It was a peculiar charge, asking members of this doomed race to prepare exhibits of how they wished to be remembered. And to what end? They didn't want to present a cultured people, a successful people.'

I sat back at the computer. Ruti leaned over and clicked through several pages, typing in passwords or search phrases, all the while railing against the irrationality of Hitler's great museum. 'We have other Privileged Jews on file, but it is possible this was a secret privilege. Why give glory to the curators? Better the future generations come through the museum and think the Nazis themselves had documented this extinct race. Absurd. Ah.' She paused. 'This is the Jakub Rand you want.'

And there he was. My Jakub Rand.

His file fits on a single index card: *International Tracing Service Master Index R18, T/D 450 723*. A jumble of names and dates that claim to account for three years of his life. There is nothing to say what he did at any of those places, how he survived. No mention of teaching children, or sorting through books, or a designation as a Privileged Jew. By this card alone he

T/D 450 723

Name: R A N D Jakob
oder RANDA Jan Dr. jur.
Elt: Aron und Augusta geb. Rosenberg
BD: 25.12.11 BP: Turka/U.R. Nat: -Rel.jued.

18.12.42 Gh. Theresienstadt transp. CK.
1.6.44 KZ.Auschwitz Nr. A 1821
15.7.44 KZ.Schwarzheide
Kdo Oranienburg, Sachsenhausen
3.45–8.5.45 KZ.Sachsenhausen, d.d. Russen befr.

URO Ffm.

ITS, Master Index, R 18

Dio.

YAD VASHEM ARCHIVES

should have died and yet there it is, on the last line: *KZ Sachsenhausen d.d. Russen befr.* He was liberated by the Red Army from Sachsenhausen, after spending almost eight months in Schwarzheide, a subcamp just south of Berlin that provided slave labour to the *Braunkohlen Benzin AG* (BRABAG) plant to make gasoline and diesel fuel from lignite coal. After liberation he lived in an unspecified displaced persons camp under Russian supervision before returning home to Prague.

'This is interesting,' Ruti said. 'You can see here that he was taken from Theresienstadt to Auschwitz on transport EB in May 1944. That was a special transport, to the so-called Czech Family Camp.' I had not heard of it, but I kept silent. It felt now as if she was in a trance, oblivious to my presence beside her, lost in a story she seldom had the chance to tell. 'For the Nazis it was Plan B. They had invited the Red Cross to visit Theresienstadt to see how wonderful life was for their Jews. They were confident it would work but there was a risk the inspectors would ask to see another camp. Word had already leaked out about the dreaded Auschwitz. Maybe they would want to go there too. So the Nazis made this Czech Family Camp in a corner of Birkenau, with its own entrance, its own rules. There were no striped pyjamas, no shaved heads. Conditions were atrocious, disease killed off many of the prisoners, but it was a paradise compared with what was happening only a few metres away. A small society of the damned, living in an outer ring of Hell. This is how your grandfather experienced Auschwitz.' She pointed to the next line, *15.7.44 KZ Schwarzheide*, and said, 'When the ruse was no longer needed, the camp was liquidated and the few prisoners still deemed strong enough moved on. The rest…straight to the gas.'

I had always thought that my grandfather was liberated from Auschwitz. It is where the family story ends, before picking up again in Prague. It is also the last place he is listed in the *Theresienstadt Memorial Book*, the massive tome charting the fates of all who were sent to the fortress town. In my mind, my grandfather's survival at Auschwitz had been the very essence of his Holocaust experience. Looking at the index card, however, I could see that he was there for just over six weeks, scarcely long enough for the tattooed skin on his forearm to blister, scab and heal. Then he was gone.

'Oh…' Ruti's voice pulled me from my thoughts. She tapped at the screen. 'Look here. I took the liberty of cross-checking the address. Four people lived with your grandfather in Biskupská Street before the occupation. At a guess his mother, a sister and two brothers. They were all included in the Community Register. But see—' She brought up two cards. 'For these two, Hermann and Růženka, there are no transport records. And no exit permits issued in their names either. Which means they died in Prague or—'

'I knew Hermann. He came to my *bar mitzvah*. I visited him in Austria a few years ago and then we lost contact. He just disappeared. When he escaped from Prague he managed to reach Palestine. His boat was scuttled as it neared the harbour. Most of the passengers drowned. He survived, joined the *Irgun* and, when the war was over, made his way back to Europe. Růženka, I can't say. She fled to America. I never met her.' I looked away, unable to tell her the whole story: that my grandfather fell out with his sister after the war; that her husband, a tailor, made him a suit that did not quite fit and he refused to pay; that she cursed him across the ocean and he cursed her back. That something so petty was enough to sever the bond of survival.

'I'm afraid that's all I can find,' Ruti said as we watched the printer spit out a copy of the card. 'The Tracing Service doesn't have all the answers. For most it's a start, nothing more.' She scribbled an address on the bottom of the page before handing it to me. 'About the library, the museum… Maybe you should also try here.'

Located less than an hour north of Tel Aviv, in the grounds of Kibbutz Givat Chayim Ichud, Beit Terezín is the only research and memorial facility specifically dedicated to the Nazis' 'model ghetto'. That it exists at all is the consequence of a particular historical condition: in the 1950s, the Czech Communist regime was recasting the Holocaust to exclude Jews as the primary targets of Nazi barbarism. It was, therefore, left to those Jews who had fled Czechoslovakia after the war to set the record straight.

The building that houses Beit Terezín is in every way unexceptional: a plain beige brick structure, a testament to the era in which it was built. The kibbutz's socialist enterprise had given birth to precisely the sort of buildings that were simultaneously popping up behind the Iron Curtain. If Beit Terezín had been created to give back a voice silenced by Communist Czechoslovakia, it was a ham-fisted aesthetic homage.

'Do you know what it meant to be a Privileged Jew?'

Věra Obler is the last of the survivor archivists. She is ethereal, a wisp escaped through a crack in the dark space of history. Her silver hair is in a bob that, when she flicks it to the side, reveals the nape of her neck—impossibly smooth for someone well into her eighties. A red, knitted cardigan clings to her slight frame.

'Not just a Jew with privileges,' she adds, 'but to be designated a Privileged Jew? A *Prominenten*?'

I had never really thought about the concept as anything more than colloquial, a way to describe those who, for one reason or another, were given a reprieve, so they could witness their people's suffering for a little longer. The writer Bruno Schulz was a Privileged Jew. For such an honour he was shot dead in the street while returning home with a loaf of bread—because his Nazi protector, Felix Landau, had murdered another Nazi's Privileged Jew. That is what it meant to be privileged: you were the currency in a malevolent system of exchange.

'On this computer,' Věra continued, pointing at the glowing green screen, 'I have all the Nazi records at my fingertips. Gone are the days I would have to trawl through paper files.' She tapped away for a few seconds then looked up. 'See here. This file is mine. I worked on the camp's outskirts, tilling the fields. Can you read it? Come closer. *Obler, Věra. Garden detail.* My point is, if you had a job, I have your record. Now, there weren't many Privileged Jews. Most of them we knew already, by name. They were the *Judenältesten*, the organisers, those with special skills, who could help the Nazis achieve their aim. Vital cogs in the machine,' she said before bringing his name up on the screen. 'Your grandfather was not one of them.'

Věra flicked a switch and I watched the words disappear. 'His name is mentioned once, on a request for exemption from transport. Your grandfather and, by association, his mother and his brother. It came from the *Jugendfürsorge*, the Youth Welfare Department. I can see where the misunderstanding lies. He was, it appears, a teacher. For his work he was afforded some privilege, but that is quite different from being a Privileged Jew.' She rummaged through some papers on the desk and handed me a sheet. I scanned the German until I found them:

Jugendfürsorge — Waad Hassafah

An die Transportkommission.

Wir bitten Sie, folgende Mitarbeiter nicht in abgehende Transporte einzureihen, da deren Verbleiben im Ghetto zur Aufrechterhaltung der hebräischen Arbeit unbedingt notwendig ist:

Mitarbeiter: — Familienangehörige

Aus dem Altreich:

Mitarbeiter			Familienangehörige			
Braunfeld	Schaje	IV/13-845	Braunfeld Taube	IV/13-844		Schwester
Frucht	Deborah	IV/13-434	Frucht Dr. Jak.	IV/13-433		Gatte
Kästenbaum	Prof. Isr.	IV/11-559				
Koschland	Dr. Isr.	I/74-9443				
Rosenthal	Frieda	IV/10-905	Rosenthal Ethel	IV/10-904		Schwester

Aus dem Protektorat:

Mitarbeiter			Familienangehörige				
Borger	Rosa	257/AAm	Borger	Paula	256/AAm	1890	Schwest.
Ehrlich	Hanna	791/S	Ehrlich	Frieda	790/S	1899	Mutter
			Ehrlich	Eva	792/S	1926	Schweste
Graus	Franz	287/G	Graus	Ada	286/G	1897	Mutter
			Graus	Friedr.	288/G	1924	Bruder
Hatschek	Kurt	512/Ai					
Herrmann	Josef	831/U	Herrmann	Grete	832/U	1911	Gattin
			Herrmann	Akiba	833/U	1934	Sohn
Löwy Dr.	Karl	46/S	Löwy	Vera	45/S	1919	Gattin
Metzl	Paul	959/U	Metzl	Olga	958/U	1890	Mutter
			Metzl	Ruth	960/U	1924	Schwest.
Müller	Aron	954/U					
Rand Dr.	Jakob	572/Ck	Rand	Gusta	571/Ck	1892	Mutter
			Rand	Sam.	451/Bf	1923	Bruder
Scheck	Abraham	31/Bd	Scheck	Rachel	372/AAc	1884	Mutter
Steinberg	Ida	542/Ba	Steinberg	Ludw.	543/Ba	1910	Gatte
			Steinberg	Amos	541/Ba	1938	Sohn
Weiss	Eugen	576/Ai					

Jugendfürsorge: — Waad Hassafah:

Rand Dr. Jakub 572/Ck — *Rand Gusta 571/Ck 1892 Mutter*
Rand Sam. 451/Bf 1923 Bruder

Věra waited a moment before continuing. 'He also sent some correspondence to us sometime in the late 1980s. He makes mention of this task, with the books, and he names a few people we know were involved with the Central Library at Theresienstadt. But if you want my opinion, these are just names dropped willy-nilly.'

I wanted to protest. In her eyes I could see sympathy, pity even. She tried to explain: 'I was there and I can tell you quite definitively it didn't happen. I would have seen it or heard about it. We knew all the goings-on, we were a fully functioning society, an entire metropolis piled into a matchbox. We lived on each other's shoulders, quite literally. Nobody kept secrets; to do so was pointless. There was a library, that much I know. We have lists of those that worked there. Jakub Rand was not one of them.' She reached into a plastic pocket next to the computer and pulled out what appeared to be an earlier version of the newspaper article. It was in Yiddish, clipped from the *Canadian Eagle* in 1987. 'This, I am sure, is what you were speaking about when you first contacted us. What can I say? It is a good story, but there is no truth to it. Murmelstein, Eppstein? Two of the most famous names in the camp. They were the *Judenältesten*, the Camp Elders. It's impossible. They couldn't have left Theresienstadt, couldn't have gone to Prague. And Muneles? That was also an important name, but not until after the war. When the camp was liberated, while he was still there, he wrote some short reports but said nothing of any Museum of the Extinct Race. Once he returned to Prague he was one of the key figures who helped to establish the city's new Jewish Museum. That's why he is remembered. That's why this article mentions his name. You want to see the true story about Theresienstadt? You want to know where your grandfather was? Be my guest. Head outside. The exhibition is just along the path.'

I stood in the hall of Beit Terezín's museum, reeling. The exhibition was just one room, cavernous but maze-like, intended to make visitors feel as if they were in a cramped ghetto. It was the exodus, in reverse, a peculiar miniature. It lacked both the grandeur of Yad Vashem and the power of visiting the camp itself. I couldn't help but think this memorial redundant, a minor relic from a time in which the horrors it depicted were not accessible.

I stood against the wall, next to a picture of Rabbi Benjamin Murmelstein, the most maligned of the *Judenältesten,* and tried to work out how long I was obliged to wait before I could leave without appearing rude or ungrateful. Murmelstein's smug, swine-like face stared out across the room to pictures of filthy streetscapes on the opposite wall. Legions of emaciated ghetto folk craned from the windows of their overcrowded rooms. As the hall spun around me, their heads moved from side to side like ceramic carnival clowns.

I steadied myself and looked into Murmelstein's eyes, hoping for some clue, but instead Věra's words echoed in my head. *I was there.* She had lost interest in my quest and offered to look up other family members as a consolation. For the next half an hour I listened to the scraping of a dot-matrix printer. When she had finished, Věra stood up triumphantly, tore the tooth-holed strips from the side of the paper, and handed me the printed index cards of the rest of my family. 'I'm sorry you didn't get what you wanted but it wasn't a complete waste.' I thanked her and said that she had been very helpful. She walked me out to my car.

I had already started the engine when she tapped on the window. She waited until I had rolled it all the way down before leaning in close, as if to whisper, but her voice resonated in the small space: 'It is, I suppose, the great danger of exhuming someone you love. You must first displace the dirt. And even then, when you lift the lid on their coffin, you won't always find a familiar face.'

Who was I to question Věra's experience? I could hardly challenge her, say that she was merely a gardener, while my grandfather was a highly regarded intellectual specifically tasked with overseeing one aspect of a top secret project. Perhaps my mistake was semantic, a belief in his status as a Privileged Jew when all available evidence clearly suggested he was not. Věra seemed to think in absolutes: because my premise was wrong, so, too, was the rest of my story. Especially considering that it conflicted with her own. I would not have expected her to know of these few individuals, locked away sorting through crates of stolen Judaica while she plucked potatoes from the ground. My grandfather and Věra had survived two different Theresienstadts, on parallel but competing plains in the multiverse that was the Holocaust. No matter what evidence I brought forward, his experience would always seem fanciful to her. And so here, on this kibbutz dedicated to the commemoration of the camp in which my grandfather briefly disappeared from history's view, I found myself up against the great Perspex wall of Holocaust ownership, the barrier encountered by every member of the second and third generation who tries to make sense of what happened to their family.

What arrogance, to say that we, not those who survived, know better. How can we claim to stand back objectively and collect evidence like police poring over a crime scene? How can we claim that there *is* an objective narrative, floating above individual experience? Who are we, the ones reaping the benefit of their sacrifice, to dare suggest that their view was obscured by the plumes of smoke wafting skywards with the souls of their children?

And yet…it is our duty to confront the silences, to break open the cracks that have thus far only allowed flashes of light to pass. With the luxury of time, distance and technology we can deconstruct those we loved, in order to try to set the record straight. But in doing so we risk inadvertently fanning the flames of Holocaust denial, that horrid beast that feeds on the doubt we might create. Such is the historiographical tightrope we walk.

So we search, we sift, we question, we beg, we scream, we suffer, we smash at doors with our shoulders, until we hold those pieces of evidence in our clenched fists. But even then we are left to wonder: whose stories are they; who owns the experience; to what end can it all be used? And still there are the schisms when—like the man who comes before the law in the parable told to Josef K by the kindly priest—we reach the door meant only for us and confront a guard who will not allow us to pass. We cannot wait there forever until the door is closed. Neither can we just barge through. Such was the impasse I had reached with Věra. I couldn't bring myself to say that perhaps she was wrong. For in the end, as I drove away, I knew that the truth of my grandfather's story was not more important than the peace she had found in her own survival.

I returned home via Prague, to visit my mother's cousin Ludvík and search for what my grandfather might have left behind. It had been almost thirty years since my last visit, when Communism still cast its pall over the city's majestic beauty, when I stood in line, holding my great-grandmother's hand, waiting an hour to buy the lukewarm carcass of a chicken that would become our dinner. She did not live to see the city reborn. A year before the regime fell, she took ill and died. Her ashes were scattered in the forest around her holiday home in Sudoměřice. Within months my cousins began to write of new landmarks, fast food chains, international brands. Of freedom and excess. The Czech people had a new hero, the poet and playwright Václav Havel, a resurrected Christ, a modern day Tomáš Masaryk. He had brought light to the city, chased away the forty-year night. It was in this new Prague that I could at last hope to find traces of my grandfather, in the streets, in books, in the recesses of untapped memories. And, of course, in the labyrinthine corridors of the Prague Museum.

> Thank you for your email. I can of course meet you but since I am quite sure that your grandfather did not work in the museum during the war I am afraid that I will not be able to help you with any new information.
>
> MARTA HAVLÍKOVÁ
> DIRECTOR

I didn't write back.

'Maybe visit for nothing,' Ludvík said in his strained English. 'Or maybe this interests you.'

Had Ludvík's mother been taken to Theresienstadt like her sisters, she too, might have fled to the furthest corner of the world and made a home in Australia. But fate played a cruel trick on Hana Rubíčková. She was spared the horrors of the Holocaust only to have her son—the boy she named after her father—cast into the jaws of another vengeful God, Communism. He would not know childhood as his cousins knew it. He would not be free to play the same games, learn the same lessons, make the same mistakes. And yet Ludvík was a cheerful boy, adventurous and cheeky, making do with what little he was given. In some ways he was also lucky; the bureaucratic wheels turned in his favour. When his classmates were sent off to train for menial jobs in the greater party machine, Ludvík was singled out to study engineering. It guaranteed him a steady income, enough to help his mother get by, enough to make a start on a family of his own. Throughout it all Hana remained his one constant, and he repaid her sacrifice with absolute devotion. Her death a few months before my visit had left him bereft. He had not ever imagined a world without her.

'At the back of cupboard in Biskupcova house I see box for shoes my mother kept. Inside is this.' Ludvík reached into his front pocket and pulled out an envelope. 'It is not grandfather so maybe not important for you.' He unfolded the paper, flattening it against the metal table. The pencil strokes had faded, and were almost invisible. 'Letters. From grandmother of you, Daša. It is from the camp. Maybe Oświęcim. You know? Auschwitz?' Ludvík bent down to examine the pages, his finger scanning each line before coming to a stop. 'Here. I try with translate. *We have escaped with our lives...I tell you gas is used on large scale.* If you want, maybe I make copy.'

All this time I have fixated on him, his story. Daša has been there too, but only in the background, as a subplot. When the article about my grandfather was published in the *Jewish News*, it did nothing to displace her from within the comfortable narrative our family had come to accept. The eldest daughter of a convert, she and her sister Irena were sent to Theresienstadt then Auschwitz. Somehow they managed to stay together. Somehow they survived. We built stories around her strength—she laid train tracks, dug ditches—and around her Aryan beauty. We tried not to imagine all that the latter might imply. In the camps, she carried a gold ring—in her hand, her mouth, wherever it could be hidden—waiting for the moment when she would have to trade it for her life. The moment never came.

Not once had I considered her mother and two youngest sisters waiting for Daša and Irena in Prague, praying for their safe return. I certainly hadn't thought they stayed in contact. The very idea seemed impossible. I knew of postcards that were sent from the camps, usually to further the ruse of resettlement, but full letters, uncensored, untouched?

'You don't know?' Ludvík said. 'Babička Františka visited them in Terezín. Together they made Christmas.'

I wander the streets of the Old City hoping to find them. Could it be that, in walking where they, too, once walked, I might feel them again, in a warm gust of air, a tightening of the hand, a familiar scent drifting from a nearby restaurant? I stand outside 3 Jáchymova Street, then make my way east towards my grandfather's home in Biskupská Street. How many times did he make this same journey? I reach the corner where there is a large church fenced in by iron spikes. I loiter outside number five. A shopkeeper comes out and stares at me. I wait; the air is still. My grandfather will not come. As I head back to my hotel, I am taken by the strange similarity in the names: Biskupská, Biskupcova. As if Jakub and Daša had almost lived as one.

'Before you go, there is one place I take you.' Ludvík and I were sitting at the kitchen table in his mother's old apartment at 13 Biskupcova Street. It was almost exactly as I remembered it from when I had visited as a child. More than anything, it struck me as a shrine to Babička Františka. In the twenty-odd years that Hana had lived there, she did almost nothing to make it her own. Even the table, formica-topped with streaked aluminium legs, was the same. It was here that my mother walked in and caught me smoking. I was five years old. Babička Františka, unable to otherwise communicate with me, saw it as something we could do together. Ludvík shook me from the cloud of memory. 'Come. We go now.'

The radio blasted Euro-pop as we headed into Nové Město, Ludvík mounting kerbs and jumping traffic lights. We pulled into a spot opposite a grand, pale-yellow building. I stepped out of the car and peered across the street. Flowers—red, blue and white—lay in bunches beneath a pock-marked slab of large cement bricks. On top of a single rectangular window, its frosted glass covered in dust, there was a plaque, guarded on one side by a soldier, the other by a priest, cast iron sentries with their heads lowered in a show of respect.

'Is important church,' said Ludvík. 'Saint Cyril and Methodius. Here is Czech story for Nazis. After operation to kill Heydrich, paratroopers hide here. Bastard traitor betray them. There was big fight. Nazis pour in gas and water but men don't give up. Finally, Nazis break inside. Men are brave. Shoot themselves. This is Czech man. Now we go look.'

I followed Ludvík across the road and into the church. He was almost running, the patter of his feet echoing back up the stairway that led into the crypt. Inside, it was dark and musty. Along the walls were stone inlets, like hives, where coffins once lay. There was an eerie silence, broken only by the odd snatch of wind that sounded disconcertingly like a voice. I tried to imagine the paratroopers, knowing they were surrounded, wading through

the water that was being pumped in from the window above. I wondered if they knew, when they first heard the sirens, and the German orders barked from outside, that it was hopeless. Did they count their bullets, calculating how many they could spare before turning their guns on themselves? Ludvík walked slowly along the gravelled corridor. He stopped at each bronze bust that marked where one or another of the paratroopers had died. He caught up with me at the other end, near the door leading into the main body of the church, the door the Nazis finally breached. 'This one is my story,' he said, his soft voice reverberating through the crypt.

I returned to the vestry, where the story of Operation Anthropoid is told on a series of posters, the tone sombre but with an undercurrent of pride. I read each poster in turn. The Nazi occupation. Heydrich's rise to power. The training of paratroopers in England. The planning. The fateful attack. Heydrich's survival. Then, soon after, his death. I stared at a photo of him lying in state—his thin, angular, insect-like face—and turned to the next poster:

> [The] resistance group, together with several members of the former Masaryk Resistance League Against Tuberculosis, provided the paratroopers with safe housing in Prague and all the necessary assistance...The paratroopers' main bases were the flats of the Zelenka and Moravec family in Biskupcova Street in the district of Žižkov. The paratroopers' most selfless helpers included at first sight ordinary, inconspicuous Czechs who refused to reconcile themselves with the reality of Nazi occupation and were prepared to risk not only their own lives but also those of their closest relatives...Without a single exception, their members were either executed or chose suicide.

'Ludvík!' I gasped. Across the room, he looked up from an installation recreating the bicycle and overcoat that had been displayed in the window of the Baťa department store immediately following the attack. I pointed at the poster, at the words. *Biskupcova Street in the district of Žižkov*. 'Is it...?'

'Same Biskupcova Street? Daša. Yes,' he motioned around the room. 'Here, it is your story, too.'

Back in Australia, I floated on a paper lake, trapped in a gorge of boxes. One small storage container in a building full of them. A vast hall of souls, memories that people could not cast off, but probably don't ever visit. We are all hoarders when it comes to the lives of those we loved. The room was two metres by two metres, smaller for the encroaching mountains of cardboard.

Files shifted like tectonic plates around me. When I rolled up the door, I expected to see their house in miniature. I wanted my grandfather's leather recliner, with its extendable footrest. I wanted my grandmother's card table, on which she always kept boiled lollies hidden under a tea towel. Most of all, I wanted my grandparents back.

The air was dead, a low hum of fluorescent lights echoing in my head. Alone there for two days, I sifted through it all. My grandfather was a prolific correspondent, but any order in which his papers were once kept had been lost in the rush of the clean-out. It was all there. Letters to doctors about my grandmother's treatment for Post Traumatic Stress Disorder. Letters to the German government, fighting over every cent they refused to give. Letters to former employers about monies owed and copyright infringed. And then, between some letters to the local council about a proposed halfway house and some legal documents relating to his property investments in Surfers Paradise, I found it. A bushel of papers with letterheads I recognised. Beit Terezín and Yad Vashem. He had written, and they had written back, just like Věra Obler had said. It wasn't a journalist's act of ventriloquism. It was his own voice.

For the first time I would be hearing my grandfather's side of the story.

On 11 January 1983, my grandfather sat down at his desk, took fresh sheets of paper from the pile in his top drawer and typed out the same letter twice. One was addressed to Yad Vashem, the other to Beit Terezín. It was the first time he had contacted either institution. Despite going to Israel on a number of occasions, he had never visited either place, an omission that he explained in an almost offhand way: 'I freely confess to having tried as much as possible to avoid it,' he wrote, 'so as not to resurrect the past in my mind, in my conscious mind at least.' There is a certain humility in the sentences that follow, a desire to contribute to history and, perhaps more importantly, a palpable need for their author to understand his place in the wider Holocaust survival narrative. The letter is less than a page long and sums up three years of unimaginable suffering in a single matter-of-fact paragraph. 'My personal data and my experience,' he wrote, 'are of no particular significance.' At that stage the modesty was genuine. The lid was still shut on the box of his memory, the lock still in place. My grandfather was, for the first time in his life, daring to whisper out through the keyhole. It had taken him thirty-eight years.

I scanned the letter for any mention of the Museum of the Extinct Race but there was nothing. Instead, this: 'While my memory still serves me I should like to find out whether your documentation files contain the title *TALMUDKOMMANDO* and if not, does Murmelstein mention this group in his book about Theresienstadt?' I read over that word, sounded each syllable out loud: *TALMUDKOMMANDO*. 'I was a member of that small group of Rabbis and Hebraists selected by Murmelstein, our object was to catalogue and comment on all books and manuscripts that were stolen from all over Europe.' The letter concludes with a few lines about his movement between camps and his arrival in Australia. Then, his signature in shaky script.

My grandfather received almost identical replies from both institutions, albeit some five months apart. No files could be found on the *Talmudkommando*. The work of cataloguing Hebraica in Theresienstadt was documented, although not in any detail. Yes, there was mention of some sort of ghetto library in Murmelstein's memoir, but it was only in passing, a mere paragraph. 'We would appreciate it very much,' wrote Esther Aran of Yad Vashem, 'if you write to us and give us more details about this work.' The head archivist of Beit Terezín at that time, Pinda Shefa, was more effusive in his reply, but it amounted to the same thing. He knew nothing of this *Talmudkommando*, was sorry that he could be of no real assistance, but was keen, nonetheless, to learn more.

And so my grandfather's first attempt at entering the wider discourse of Holocaust survival was, at least in his mind, a failure. The institutions he had finally gathered the courage to approach saw him as just another voice in an ever-growing crowd. He refused to sit in his office writing it all down, only to have it disappear into some bottomless pit of paper, where it would never be read.

Turning away from the keyhole of memory, my grandfather retreated into daily life, where mundane concerns served to suppress his demons. He still had a full-time job. He could still revel in the time he spent with his family. His health was still relatively good. He was still actively involved in the community. He could still enjoy his operas and action movies. Yad Vashem and Beit Terezín didn't need him and he did not need them.

That all changed in 1989. Completely unprepared for retirement, my grandfather was desperate to find new ways to fill his days. He was bored and angry. His body was starting to fail him. It was time to pick up the trail he had abandoned six years earlier.

This time, however, he had a new weapon in his arsenal. Evidence. The article about his role in the Museum of the Extinct Race—the same one I would discover when it was reproduced in translation in 2005, after he had died—was published in 1987 in the Yiddish supplement of the *Australian Jewish News*. Although it did not cause the international sensation my grandfather seems to have believed it did, it certainly created ripples. The article was republished in Yiddish newspapers around the world. America, Canada, Germany, Czechoslovakia. My grandfather figured that if he showed it to those who had previously dismissed him, they might now give him the credit he was due.

'Dear Sirs,' he wrote to Beit Terezín in 1989. 'I refer to our previous correspondence…' As if no time had passed at all. 'I have been asked to shed more light on that little known *Talmudkommando*, of which I was a member from its inception in 1943 under Dr Murmelstein right to its liquidation in the spring of 1944.' He was not averse to puffery, presenting them with a carrot of exclusivity. He would not talk to the press if Beit Terezín wanted to speak to him.

The response was prompt and, for my grandfather, completely unexpected. Although it reiterated Pinda Shefa's inability to shed further light, its sender was the new archivist, Alisah Shek, wife of Beit Terezín's founder, the late Ze'ev Shek. According to Alisah, Ze'ev Shek had been the youngest member of the very group about which he was enquiring. 'You might remember my late husband,' Alisah wrote. Although there wasn't documentary evidence as such, she did have some personal information that might assist. 'All I know is what I remember vaguely from his stories about the place.' After the war she travelled with Ze'ev to various castles in the north of Bohemia 'where we found vast quantities of books, which the Germans dumped there in heaps and mountains, but I don't even remember if some of them were marked by the *Talmudkommando*.'

It was a promising development. My grandfather had found a reliable correspondent who didn't dismiss him out of hand and who, thanks to a personal connection, had a special interest in his *Talmudkommando*. Any satisfaction he might have felt from Shek's first letter, however, was soon shaken by her second, sent immediately afterwards. Being Czech, the archivist possessed only a rudimentary grasp of Yiddish and hadn't actually read the article before her initial response. Now, having deciphered it, her curiosity turned to doubt. The tone of this second letter was completely different, terse and interrogative. It bordered on accusation. 'Sorry to bother you,' she began, 'but I would like to know the following facts.' What came next was a series of pointed, suspicious questions, which cast doubt on everything from his knowledge of the *Talmudkommando* to his very identity. 'Is the index card which is nearest your name really you?' she asked. And then, twisting the knife, 'We have no "Randa" matching you.' The other questions sprang from her intimate knowledge of the group, which clearly did not accord with the facts as presented in the article. 'When did you go to work in the Prague Museum? When did you get back to Terezín? You mention Dr Murmelstein, who was the last *Judenältester* and was in charge of the *Talmudkommando*, but you also mention Dr Eppstein, who was *Judenältesten* before and, to my knowledge, never worked there.' In signing off, she threw down the gauntlet. 'We shall be most grateful if you will answer our questions and until then we wish you all the best.'

The gambit had failed. In bringing attention to this 'little known' group, and then relying on an article that he must have known took considerable liberties with the truth, my grandfather damaged his chances of being taken seriously by those in the know. I imagine that those two or three months in 1989 must have been both intellectually and emotionally tormenting. Only two years before, his story had become an interesting historical curiosity. People knew him as more than 'that teacher' at Mount Scopus College in Australia. He must have hoped against hope that he would never come across someone like Alisah Shek.

When it came to Yad Vashem, my grandfather was much more frank. Already on the back foot, he realised that he had to flag what Shek already knew if there was any chance of him being believed. He enclosed the article, but this time with a caveat. 'As the result of a series of conversations,' he wrote, 'an article was published in the *Australian Jewish News* on 6.2.1987, which unfortunately contained many inaccuracies.' Perhaps most curious, however, was his pursuit of one aspect of the article that seems hardest to verify. 'Would you have any clues who was that high ranking SS officer/ Hauptsturmbannführer/ who arrived in 1943 and put us though an examination over an open volume of Maimonides/?/ in order to select the final small group of Hebraists?' Is it possible he felt a debt of gratitude, that he wanted to repay the man for saving his life? 'Rumour had it that he was from the Preussische Staatsbibliothek or a professor of Semitology from Berlin.' Unfortunately, his frankness was to no avail. A month after sending the letter, he received an even more curt reply from Yad Vashem. They thanked him for his letter and the article but could find nothing more than what they sent in 1983.

There must be another letter, but it has been lost. It contained something that changed Alisah Shek's mind. If I were to guess, I would say it was an admission, like the one my grandfather made to Yad Vashem, that much of the article was untrue. On 2 August 1989, Shek wrote to my grandfather one final time, a warm and detailed letter, mostly about her husband. It is clear from the tone that her suspicions had been allayed. As quickly as she had turned against him, she was now his friend. She thanked him for that missing letter. She didn't really know much more but put him on to two other people who were involved in the *Talmudkommando* and who might have been able to help. Frau Kornelia Richter—'who does research about it' —and Dov Herschkowitz.

He never followed up with either of them.

I have tried to track down both Frau Richter and Dov Herschkowitz, but it is too late. Richter has disappeared and Herschkowitz died. The trail ends there, with them, in 1989. It is one of the great frustrations for family of those survivors who could not tell their stories. We, who have been entrusted to perpetuate their memory, to uphold the great refrain of 'Never again', who have stood by and watched in horror as it has happened again and again, in Cambodia, in Rwanda, in the Former Yugoslavia, in Darfur, in the Middle East, are left impotent in their silence. We understand it. We cannot be angry. But it is there. And we have stood in its vacuum for too long. We didn't question. We were too young to understand. We thought them immortal. We cannot ask them, our grandparents, our great-uncles and great-aunts, their friends, because, at the time, they chose not to speak and now they are gone. And we cannot find the pieces of the puzzle that make up those few years of their life, for they, too, are gone.

So I will not meet those learned men who sat on either side of my grandfather, also sorting books, praying to God that there might be more collections to be plundered, so that this menial process might go on long enough for the Messiah—any Messiah—to come and free them. I will not meet the people who slept next to him, infested with lice and covered in boils, on the wooden-slatted bunks of Auschwitz. I will not know the passengers on the cramped, shit-stained cattle trains, their feet burning on a carpet of quicklime, or the workers in the munitions factory, forced to carry gnarled shrapnel in their emaciated arms.

All I shall ever know will be hearsay.

I turn back to that line in the letter to Yad Vashem.

'Unfortunately it contains many inaccuracies.'

Occupation

I

'Arnošt Flusser!' The teacher called out from the front of the room. 'Hands on your head this instant. We do not wave at wasps.'

The boy stood at the window, his right arm hoisted awkwardly in limp salute. It wasn't clear to his classmates if he was welcoming the troops as they rolled in below or simply wiping clear the film of mist he created with each breath. Arnošt was that kind of boy. Everything he did seemed ambiguous. 'A fine bed he makes…' His teacher now spoke in a soft thrum. 'Turning down the sheets so that the lice might be more comfortable.' A pause. Some giggles, stifled. His teacher, louder: 'He has yet to consider how he will sleep.'

Arnošt Flusser stood still. Was it defiance, fear or boyish fascination? He knew the teacher was pointing at him, but could not turn around. With his nose pushed against the glass, he did not see wasps or lice or insects of any kind. He saw three-headed newts, like in the story his father had told him the night before: salamanders that slithered across the bridge in perfect formation, their sleek bodies hiding the mechanical movement of their feet. They made no sound. The snow swirled fairy dust dervishes around them, settling on the cobblestones or disappearing into the river, but never gathering on their leathery skin. The newts did not stop to feast on the slugs that had gathered on either side of their columns, enthusiastically extending their antennae. Little Arnošt glimpsed stuttered movement in the whiteness of Křižovnická Street. He turned to look in the direction of the university, and saw clusters of chameleons changing colour as they tumbled forward: one moment grey, then a fluttering white, and, as they came closer to their reptilian brethren, red and black. How strange nature can be, he thought. Another puff of mist. Again Arnošt wiped it away.

The teacher sat at his desk watching as the young dreamer surveyed the dawning of a new city. Was the boy recalcitrant, touched or, as he often suspected, blessed? Either way it amounted to the same thing. Arnošt Flusser was a nuisance. It was not within the teacher's powers to instruct such a child. At most he could help the boy survive, making sure he was not the butt of the other children's scorn. But there were limits. Every few days he would send Arnošt to stand in the corner because, the teacher would tell himself, examples must be made.

'Master Flusser! To the back. Now!'

Not that it seemed to bother the boy. On the contrary. The teacher suspected that he relished the opportunity to escape into his imagination, that he saw it as a reward. He could never tell. Best to leave him be. But today was different. Today the teacher wanted to storm to the corner and grab Arnošt by the ear, shake him and scream at him: '*Can't you see what you're doing?*'

For everyone else in the room nothing had changed. Why then must this one child insist on reminding them that the streets were no longer their own? That the moment the bell rang, and the doors flung open, they would step out into purgatory—and Arnošt, the only Jew, into hell? And yet the teacher did not have the strength to stand up, to walk those few steps, to take hold of the boy. Slowly, he exhaled. He had not slept in days.

At four-thirty that morning the teacher had rested the wireless on his lap, adjusting the frequency, hoping to hear the message without interference.

It was from the State President and the Minister of Defence. '*German Army infantry and aircraft are beginning the occupation of the territory of the Republic at zero six hundred. The slightest resistance will cause the most unforeseen consequences and lead to the intervention becoming utterly brutal. All commanders have to obey the orders of the occupying Army. The various units of the Czech Army are being disarmed. Military and civil aeroplanes must remain on their aerodromes and none must attempt to take to the air. Prague will be occupied at six-thirty.*' If only it were a hoax, a radio play, like last year's Halloween broadcast that had caused panic in distant lands. How he had laughed when he heard. But not now.

The teacher had already resigned himself to the occupation. He knew it was coming. First the Sudeten, then the Slovaks. Only yesterday there had been an attempt to start riots in the streets, to incite his countrymen to fight and make victims of the German minority, victims that the little madman's army might swoop in and rescue. Of course it failed, the Czech people would not rise to petty provocations. But it did not matter. The rescue was already underway. And as he prepared for that chunk of earth that was Czech without Slovakia to be tacked once again onto its northern lands, all the teacher could think about was that six o'clock was a terribly inconvenient time. How was he supposed to get to school to instruct the children?

The teacher made sure to leave home early. He did not want to be held up at roadblocks or, worse, crushed by some wayward tank. He gathered his books and stepped out the front door. Orbs of hazy light seeped from the street lamps, struggling against the unforgiving Prague night. The teacher could just make out others who had put forward their daily schedule by an hour or two.

'*Ahoj*,' someone called out.

'*Ahoj*,' he replied into the darkness.

This is what it took to be normal, to ignore the occupation, to show that life went on. The teacher listened for signs, explosions, the thunder of gravel crunching under wheels. But all he could make out was a howling gale as jagged shards of tiny icicles smashed into the side of his head.

And yet, on the wind there were whispers he could not hear. The conquering forces had been delayed. There was resistance. Their vehicles were breaking down. They were lost. The sun had begun to edge over the horizon and there were no tanks, no guns, no motorcycles, no planes. Prague was still free. The teacher made his way down Platéřska Street and turned into Křižovnická. He hurried, his collar pulled high. At the school's entrance, he fumbled with his keys, then strode down the corridor to his classroom. All was as it should be. Soon the radiator would come on and the thaw would begin.

The teacher jumbled the sticks of chalk, making sure that there was no discernible order because, he thought, *chaos is freedom*. He wiped the top of his desk, although it was not dirty. That is what a free man can do. And then he slumped into his chair and awaited the arrival of the sun, of children and tanks, wondering which would come first to snatch this precious freedom away.

'Children, please,' the teacher said. They had stopped listening, and turned instead to watch Arnošt Flusser and revel in his mute rebellion. How could the teacher hope to impart knowledge anyway, today of all days? The bell had sounded, and he had tried to call them to order, but it was too late. The storm was finally upon them. *Peace in our time*.

Groups gathered in the street: student fascists from *Vlajka* in dark, starched uniforms, like-minded Germans and *fräuleins*, clutching bouquets of forget-me-nots to their sparsely covered breasts, flowers to throw upon the advancing soldiers on the off chance that their bodies failed to attract the desired attention.

The *Vlajka* students marched onwards to meet the approaching army, drunken fire still raging in their bellies from a night spent fighting with police outside the Deutsche Haus on Na Příkopě Street. There was no satisfaction to be had in that fracas. It was not like September, those few glorious months after Munich, when they had stormed the streets with impunity and given the Jewish parasites a taste of what was to come. It now seemed a lifetime since their nostrils had filled with the sweet smell of smoke from Jewish shops and synagogues. Five months. Yes, a lifetime.

Now, in the presence of their saviours, they would be born again.

And so they marched on, these fledgling fascists, brushing clumps of snow from their shoulders, gazing at the columns of motorcycles, each with three soldiers, that were riding towards the centre of the Reich's newest city. They marched in anger, in shame, that the whole city had not come out to welcome their new masters. Only one of them stopped and turned around, catching sight of something that filled him with hope, with happiness. There in the window, three floors up, was a little boy, an honourable citizen, holding his hand high in salute.

Heil Hitler.

2

'To Anděl Richter and his festering cesspool of the inferior race!'

A chorus of cheers erupted from around the room as glasses were thrust into the air, waves of beer spilling onto the floor. Anděl Richter shook his head, made a bow and turned back towards the kitchen. To those crowded inside he was a hero, a joker and quite possibly the shrewdest businessman in all of Prague. Across the city, at Café Manes and the Hanau Pavillion, on Slavic Island and at national clubs as far out as Smíchov and Strašnice, signs were popping up forbidding entry to Jews or quarantining them to sections away from the general view. But not at Café Palivek. Richter had refused to put up a sign, kept it all intentionally vague. Within days of Reichsprotektor von Neurath's August expansion, Café Palivek was seen as an escape from the occupation, a place where patrons of all kinds could mingle unmolested. No doubt things would have continued as such had an off-duty German soldier not wandered in one evening and taken offence when asked by a tipsy Jewish man for a cigarette. A shouting match ensued and was about to turn violent when four quick-thinking patrons surrounded the soldier and bustled him out. As the man slunk into the dark streets, Richter was still at the door, waving his cleaver and shouting obscenities.

The following morning he was visited by the Gestapo. 'If you wish to permit Jews inside,' said the larger one, 'you will put up a sign restricting them to a particular area. Don't test us, Herr Richter. The rules are very clear. Any further breaches will result in the immediate transferral of this business to somebody more amenable. Good day.' Richter obeyed, but in a way that was very much his own. He drew up a large sign and placed it near the entrance so that only two booths in the café were not 'For Use By Jewish Patrons'. Then he sent his waiters, his chefs, his cooks, his friends, everyone he could possibly muster, out on the streets to spread the legend of Anděl Richter and his minor rebellion. As some told it, he had kicked out Reichsprotektor von Neurath himself and lived to tell the tale. Business began to boom, so much so that Richter was forced to employ new wait staff. He genuinely came to like these Jews. He liked the air they brought to his establishment. They smelled like money.

Jiří Langer dug in his pockets and pulled out a wad of notes. 'Richter will swing one day,' he said. 'Old Konstantin will come down personally and drag him by the ear to Hradčany Castle. You'll see him hanging from the tallest turret, flapping in the wind like a white flag.' He slapped the cash onto the beer-soaked table. 'Here,' he said. 'Help a man into poverty.'

Georg Glanzberg reached across and grabbed the money. 'Another round? Dr Jakobovits? Jakub?'

Jakub R sipped at the cloud of bitter white froth that floated across the rim of his glass. Georg shook his head and laughed. Tobias Jakobovits downed what was left of his drink. 'Something smaller then,' Georg said. 'A tumbler. Maybe a thimble. Try to keep up.' Jakub watched his friend disappear into the crowd.

'I've had another letter,' said Langer. 'Max has finally settled in Tel Aviv. A nice apartment, he says, for a fledgling city. Elsa still berates him that he chose to take a suitcase of papers. Every day she rattles off the list of what they left behind. Of course, he couldn't have taken anything valuable but she won't hear it. She has banished him and his suitcase to the smallest room in the apartment. Meanwhile, he busies himself with the theatre. It's the only art form he still abides.'

Langer dabbed at his lips with a napkin. His weary eyes lent him a distant air, as if his presence in Prague was now only physical. His announcement that he intended to leave for Palestine came as little surprise. He had long been a spiritual nomad: a committed Jew who could not decide which of the various images of Gods was His true face, and who was willing to walk to the ends of the earth to find out. As a young man he had ventured to Belz and immersed himself in that community's strange interpretation of Hasidism. It was, if Jakub had read Langer's account correctly, more akin to the mysticism practised in the Far East, complete with transcendental meditation and levitation. In other words, utter nonsense. When Langer returned to Prague, his own brothers hardly recognised him, and within months he journeyed back to Belz to finish his apprenticeship. It passed through him like a fever, and while he still professed a strong interest in Hasidic ideals, he returned once again to the city, shaved his beard and nestled up to a new god, Zionism. He now proposed to follow his old friend Max Brod to Palestine, not to escape any potential threat—Langer still had faith in the essential decency of the Czech people and was sure they would protect the Jews from harm—but to sow the seeds, quite literally, of an eternal homeland. He would not wait for the coming of the Messiah or the construction of the new holy temple, because Palestine was itself the Messiah, and fertile fields would be temple enough.

'Sorry I'm late.' Otto Muneles eased his portly frame into the booth beside Jakub. 'Duty called.' Short and ruddy-faced, Muneles spoke with a voice more accustomed to conversing with the dead: soft, low and without any discernible inflection. It was something he had honed while travelling with Langer among the Hasidim, when he was expected to exude no aura, make no mark, speak with no one. Back in Prague, he all but disappeared from communal life, unable to relate to those around him. When the head of Prague's *Chevra Kadisha*—the Jewish Burial Society—died, Muneles was named his successor. Now his days were spent sitting and watching over the bodies of the recently deceased, patting them clean with a white cloth, and preparing them for their return to the earth. Only the news of Langer's imminent departure had lured him from his kingdom of boxed pine. He was not even aware of the curfew that was to begin the following day. It was of no consequence; his life was already spent casting shadows.

'So we heard,' said Langer. 'Bad news travels.'

'Fuchs?'

'Poor fellow,' said Jakobovits. 'He left a note?'

'Only one line: *We have no homeland.*'

Jakobovits leaned in to the group. 'See what becomes of a soul without stimulation?' he said. 'They took away his country. They took away his business. And he loved both of those more than he loved life itself. Give a man time with his idle thoughts and soon enough he'll conjure a noose.'

'He jumped,' said Muneles.

'A cleaner end, for sure. And more certain. Perhaps he left it to God. *Here, you choose.*'

'A dilemma for our dear rabbi, I suppose,' said Langer. 'Where to put all these suicides? The corner must be full by now.'

Muneles's eyes narrowed, and he pushed his glasses to the bridge of his pug nose. 'Fuchs was buried like any other man. In these times we need not make excuses. To jump from a window is a natural death. The widow cried, but only because he hadn't dragged her out with him.'

'Natural, indeed,' said Jakobovits. 'If the Community Council hadn't found me something at the school when they closed the library, heaven knows what I might have done. This city is my life.'

'And Palestine?' said Muneles.

'Is suicide of a more protracted kind, where you die clinging to an idea. Isn't that right, Jiří?'

'There is no limit to what an idea might sow,' said Langer. 'From some grow beautiful crops. Herzl was an idealist. There can't be much more labour in building a state than in tearing one down. Look at us here. In our own lifetimes we have lived in four different countries. And we didn't have to move an inch.'

'Masaryk would be turning in his grave.' Tobias Jakobovits sat up and tugged at his lapel. 'While we are being legislated out of existence, he is in heaven crying. Every time it rains I lick my coat cuffs expecting to taste salt.'

'Here.' Georg returned to the group cradling four glasses of beer. 'Oh.' He looked at Muneles. 'I didn't see you come in. I can—'

'Thanks, no,' said the other with a dismissive wave.

'So which dune in the stinking desert will you call home?' continued Jakobovits.

'I'd always picked you for the Jerusalem kind,' Jakub said.

'I go where the wind takes me,' said Langer. 'The city, a kibbutz...I'll find my feet. Max says he has a few leads for my book. I'd like to be published there. It's a fine way of putting down roots in a new homeland.'

Jakobovits shook his head. 'Until the dirt shifts,' he said.

'Who knows what will be?' Langer turned to Jakub. 'You of all people should understand. A teacher? Who'd have thought it? One week you graduate law school and the next...Here you are. Taking my place. Come on, Tobias. Admit it. You're happy to have him.'

'Of course I am. But, Jiří, it's a poisoned chalice you pass on.'

'Rather his poison than theirs,' said Georg.

'Exactly,' said Langer. 'Theirs is a crooked jurisprudence. Even the simplest act of conveyancing is theft. How would Jakub spend his days? Transferring Jewish factories to Aryan hands? No, don't pity him. He's been spared. You should pity his poor classmates instead, having to submit to the dictates of our new rulers. He should teach.'

'And stay to fight,' said Jakobovits.

'Jáchymova is hardly the resistance,' said Langer.

'But you're wrong,' said Jakobovits. 'Staying in Prague is an act of resistance. This entire city simmers with rebellion. This is not Poland. And meanwhile you abandon ship and we gather here to smash a bottle of our finest wine on the hull of your lifeboat.'

'I wish I shared your faith,' said Muneles.

'You do, Otto. You're staying. Look, this is not the time for petty tribalism. Zionism is a golden calf, weakening us in the face of a terrible threat. We divide, they conquer. Where does your loyalty lie, Jiří? To the people who continue to stand by us even while their own freedoms are compromised, or to some idea that seeks to place our entire people in a sandy ghetto? I will not leave Prague. None of us will. This is the seat of Jewish life, with or without their laws.'

'Please, Tobias,' said Muneles. 'Jiří is an ideologue, a poet. He is not a deserter.'

'No,' said Langer. 'I'm a realist. Reichsprotektor von Neurath has gelded us with his decrees. I do not intend on spending this war in quarantine.'

'You'd prefer to wilt in a faraway desert,' said Jakobovits, 'digging ditches and being accosted by camels.'

Jakub laughed and wiped his mouth with his sleeve.

'*L'chaim*,' said Georg, raising his glass. 'To our friend Jiří Langer and his ever-shifting ideals. To the last great wandering Jew. I think what Dr Jakobovits means to say is that we'll miss you.'

'Why?' Jakobovits would not let go. 'He'll be back soon enough. In the meantime you and Jakub will keep his seat warm. That's why you worked like dogs, right? Earning your fancy doctorates in disciplines now forbidden to us just to be stuck at Jáchymova?'

'It may not be their first choice of profession,' said Langer, 'but in times like these it will do.'

'Does that make it easier?' Jakobovits interrupted. 'Will you sleep better on your journey knowing that you sail on the winds of their broken dreams?'

Jiří Langer reached across and put his hand on Jakub's arm. 'Forgive him, Jakub. The Rebbe of Belz once told me that sometimes learning is an end in itself. I know you'd hoped for more and, to be frank, I don't know what I'd do in your position, if all I'd worked for came to nothing.'

Tobias Jakobovits leaned back and stroked his goatee. 'I suppose you'd go to Palestine,' he said with a wry grin. 'On a ship of fools.'

3

Františka Roubíčková sat at the kitchen table and watched as her cigarette burned a mournful halo at the base of the mottled black filter. For eleven years now she had been one of them, eaten their food, partaken in their rituals, hidden from their God, but not once had she longed for their cursed embrace until the day Ludvík marched her and the girls to the new Jewish Community Council office to sign the local register. 'Not you,' he said, gently wresting the pen from her hand. She stepped back, watched the nib as it spilled out his name in black ink. When he had finished he held the pen over the page and looked up at the clerk. 'The girls?' Ludvík said. 'Their mother is…' The clerk glanced at Františka, then nodded his head. 'Them too,' he said. From behind: whispers. The indignity, the finality of that word, *mischlinge*, half-breed, an umbilical tether, fusing flesh and blood. Her flesh. Her blood. Františka trembled as Ludvík added their names. How she wished to see hers beside them. Yes, it was true. At last she knew what it meant to be singled out among the nations, what it meant to be chosen.

And to think that good fortune had briefly touched upon her family. Two months before the Germans strutted in and set about choking the city, Ludvík had secured steady employment with Pan Durák, a distributor of women's clothing. Finally he had a job that would allow him to return home to his family each night. Soon after *they* came, Jews were forbidden to leave Prague without a visa and Ludvík's new employment proved an even greater stroke of luck. Had he not found Pan Durák when he did, had he not charmed the affable Sudeten with his half-truths of past business conquests, the girls would almost certainly have starved.

Pan Durák, too, found fortune in the German occupation and was eager to share it with his employees. On a spring evening in April, they gathered at a tavern in Nové Město to hear the distributor lay out his plan. 'Enough with the dowdy salons that take our stock on consignment,' he said. A waiter swept by and left a plate of beer cheese on the table. 'Enough with the long journeys, the late nights. Here in the city we now have an army of customers.' The men leaned in closer. 'I know their type. I've fought alongside them and I've fought against them. It's always the same. They care only for conquest then go blind in the afterglow. So, too, in commerce. You must make them think they've won. Let them stab you in the heart. You'll see.' He spat a fleck of rind to the table. 'We'll bleed crowns!'

Ludvík's confidence grew with the warmth of spring and by the end of the first month he had sold more dresses than any of Pan Durák's salesmen. Františka began to recognise in the man who shared her bed the boy who had once charmed her with his dreams and promises. Every night over dinner he regaled the girls with stories of danger and daring, so that they wanted nothing more than to see this brave knight in action. 'Mama, please,' said Irena on the first day of the summer holidays. What choice did she have? Excited children are like unexploded bombs. They must be defused or they will wreak havoc. She filled a hamper with dry biscuits and sliced meat and told the girls to get dressed. 'Be sure to look smart,' she said. 'For Papa.'

At the sight of his family, Ludvík stood tall in the square. He waved, smiled, danced a clumsy two-step before straightening himself and charging into battle. Františka and the girls found a quiet place beneath the awning of a corner café from where they looked on as he haggled with the passing soldiers in their stiff grey uniforms. With every sale Ludvík turned to his family and winked. They clapped and cheered. Františka marvelled at the way the soldiers parted with their money. 'I'm telling you,' said Ludvík when he joined them for a quick lunch. 'Prague has become the Nazi clearance store!' That night the girls looked upon their father with a new reverence. Františka also felt a certain warmth, perhaps even pride. She would write to her family in the morning, invite Emílie to visit.

When it became apparent that the occupation was truly entrenched, that the world really had abandoned his little country, Pan Durák invited Ludvík and Františka to dinner at his apartment, to discuss *a certain matter* in private. 'Please,' he said as they entered. 'No formalities. Here I am called Bedřich.' The first two courses were devoured in good cheer. Paní Duráková—Františka never did catch her name—was a competent cook, skilled in technique if lacking in soul. Pan Durák talked of his time on the various fronts, and of the lessons he had learnt in war. 'It is life,' he said. 'Only smaller.' At her host's instigation, Františka spoke of her millinery. He probed her about the source of her fabrics, her manufacturing process and likely yield. By dessert, Ludvík was all but a spectator to their exchange. Paní Duráková, too, had retreated to the kitchen to grate hard white cheese over a second batch of fruit dumplings. Františka was, she realised, cornered.

'Consider a partnership,' he said at last. 'I'll take whatever you can manage. Sixty–forty. In your favour, of course.' He pointed across the room to a floral dress made of coarse fabric that was hanging from a doorhandle. 'These soldiers, they are happy to buy whatever we show them. What do they know about materials when my salesmen speak with silver tongues? Think how much more we could make if your husband were to offer them a matching hat.' Ludvík bit down on the silver cake fork. Františka pawed nervously at her napkin. 'Pan Durák…' she said. The Sudeten let his name linger in the sweetened air. The clink of plates and silverware chimed from behind the kitchen door. 'Bedřich,' he said when he saw she could not go on. 'It is not something you must decide right now, though I can't see what there is to think about. Your husband has made me good money. I owe him. Both of you. It is a fair offer.' Františka blushed. 'I know, yes. It's just that… my hats…they…' Pan Durák grunted and turned towards the kitchen. 'It's late,' said Ludvík. 'We should be going.' The gentle strains of a Dvořák tune filled the room as Paní Duráková reappeared with the steaming balls of dough. 'My husband's mother claimed to be related to the composer,' she said, before registering the change in mood. 'Yes, yes,' Pan Durák said. 'A cousin.' The dumplings were consumed in haste and the night ended with handshakes and kisses. Pan Durák helped Františka with her shawl and squeezed across her shoulders. She pulled herself free and hurried out the door.

'Is he mad?' Františka said as they made their way home. 'Already he fills our house with his rags. And now this? He mocks me, Ludya. Right there in front of you. And what do you do?' They walked on without speaking, the silence broken only by the rattle of passing tramcars.

The idea was quickly abandoned and Františka's rage subsided as money continued to tumble in faster even than Ludvík could drink or gamble it away. He had returned to his ways, she knew it, but each time she stood in the square, the girls by her side, and saw how they cheered and blew him kisses, how he stole moments to sneak across with a boiled sweet or pastry, she thought it enough that he was a good man, a good father. Pan Durák, too, was unfazed. Other than a return to formalities—he curtly corrected Ludvík the first time Ludvík tried the familiar *Bedřich*—the Sudeten seemed pleased with his continuing success. It was a blessing that these brutes who watched over their city appeared to know nothing of taste. That was until they began to approach Daša.

Ludvík's blood flowed weakly in Daša's veins, much less so than in her sisters'. His dark, wavy hair, brown eyes and stooped gait were not evident in his eldest child. In the past, Františka had seen it as a cause for concern. There were whispers, she knew. Not just the girl's looks, but her prospects. She had heard them. 'Nonsense,' Ludvík had said. 'It will do good to bring some fairness to this community.' She understood; it was an apology of sorts—she needn't have been dragged into this mess. But what was done was done, and now the girl was being looked upon as a prize Czech artefact, another spoil of war.

She is a child, Františka thought. *Have they no shame?* But they, too, were children. And they spoke to her daughter with such reverence that it was hard for a mother's heart not to be moved. 'Frau,' they would say, doffing their caps first in her direction before clumsily trying to engage Daša in her own language, never considering that she might be fluent in theirs. Watching these scenes, innocent teens giggling, reminded her of her own childhood, when she was courted by the boys at the lake, only to be scolded by her mother. 'Františka!' Paní Vrtišová would say. 'You are destined for higher things.' The city, that was her destiny. But fate had its own way and so, while her mother was right, she could not have known that, viewed from the wrong angle, Prague was just another Potemkin village; often behind the grand facades of high society lay empty plots.

And Františka's empty plot was called Žižkov.

Two raps at the door, a pause, then another. Františka Roubíčková stubbed out what was left of her cigarette. From the next room, silence. 'Sleep, little Handulka,' she muttered. More knocks, the same pattern. Františka fastened her apron and headed to the door. It was Ottla B.

'May I—'

'Of course. Please.'

Ottla B seemed only to exist in the reflected light of her son. Everything about her was muted: the matted brown hair that drooped from her small head, her eyes, which drifted from hazel to grey and back again, and her curved posture, as if she were in constant repose. Even her words curled back into her throat when she spoke.

Františka didn't intend to become her friend. Theirs was a bond born of necessity, conceived in a fit of Ludvík's indignation. From the day Bohuš first arrived to escort the girls to their new school, Ludvík had taken to spending his evenings alone in the corner of the local tavern, drinking the cheapest beer and picking at a plate of limp pickles. Jiří B watched the sad performance for a week until he could bear it no longer. Snatching up his glass, he walked across the room, settled onto a stool beside his neighbour and offered to help.

'Don't be so proud, Ludya,' he said. 'We all make mistakes. So your fortune won't be measured in crowns. You have something far more valuable.' A sip, for effect. 'Each child is a blessing for which the father pays dearly. Unfortunately, the greater the blessings, the poorer the house. It is God's way of keeping balance. My wife and I have been spared, I suppose, though I can't say whose fortune I'd rather. Ottla would trade all the honour Bohuš brings us to have just one more, but it isn't to be. And so our pockets grow full while our house remains empty. Such is our lot.' Jiří plucked a pickle from the bowl. 'Look, Ludya, I can help. I want to help. What good can it do me while a friend suffers? Just take it and move on. Or consider it a loan. Pay me back if you like, whenever you can. I won't come knocking.'

Jiří went to put his hand on his neighbour's shoulder but Ludvík shook it off, slammed his glass on the table and put his face right up to Jiří's. 'We don't need you,' he hissed in a rabid whisper. 'We don't need your son. And most of all we don't need your charity.' He stormed out of the tavern.

The rage simmered inside him with every step and by the time he opened the front door he could no longer contain it. The girls cowered behind the gauze curtain as Ludvík thundered at his wife. 'Who does he think he is? Such a big man, taking pity on us. That bastard so much as looks at our family and God help me—' Ludvík grabbed a saucer from the counter and threw it against the wall. 'Do we starve here? Are we not content?' Františka went to sweep up the ceramic shards but Ludvík seized her shoulder and spun her back around. 'What does he have, anyway? That mouse of a wife? A son who has grown so large his fall will be heard in Moscow? Let the girls take themselves to school. They are not babies.'

If Ludvík was too proud to accept money from his neighbours, Františka had no such qualms. Back in Miličín, when she was a girl, the townsfolk always rallied to help one another. That was, according to her father, the very essence of community. Mother Nature was erratic; she would test each farmer in turn, destroying this one's crop one year, causing pestilence in that one's cattle the next. If it weren't for his neighbours, each one would be left destitute when his time came. 'Take this to Pan Sedlaček,' her mother would say, handing her a pot of their freshest honey. 'Wish him a sweet harvest. Now go.'

Why should it be any different in the city?

And so, the following afternoon, when Ludvík went out to search for yet another job or maybe just to drown his sorrows in a faraway bar, Františka Roubíčková tucked Hana into bed, kissed her forehead and walked proudly into the entrance hall of the nearby building.

'Františka!' Ottla could hardly contain her excitement when she saw who had been knocking. She beckoned her neighbour inside and pointed her towards the sitting room. 'Tea?' she said. Františka smiled and shook her head. The two women sat for a while and spoke of their children, then of their families, the street, fashion, current affairs, the rising price of fresh produce, music, millinery, theatre; in other words, everything except what they both knew had to be said. At last Františka came out with it. 'This business with the car…it has made a shell of him. He tried. I know he did. If only he prayed to a god more generous than luck. Maybe now…Look, Ottla, we appreciate Jiří's offer. Ludvík appreciates it. He just doesn't know how to say yes.'

'What of his parents?'

'I haven't the heart to ask. He has brought disappointment enough.'

Ottla was relieved. When Jiří had recounted the events of the previous night, how he had been afraid Ludvík would punch him or, worse, harm himself, she feared a great feud. But now here was Františka, in Ottla's apartment, not in the corner store, not at the tram stop, not making idle chatter on the street. 'It is still on Jiří's dresser,' Ottla said. 'Wait a moment.'

She returned, holding an envelope with the monogram *J.B., Proprietor* printed in the top corner. It occurred to Františka as she read those words that she didn't know what Jiří did, how he came by his money. Ludvík had never spoken of it. But this was not the time to ask. Františka took the envelope. 'It is only temporary,' she said. 'I will pay you back, I swear. Not only in crowns, but something more. A token of our friendship.'

For three months Františka toiled at her machine until she had saved enough to repay the loan. She regretted her promise of a token, but more so of friendship, and waited before rifling through her cupboards for something she could spare. Nothing too fancy, but enough to satisfy the hope in her neighbour's heart. She found it underneath a bolt of linen in the corner cupboard: the hat—grey felt, with a red bow—that had stood on her dresser table, watching over her as she nursed baby Hana, taunting her with its tangle of thread, board and cloth. Once the child had left her breast, she had finished it after all and immediately hid it away. Now she held it up to the light. Yes, with a brush to remove the dust, it would make the perfect gift.

Ottla gasped when she saw it and immediately placed it on her head. Františka feigned pride in her work. To the untrained eye it was a beautiful object, but beneath the band lay the signs of professional neglect—missed stitches, slight overcuts, spilled glue. Františka saw in it a map of time, innumerable separate periods etched as clearly as the rings on a felled oak. That it had come together, she thought, was a credit to her perseverance, not her talent. To that, it was an insult.

Ottla donned the hat like a crown through the streets of Žižkov. She began to speak of Františka as her dearest friend, and would try to be seen in her company. Františka, on the other hand, hid away, waiting anxiously by the window until Ottla disappeared back into her home or onto a tram, before heading outside. To her, the business was done. Then, one morning, she opened the biscuit tin to find her money gone. Ludvík was nowhere to be seen. Františka set off across the street. They would be friends after all.

'Quickly,' said Františka, stepping aside so Ottla could shuffle past. Františka pressed her eye against the crack in the door, peering out to make sure nobody was watching.

With the occupation had come a shift in the atmosphere of Biskupcova Street. Eyes no longer met, trust was undermined. Františka could not help but notice the way Jáchym Nemec from number nine would stand a little too close to conversations that didn't concern him, or how Štěpánka Tičková from number twenty-two was quick to spread outlandish rumours, or Žofie Sláviková watched over every purchase made by the customers in her corner store, sometimes noting them in a pad she kept in her shirt pocket, separate from the business ledger. Even Marie Moravcová from number seven, the volunteer sister of the Czech Red Cross, lovingly dubbed Auntie by most of her neighbours, had become secretive and aloof. The disappearance of one of her sons was the subject of persistent scuttlebutt. Štěpánka Tičková had it, on good authority, of course, that he had fled to join the army and, although she could not be certain, she suspected it was that of their oppressors. Auntie Marie, insisted Štěpánka, was now hiding in shame.

The darkness had also enveloped the entrance hall of number thirteen. Františka was convinced that those in her own apartment block were watching her through their peepholes. And while the visits from Ottla B were nothing more than the meeting of two friends in troubled times, to a more fanciful imagination they might be taken for conspiracy.

Františka Roubíčková let the door click shut. For now she was safe.

'Smoke?'

'Please.'

Ottla had grown into their friendship but, even more, she had grown into the occupation. There was a new confidence about her, a brashness, even pride, as if all she had ever needed in order to be noticed was a diminution in those around her. Františka's kitchen had become her staging ground. It was the unspoken interest on loans long since repaid, a chance to extend beyond who she had once been. Františka, for her part, had come to delight in her neighbour's peculiarities.

'Filter?'

'No need, thanks.' She leaned forward as Františka struck a match. A plume of smoke rolled up her face. 'It's nice, this,' she continued with a meaningless gesture around the room. 'We have some freedom now. I used to worry. I didn't want you to feel—'

'*Pshah.*' Františka waved away the smoke. 'You know how it is. This too shall pass.'

'Jiří is pleased for me…for us. He says the company has reddened my cheeks. Meanwhile he grows pale in the shadows. I swear the man is a chameleon. Not that he talks about it. I know only that he has associates. Nothing more. I've half a mind to sniff at his collars, but if there's a mistress it's she who is being cheated. I can't see my dresser for his gifts. *Search out every opportunity*, he says. *There is money to be made in the occupation.*'

'And the boy?'

'He listens to his father. Then, the moment Jiří leaves in the morning, he, too, is out the door. I worry about him but what can a mother do? He is of that age.'

'Maybe he is right. Ludya too. Personally, I dread these new opportunities. Here we are, more secure than ever. The girls, happy, fat. But we are feasting in the eye of the storm. One way or another it will come undone.'

'You fret too much.' Ottla smiled. 'It's like you no longer trust comfort.

But look at you. How long has it been since you've come to my door? When did I last see you duck beneath the window ledge as I passed by? Now we go to cafés, the cinema, sit by the river. You fill your ration cards with money honestly earned. Face it, Frantishku, this occupation suits us. Now gather your things. The children will be home soon and we have a date with Lída Baarová. I didn't much care for her in that last movie...what was it? *Virginity*. Yes. But this new one, a romance, they say...I might have to reconsider.'

'She's awful.'

'It's our national duty.'

'To wallow in the muck of bad taste?'

'Oh Frantishku, you don't know? Lída Baarová...She's taken Goebbels for her lover.'

4

Each night, as its inhabitants slept fitfully behind windows blackened to hide them from enemy pilots, the city transformed into a new and ever more frightening beast. Hideous plates of armour settled on the walls of its grandest structures, weighing down gargoyles and statues, and trapping the air so that the stench of half-digested hope hung on the dawn.

Behind a grey door on the second floor of an apartment building in Biskupská Street, Jakub R rose with the jangling of the alarm clock. In the darkness he felt the comforting presence of his mother, who still saw in him the future of their rabbinic dynasty, and the aura of an absent, yet omniscient father.

Jakub pushed the sheet aside and unfolded the nightgown that had protected his head from the wooden floor. It was still an hour before he would need to leave for work. He now had a rigorous, if not lucrative, routine—four days at the school in Jáchymova Street and two in the community archives—so Jakub R continued his dreams in the cramped kitchenette, stirring his coffee and telling himself that perhaps, when he stepped outside, he would find that the world had not changed for the worse.

A cough from the next room.

One never escapes, he thought. There is always a trail. The hopeless, the weary, the heartbroken: eventually they will follow. And they did: Gusta, Růženka, Hermann and little Shmuel. Until the occupation, their presence had mostly gone unnoticed. He had taught them to get by in the city. But after four years of familial responsibility in the tightening vice that was his home, Jakub found himself trying to stave off resentment. His landlord had recently increased the rent—'On account,' according to the letter, 'of the additional tenants and the decrease in security of a Jew seeing out a long-term lease.'

It was his penance, he knew, for having deserted his sick father, for not having come sooner to help his family. Now, for his recalcitrance, his mother lay in his bed in Biskupská Street with Růženka, while Hermann and Shmuel slept on the couches. The village folk had been good to his family, it was true. When they finally came to accept that their rabbi was not long for this world, they had made a collection of coins for his care in the city. Even some of those from across the bridge contributed. But word of pogroms in not-too-distant lands had tightened their purse strings and so, despite the best intentions of a community who owed the good tidings of their souls to this man, Rav Aharon and his family departed with little more than their carriage fare and the warm wishes of a terrified people. It was a mercy that the village folk never learned that their beloved rabbi died in a bleak hospice, writhing in agony as his helpless wife wailed beside him.

Jakub R tried his best to shield his family from the snide remarks of his neighbours. It was clear that they had come to begrudge the extra bodies. Tempers flared, most often outside the water closet that all the inhabitants of the second floor were forced to share. 'What is this,' said the widow Žuženka, 'some kind of ghetto?' Most aggrieved were the younger Jewish tenants. 'Yesterday I was late again,' said Albert Weil, the paper trader. 'They gave me my second warning, you know. These people need not look for excuses to fire a Jew. Now my future is hanging on your mother's bowels!' Jakub explained to Gusta and his siblings that things had changed, that they might have to wait until after eight before venturing into the corridor. Gusta just shook her head, unable to comprehend city life.

On the day of the first student demonstration, Jakub R returned home late, national colours pinned to his lapel and Masaryk cap in hand, only to find his little brother curled up against their mother in tears. 'I want to go home, Jakub,' Shmuel said between sobs. Jakub patted the boy on the head and turned to Gusta. 'Is Heju here?' he asked, but did not wait for an answer. He already knew. Hermann would still be out among the students. He fancied himself one of them. *Soon I will go to medical school*, he once announced with certainty. But there was no money to send him to Charles University. So, instead, each day he followed Jakub through the winding streets of Nové Město to the National Square, before heading off south towards Kateřinská to loiter outside the medical faculty. Hermann made friends easily. The students let him into their clubs, their dormitories, their homes. He would often disappear late into the night, well past curfew, while Gusta sat quivering by the door until he stumbled home, invariably drunk on the potent brew concocted in the university's chemistry laboratories.

The door swung open and they all turned around, expecting Hermann. It was Růženka. Like most nights after curfew she had been downstairs, in the Zahradníks' apartment, her ear against their radio. 'That box is cursed,' Gusta said when she first arrived in Prague and heard the disembodied voices crackle from the strange contraption on Jakub's dresser. 'How can one trust words when the speaker hides his face?' she asked. 'It is all *lashon hara*, malicious gossip. For that box we will have to repent.' Her relief was palpable when the decree came for all Jews to hand in their radios. 'Now you will see,' said Růženka. 'From this day it will only be gossip.' She did not speak to her mother for a week, as if it had been Gusta's fault. She refused to join the family for dinner, instead knocking on the doors of their non-Jewish neighbours, asking if she might listen to the nightly broadcasts. Every one of them declined, some politely, others less so, until Kryštof Zahradník stopped her in the washroom one day and whispered that she should come to his apartment after sunset. Kryštof and Karolina didn't seem to care that they were helping a Jew break the prohibition; they were listening to Jan Masaryk's dispatches from England, which itself was punishable by death.

'There was shooting,' said Růženka, more a statement than a question.

Jakub nodded. 'Yes, after the march. We cleared the streets, the SS held their weekly peacock parade through Wenceslas Square, and then the crowd reconvened. I kept my distance and lost sight of Heju early. He headed to the square with his friends. Then the soldiers arrived.'

'They are saying a man is dead. A baker. And fifteen others in hospital, mostly students. Some National Festival.'

'He opened the window and watched as they ran past,' said Gusta softly, tilting her head towards Shmuel. 'They came in bursts, with fury in their eyes. They were screaming. He was screaming. It was like the plague of the firstborn. Only divine intervention stopped them from coming through the door and dragging us from this place.' The boy was now dozing against her arm. 'Tomorrow I may still mourn a son.'

'Mother,' said Růženka. 'They were nowhere near here!'

'They were. Or their evil spirits. They came from the gates, behind the church, to take us all away.'

At dawn, a dishevelled Hermann tried to sneak through the door, but his mother and siblings surrounded him. He barely had the strength to recount the story of his arrest and immediate release by the Czech police, and the promise he had made to the officers that he would stay off the streets until the situation had calmed and the Reichsprotektor ceased baying for student blood. 'It was past curfew,' he said as he lay down on the couch. 'The streets were filled with German police detachments. We hid out near the hospital. Some of our friends were hit.' Hermann pulled the sheet over his head and was asleep before his mother's next question.

Gusta R experienced the occupation from the window in the bedroom of Jakub's apartment. She was frightened among the masses. Whenever Jakub tried to convince her to go outside, insisting that the city could yet be her home, her eyes narrowed and she said, 'This is exile. At home I knew everyone's name.'

A month into the occupation, Jakub could see that even the corridors of the apartment building had become foreign to her. She stopped speaking to the neighbours. It was a mournful quarantine, but she had taken to it with determination; she wore only black, sat on the lowest chair, took off her jewellery, and kept her head covered with a threadbare shawl. From time to time, Jakub would come home and catch his mother in conversation with the one picture that remained of her husband. She still counted on him to protect her, and would sleep with the picture under her pillow so that his spirit might watch over her dreams.

In the fortnight following the student demonstration, Gusta Randova began to wonder if her mind was playing tricks on her. Black water seemed to trickle under doors and windowsills, and, in the puddles that crept towards the cracked walls of the apartment, she thought swarms of cicadas were breeding, clinging to the wooden beams behind the plaster, and rubbing their wings in chorus, until they sounded the news that Hermann and his friends had waited for in shrill alarm.

The student, Jan Opletal, is dead.

Gusta pressed her hands against her ears. Růženka crackled like the radio with words that were not her own. Hermann raged with the voice of a thousand students. There would be another demonstration, this time bigger, a wake like Prague had never seen, a wake worthy of a martyr. Only Jakub spoke softly, but it was his voice that cut the deepest. 'You mustn't go,' he said to Hermann. 'They will be looking for an excuse. It is suicide.'

For two days Hermann stayed in the apartment and kept to himself. On the third, he grabbed his coat and cap and rushed out the door.

The city raged in defiance and then fell quiet. Jakub set off for work and immediately sensed the presence of a malevolent seraph stalking the streets of Prague. The night had stolen the drunken, rebellious cries of the previous day and carried them, without trial, to a secret slaughter. But their spirits would not stay silent: the wind moaned with the ghostly echoes of young voices. The seraph continued its rampage into the new day, feasting on fear and anger, breaking open doors, chasing its prey from windows and grabbing those who hid in corners.

Jakub looked over his shoulder, checking for the beast, ensuring that it was not heading back towards Biskupská Street in search of Hermann. The boy was courting trouble; he had fought with the police outside the law faculty, and had driven them back over the bridge. Jakub could only hope that the *mezuzah* on their door might offer some protection.

At last Jakub reached the square, and his old spirit guide Jan Hus. The great martyr covered his eyes with a giant, bronze hand while the Hussite minions tended to a cemetery of rotting garlands below. The national colours had melted into each other, and ran like bloody tears through the gaps in the stones. A blast of warm wind tore across the square from the south and Jakub knew the seraph was near. Taking his leave from the monument in five backwards steps, as he was still conditioned to do, Jakub turned and rushed up Pařížská Street, hoping to hear the sounds of children at play. But there was only one other person in Jáchymova when he arrived: Georg Glanzberg sitting on the kerb, waiting.

'School's out,' said Georg. 'The whole city is in lockdown. Father sent me here; he knew you'd come. We need to get off the street. Now.' Georg grabbed Jakub's cuff and led him the two blocks to the family's home on U Starého Hřbitova. 'Von Neurath was summoned to Berlin with Secretary Frank as soon as Hitler heard. He won't allow such weakness. In the past month he has survived three assassination attempts. And now this. He is celebrating his invincibility the only way he knows how, with an orgy of violence. The reprisals are already underway.'

'This simmering calm,' Professor Leopold Glanzberg said as he turned from the window. 'It cannot be trusted.' Jakub and Georg were standing near the radiator, still brushing the snow from their jackets. From the next room, the clattering of plates and a woman's merry singing. Leopold walked towards the cabinet and reached for a bottle. 'For your nerves,' he said as he passed a tumbler to Jakub. Georg picked up his violin and tapped anxiously at its strings. Leopold poured one for him too.

'A drink to luck,' said Leopold, raising his glass. '*L'chaim.* A year ago and it could have been the two of you.'

Georg gulped down the whisky. It troubled him to see his father like this. The old man was quick to despair; he had retired from the bustle of academic life, found peace at the nearby Jewish Museum—dusting the plinths, straightening the exhibits. Professor Leopold Glanzberg came to rely on the daily ritual and, when not at the museum, would stand anxiously by the window, staring across the street at its ceremonial hall, pleading with his charges not to surrender themselves to the gathering dust. That his name had once echoed through the most hallowed academic halls of Bohemia, that he was once consulted by community leaders, rabbis and politicians alike was no longer of any consequence to him. He had given up the care of human souls for that of ones less finite.

'The streets are almost deserted,' said Georg. 'Shopkeepers have not lifted their awnings. There is only the sloshing of buckets: German soldiers plastering the walls with posters. Another decree, of course. On my way back I saw an old classmate, who said the Germans have emptied the halls of residence and expelled anyone they suspect of involvement with the Opletal wake. Karl Frank wants to take Prague for himself—it is plain to see. The demonstrations made Von Neurath look weak so, while he was still trying to explain himself to Hitler, apparently Frank commandeered the official plane with a list of names in his hand. At this point my friend began to cry. If only it was expulsion, he said. Last night the student union meeting was stormed and the leaders taken away. As were some of the professors. Nobody has heard from them since.'

Leopold resumed his position against the window. 'They're dead, no doubt. And soon enough their loved ones will be receiving the bill for their executions. Boxes and bullets don't come cheap. We pay in hard cash for this occupation.'

Georg stood up to pour himself another drink. 'On Maiselova one of the posters says they're closing the universities. It is not enough that they kill our students; they are murdering the institution itself.' Georg raised his glass. 'To the death of knowledge. And, of course, to you, Jakub. My friend. Quite possibly the last Jew to attain any. May they put you on a plinth across the street so that my father can dust your shoulders.'

They played chess late into the afternoon. Each game lasted as long as Georg decided it should, allowing him to test out new gambits before moving in for the kill. Jakub's defences were clumsy, but occasionally Georg would sit back and look over the chequered battlefield, forced to reconsider his next move.

It was dusk when Leopold returned to the room. 'The patrols are more frequent,' he said. 'Jakub should leave while it's still light. His mother need not worry about two sons.' Jakub considered his impossible footing on the board. Once again, every piece was in danger of falling to Georg's perfectly positioned army. 'Stalemate, then?' he said as he got up.

Life had yet to return to the streets. Snow muffled the footsteps of the German patrols. Windows fell shut as Jakub raced the sun to Biskupská Street. There were still hours before curfew, but he did not trust the dark, the silence. The day had brought phantoms enough.

When he opened the apartment door and saw Hermann on the couch, Jakub stopped to kiss the *mezuzah*. The angel of death had passed over their home.

'I should be on one of those buses,' said his brother. 'I should be with them.' He had rushed to the dormitories when he'd heard, found them empty, saw the carnage. Books strewn across the floor, desks toppled onto their sides, broken glass and blood in the flowerbeds. Hermann began packing as soon as he got home. A few clothes, books, a spare pair of shoes. A blanket. He would need to travel light. There was no money for a train fare, let alone the migration tax. Anyway, Gusta would need it just to live. His only option was to walk, to stow away. He would make do wherever he landed. England. America. Palestine. He would join the army, the medical corps. One way or another he would be initiated on the front line.

Gusta cursed, then pleaded, then cursed again. Hermann sat by her side, explaining his reasons in his soothing voice, while she gazed at the picture on her lap, as if Rav Aharon might offer counsel. Their last hours together were spent planning Hermann's journey, inventing adventures in foreign lands. Scheherazade in Biskupská Street. The sun arrived to take him, and they all stood at the door. Only Shmuel failed to appreciate the gravity of the moment; in his eyes his brother was a storybook hero.

5

Their black robes disappeared into the curtains on the surrounding walls. Three stern men: disembodied heads and hands. On the table before them lay a dossier—the indictment, only a few pages, provided in triplicate. The men read in murmurs, stopping only to ask a question of the officer standing at attention behind the desk nearby. He answered through a police interpreter. The men returned to the papers, the *clickety-clack* of a typewriter continuing throughout. They looked up as one, a single organism, at the condemned man, crumpled on a steel chair, his hands tied with cord. The three heads of Cerberus, guarding the gate to Hell. Five days of interrogation, then here. It was not their place to consider what he had endured. They knew enough—that in the nearby palace the interrogative method was refined torture. Here, in the single courtroom of Pankrać Prison, it was their job merely to make a show of justice. The charges were unremarkable: clandestine sales, forging ration cards and making black market purchases. A profiteer. Nothing more. The trial would take less than ten minutes.

When they first came to arrest him, Jiří B assured his wife and son that he would be back that afternoon, that it was a misunderstanding, that he was a simple businessman trying to get by in difficult times. It was a calculated charade, designed to fool the Gestapo men who had knocked at the door just as his family were finishing their breakfast. The men spoke no more than was necessary and waited by the entrance for Jiří to gather his things before ushering him outside and bundling him into a waiting car. Ottla lingered on the porch, trying to catch a glimpse of her husband. The car idled by the kerb just long enough for her to see the larger of the Gestapo men fasten a blindfold over Jiří's eyes. It was an unnecessary caution. Everyone in Prague knew where these unannounced visitations ended and, anyway, Jiří was familiar with every pothole on the short drive to Peček Palace in Bredovská Street. He had banked there briefly before the war, and stood outside its imposing black facade during the recent demonstrations while the crowd demanded the release of his friends.

He thought it easiest to confess, to name names, not out of fear or spite but out of expedience. It would be enough to deny his captors the pleasure in their cruelty; he wanted to watch the dissatisfaction in their gaze as they slid the sharpened bamboo reeds under his fingernails, or stubbed out their cigarettes on his cheeks, or touched the electrodes to his exposed balls. These men in their black shirts and pants were merely playing out scenes that had, through constant practice, been rendered almost natural. Only their hands gave it away: the men were always unsure what to do with them, where to position them. It was uncomfortable watching them. Jiří saw no need to prolong it. Let them do their jobs. They didn't want to be here any more than he did.

When they were finished with him, when they were ready to bring him before the court, the blood and the bruises would render him almost unrecognisable.

The girls slept soundly, the train's rhythmic rattle dissolving into dreams of summer play as it carried them back from the country. Františka Roubíčková let her eyes drift to the passing fields. How quickly one can fall under nature's spell, she thought, to believe in the promise of peace. Somewhere beyond it all a war was being fought, one in which they were all expected to do their part. Even in her little town of Miličín, where the birds still sang and the honey still flowed, men watched over crops like fretful parents. There were records to be kept, quotas to be met. Penalties to be paid. 'They've conscripted us all,' Emílie had said while they sat outside on the veranda in Sudoměřice, watching the girls splash in the lake. 'Even the bees.' She took a sip of tea and placed the cup back on the saucer. 'And you?'

Františka could not tell her sister how it was in the city, not the truth, anyway. Two months had passed since Pan Durák closed his business, casting Ludvík back into the grips of his affliction. Most days now, Františka sought comfort in the hum of her sewing machine. Only when the girls returned from school did the clamour of life resume. She saw little of Ludvík and had stopped watching the clock as curfew came and went. So seldom did he lie beside her at night that he did not notice the small gap Františka had made, pushing their single mattresses apart.

'Yes,' she said. 'And me.'

'What about that husband of yours?'

'He gives what he can. He has other concerns.'

'So nothing, then.'

'His parents are suffering. The factory is gone, sold for a pittance to a manager who promised to keep Papa Roubíček on in the storeroom. Four days it lasted before he was fired. Now he puts on airs so we don't think them a burden, but we can sense the despair behind his crooked smile. To think all this time they've helped us get by and now, in their need...We try to help. I try to help.'

'Frantishku, please. At this rate you will all starve and I won't have that on my conscience. For years I've held my tongue. Oh God, how I wanted to say something while you scampered around in the dirt like a fieldmouse trying to make ends meet. But no, it was your choice, your doing. You wore Ludya's sickness like a girdle. But this is different. Elias and I have talked about it. We want to help. We have our obligations to their Reich, but it is a good season, this year. The hives flow freely and the earth is burgeoning. Our larders are full and those bastards are none the wiser. When you leave you must take whatever you can. My dear, it's enough that you insist on calling yourself a Jew, but you need not live like one.'

'I couldn't possibly—'

'Damn your pride. Take. And when it is gone, send the girls for more. Give their barren aunt some joy.'

~

Františka Roubíčková knocked on her neighbour's door. From the stairwell behind her she heard the click of a latch, a slow creak and the snap of a tautened chain. Františka held her package close to her chest—a square of butter wrapped in baking paper, a jar of honey and what remained of the salami she had sliced for her lunch, bundled in a dishcloth. It was only right, she thought, to share this first bounty with her friend. But why? The debt had been repaid, forgotten. Yet each act of kindness was still stained with her disgrace. What would it take to right the order of things? Kindness, time, gifts, friendship: she had tried them all. No. Absolution would have to come from within. She would first have to forgive herself her original sin of weakness.

A faint scratching came from behind the door. 'Ottla?' she whispered. The scrape of metal hissed through the landing as a series of locks were unbolted. The door swung open to reveal her friend, unkempt, pale and drawn. Ottla pulled her close, heaving as she sobbed. Františka felt the damp warmth of tears seeping into her collar. In the flat light of the corridor, she saw swirls of dust above the litter on the floor. The sobs receded and Ottla stepped back. She took Františka into the sitting room and, as she sat on the couch, Ottla began to mutter, as if a valve had been twisted loose.

They had come for Jiří soon after Františka left for the country. For the first two days Ottla waited by the door. On the third she pulled down the blackout blinds and fastened them to the windowsills with tape. Until he returned it would be night, for that was when Jiří usually came home, when they would sit together as a family for their evening meal and talk of the day's events. She scolded Bohuš when he complained about the gathering grime. Her bed grew cold, unwelcoming. When Jiří had not returned for a week, she took her pillows and a blanket to the sitting room and lay them on the couch. The slightest noise would wake her and she'd rush to the door. Mostly it was nothing but, if it was Bohuš, she scolded him again: for staying out late, for breaking curfew, for giving her hope. Exasperated by her moods, he carried the pillows and blanket back to her bed. 'Let me wait up,' he said. And so she slept for the first time, but her head filled with horrible dreams: the fatal shot, the swing of the trapdoor, the snapping of his neck. In the morning, she checked the mailbox. There was no letter. She went out to check on the lists of the dead plastered across the city walls. Jiří's name was nowhere to be found. It became her daily ritual. Bohuš spent less time at home.

Official notification of Jiři's fate came three weeks after he was taken. He had been sentenced to six months' hard labour in the south. Matthausen. He would return in the winter, if he returned at all. Ottla could send him provisions but, given the nature of his crimes, all packages would be scrutinised. Anything for which she could not give a proper receipt would be confiscated and she would be brought in for questioning. She had yet to send him a thing and could hardly eat for the worry and the guilt. Bohuš couldn't understand and had taken to treating her like an invalid, forcing food into her mouth. Sometimes he looked at her with disdain, like he was already an orphan, tethered to the graves of his parents. He could not wait to escape, to run to his friends at the SOKOL youth club.

'But he comes?' said Františka.

'Yes,' said Ottla. 'He comes.'

Františka knew she would spend the afternoon here; she would tear the brown tape from the curtains, let the day back in. She would go to the kitchen, find bread, cut away the mould and prepare a meal. Tomorrow she would return and do it again.

All this time she had been mistaken: absolution does not only come from within. It is also found in the depth of another's despair. There is no satisfaction, no pleasure to be had. Absolution is a shrivelled kernel of shit: hard, unpalatable. It chokes away what is left of your soul. But it restores the balance. It silences debt's echo.

Every day it starts anew. The morning siren howls across the camp, but they are already awake. At night, exhausted, they had prayed for sleep. And still they lay there, staring into the dark until the whispers began. They spoke of their families, but not of their crimes. The night is no confessional, it cannot swallow shame. What is there to say, anyway? That what they did was of no consequence? That if only they'd had more strength, more courage, they might have done something that warranted death? Here they broke rocks, or the rocks broke them. Here they served their sentence, one day at a time. Each day an eternity.

Jiří B counts the drops of piss as they fall onto his blanket from the bunk above. He does not know how long he's been here, how much of his sentence he's served, only that it is enough not to be bothered by the failing bladder of a dying man. Soon they would take the poor soul to the infirmary, from where he would not return. Jiří pushes the blanket aside and gets out of bed. His face is level with his bunkmate. The old man smiles and holds out his hand. Jiří takes it and brings his cracked lips to the knuckles. 'Sleep, sleep,' he says. 'There's still time.' The old man mumbles and closes his eyes. Jiří rushes to the mess hall. A cup of tepid coffee and a crust of stale bread: fuel for a day in the quarry.

As the leaves turned yellow, the laughter of young girls danced on the cool Miličín breeze. They tried to outdo each other with their adventures. If

Marcela smoked out the hives, Irena dived in the lake. If Daša slept alone in the attic, Marcela slept on the floor beside her aunt. For those short visits they forgot the occupation, forgot what it meant to be a Jew, and when it came time to leave, their souls were light and their cases heavy.

At home, too, their stomachs were full. Even Ludvík who, despite all his failings, knew better than to ask questions, ate like a free man. But he took without giving, and for that Františka grew further away from him.

Ottla counted the days until her husband's release, scoring each one on the 1940 Baťa calendar that she kept on the kitchen bench. There was solace to be found in numbers, comfort in the shifting weight of time. Ottla did not blame Jiří for what had happened nor did she entertain the possibility of his guilt. *It is no crime to provide for your family*, she said. She was not bothered either by the appearance of so many familiar names—men she had not met but who she knew were important to her husband's dealings—on the lists of the condemned. A wife ought not assume the worst of her husband for the company he once kept. Where were they in her time of need, anyway? They had not come to console her. They did not bring her groceries or anything that might help her get by. Curse them and their fair-weather ways. After all that Jiří had done for them! Ottla stood and straightened her skirt. She picked up her pencil, leaned over the calendar and crossed off another day.

It was almost November when the first dusting of snow fell on the city. Františka opened her pantry. The girls had returned from a weekend in Miličín but this time there was not enough to fill the shelves. The frost had come early to the fields. The bees, too, had taken to their hives and would not come out. Daša spoke of a strange hush in the yard, the stillness of hibernation. *What a privilege*, Františka thought, *to sleep through the war, to not know hunger*. She had been expecting this day and had hoped to be better prepared. They would all have to make do with less. But how? Already, she could hardly recognise Ludvík's parents, with their distinguished clothes now so ill-fitting. How mean she would feel watching Papa Roubíček kiss the sachets of rice or barley that she brought, knowing that she could have given more. And what of Ottla B? Until the ground softened and sprouted again, it was not Františka's concern. Let them fend for themselves. So long as her girls were fed. *It is no crime to provide for your family.*

~

On the day designated for Jiří's release, Ottla resumed her vigil by the door, but he did not come. She waited through the night and the days that followed, afraid that the moment she stepped away he would stagger into an empty hallway and think she had abandoned him. Still he did not appear. Bohuš came and went like a house cat, to feed and attend to his bodily needs. He often smelled of fertiliser or gasoline or sweat. He was a man now and she was proud but also afraid. More than ever, he needed a father to guide him. Her Jiří: provider, survivor and, dare she say it, hero. Ottla stood by the door and waited.

Františka Roubíčková stopped on the pavement outside 13 Biskupcova Street and looked at the building on the other side. A white winter's sun shone in the clear sky. It was strange, Františka thought, that she had not heard from her friend. She had knocked on the door, whispered through the keyhole. Nothing. She left a small package on the mat—enough for a little cake to celebrate Jiří's return—and headed back downstairs. As she stepped onto the street she thought better of it and ran back. The package was gone.

Could the rumours be true? Štěpánka Tičková had spoken of a spectre that had recently crept through Biskupcova Street. It shielded its face from the light, she said, as it stumbled forward, tripping on the pants that hung from its cinched waist, before disappearing into a nearby building. Heavens above, Štěpánka insisted, there was no mistaking it. That sickly creature was all that remained of Jiří B.

'She buys disinfectant,' said the shopkeeper to the small group gathered at her counter. 'Mostly iodine. And bandages. Sometimes she takes apples, razor blades. She refuses to talk. Just goes to the shelves, takes what she needs, and pays. I ask after the husband, but she will not be drawn. He is sick, that much is for sure. I suspect he has been quarantined, which suggests only one thing: consumption. She is taking the right precautions, sterilising the house like that, but watch yourself near their building. This is no time to be stricken.'

'Syphilis!' said Jáchym Nemec. 'It was the same with my uncle. Caught it from a whore in Bratislava on one of his business trips. One day a car arrived and two men whisked him away to a spa. It was my aunt who called them; she wanted it all taken care of with a minimum of fuss. He stayed there for months while worms bored holes in his brain. They stuck him with so many shots of Salvarsan that he had to sleep on his stomach for the first few weeks. But there was no improvement. He ended up covered in rashes and pissing blood. His death was attributed to liver failure—that's what the doctor put on the certificate—so at least my poor aunt was spared the humiliation. They even gave her back his amputated arm free of charge. It was still fresh—he only outlived it by a fortnight. Every man who glimpses Armageddon in this occupation runs to the nearest whorehouse. Poor Ottla, she is now left to nurse that bastard while he oozes his infected discharge over her bedsheets.'

'It is obvious how she survives,' said Štěpánka Tičková. 'Look at her, all quiet and pious, hiding her face in a shawl as she canters past. I'm telling you, it is different across town in Holešovice. There she wears much less. I wouldn't be surprised if that's how he caught it in the first place. Did you never ask yourself how they could support such a life? Always grandstanding, he was, but I have it from a reliable source that there was no company, no business to speak of. Such shame that family brings to our street.'

A sharp rapping on the glass. Františka recognised Bohuš's shoes immediately—from her sunken vantage point it was how she knew the comings and goings of most of her neighbours. She rushed down the hallway and into the foyer. Bohuš was peeking through the mail slot as Františka approached. 'Please, Paní Roubíčková, you must let me in.' She fumbled with the lock until it slipped free. Bohuš pushed past, crouching as he ran. Františka closed the door and followed him.

'Bohuš.'

'I've come for—'

'Your mother?'

Bohuš shook his head. 'She doesn't know I'm here.'

Well dressed, in suspenders and a loose-fitting shirt, Bohuš had the beginnings of a dark moustache and a wispy beard. He was growing into a fine young man, with a serious and determined manner. And yet there was still something childlike about him: scuffed shoes, a soft hat perched over unevenly trimmed hair, a crooked smile not yet dulled by the demands of adult life. As he shifted from one foot to the other, Františka saw his maturity ebb and flow: first a man, now a boy, now a man again. His essence was elusive. He could be a panhandler, a student, a layabout or the son of a banker. He would blend into any street, any environment. He reminded her of Daša in that there was nothing that marked him out as a Jew. Františka looked at him with fondness. It was only their kind, she thought, who had a future in Prague.

'Is it true what they say? That he is back?'

'Yes. No. He is not the same. The one who returned…he is not my father.'

'Štěpánka says—'

'All his energies are spent moving from window to window, peeling away the edges of the tape, peeking out from behind the blinds. At night he covers his face with pillows.'

'I have tried to come. Ludvík too.'

'You would have seen a cripple scrambling to hide under the table, Paní Roubíčková. With every knock he thinks they have returned. I try to leave the house but his eyes fill with tears and he whispers: *They are watching.* So I wait until he sleeps and then—'

'You do what you can, I'm sure.'

'No. I'm ashamed.'

'Bohuš, please. It is nothing to—'

'Of him, Paní Roubíčková. I'm ashamed of him. Of Mama too. So I've come because a son is supposed to honour his parents. Even when he has grown to resent them.'

'Bohuš!'

'I know you bring things from the country and share them with us.

I am here to collect what is ours. I won't stand by and watch my parents in this state anymore, Paní Roubíčková. I have ration cards if you want.' Bohuš shoved a hand into his coat and pulled out a ration book. 'Here,' he said, holding the dog-eared pages out to Františka. 'They're worthless to us.'

Františka pulled a chair out from the table. 'Sit, Bohuš. Calm yourself.' He slumped down. 'Look,' Františka continued, 'I'm glad you've come. Your mother is like a little sister to me and Ludvík misses his friend. It's just that winter...' Františka scanned the pantry shelves. 'Why don't you stay for a while? I'll prepare something nice. And what's left you can take back to your parents. Go to the lounge. Lie down. Rest. It's too much for a young man, all this responsibility. The girls should be home soon.'

Bohuš dozed, breathing in the soothing aroma of warm milk, onion, butter and allspice. When the meal was ready Františka nudged him awake. The girls were already seated when he came to the table. They all pushed the bread dumplings around, soaking up the watery stew, stabbing for meat that wasn't there. The girls laughed and chattered and Bohuš endured their questions with good humour, all the while exchanging coy glances with Daša. When they had finished, and their plates shone with an oily lustre, the two younger girls excused themselves and headed to bed. Daša and Irena began to clear the dishes. Bohuš went to grab the glasses but Františka took them from his hand.

'Tonight you are our guest,' she said. 'My husband will be back soon and I don't expect he'll be in any state to entertain.' She scraped what was left of the stew into a fresh pan. 'For your parents,' she said. 'Tell them...tell them I'm sorry.'

The Nazi standard hung over the great pylons of the National Museum, imprisoning King Wenceslas and his stallion in its tricolour bars. An unwelcome air of celebration was filtering through the streets of Prague like the fingers of the tenth plague. The soldiers marched in sharper step, flags frozen in position by the barrage of sleet. In one month it would be the second anniversary of the occupation, and still none of the neighbours had chanced to speak with Jiří B. Ottla no longer frequented Žofie Slávikova's store. 'It is worse than we thought,' said Štěpánka Tičková. 'At night I hear the cars pull up at their kerb. The engines idle for a few minutes and then they speed off. There is only one kind of person who attracts such visitors: collaborators!'

'Enough with your rubbish,' said Jáchym Nemec. 'I have not heard these engines.'

'That's because your wife snores like a donkey. Half the neighbourhood shoves cotton balls in their ears thanks to her. You will see, Jáchym. Jiří B has become one of them.'

'Štěpánka! Have you no heart? The poor man suffered in a camp. It is on the public record.'

'You fool! It is common knowledge that he went to Peček Palace. I have it on good authority that he was down in the basement, in the old cinema, sitting against the wall by himself while all the other prisoners sat on pews, waiting to be poked with metal rods. Not him, though. He sat near the heater, face to the floor, too ashamed to look a single one of those martyrs in the eye. They were supposed to believe that he, too, was a victim. But the facts speak for themselves, Jáchym. Six months he was gone—exactly how long it takes the Gestapo to train its civilian operatives. And why him? Well, if you opened your ears for once you might already know. Biskupcova Street is a hotbed of resistance activity. Yes, can you believe it? Our Biskupcova! And who better to report on it than the man who waves around his copy of *V Boj*?'

'A month ago he had caught syphilis from his whore of a wife. Now this?'

'Yes, there is no end to the shame. And the boy? Coming home covered in paint the same morning we woke to that awful graffiti. What were they thinking, provoking the Germans? I have half a mind to report it.'

'You will do no such thing. Leave them be.'

Štěpánka Tičková pulled her coat tighter around her and screwed up her face, as if she were ready to spit. 'A scourge on the whole family, I say.'

A lone figure, cloaked in grey, walks along the Charles Bridge, his head bowed. Snow has begun to fall, and the sentries positioned along the path breathe lassos of vapour, as if to ensnare the flakes. They laugh at the patches of white on the statues. The man keeps walking. He could be a resistance fighter, an assassin or a saboteur. But he is not. He is just a man, crossing a bridge, relying on a thick cane to hold him upright. He is neither old nor young. His footsteps are quickly erased. The soldiers pay him no heed. Their guns, strapped to their left shoulders, point skyward. There is peace on the streets again; guns will not be needed for now.

The man carries his burden past the saints on the north side, pausing at this one and that, as if to pay his respects. Sometimes he takes pity on his cane and stops to rest against the uneven stone balustrade. He puts one hand on the cold surface and gazes down at the raging Vltava below. When he reaches The Crucifix and The Calvary he pauses to mutter the words spelled out in an arc of gold—Holy Holy Holy Is The Lord Of Hosts—in his broken Hebrew, a language he has forsaken since his youth. His voice alerts nobody. Snow falls, its trajectory unaffected by the shift in the air.

Neither soldier nor saint nor cobblestone notices when this husk of a man tumbles from the bridge near the eastern bank, and lands with almost no sound in the water below. Even the Vltava has become accomplice to his disappearance, spitting him out on the shore far enough downriver to ensure that nobody could recognise him. The shopkeeper who drags the body up from the mooring pole on which it has become snagged does not send his assistant back across the bridge to alert Otto Muneles at the *Chevra Kadisha*. Instead he calls the local police, who grudgingly come to collect the body and take it to the city mortuary. There it lies for three days, after which it is consigned to a pauper's grave in the back corner of the Olšany Cemetery along with several other indigents.

And so it is that no stone will ever mark the final resting place of Jiři B. He has been erased from history.

6

They huddled behind the chipped wooden pews, these prisoners of Babel, flotsam from the outer reaches of an empire that was devouring faraway lands while constricting around the throats of those trapped inside. Here they were all castaways and immigrants, a jarring symphony of mashed syllables, from Žižkov, from Nusle, and from the Sudeten, Vienna and Munich as well. They came in shifts, one in the morning, one in the afternoon; what had been a spacious if Spartan, school eighteen months before, was now an over-crammed warehouse for the unwanted.

Jakub R thought of his own childhood in the village, when every word from his teachers' mouths had been spoken first by the sages. *To save just one life*, it is written, *is to save the entire world*. That was how sacred each person was to God. Yet here at Jáchymova, where he had been a teacher and was now more like a cattle dog, fifty worlds collided in every classroom twice a day, and the result was a confined catastrophe. They looked like vagabonds, gutter-dwellers. For more than a year they had not been permitted clothing vouchers. Jakub could see the seams where the shirts had been let out, and the shorts patched with strips of curtain. Even young Herschmann, the refugee boy from Munich, who lived with his uncle, the cobbler, had holes in the leather of his shoes. Only the cloth stars still looked new: golden, beaming like suns from the fading greys and browns onto which they had been stitched.

'Children,' said Georg Glanzberg, 'please form five lines. Be quick about it.' They rushed into their cliques, a small society with its own pecking order. Jakub noticed each group, and would listen in to their conversations. Up front were the Czech children, who considered themselves above this corral of foreigners. They still had parents, homes, the semblance of a settled life. Their mothers cooked in the same pots they had used for the past twenty years; their fathers sat on armchairs into which the impressions of their bodies had been imprinted. These children asked one another if they, too, had begun to smell. More than once Jakub found that peculiar boy Arnošt Flusser in the bathroom frantically scrubbing his hands. For those like Hana Ginzová, the daughter of a Jewish father and Christian mother, the insult was enhanced: by Jewish law she was not even one of them and yet here she was, at the Jewish school, forced to share in the bread of their affliction.

The German and Austrian refugees gathered in the third row, looking as confused as they had on the day they arrived. Some had been in the city for almost four years, but they had yet to properly assimilate. Their parents had enrolled them in Prague's German schools in the hope of easing their transition, but they soon fell victim to mockery and physical attacks. It was as if these schools were sovereign German territory, with all the attendant prejudices and proclivities to violence. Their expulsion at the end of the previous school year had been a relief, and they looked forward to finding their feet at a Jewish school in which they would be the superior class. The reality, however, proved a shock: they were jeered by their Czech classmates. Cast adrift in a hostile city, they would often speak of their homeland, but they meant Palestine, not Hitler's vile dominion. Jakub once overheard two of the boys, Herschmann and František Brichta, reminiscing about a camp they had enjoyed when Jews were still allowed to ride the trams as far as the country terminus. The boys had gone on long walks, practised tying knots, sung aspirational songs and roasted knackwursts on a stick. 'I swear,' young Brichta said, 'this is how it will be in Palestine. This is what it is to live on a real kibbutz.' Jakub hadn't the heart to tell them of the letter he had received from Jiří Langer: his mentor had contracted a chest infection on the boat over and spent the first eight months of his spiritual homecoming convalescing with consumptives and hypochondriacs. *There is no need for Hitler in Palestine,* he had written. *The desert air has spite enough. It is like I never left, and yet I am free.*

The Sudeten refugees did not speak of Palestine. The very concept of home had lost its meaning; they had seen how one day their state could exist and the next it could disappear. Most looked within themselves for a sense of belonging. They were as uncomfortable among their Czech classmates—who rebuffed them as traitors or deserters—as they were among the Germans.

Some students tended towards truancy, like Frederick Fantl, son of the journalist and conductor Leo Fantl. Jakub R and Georg Glanzberg had often spoken of the boy, his potential, his sporting prowess—the boy could run faster and jump higher than anyone else in his class—and his fine intellectual pedigree. But Jakub did not question absence anymore. Invariably they came back, all except one, the Viennese boy Kurt Diamant. His disappearance in late April shook his fellow pupils; he was the first of them to be deported along with his family. The class was poorer for his absence, not only because he was a friendly and intelligent boy, but also because his mother was a skilled dressmaker who would often help with the children's rags, turning them into something presentable. Jakub, too, had availed himself of her services. A few weeks before his sister Růženka left for America, he took her to visit Gisela Diamantová at her home in Valentinská Street. Kurt's mother was a stocky woman, her strawberry hair cropped and pinned to her head. There were folds of skin beneath her eyes from years of squinting at needles and thread. Růženka had brought with her four dresses, ample material for Gisela Diamantová to assemble one piece. 'I can't carry much,' said Růženka as she laid the dresses on the table. 'Only one case, and what I have on my back.'

Gisela was stern and businesslike but these riches of material brought a smile to her face. She measured Růženka, occasionally turning to Jakub to ask about Kurt's progress at school. 'An amiable boy,' Jakub replied. 'In sport, I am told, he excels. Had things been different he might have made a promising boxer.' Ten days later Jakub and his sister returned to Valentinská Street to collect the dress. It was sturdy but modest, something that would allow its wearer to meld into the greater whole without catching the eye of a swindler, cad or gendarme.

Otakar Svoboda disappeared under the black cloth behind his camera. 'Little girl in the third row,' came his muffled voice, 'we cannot see your pretty face. Please move a touch to your right.' Jakub turned to see Markéta Fischerová edge gingerly out from behind the Kleinová girl. The poor child still bore the scars of having lost her dog Schnitzli last year. She was not the only one; when the decree came that Jews could no longer keep pets, several of the children had to find new homes for their beloved creatures. But nobody had wanted Schnitzli. The mangy thing was old and incontinent, and used to snap at whoever reached out to pat it. Only Markéta could calm the dog, and would let him sleep on her bed, cleaning up whatever he had left behind in the morning. The deadline loomed, and word got out that the Germans were planning to euthanise all remaining Jewish pets. Markéta's father grabbed Schnitzli by the scruff and told the girl to bid the dog farewell. Schnitzli wheezed and growled as Markéta held him close. 'It is the right thing,' said her mother. 'At least we can be sure he won't suffer.' The poor creature did not make a sound when Pan Fischer took him to the bathroom and drowned him in the sink.

'Smile!' said Otakar Svoboda. He held up his flashbulb and pressed on the switch. It would be the last picture of Jakub R before he returned,

almost four years later, from the hell into which he was cast. For Georg Glanzberg and for most of the students, it would be their last photo ever.

7

The many possible fates of Jiří B remained the talk of Biskupcova Street until even Štěpánka Tičková ran out of theories and, instead, turned her attention to a more urgent threat: resettlement.

It had been tried before. The entire community had been shaken by its brutality: a thousand Jews sent to a small agricultural compound in Nisko, near the Polish town of Lublin. Within a few months, six hundred of them had either frozen or starved to death. The rest were sent back to their homes, only to find them occupied by strangers. The Jews had rejoiced in the plan's failure but its spectre continued to haunt them. Day after day they now lined up at the head office of the Jewish Religious Council of Prague, demanding assurances from Dr Emil Kafka that a similar fate was not in store for them. 'He speaks in circles,' said Jáchym Nemec, to nobody in particular as he walked back down the steps without an answer.

Soon it was summer and the city gleamed. Posters adorned the walls and pylons. Another decree, in black and red. All Jewish inhabitants of the city's outer reaches were to come to central Prague, where they would be housed in one of three districts. Similar directives were issued for the Protectorate's other major cities. There would be resettlement after all, but it was to be a more contained affair. The most affluent Jews were particularly put out: evicted from their homes and moved to rundown tenements, they found themselves worse off than even the poorest of their brethren. They clung to the trappings of their former lives, many choosing to don suits and ties as they undertook the menial jobs found for them by the Council. And so it was that for a few short months the city had the best-dressed street sweepers and garbage collectors in all of Europe.

Then Von Neurath fell out of favour with Berlin and was replaced—in practice, if not in title—by a far less forgiving man. Štěpánka Tičková found out as much as she could about this new Acting Reichsprotektor, and what she learned she did not like. His reputation for savagery on the Russian front was the stuff of Nazi legend. *He rides a chariot and hunts Jews for sport.* Štěpánka rushed to warn her neighbours, but there was no need; from the moment he assumed control of the Protectorate, Reinhard Heydrich wasted no time in proving his mettle. Before the first week was out he had ordered the execution of close to a hundred people, closed down all of Prague's synagogues and, by stepping up the frequency and brutality of German patrols, effectively decimated the resistance. By midway through the second week he had already set in motion the complete Aryanisation of the Czech lands. The Jews would be first to go.

Heydrich was able to avail himself of the existing arrangements. Adolf Eichmann had overseen the Central Office for Jewish Emigration since the beginning of the occupation and had successfully encouraged a minor exodus of Jews. It was also Eichmann's office that had coordinated the concentration of Czech Jews into the major cities. The key to the next stage, figured the Acting Reichsprotektor, was simply to remove the element of choice. For several hours, Heydrich, Eichmann and Von Neurath's former deputy, Karl Hermann Frank, pored over maps and schedules and lists of addresses, drawing up a plan of action. When it was done, they drank a toast to the Fatherland, to their own efficiency and to absolute victory, and then sent their instructions to Dr Kafka. Heydrich's wishes were to be enacted forthwith. Kafka was also to establish a Jewish Community Trust, to deal with abandoned property.

The cramped offices of the Jewish Religious Council exploded with activity as directors and secretaries alike sat hunched over their desks, frantically compiling lists and transcribing the information onto index cards. On each one was printed a name, an address, a date and the same location: Wilson Station. Those summoned were to bring a single suitcase. A combination of warm clothing and valuables was recommended. On some, where Dr Kafka recognised the name, he printed a short message. *Forgive me.*

The cards went out en masse. Their arrival was met with confusion, but the news soon spread and within days an unexpected knock at the door became the most feared sound in all of Prague. In this way, five trainloads of Jews, some five thousand people in all, mostly academics, professionals and aristocrats, were resettled in the Polish ghetto of Łódź. Among them were Ludvík's parents, Papa Roubíček and Mama Roubíčková.

What Von Neurath had sown, Heydrich reaped. The entire harvest took less than three weeks.

'Victory for the Zionists! We shall have a homeland after all.' Jáchym Nemec dropped a small bag of potatoes on the shop's counter.

'Enough with your glibness, Jáchym,' said Žofie Sláviková. 'It does not become you.'

'And why not? They have cleared the town. Even Kafka won't deny it, the damn flunky. Trains full of Czech peasants flooding into Brno and the Sudeten, wherever there is space, proudly doing their civic duty. They are offered our property as incentive. It's a fine trade they have made.'

'The prospect is not without promise.' Žofie Sláviková pulled the ration clip from her apron.

'Yes, to live like wildlife on a reserve, left to fend for ourselves. Look at us, Žofie, and tell me how long we'll survive. We are city folk now; the farming life is foreign to our kind. We count on people like you, with courage to sell us what we need from under your counters.'

'You'll survive,' she said as she clipped Jáchym's ration book. 'I would be glad to see the back of this overflowing sewer. Banish me to wherever, just leave me in peace. Eventually this war will end. I almost envy you Jews.'

'But a military garrison? When Štěpánka told me I didn't know whether to believe her. It sounded so...so—'

'Obscene.'

'Yes. I thought maybe she had misheard. You know how she is. But she insisted, said she'd heard it from the Council herself. *It has begun*, she told me. *Go see for yourself.* So I did and, sure enough, they were there at the precise hour she had said. Young men, strong men, huddled together, sitting on their suitcases, some playing cards, a few smoking, all looking bored. At last the wait was over. A crowd had gathered, watching as the men boarded the carriages. The direction of the tracks did not escape our attention. The train was headed north, not east. These young men would remain in the Protectorate. The rumours about Terezín were true. A hundred faces, more, rolled by as the train set off. They all blended into one until, suddenly, I saw him. Leaning against the window, staring right back at me. Bohuš B. Older, broader. But I'm certain it was him.'

Františka Roubíčková woke from a night of fitful dreams to glimpse the silhouette of her eldest daughter scampering across the window bench like a frightened animal. The girl's thin arms swatted away the curtains so she could peer at the street.

František slipped from the bed, careful not to wake the others. The pale light of an early dawn cast eerie shapes on the far wall, nightmare visions of the avenging angel that had descended on the city just hours after the attack on Acting Reichsprotektor Heydrich. With each of Daša's jolts, the shadows shifted to reveal momentary scenes of horror, ever more ghastly as the tyrant succumbed to his infected wounds.

A pushbike and a leather coat dancing a slow waltz in the window of a city store.

Conspirators cowering behind a closed door, hoping to hear a familiar voice.

A praying mantis, encased in wood and red silk, blind to the wailing masses filing past its mangled corpse as they mourn their own impending deaths.

An entire village engulfed in flames.

'Daša?'

The girl continued to twitch against the glass.

Františka moved towards her. Any moment now Daša would turn around, let out a gasp or fall from the bench. The sound would set the neighbours howling with fright. The sentries would be alerted; a detachment would turn up at the apartment. They'd find what she kept hidden.

Daša reached out and snatched at the air between them.

'Mama,' she whispered. 'I heard cars doors slamming. And voices. I ran to the window. There were legs, in suits not uniforms. Polished shoes.' Františka crouched beside the bench and put her arm around Daša's waist, but the girl pulled away. 'Look towards Mladoňovicova. There. It is still curfew and there are people at the crossroads.'

The girl was right. Františka wedged herself into the corner, her cheek and nose squashed against the glass. Down the road, people were milling about. Two black cars were parked at the end, obscuring her view across the thoroughfare to number seven. Františka put a finger to her lips, nodded in the direction of the door.

They went to find their coats. On the small table by the rack, a crumpled handbill taunted them with the promise of unimaginable wealth *for any information*. When Ludvík had taken it from his pocket yesterday and held it up, he looked imploringly at Františka. 'Maybe you've heard something,' he said. She shook her head, tried to turn away. He would not let it pass. 'We have five days, then more reprisals. Harsher. It's not about the money, Frantishku. They're killing people. What happened to Heydrich, it isn't the salvation we had hoped for.'

She looked at him, steely, then scrunched the paper.

Who was he, anyway, to ask such things? Most nights he wasn't even home and, although she tried to hate him, hate the idea of him, she would find herself praying for his safety, praying that he was sleeping on a friend's sofa or on the floor of a barkeep's apartment. Since the deportations had begun, it was not unusual for people to just disappear. Family members and friends would rush to the assembly grounds near Stromovka Park, hoping to catch a glimpse of their loved ones, to know that they were still alive, and that perhaps, when their own time came, they would meet again. Františka, on the other hand, knew to wait. He would return.

The morning sun cut through Biskupcova Street in its summer splendour. Weeds unfurled in the pavement cracks and birds chirped in the dense bloom of linden trees.

Františka and Daša Roubíčková ran to the corner and elbowed through the crowd. Several men in suits, with long black trench coats and gloves, stood guard at the kerb, forcing back the occasional surge from the anxious neighbours. Beneath peaked caps, beads of sweat lined brows framing dead eyes. Daša watched the bustle on the opposite corner as sharp-faced men in identical garb weaved in and out of the door to number seven. Františka listened to the panicked whispers around her. Names were bandied about, most of which she had never heard. How could she live so close to this many strangers? But there was one name that kept recurring: Moravec.

Moravec. Moravec. Moravec.

'To think I sold her supplies.' Františka recognised Žofie Sláviková's stern voice. 'I hope they don't take me for an accomplice.'

'I knew it.' This time, Štěpánka Tičková. 'Didn't I tell you I knew it?'

Then Jáchym Nemec: 'You wouldn't know it if the entire resistance was operating from your kitchen.'

Františka felt her daughter's grip tighten around her wrist as she was pulled to the front of the crowd. The bodies parted to afford her an unbroken view across the intersection. Gestapo men surged out of the building and stood at attention beside an idling car. A moment of absolute stillness. All eyes fell on the door, as they waited to see what would emerge.

In the days that followed, Štěpánka Tičková would tell how Alois and Ata Moravec held their heads high in defiance and marched with singular purpose as they were escorted to the waiting car. No one in the crowd would have the heart to say otherwise—it does not do well to speak ill of the dead—but they would all remember a middle-aged man, glasses askew on his sunken face, walking beside a whimpering youth with unkempt blond hair, both in shabby pyjamas, their hands tied behind their backs. It was only a few steps to the kerb and it was over in a few seconds. The car door slammed, the motor revved, and they disappeared in the direction of the Old City and, inevitably, Peček Palace. 'The men should be ashamed of themselves,' said Jáchym Nemec, 'walking to their slaughter like that.'

'She's escaped,' whispered Štěpánka Tičková. 'I knew it. Stole away in the night and left the others to pay. That is what becomes of—' She would have continued cursing her neighbour, regaling those who remained on the corner with tales of the woman's descent into moral ruin, had everyone's attention not been drawn back to the open door. From where they stood, it was almost comical: a uniformed soldier tripping backwards over the threshold, out onto the pavement. In his hands, two feet, then came a torso and at last the strange sight of another soldier gripping his load under the arms, his chest melded to its shoulders, obscuring the head and creating an obscene sideshow attraction of flailing limbs.

The two soldiers released their hold and the body of Marie Moravcová fell with a dull thud to the ground. Much would be said about her after the siege at the church: her involvement in the plot to assassinate Heydrich, her bravery in biting into the cyanide pill, the beheading of her corpse at Peček Palace. Word would soon spread that the bloody tendrils hanging from his mother's neck were the last thing Ata Moravec would see before breaking down and telling the Gestapo everything he knew. They would try not to blame him; after all he had delivered them from a violence Prague had never seen and still paid with his life.

When the clock struck curfew's end, and Biskupcova Street filled again with its usual bustle, Františka would return to the corner and look across the street, remembering the face of Alois Moravec. This, she thought, is the measure of true worth. This is a man.

8

Jakub R curled up in the corner of the cart, arms locked around his legs, the jolt of every cobbled stone like a bayonet in his spine. It was his turn to rest now—to lean against the pillows and couches, the steamer trunks, the sacks and boxes—while the cart lurched through the street, pulled by two horses, and Georg Glanzberg holding the reins.

Jakub pressed his eyes to his knees and was back home, in his village. It was deserted now. Only the *clack clack clack* of a horse's shoes on stone could be heard. From nowhere, four children appeared, rushing towards him. 'A newspaper,' said the oldest, holding out his hand. Jakub rummaged through the bric-a-brac, but all he had to offer was *Der Stürmer*, that awful gutter rag whose very ink was venom. Still they took it, just to have word from the outside. They thanked him, and ran to the river to imbibe its poison. He watched, waited. Then he laughed, his entire body quaking, as they lay down and died at the water's edge, their bodies sinking into the mud.

Clack! Jakub sat up, startled. They were gone. They were never here. The pile of newspapers rested beside him, held fast by thick twine. It was not for reading, but wrapping. *Anything fragile, anything of value.* So said the director.

Beside Jakub was a black folder, a record of the accumulated worth of those who had moved on. Each page told a tale of frantic packing: decisions made, then taken back and made again. Words were crossed out, others scribbled in the margin. Fights between husbands and wives. Pleas from children. What to take, what to leave behind. Jakub closed the folder between each stop, so that the echoes of these sorrowful cries would not frighten the cherry blossoms from their branches. And, as the cart rattled through the streets, from house to house, collecting things left behind by his people, he knew that he, too, was just another forsaken item.

'Like Haman,' Georg had said when taking the reins. 'The vile prince of Amalek.' And he was right, thought Jakub. The ignominy of it all, parading through the streets of Shushan. It was always the same: his fellow employees of the Jewish Community Trust waiting in the doorways for the cart's arrival, hoping that this time, at this address, it would not be their colleagues, their friends, their families.

For a third time Jakub had been saved. By Emil Kafka, Jakobovits, perhaps even Muneles. The cart floated on Pařiszká Street like a lifeboat. The waters below: boredom, hard labour, despair. But the cart was protection from the index cards that sealed the fate of those less fortunate than him. His harbour, still, was Jáchymova. 'I am sorry, Jakub,' said the principal when it was decreed that the school must close. 'We will find you something else.' That was in June. The young teacher was soon summoned to the Religious Council with Georg. Their employment would continue, in a new role. A scrap of paper with that familiar address: *3 Jáchymova Street.* 'Report tomorrow to the stockroom,' the secretary said. 'We are struggling to keep on top of the transports.'

Jakub barely recognised the place. The school had transformed overnight into a maze of scaffolding. Shelves lined every wall and there were vast piles of goods, fragments of broken lives. The rooms were arranged by contents. Never before had he seen in one place so many clocks, so many sewing machines, so much silver cutlery. In some of the items he saw his students' faces. This book is František Brichta, that rocking horse, Hana

Ginzová. He would meet them again, in photo frames, portraits, as he emptied their houses, always struck by how little they had. *So few items by which to remember you*, he would think. Some of the children were still in Prague; he would see them in the street making mischief, bored, and he would turn away, hoping they didn't notice him.

Only one more stop for the day, unscheduled. A boy had come to the house in Břehová Street with a message from the Council that there was an urgent assignment. The cart was already full, but there was no choice. The horses strained to heave the load along the uneven street. Jakub was now walking beside Georg, so that he did not add to the poor creatures' suffering. They were all exhausted, these four beasts of burden. Sometimes they tugged on the bridle; the horses halted and they all waited until the pile no longer swayed.

The two friends had to reach the house on V Kolkovně Street, empty it and return to Jáchymova with enough time to get home before curfew. When they arrived, another cart was already there, as was one of the few delivery trucks still owned by the Trust. Weary packers leaned against the wheels or sat in the gutter. Only one man was standing, hands buried in the pant pockets of his suit, impatiently tapping his feet. The foreman. Jakub had not seen him before, but he knew to fear the man's presence. He was the only one in the Trust's employ without calluses on his palms.

'You are late,' said the foreman. Jakub stared across the street at a shop-front that had been sealed off with planks of wood. Someone had scrawled a crude Star of David on the middle plank. The foreman continued: 'The Gestapo came earlier. There were reports of sounds, movements. Impossible for an empty house. The Landsbergers lived here, but they were transported over a month ago. We should have already been here. An oversight. A neighbour became suspicious, called the authorities. The Gestapo wanted to make sure there were no Jewish ghosts hiding in the walls, if you know what I mean. They snooped around for two hours. Then they came out, said it was clear for us to start. Of course, they put a few boxes in the back of their car and crossed the valuable items from my list. Here,' he said as he handed the clipboard to Georg, 'take it.' The other packers had already begun to gather near the entrance. 'You have an hour,' said the foreman as he opened the door. 'Maybe less.'

They rushed up the three flights of stairs, spilled onto the landing and waited at the door marked *5*. Ten men, more than could possibly be required. Jakub was relieved that he wouldn't have to drag the furniture down with Georg. Neither of them was cut out for it. Georg ran through the inventory, divided it among the packers. The bigger men would be responsible for the heavier items: tables, couches, beds and the like. The slighter men could handle the kitchenware and religious artefacts. The books would be left to Jakub and Georg. 'You heard him,' Georg said. 'Time is against us. Take your items, wrap them up, whatever you can find. Someone else will sort it at Jáchymova.'

They had once lived well, the Landsbergers. That much was evident. The name was revered in Prague; it could be traced back over five generations. Maximilian Landsberger, his son Aleš, and Aleš's son Matěj had all been in shipping. Then came Max, named after his great grandfather, who steered the course of the family business away from what he called *yesterday's fancies*. Max was a man of his times; electricity was his passion but, to his dismay, it was not shared by his own son, Heinz, the present Mr Landsberger. His love was steel. Czechoslovakia, still in its infancy, was booming thanks to foreign investment and local naivety. Heinz seized the opportunity and used his inheritance to partner with the great Max Bondy. To many, Heinz symbolised the fledgling nation: something new forged from a turbulent past. Such was his renown that Karel Čapek had wanted to make a character of him, and even went so far as to work him into the first draft of his lizard book. Landsberger vetoed the idea, and told the author to use Max Bondy instead. 'He prefers the attention.'

That was before the occupation. Like all business owners, Heinz Landsberger sold his interest to a non-Jewish administrator for a pittance and was surprised to find that it did not bother him. He already had what he wanted. A wife, two children, the trappings of comfort. He also had the luxury of time to take stock of his life. With each decree he gave away more of his possessions, and came to appreciate the humbling effect of austerity. By the time most of Prague's Jewish aristocrats were forced from their homes, he had already taken up more modest accommodation in the Old City. The change pleased him. What had begun to look sparse in the great mansion in Smíchov fitted perfectly in his new home on V Kolkovně Street. They didn't come looking for him when they rounded up the Czech gentry; he was no longer counted among them. Rather, Heinz Landsberger was a fatalist and an ascetic; any remnants of his former life were merely nostalgic, and mostly his wife's. He was resigned to the same fate as every other ordinary Jew.

The packers went about their duties like drones, not a word exchanged between them. Georg crossed each item in turn from his list. One by one the packers disappeared, makeshift sacks slung over their shoulders. The hour was almost up, and only Jakub and Georg were left inside. Below, the foreman was standing alone in the street, guarding their cart.

'Did you hear that?' Jakub said.

Georg shook his head.

'There. Again.'

Georg continued to wrap an old, leather-bound volume. 'Rats,' he said.

Jakub headed to the empty bedroom. He looked around—door to the bathroom, door to the closet, door to…He gasped. Another door. Had it been hidden behind the dresser? It was small, granted, but how did they all miss it? Again, shuffling sounds from above. Jakub rushed to the door, put his ear against it. Louder. He turned the knob. Behind there was only blackness. Jakub reached inside and grasped something cold, metallic. A rod. He slid his hand up and felt a flat surface, coarse like sandpaper. His hand glided further, then reached another flat surface. Then another. Stairs. *Impossible*, he thought. *I am already on the top floor.* Jakub stepped inside; there was enough space for one person, no more. He edged his foot forward. A sudden flash of pain. He had kicked the first step with his shin. It was one of those spiral staircases: only the steps themselves and a twisted rail for support. Jakub waited for the pain to subside, then began his ascent.

There was no light above or below and his eyes could not adjust. Outside, it might already have been dusk.

At the top he gingerly poked his foot around to find solid ground. There were beams, boards slung between them. The sound of someone breathing, soft, shallow. 'Hello?' he said. No reply. 'Hello?' He ventured a step, steadied himself against the sloping surface of the roof. He stopped again, listened. A single breath, like water down a plughole. Then a loud rustle and he was thrown backwards by a terrible force. It took Jakub a moment to realise that he had been tackled to the ground. Something was on his chest, crushing him. *Is it man or beast?*

'Who are you?' said his attacker.

'Jakub…Jakub R.'

'What is your medium? Charcoal? Oil? Pencil?'

'I—'

'A sculptor? I knew it!'

'No, no.'

'Who sent you? The guild?'

'I can't breathe.'

'Don't move.' Jakub sensed it was a man's hands running along his hips, slipping into his pockets. 'All right,' the man said. 'You are not armed. Not even a chisel.' Jakub was still trapped between the man's thighs, but it no longer felt like a vice. 'So you are not an artist at all?'

'No.'

'Then I take it you are with them?'

'The Gestapo?'

'No, the ones clearing out the Landsbergers' place. I've been watching it all through the air vents. A real pity, I say. But they have no more use for it.'

'You know the Lands—'

'Of course. Every artist knows his benefactor, even if the opposite is not always true. Follow me.'

'I—' A sudden rush of air. Jakub felt the man's knee brush across his sternum. A soft hand took his own and helped him to his feet. The two made their way across creaking boards. 'Watch your head,' the man said.

Jakub reached up and felt the roof come in at a sharp angle before opening up again. After a few minutes, the man stopped, grasped Jakub by the shoulders and turned him to his left. 'Here,' said the man. Shafts of flat light came through cracks in the roof, and forms began to emerge from the darkness. In front of him, on an easel, was a huge canvas.

'You weren't meant to find this place.'

'There was a door.'

'Someone got lazy. Every entrance was supposed to be sealed off. We were quite content to be left alone.'

'We?'

'Artists, my man! After the occupation, it was too dangerous for us on the streets. We came up here, to the crawl spaces in the roofs. They are all connected, you know. We colonised according to medium. This part of Josefov was for painters, though the various schools kept to themselves. Realists, Expressionists, Romanticists. We were spread out as far as Pařiszká, Kozí and Vězeňská streets. There was even one colony in Benedíktská. All satellites rotating around our last remaining sun, the gallery owner Avram Becher, God rest his soul.'

'Across the street. The boards—'

'Yes. It was inevitable, I suppose. When the army arrived, the city lost its colour. Only the Realists rejoiced. Their landscapes and fruit bowls would be the toast of occupied Prague because that's all the new masters would permit. The rest of us just sat here, staring at our blank canvases. Then Becher lit the fuse of hope. *Never fear*, he insisted, *there is another space for more discerning patrons. Let our presence there be an act of defiance, for artists do not take up arms*. Or some rubbish like that; he always spoke as if hoping to be quoted. Still, it worked. His words halted the creative paralysis. The rooftop city sprang to life.'

'But there's no one else here.'

'Yes. I owe that to one person: Yitzik Berenhauer. A tragic end.' The artist let out a slow sigh. 'And a debt I shall never repay.'

(The Brief, Sad Tale of Yitzik Berenhauer)

They came because of him and they left because of him. The mad modernist of Josefov. He appeared among us one day and set up his easel. What took shape on his canvas—a traditional manger scene—had been done a thousand times, and we were ready to dismiss him. Then we noticed a fourth wise man standing over the baby. In his hand was a dagger, its blade flushed crimson. At first we feared a blood libel. Was this painter trying to have us all killed? But, then, a daub of purple near the child's lips. Wine. This was Christ at circumcision. The painter signed his name across the bottom: Yitzik Berenhauer.

He painted them without pause, the others in his series: Jesus the Jew—Jesus at Bar mitzvah, Jesus under the Succah, Jesus prostrating himself before the ark on *Yom Kippur—and when each was done he would turn around to find an ever-larger crowd gathered around him. By the time he set to work on the final canvas, a replica of Da Vinci's* Last Supper, Jesus at the Passover Feast, *the roof space was full.*

Only I was not under his spell; my mind was elsewhere. In necessity I had found inspiration. While pushed up against the wall, I had moved aside a tile so I could breathe, and when I drew my hand back from the cold Prague night it was black: pages from our holy books, set ablaze on some distant pyre and returned to me as char on the wind.

I gathered strips from the garments of the huddled mass around me, stretched them across a large wooden frame and began to paint. Layer upon layer of ash, it defied perspective, each scene disappearing into the next.

Lost in exquisite blackness, I was interrupted by an ungodly cheer. Jesus the Jew *was complete. I watched as Berenhauer put down his brush, rubbed his hands on a rag, and walked towards the exit. The carnival of acolytes followed, hooting and whistling as he led them out of this rooftop captivity and down into the streets. I perched on his plinth and pushed aside another tile so I could watch. A figure appeared in the door opposite: Avram Becher, arms out to greet them. That was enough for me. I put the tile back, stepped down and looked around. I was alone.*

I fell into a sleepless routine, painting the entire city. Occasionally I stopped to watch the scene at Becher's gallery, the same every day. Visitors came to see Berenhauer's pictures but Jesus the Jew *was nowhere to be found. They begged Becher, chastised him, but he would not be moved. He was too cunning for that. There had already been a raid. Two. Three. They found nothing, but I knew it was inevitable. To the hum of the disappointment below, I devoted myself to my portrait of our city—I wanted to be hung alongside Yitzik Berenhauer before it was too late.*

First came the river, its waters turned to blood. On either side, the city sprawled outwards, its streets and buildings, castles and parks, covered in a dirty shroud. This cartographer's nightmare would serve as a backdrop for the faces of those trapped within. They came to me like revenants, demanding to be seen. Jan Kohout, a student of weak will and shifting passions who might just as well have stood at the bridge with armbands but instead mounted the barricades, now imprisoned in Oranienberg, waiting for the city to pay his ransom with its surrender. Our dear Mayor Otakar Klapka, blood oozing from his wounds like stigmata, executed at the Ruzyně Barracks for treason—for placing a wreath at the tomb of the unknown soldier, and for running a resistance cell from City Hall. Petr Bamberger, set upon by Nationalist thugs for failing to display his star in public, and for failing to vacate a tram at peak hour. The terminally serious Feliks Kral, sweating in an isolation cell, accused of making jokes about Hitler, wishing that he had not beaten the vindictive Marek Zalenka to that promotion. And so it went, the march of the damned. But behind each heroic moment was something less noble, something disturbing; it was only when I reached the end that I saw what it was. A loss of hope, of faith, of dignity. The betrayal: their society had been relinquished to the sympathisers, collaborators and opportunists.

I sat against the wall and stared at the canvas. For all its horror there was still something lacking. At my first encounter with Becher, seven years ago, he glanced at my work then shook his head. 'You have skill,' he said, 'but I don't want architecture, I want soul!' Yes, populated by so many souls, my grand portrait lacked one of its own. How was I to know that the ill-starred Becher would provide it?

The screech of tyres, the slamming of car doors, a gunshot. A chorus of screams, then a terrible wail. The blood left my body. It was Becher. They had found the other gallery.

I rushed to my perch, pushed aside the tile. Becher stood in the street as four Brownshirts boarded up the windows. And Berenhauer. Poor

Berenhauer. Throwing his arms into the air. Screaming profanities. He tried to pull down the boards, only to be met with the butt of a pistol. That shut him up. The soldiers escorted the men back inside. Soon they appeared again: Avram Becher with his wife and their four children, dragging suitcases, pillows, blankets. The soldiers herded them all into the back of a waiting truck. And then Berenhauer and his last four apostles, carrying a stack of half-finished paintings. A few soldiers stepped forward. There was a scuffle, but it was no use. The canvases were stomped on by polished jackboots.

The engine started, but there was still one more indignity in store. A Brownshirt dragged out little Chana Becherová by her scraggly hair and, to punish her for being her father's child, to show her that anyone could paint, but that not all painting should be considered art, he made her daub the boards covering the entrance to the gallery with a giant Star of David. Then he grabbed the child by her leg and threw her into the truck. The engine revved and they were gone.

The other cars drove off. A lone soldier stood over the broken canvases. He kicked the pieces into a pile, picked up a bottle from the gutter and splashed out its contents, fumbling in his pocket for a lighter. A flash. The canvases screamed the last testament of Yitzik Berenhauer. I reached out to pull the flames towards me, the embers scorching my fingertips. Before they cooled, I sketched what I had witnessed: God shutting His eyes.

'But it's—' Jakub started. 'It's—'

'Completely black. To the unknowing eye, yes, I suppose it is.' The two men stood there, mute. A distant chime. Six. 'Now take it. Tonight I'll make my escape to the south, but I must know that it wasn't all for nothing.' The artist snatched the canvas from the easel and forced it awkwardly into Jakub's hands. 'Take it,' he panted, pushing Jakub backwards. 'Let it be among the things you confiscate from the Landsbergers. I've seen how your lists work. Add this, cross out that. What's another painting? Give it life, let it be seen. Take it! Take it!' he began to shout. 'TAKE IT, JAKUB!'

'JAKUB!'

He woke to find Georg standing above him, shaking his shoulder. The room was empty, just as he remembered it. A door to the bathroom. A door to the closet. That was all. Jakub was lying where the other door should have been, but the wall was smooth. 'I heard a sound. You collapsed,' said Georg.

'The door—'

'Stay there, I'll get you some water.' Georg disappeared into the living area and returned with a glass. 'Here. I think you're dehydrated.' Jakub took a sip, then gulped down the rest. 'Today was long. Too long. We must get the cart back before curfew.' Georg helped Jakub to his feet. In the entrance hall, a barrow was filled with clumps of paper. 'I wrapped them all,' said Georg. Jakub walked slowly down the stairs, holding on the railing for support. Georg followed, backwards down each step, dragging the barrow, wincing every time it landed with a jolt. At the bottom he shuffled around to the other side and pushed it towards the door with his foot. The barrow slid down the steps of the stoop and came to rest in front of the foreman.

'Your friend is sick.'

'He is fine.'

'If he were a horse, he'd be shot.'

Georg handed the man the folder. The foreman glanced over the pages, nodding. On the last page he signed his name with a flourish, gave back the folder, and headed off. Georg waited until he was out of sight then went over to Jakub, who was leaning against the back of the cart. 'He's right,' said Georg. 'You're sick. Just wait there while I unload the barrow. We'll get this to Jáchymova then get you home.'

'You'll break curfew.'

'Don't worry about me. I have my ways. Curfew is a game of strategy like any other.'

Jakub slept a week, a month, maybe more, scarcely registering the presence of his mother as she tended to him. Georg came but Jakub did not understand what his friend was saying. There were sensations, hot, cold, a fever, and he feared that he was sinking beneath the surface, choking on his own sweat. It was all a haze until this: the sound of approaching footsteps and a knock at the door. He heard his mother speaking with someone, then crying out to the corridor. They had been summoned for transport.

9

Františka Roubíčková rode the tram towards the small civil registry office in Nové Město. She sat in the front carriage, peeking into her bag from time to time, checking that the papers were still tucked inside. It had not occurred to her that she ought to have been in the back. Snow muffled the clatter of the wheels as they chewed into the rusted tracks; beyond the pavement, the buildings anchored the streets to a bygone era. As each grand edifice gave way to the next, Františka considered her strange limbo. The occupation would continue, but for her soon it would be different. *It is his idea. It's what he wants.* 'I am the lens through which they will see you,' he had said. 'Please, for the girls.'

The tram came to a halt at the corner of Jindřišská and Panská streets. Nobody paid the handsome woman any attention as she weaved her way through the carriage and out onto the pavement. At Nekázanka Street she picked up her pace. Again she said it to herself: *It is his idea. It's what he wants.*

The registry office was halfway down the street, hidden on the second floor of one of the smaller buildings. Františka made her way up the stairs and let herself in without knocking. 'Yes?' said the woman behind the desk. Františka didn't know how to say it. An awkward beat, then: 'I'm here about my marriage.' The woman motioned to the one empty chair, against the wall. 'Take a seat. You will know when he is ready.' Františka sat down and looked around the room. The others did not acknowledge her presence. She understood. To be here was a capitulation, a disgrace. They sat together, in conspiratorial silence, waiting for a knock, a chime, the buzz of a phone, anything to signal the end of this purgatory. But there was only the faint whistle of the clerk's breath, the scratching of her pen on the stack of paper.

Františka saw the passage of time in the changing height of the stack.

Every now and then, one of the other women would stand and go through a door marked 'Private'. There was an order, to be sure, but Františka did not know her place in the queue. She tried, once, twice, shuffling forward on the chair, arching her back as if preparing to rise, but the clerk swatted at the air. She sat back down, inspected her shoes. On her third try, the clerk did not stop her. Františka pushed open the door and stepped through.

'Name?'

'Roubíčková, Františka.'

'Roubíčková...Roubíčková. A Jewess?'

'Yes. No.' Františka fumbled with her bag. 'That is why I've come here.'

The registrar put out his hand, took the papers. 'Married to Ludvík Roubíček.'

'Yes, sir.'

'In Žižkov. Not the ghetto. Children?'

'Yes, sir. Four.' And then, as if that was not enough, 'Girls, sir.'

The registrar leaned back in his chair and held the papers close to his face. His glasses remained on the desk near the ink pots. 'For convenience, then?'

'No, sir,' said Františka. 'You don't understand. It is a long time coming. He is a fine man, mostly. But there are problems. This...it is his idea. It's what he wants.'

'I am not here to judge you, Paní Roubíčková. How you choose to survive these times is your own business. There are consequences, of course.'

'Yes, sir. I understand. He has already taken residence elsewhere. The address there, that is mine. Any correspondence to my husband should be forwarded to 20 Cimburkova Street. He stays with an associate. There is no point in renting, he says. His time in the city is short.'

'Hmmm...it will take a while to stop using that term, husband.' The registrar recoiled as if the very word was sour on his tongue. 'You should forget him now. A pretty girl like you will have prospects when this all blows over.'

'Yes, sir. It's what he says too.'

'But for now...well. Look, Paní Roubíčková. You mustn't feel unfaithful. Our vows have been reduced to nothing. One cannot betray that which does not exist.' He scribbled on his blotter. 'And the children?'

'I'm sorry?'

'I suppose you wish to report that this man'—the registrar looked at his notes—'this man, Ludvík Roubíček, is not the father.'

'But of course he is.'

'Paní Roubíčková, I'll ask it again. Are you absolutely certain that these children belong to your husband and weren't conceived out of wedlock with another man? Let's say...an Aryan man?' When there was no answer he continued: 'It is a simple question. They have made whores of you all, no matter how you respond. All I need to know is this: are you the kind of whore who deserves mercy?'

They had not discussed it. In all their conversations—his pleas for her to cast him aside, to save herself and the girls, her stubborn refusal to grant him such easy absolution for their years of penury—not once had they even considered it. To vitiate their bond, that was one thing. But to expunge his very existence? It was unthinkable. She couldn't do it.

'Ludvík Roubíček is the father. I am certain.'

The registrar shook his head and leaned forward, deflated. 'It will be done in a few days, then. He will no longer be protected by his marriage to an Aryan woman and you will be free to disappear into the general population. As for your children, they will remain *mischlinge*. But without the millstone of their father they might yet escape this madness. I hope for their sake that you have made the right decision.'

None of them heard the footsteps in the foyer, but three sharp knocks at the door told them enough. Daša got up from the table and walked calmly down the hallway. Three more knocks, impatient. She stood at the door a few seconds. The man on the other side stumbled backwards when he saw her. 'Paní...' Daša said nothing. Let the man squirm, she thought, as she leaned against the doorjamb, her hips pressed against the frame, pushed forward in a pose he might mistake for seduction. The man was short and scrawny, his clothes dishevelled from an evening spent playing the devil's postman. He looked from her to the scrap of paper in his hand then back. 'I am sent from the Jewish Council,' he said. 'I have just been to an address'—again he looked to the paper—'Cimburkova 20. But there was no one. I was also given this address. Perhaps...' The envoy was sweating. 'Perhaps you know the man I'm after. Ludvík Roubíček. He is not registered here but I am told I might find him.'

Daša glanced behind her. In the kitchen the family sat huddled around the table, picking at their meal. She would not disturb them. 'Yes,' she said. 'He is here.'

The man knelt down and opened his briefcase. Inside, there was a wad of pink papers, tied with a red ribbon. He unfastened the knot and fanned through the papers. 'Yes...Wait...I know it's—' He pulled out a single pink slip, followed by several forms from a secondary pocket. The click of the briefcase lock reverberated through the stairwell as the man regained his composure and got to his feet. 'If I might speak with him—' But he knew better than to expect an answer. 'In that case, please pass this on. He is to report to the trade fair grounds in three days' time for relocation. The details are all on the summons. If he's late, it will no longer be in our hands. Acts of resistance do not go unpunished. As it is, I should report him for failing to be at his registered address after curfew.'

The man shrank back as Daša snatched the papers. She slammed the door, but his voice could still be heard in the distance, rattling off ever more fanciful warnings.

The night before he was to leave, Ludvík Roubíček sat in the cramped lounge room of 13 Biskupcova Street with his two eldest daughters, while Františka busied herself in the entrance hall packing, unpacking and repacking his suitcase. Fifty kilograms. That was the weight of a man's life. From the kitchen, the smell of condensed milk on the boil, fresh bread and onions. As the hours wore on, they did not speak, only listened to the sounds of Biskupcova Street that Ludvík had long ago stopped hearing. Behind the gauze curtain Marcela and Hana snored softly, dreaming whatever young girls dream.

~

The sled was Irena's idea. 'There's a plank of wood on Rečkova Street,' she said, breaking the evening's silence. 'Perhaps if we tied a rope to it we could drag Papa's suitcase.' Ludvík continued to go over the transport forms, filling out his details as best he could. He didn't have a home to hand over. Or personal property. Everything had already reverted to Františka. He had no keys to give them, no inventory to be traded for the privilege of this transport.

At first light, they woke Marcela and asked her to prepare the cardboard label that was, according to the summons, to hang around Ludvík's neck. She took to the task in earnest, practising each letter of the identification number several times before finally inscribing it on the brown rectangle: *CC-109*. She held it up. It was perfect. Ludvík could not possibly get lost. He would reach his destination and send her exotic gifts. Marcela searched her mother's sewing drawers for a knitting needle. She held it against the top corners of the cardboard, punched two holes. After she had threaded the string and tied it off, she ran back to Ludvík. 'Papa, put it on,' she said. But he ignored her, continuing with his papers. 'Papa, please,' she said. 'I made it for you!' Ludvík slid it over his head and slumped forward, resting his cheek on the table. 'Show me, Papa,' said Marcela. Františka pulled the girl back by her shoulder. 'That's enough, Marcela. Papa must be left to prepare now. We will be leaving soon.'

'For the circus?' The girl had heard them say it, taken the term literally. How was she to know that's what they all called the trade fair grounds?

'Yes, for the circus.'

They set off in the morning chill, the sled leaving a path of discoloured snow in its wake. They took it in turns to pull it along, first Ludvík, then Františka, then Daša and Irena together. Little Hana sat at the front, her legs hanging over the suitcase, smiling and waving to passersby. Marcela skipped around them, clapping and singing. Ludvík Roubíček did not look back at his old home, nor into the eyes of his wife or daughters. He held his head high, his gaze fixed in the distance. Františka kept the cardboard label inside her coat, to protect it from the falling snow, but also so that he could walk the streets as an unmarked man as they made their way towards the Hlávka Bridge. When they reached the clearing at the southern bank, Františka could see other families, other sleds, and the tracks of those who had come before.

They arrived at Výstaviště Trade Fair Grounds to the fading sound of church bells. Ludvík looked at the clock on top of the central turret of the Industrial Palace; it was just after noon. They had been walking for almost two hours. A swirling grey mosaic of stone tiles lined the grand promenade, rubbed clean by a constant stream of shuffled feet. 'Wait,' Ludvík said. Daša and Irena stopped dragging the sled. All around them, groups of people huddled together. Some came from the road, others alighted from the back carriage of trams. A few talked, a few cried, but most proceeded in mute resignation, cardboard labels around their necks, all marked with the same two letters, *CC*. Ludvík let them pass. There was no hurry. They were not heading for the towering ceilings and slate floors of the Industrial Palace, which for over fifty years had been the envy of barons and princes alike. Instead they would be shunted to the Radio Mart exhibition hall, the wooden annex that had last been used to house the electronics trade show. How many times had he come to these grounds as a younger man, to tout the wares of whatever charlatan would have him, to revel in those carnivals of abundance? Back then he would skip to the gate. Not now. Let them pass, he thought.

The nearby Stromovka Park, once a royal game reserve, lay dormant; no one dared venture near the assembly point lest they find themselves dragged in to make up the numbers. There were no children playing, no young couples exchanging sweet nothings. Only the wagtails and rooks still swooped towards the frozen fountains. Their numbers had thinned; there was no one to feed them.

Ludvík took hold of the rope handle and pulled the sled. It was his burden now, this bundled life. The others followed in single file, up the promenade towards the barbed wire fence. Ahead was a long line of people ending at a table placed in front of a flimsy metal gate. A lone clerk from the Community Council sat up straight, tugging at his coat, trying to fend off the icy wind. Nearby, a policeman leaned against the fence, chewing on a wad of tobacco, oblivious to the brown spittle dribbling down his chin. Ludvík stepped forward, joined the line. Those who had already passed through to the other side of the barbed wire now milled about, puffing on cigarettes. Some stopped to barter—a gold watch for a tin of condensed milk, a razor for some onions, whatever might help them in their new home. Wandering policemen joined in the transactions, or, when they did not favour the exchange, simply confiscated the most desirable goods.

'Papers?'

The clerk adjusted his white armband and took the pink slip from Ludvík. He checked the name and number then opened the master roll to record the new arrival. Ludvík tried to find a name he knew, someone who could keep him company on the journey, but there was none. The policeman cleared his throat and spat a glob of phlegm near the clerk's foot just as he was drawing a line through Ludvík's details. Františka handed over the cardboard number and, as Ludvík slid it around his neck, Marcela began to clap, the sound muffled by her woollen gloves. 'I made Papa's ticket. We will see the elephants.' Ludvík puffed out his chest and slid the label across to cover his yellow star. For those few moments, he still belonged to Prague.

'And you? Your numbers?'

'No, sir,' said Františka. 'We have only come to escort.'

'It's best you part ways here, then. Inside—' He gestured towards Hana on the sled, then Marcela beside her. 'It's not for them.' Františka ignored him and went to pick up the rope. Daša and Irena stood on either side of their father, each clutching an arm. The gate swung open on its loose hinges. They stepped forward. Immediately, Františka was jolted back. The policeman stomped his foot on the sled. 'From now you carry.'

Step right up, little Marcela. Here is the circus you've been so anxious to see. Is it as you had imagined? Would it help if I told you that this is just the sideshow? God knows where they have set up the big top. I suppose I'll get there in the end. What did you say? Don't cry. I'm sorry, I didn't mean to scream. It's just that

I can't hear you over this horrible din. You'll have to lean closer, speak into my ear. Even when they are not barking, those loudspeakers blare with the phantasms of our discarded radios. Now come. Follow me. Stay close.

Ah, this is the spot. CC-109. Yes. What is that you say? There is only one seat? Well, of course there is. Can you have it? No. I know your legs are tired. But this patch of dirt will not do for a girl as delicate as you. And look how the lady here spills across the line with her arm. Shhhhh! *She is old, you mustn't wake her. Can't you see that she is lying on a stretcher, that she doesn't move? Leave her be. Climb on my shoulders and we can explore this circus together.*

Queues everywhere. People queuing up for their last chance to win. It's okay. There will be plenty of time to play all the games: two, maybe three days. And you can come and go as you please. Me? No. I will wait here and hold your place. So where should we start? Let's try this one. First you must take your ticket to the clown at the table. Do you see him? Yes, that's right, the fat one with the wiry hair and nervous expression. So here, take this ticket—Yes. Yes, I know. It looks exactly like Papa's ration card, but surely you know that in the circus nothing is as it seems—and hand it to the clown. He will wave you away, no doubt, but it is all part of the game. You come back and stand with me. Then you wait and you wait and you wait and eventually he will send one of his monkeys out with a tray of delicious treats. You have to be lucky, though. Not everyone is a winner. That's a lesson you must learn. Sometimes you end up with nothing.

We'll move on, then. Look at this! A grand sculpture like you've never seen before. Spoons, forks, knives—all silver—piled higher than the old clocktower itself. Of course I don't pretend to know what it means. Modern art escapes me. It is more your mother's domain.

What is that? You want to play this game? But Marcela, look at how they stand in line. Holding their house keys in their hands? But those are no ordinary keys. Watch how the man in front hunches forward like that key is the heaviest thing he has ever held. That's because it is, my dear. If only you had one to hold you'd understand that it is the exact weight of all that he has ever owned. And we who come here no longer have the strength to carry such things. That, then is the game: a test of strength. Is there a man in all of Prague strong enough to hold his key when he reaches the clown at the table? I think not. Just look at the relief on their faces as they hand it over. As if the brass has burnt holes in their skin. This is not a game for little girls. And Papa doesn't have a key. Let's move on to the animal enclosure instead. Over there, it is that great pile of darkness in the corner.

Why do they lie there like that? you ask. Can't you see they are sleeping? Foxes and minks and beavers and bears, huddled together in peaceful slumber. They are tired like you. They've also come from far away, from all over Prague, hiding in handbags and suitcases, rolled up in mattresses. No, you cannot pet them. We are not allowed past the chain. It is for your own good. One should never wake a sleeping bear. Here's let's—

Quick. Get down. Sit. Please, Marcela. You must sit. He's here. There. Across the room. Fiedler the Lion, the most ferocious creature of them all. See how he struts, head held high, fangs peeking out from his thin lips, claws punching holes in the ground. It's a very strange act, I know. We wait here with our eyes to the floor, hoping not to catch his attention. What sort of thrill is that, to not even look at the main attraction? But the lion is a wild beast, no matter how well he's been trained. You never know when he will lash out and swipe a little girl across the face. Many have already perished by his claws.

*When he is gone I will take you to play the last game, the greatest of them all. I have the ticket right here in my hands, a piece of paper with my name and photo and a big red 'J' across it all. There are so many stories about this game. You will no doubt be told that Papa ran away and joined the circus, that he was afraid to turn around and face the lion, that he boarded the train with all his new friends and was finally taken to the big top. But they are wrong, Marcela. That is not how this game works. There is no big top. There is no show. No. In this game, when we reach the front of the line, when we come face to face with the clown who sits at his table, we hand over the ticket. The clown will take his big rubber stamp, he will hold it high in the air so you can see the single word on its inky base—*EVACUATED*—and, with a great flourish, he will bring it down. And, just like that, Papa will disappear.*

Three

FROM: JACOV TSUR, *former student of Dr Jakub Rand and survivor*
TO: FRANK BRIGHT, *formerly František Brichta, fellow student at the Jewish School in Jáchymova Street*

One day before the death march to Litomerice–Terezín in April 1945, about 70–90 prisoners were transferred from Schwarzheide to Sachsenhausen, among them J RAND.

FROM: FRANK BRIGHT
TO: DR Z S, *Australian Academic*

When I met Dr Rand (as he then was) in Prague at the end of May 1945, or over 65 years ago, I seem to remember him saying that he had to work in a factory producing poison gas for the German Army (i.e. not Auschwitz and probably Sarin), that prisoners had not been issued with gas masks and that the plant had leaked.

FROM: FRANK BRIGHT
TO: BRAM PRESSER

Your grandfather was in Sachsenhausen from 15.04.1945 till 22.04.1945, or one week. What happened after that I don't know. He must have recovered quickly enough to have made his way from wherever the Russians had taken him to Prague because that was where I met him, both of us wandering, I somewhat aimlessly, round the Old Town around the third or fourth week in May.

Interview with Berta Malachová, survivor:

> *You must stop this obsession, stop this search. Do not let it take over your life. I can see it in your eyes. It will destroy you.*

IN THE CAMPS, SHE carried a small gold ring...

She kept it with her for the rest of her life. On a chain around her neck, beneath her blouse, her apron, her hospital gown. After she died we found it tucked in a jewellery box in a drawer beside her bed. She'd put it there before we drove her to the hospital for the last time. While we still lived in hope, she had already come to terms with her fate.

I held it just once, this witness to her ordeal. It was the touchstone of her legend—stories of courage, of strength, of devotion—and yet it seemed so insignificant, resting there in my hand. I rolled it between my fingers, hoping it would reveal her secrets. So much of what we'd come to believe seemed impossible but, as one survivor told me, survival itself was impossible. *Don't be too quick to dismiss the illogical,* he said. *The fanciful, the absurd, these things happened.* Refracted through that simple, perfect circle, I could see another Holocaust. *Every story is different,* the survivor had said. *Every one of us endured his own Auschwitz.*

After her death we made peace with the silence. We couldn't have known what lay in a shoebox at the back of her sister's apartment in Prague. It took another sixteen years before I would sit at a café table watching Ludvík unfold those delicate sheets of paper, and then another few months before he sent them to me.

Here she was, at last:

Dear mother and little sisters,

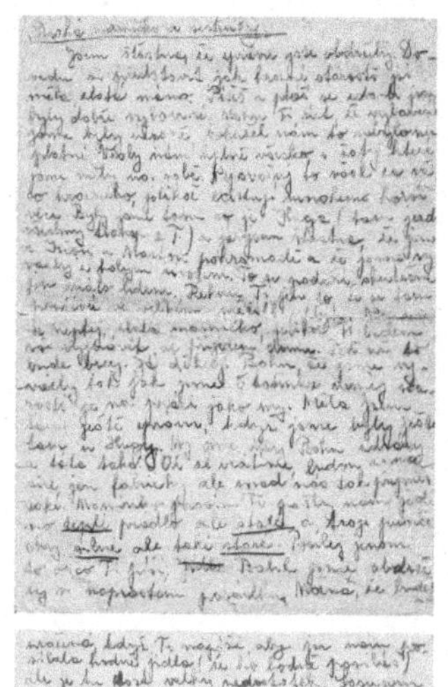

I am happy that you have received my news. I can imagine how terribly worried you must have been, my golden mother. You write and ask whether we were well kitted out. I can tell you kitted out we were wonderfully, unfortunately it was of no use to us. They took from us absolutely everything, even the clothes we were wearing. However, do not think this is something awful, since there exist much worse things. We were where all transports from T go and I am happy that we are together and that we have escaped with our dear lives. Only very few people manage this. I will only tell you that gas is used there on a very large scale. Do not ask, dearest mother, because we will tell you everything when we come home. Now I hope that it will be soon. I thank God that we are all the way we are. Do not worry about daddy, he is in the same situation as us. I still had news, when we were there. We, thank God, are in good health and daddy also. When we return, we will have become only factory labourers but perhaps you will accept us as such. Mummy, please send us one lot of warm underwear, but old, and three pairs of stockings, thick, and also old. Send only that which I have written for. We have received the parcel in perfect condition. Perhaps you will be offended if I write to you to send us lots of food (because you already are sending a lot of it), but there is quite a severe shortage here. We are issued soup at midday, in the evening soup, a piece of bread and something with it. But everything is so minimal that it is not enough for even half a day. Aside from this I work hard, and

all day outside. You must not send food in glass containers, mummy. You cannot, poor you, imagine how it is. I smuggle everything into the camp under SS watch. I have to be very careful since I know what it means for one's life to hang on a thread. And, believe me, I act accordingly. In the parcel everything was correct, except for the glass jars. Also, thanks to you, everything was wonderful. You will be able to calculate how many parcels you should send. So that it is enough for three people. You can also include food in parcels for daddy. If you are [illegible] mummy sending any meat, then not in [illegible]. Send no lard at all. Cigarettes the same as last time. Mr B is a very nice person. He also has children and a wife. I hope that one day we will be able to reciprocate to him. Mummy, please write to us about what the situation is and when we will see each other again. You cannot know how happy I would be if we were all together again. Above all, I wish you good health and to be courageous. Do not, mummy, worry about Irča. In the first place I am almost 20 years old and secondly, after such a rich experience, believe me, I am a fully grown up person. So, hold your head high.

Regards and kisses to you,
Daša

In it there is everything: what she knew, what she didn't. That she had survived, and Irena too. Perhaps even their father. She had caught sight of him in Auschwitz on the day she left. He was standing at the barbed wire fence, watching as she was herded towards the train. He waved goodbye, blew her a kiss—some tenderness, familiarity—in that place. Little did she know that he would soon be dead, shot in the head after he collapsed, his strength finally deserting him just as freedom was on the horizon.

Daša carried them, kept her mother and sisters alive. *You say that you would give many years of your life to be able to come to see us,* she wrote in another letter. *What foolish things you write. We will return in a few months' time and you would have lost years of your life. Do not worry about daddy not writing. It is sometimes not possible. And certainly, when he has the tiniest opportunity, he will write to you.* She absolved her mother: *I have forgotten something else. And that is, you write that you will never forgive yourself that you were so weak towards daddy and brought us up in this faith. It is fate and I'm surprised that a woman as intelligent as you can let something like this come out of her mouth. I hope it never happens again. And I promise you that we will return to your motherly embrace healthy and strong.* To her sisters too, humouring them, as if she were just on holiday. *My dear little golden Bumblebee.*

Words: they clung to her words in their grief and fear. Smuggled words. Words that could have seen her killed, that almost did. Words I have tried to understand. *I smuggle everything into the camp under SS watch.* But two most of all. A name repeated, a flicker of light in this darkness.

'Mr B.'

Those who survived wanted nothing more than to disappear, and so they sought refuge in faraway lands. Entire suburbs sprang up, designed to go unnoticed, to be passed over when the next catastrophe came along. Identical houses of dull, monotonous brick. The curtains, thick white filigree approximations of knotted lace, were usually closed. Inside, lives were refashioned through photographs and knick-knacks that told of every moment spent on Lazarus's back. Here in Australia, they lived and they died, one by one, until only Uncle Pavel remained.

For years he lived on, cursing each new dawn that broke outside his window. He went into a nursing home when Irena needed full-time care, and stayed after she died because he saw no point in leaving. *It's comfortable enough. I eat, I sleep. I just want to be left alone.* As he struggled for breath, as his eyesight failed, as his movement slowed, as his body shut down, he somehow still managed to cheat death. *Listen to me, darling,* he'd say to me. *Don't grow old.*

His had been a different kind of survival. Born into Czech aristocracy, a scion of the Bondy empire, Pavel's birthright proved a curse. It was his kind that was taken early, forced from their stately homes, exiled to Łódź. This was before the main transports, before Theresienstadt, when people were chosen not just because they were Jewish but because they were the worst kinds of Jews: intellectuals, aristocrats, journalists, political enemies. For Pavel, the nightmare of Łódź became a memory as he was forced from ghetto to ghetto, from camp to camp, until he found himself a *Sonderkommando* in the stoking house of hell, clearing gas chambers and throwing emaciated corpses into pits of fire. He was not afforded the small mercy of denial, of believing the smoke came from nearby brick factories. His premonition of death was pink and tangled, scratched and bruised, coated in blood and soot.

When it was over he returned to Prague and lived a sad imitation of the life he had once been promised. He married Irena, had a son. Those years had taught him to work, to seize opportunities. He took his young family to Israel, where he became a plumber and carpenter, then to Australia, where he chose to stay. But no matter where he ran, he could not escape the crematoria, the bodies. That was what he was left to relive, when they had all gone, when he woke up and saw the sun taunting him with another pointless day.

I tell him about Hana and the shoebox. He shakes as he holds the letters. He listens, reaches for a handkerchief. He caresses the page, his wife, in her youth. Irena, too, had written home. *I am writing this in a hurry, that is why it looks as it does, but you will not be angry with me, mummy dearest, will you? What do you do all the time? Mummy, please take care of yourself.* Pavel leans over the yellowing pages, his magnifying glass positioned close to his milky eye, his finger pausing on each word. Slow wheezes. The stale smell of old age. Beside some pills, his teeth.

He talks as he reads, tells me his story; the anger and then resignation in his voice will later wrestle against the tape recorder's metallic hiss. When he has finished he lets out a tremendous sigh. I wait a moment, let him regain his composure. Then: Irena and Daša? *They stayed together throughout.* Did they lay sleepers for trains? *No. They worked in fields, in laundries, then in factories. How you say? Textiles. To make warm clothes for Nazis on the Eastern front.* When they were liberated, did the Russians…? *They were bastards. But no, not that.*

'And Mr B?'

'It's been a while,' he says, heaving himself upright. 'There was a boy from the neighbourhood, a friend of the family. He went on the first transport, the one sent to turn the old fortress town of Terezín into the camp the Germans called Theresienstadt. I knew him only through stories:

that he had watched over them, kept them safe. As for his name...you have to understand, they lost so many friends, but to me each was the same as the next. Except one. Yes...there was one in particular that stood out for no other reason than that they never said it directly to me. It would only come out when they thought I wasn't listening. *Bohuš.* Maybe that was him. Maybe that's your Mr B.'

They were electricians, carpenters and builders, plumbers, machinists and masons. Three hundred and forty-two young Jewish men chosen for their skills and sent north on 24 November 1941. Transport 'Ak', the *Aufbaukommando.* They left in good spirits, clinging confidently to what the Nazis had promised: they would be able to return home on weekends; they would receive regular food; they would enjoy greater comfort; their wages would be paid to their families back in Prague. They arrived at Bohušovice station and were marched the three kilometres to the fortress town, Terezín, where they were assigned to the dilapidated Sudeten barracks. Rubbish was strewn across the cold, damp concrete. Windows were smashed, doors hung open, screeching in the wind. They slept on the concrete floors, rationed their meagre supplies. For the most part they were confined to the stables. One man tried to send a postcard home to his girlfriend but it was intercepted and he was hanged. The Nazis brought them nothing: no food, no bedding, no word from the outside.

By the time the first civilian transport arrived six days later, the *Aufbaukommando* had done little to prepare for the new inmates. Confronted by a thousand bewildered faces—Transport 'H' consisted mostly of older men and women—they turned away in shame. Then, on 4 December, a third transport rolled into Bohušovice. Another thousand men, mostly young, mostly skilled. They, too, were assigned to the *Aufbaukommando.* Officially, the transport was designated 'J', but to those in the camp it was known as 'Ak2'. Close behind it, almost unnoticed, was one more train from which twenty-three people disembarked, including Jakob Edelstein and the rest of what would become the Council of Elders.

By the end of that grey winter's day, there were two and a half thousand

Jews in the fortress town that would, for the next four years, be called Theresienstadt. One of them was this neighbour who might have been Bohuš.

Names cascade like dirty snow across the pages of the *Theresienstadt Memorial Book*. Here they lie, the reconstituted ashes of all those who were taken from their homes and dumped together on the dusty clearing beside the tracks at Bohušovice station. I look at the record of the ones who didn't come back, whisper each name, the white noise of guttural stutters filling the desolate room. First names. Surnames. There is nobody called Bohuš.

I rush back to Pavel, ask him to think again. *Who was Mr B?*

'Bohuš,' he says, this time with more confidence. 'I heard them whisper *Bohuš*.'

They reach out from the page, begging to be remembered. For months I try to conjure their voices, their stories, from a squall of dates and places. With each pass I eliminate some from the list, those who don't fit Pavel's description. This one, too old. That one, from too far afield. This one sent not to Auschwitz but another camp, maybe Riga or Dachau or Maly Trostinec. I delete them again from history, negate their brief resurrection, strip them of the lives that might have found meaning in what I write.

~~Bedřich Altschul. Gustav Bacharach. Hugo Bacharach. Erich Bauer. Bohumil Benda. František Bergmann.~~ Jíři Bergmann. ~~Rudolf Bergmann.~~ Alfred Bernath. ~~Bruno Better.~~ Erich Bloch. ~~Heřmann Bloch.~~ Pavel Bondy. ~~Richard Brauchbar. Farkaš Braun. Kurt Brodt. František Budlovský. Emil Bustina~~. Bedřich Friedländer. Bedřich Gratum. ~~Bedřich Gross. Bedřich Hoffman. Bedřich Lubik.~~ Bedřich Meisl. ~~Bohumil Reinisch.~~ Bedřich Strass. ~~Bedřich Straussler.~~ Bedřich Weiss. ~~Bedřich Weltsch. Rudolf Jokl. Nachman Basch. Leo Bass. Rudolf Bauer.~~ Vilém Baum. ~~Alexandr Bäuml. Bodhan Beck. Erich Beck. Josef Beck. Karel Beck. Louis Beck. Theodor Beck. Max Becker. Leo Beer. Mojžiš Belligrad. Bruno Berger. Ota Bergler. Alexandr Berkovic-Katz. Nathan Berkowicz. Šalamoun Bernfeld.~~ Ludvík Bernstein. ~~Wolf Besen. Hersch Biber. Ota Bienenfeld. David Bleicher. Heřman Bleiweiss. Gustav Bloch. Valtr Bodanský. Emil Bondy. Pavel Bondy. Kurt Brammer. Oskar Brand. Eduard Braun. Karel Braun. Otto~~

~~Breslauer. Jan Breth. Julius Bretisch. Bertold Fantl. Bedřich Friedländer. Bedřich Glaser. Bedřich Goldschmidt. Bedřich Grosser. Bruno Grünstein.~~ Bedřich Heller. ~~Bedřich Hirsch.~~ Bedřich Kraus. ~~Bedřich Liepmann. Bernhard Lichtenstein. Bedřich Löwy. Bedřich Lustig. Bedřich Müller. Bedřich Pick. Bohumil Polák.~~ Bedřich Pollack. ~~Bedřich Pollert. Bedřich Prager. Bruno Reik. Bedřich Reitler. Bernhard Ringer. Benno Rynarzewski. Bela Salomon. Bedřich Schnabel. Bedřich Schön. Bedřich Schöpkes. Bruno Tausk. Berthold Ucko. Bedřich Wermuth. Bohumil Winter. Bedřich Zucker. Ervín Bandler.~~ Arnošt Basch. ~~Zdenek Basch. Otto Baum. Otto Baumgarten. Valtr Baumgarten. Viktor Bäuml. Arnošt Bazes. Alexander Beck. Pavel Beck.~~ Jindřich Beck. ~~Arno Behrendt. Jíři Běhal. Viktor Beneš. Adolf Berger. Bedřich Berger. Evžen Berger. Pavel Berger. Hugo Berglacz. Josef Bergmann. Bedřich Bergstein. Josef Bernstein.~~ Jan Beutler. Arnošt Beykovský. ~~Hugo Bienenfeld. Walter Bischitzký.~~ Kurt Bleyer. ~~František Bloch. Kurt Bloch. Pavel Bloch. Arnošt Blum. Simon Blumental. Rudolf Bondy. Vilém Bondy. Jindřich Boschan. Zikmund Brauch. Heřman Braun. Leopold Braun.~~ Leo Breitler. ~~Vilém Brik.~~ Vilém Bruml. ~~Kurt Brumlík. Kurt Buschbaum. Bedřich Fauska.~~ Bedřich Feigl. ~~Bartolomeus Friedmann. Bedřich Fritta. Bernard Gerber. Bedřich Grab. Bedřich Heller.~~ Bedřich Holzbauer. ~~Bedřich Jakobovič. Bedřich Kafka. Bedřich Kaufmann. Bedřich Klein. Bohumil Klein. Bedřich Kohn. Another Bedřich Kohn. Bedřich Kollin. Bedřich Kompert. Bedřich Kraus. Bedřich Krieger. Bedřich Küchler. Bedřich Langer. Berthold Laufer. Bedřich Löwenbach. Bernard Macner. Bedřich Mautner. Bedřich Meisl. Bernd Nathan. Bedřich Pollack.~~ Bedřich Sachs. ~~Bruno Schuschný. Bertold Schwarz. Bedřich Seidner. Bedřich Stein. Bohumil Steiner. Bruno Steiner. Bedřich Sternberg. Bedřich Tetzner. Bertold Wassermann. Bedřich Weiss. Bedřich Zentner.~~

I want to run back and show the last few names to Uncle Pavel, to see if there is a spark of recognition. Bohuš is a nickname, another code word. If only Pavel could think harder, push through the fog. They must have uttered his real name. Just once Irena must have told him everything.

I want to run back but I can't. Pavel died yesterday. He finally beat the sun.

~

I had hoped to give what they could not—gratitude, recognition, for their lives, for my own—but now there is no way of knowing who he was. I settle on a name, one that did not exist, one that can be demonstrably proven false by the simple act of running your eyes down those two lists—Transport Ak, Transport J. And so I create a boy, a neighbour called Bohuš, give him a family, friends, all of whom will disappear. This representative construct might be one or all of Jiří Bergmann, Alfred Bernath, Erich Bloch, Bedřich Gratum, Bedřich Strass, Vilém Baum, Ludvík Bernstein, Arnošt Basch, Jindřich Beck, Jan Beutler, Arnošt Beykovský, Kurt Bleyer, Leo Breitler, Vilém Bruml, Bedřich Feigl, Bedřich Holzbauer and Bedřich Sacks.

Or perhaps it is none of them. Perhaps Uncle Pavel was mistaken. He was desperate to help me, so he drew together long forgotten stories, stories that he had only half-heard and, spurred on by my insistence, my encouragement, unwittingly created a composite of his own. There was a boy, as he said, a boy who helped them in Theresienstadt, in Auschwitz, but his name is lost. Might there not have been someone else too? Someone who didn't come along until much later, towards the very end, when they had been sold as slave labour to *Kramsta-Methner und Frahne AG*, a company that processed flax in a four-storey factory in Merzdorf, Upper Silesia?

The factory was situated in a village where the prisoners came into contact with the locals, as well as with other foreign workers—machinists, builders, labourers. It was from there that Daša and Irena sent the letters. Could Mr B have simply been a man who worked there too, a supervisor, a guard, a stationhand, a kindly German townsman who collected the packages sent by my great-grandmother Františka and brought them to the girls?

A man whose name was, like so many others, Bohuš.

I can find nothing more about Mr B, so I turn again to the search for my grandfather. Since the beginning I had been hoping to single out his words from the discordant noise. Those who spoke about him. Those who spoke for him. It came at last in urgent whispers, from the moulded metal tips of an antique Czech typewriter: *Unfortunately it contains many inaccuracies.* Each syllable tearing through the fabric of these projected memories. From the fissures an echo, what he means to say: *but it also contains truth.*

His description is unembellished. *I was a member of that small group of Rabbis and Hebraists selected by Murmelstein, our object was to catalogue and comment on all books and manuscripts that were stolen from all over Europe.*

Little is known about the *Talmudkommando*. In his historical overview of the camp, Murmelstein mentions it in passing. Otto Muneles wrote a brief report on the 'book sorting work' immediately after liberation, but it focuses on the minutiae of cataloguing and the whereabouts of the books. A more detailed, albeit clinical description, is given by H. G. Adler in his monumental study, *Theresienstadt*. The only insight into the human dimension of the *Talmudkommando*'s work comes not from one of its members, nor a historian, but a labourer, Franz Weiss. Initially given the job of converting an old barn into a workspace for the group, Weiss stayed on to cart boxes of catalogued books back to the main camp. He was able to observe the members at work and, occasionally, talk with them. Some considered him a friend.

It is likely that the order to establish a group to sort looted Jewish books came from Adolf Eichmann himself sometime in early April 1943. The Gestapo chief knew he could count on Benjamin Murmelstein to get the job done efficiently. The two had worked together in Vienna after the Anschluss, when the city's Jews needed to be resettled in camps. For his diligence Murmelstein was rewarded with transport to Theresienstadt and given a place on the Council of Elders. To assist him in assembling the *Talmudkommando*, Eichmann appointed an expert from within the Nazis' own ranks. There is some suggestion that it was SS Sturmbannführer Karl Burmester, the Gestapo library chief.

The selection process took close to three months, during which time the applicants returned to their previous work details. Meanwhile, crates of looted Jewish books started to arrive from Berlin, where, until Allied bombing forced a change in plans, Nazi experts had been sorting them for use in what was to be a representative library of Jewish thought known as the Advanced School of the Nazi Party (*Hohe Schule der Nationalsozialistische Deutsche Arbeiterpartei*). Afraid the books might be destroyed, the Nazis split up the collection and shipped it off for safer storage. Those already catalogued or deemed of lesser importance ended up in castles in Silesia and Northern Bohemia. The rest were sent to Theresienstadt.

Although some of its key members would not arrive for another few weeks, the *Talmudkommando* began its work on 26 June 1943. That day, they were escorted under SS guard out of the main camp to the south, along Südstrasse, until they reached a converted barn built into a hill. It was only half a kilometre but it must have felt like another world. There was no barbed wire, no moans of desperation, no crowded streets, no snarling dogs. In time, the members of the *Talmudkommando* would come to call it the *Klärenstalt*, the Clarification Plant.

Each man was assigned a place on one of the low wooden benches and told that it would be his workspace until further notice—the threat of deportation was always there. The same Nazi officer who had overseen the selection now outlined their duties. The books were to be sorted using the Prussian cataloguing system. They were to be given the designation *Jc*, followed by a number, and a brief bibliographical description. Then they were to be put in a crate for storage and, ultimately, returned for use in the Advanced School. Any works of particular rarity or value were to be set aside and reported to the SS for individual collection. No book was to leave the *Klärenstalt* in any other way.

For almost two years the *Klärenstalt* proved a silent haven for those locked inside. They worked with a diligence bordering on fever, the mind-numbing monotony broken by the beauty of the books that came before them: illuminated manuscripts, handwritten tomes, works dating back over a thousand years. To think these might survive, even if the scholars would not. It was consolation enough to urge them on. By war's end many of the scholars had been transported to Auschwitz and killed. They left behind a catalogue of wonders, numbering some 28,250 volumes that would live on.

~

The Advanced School never came to be. When the war was over, 257 crates of books as well as another 237 tied parcels were found in the outer fortifications of Theresienstadt. Still more were found in the *Klärenstalt*. They were shipped to the Jewish Museum of Prague, where they joined the countless Jewish artefacts that had been plundered from the homes, synagogues, libraries, community centres and businesses of those sent to concentration camps.

Of everything in my grandfather's story, only the books remain. It is to them I must go.

The streets of Prague's Old City teem with tourists. Here, among the cobbled stones, the buildings and the graves, they will find what they need. A name on the wall of the Pinkas Synagogue, hidden among the 80,000 who perished. A fine silver *Torah* pointer from a village that is now just a field. Rabbi Judah Löew, reduced to the etching of a lion on stone. Even Franz Kafka himself, cast in bronze, sitting on top of a headless man, just as he prophesied in *Description of a Struggle*. There is only one thing that eludes them, the one thing they'd hoped most to find—the *golem*.

The tourists pay little attention to the modern building just around the corner from the Spanish Synagogue. Metal-encased lights hang from the ledge above its fortified glass doors. To the left, a grey intercom unit. Only a small chrome plate, with the Star of David perched on two stone tablets, gives a clue as to what is inside: the inner sanctum of the Jewish Museum of Prague. I push the button and wait. A crackle, then a soft voice: '*Ahoj*.'

'*Ahoj*, yes. I am here to see—'

Another crackle. The doors slide open with a mechanical hum and I step into a brightly lit alcove, a security lock. 'Identification?' She startles me. The same voice, still soft. The woman is sitting at a counter behind streaked glass, staring at a bank of video screens on which I can be seen from various angles.

I hand over my passport and driver's licence. She looks at me, at the documents, then back at me, before sliding a white laminate pass through the hole in the partition. From behind I hear a shrill buzz and a click.

Identical grey doors stud the drab walls of the administrative centre. The offices are like cells for those cloistered inside. It is deserted, a hollow heart. On the third floor I see an office door ajar. I knock, wait. 'Come in.'

I enter and am already beside her. The director of the Jewish Museum is much younger than I had expected. Waves of brown hair spill across her face and she brushes them aside as she stands to greet me. She sits back down and gestures to the chair on the opposite side of the desk. I have to squeeze past. There is no natural light; it is a fortress of books. Papers are scattered across the floor. Only her desk is clear, except for a single page. I see him, my grandfather, staring up. It is the original article.

'So you're done chasing phantoms, then?' she asks.

'The Museum of the Extinct Race,' I say. 'This is it. A phoenix?'

'Yes. After the war everyone was searching for meaning: Why? How? And here in Prague, particularly. What to make of this great collection of books, of artefacts, of treasures stored in our synagogues? Why would the Nazis do such a thing? They allowed a functioning Jewish museum to stay open under their watch? It simply did not make sense.'

'Unless there was a greater purpose.'

'Some secret plan, yes. But there wasn't. For three years it operated, until the end of forty-one, when the Nazis closed it down. By then the transports had started and they needed the space to store all the property they were confiscating. Warehouses. That's what they made of our synagogues. The Jewish community, however, was quick to rally. Its leaders saw what was going on, the liquidation of satellite communities, the transports out of Prague. They convinced the Nazi authorities to ship all Jewish artefacts—*Torah* scrolls, books, silverware, anything that related to Jewish life in Bohemia and Moravia—to Prague and allow them to select the most precious, the most valuable for exhibition in a "new" museum—'

'—of the Extinct Race?'

The director smirks. 'The Nazis agreed to the request but they didn't really care about it. They didn't actively involve themselves in its operation. Thousands of artefacts poured in and the Jewish staff catalogued them with exemplary care and skill given the circumstances. By November 1942, the curators had prepared the first exhibition of manuscripts and books and the Central Jewish Museum, as it was now called, was opened for business. Needless to say it didn't get too many people through the door, but that wasn't the intention. For the curators, it was an act of preservation. For the high-ranking Nazis who made up the majority of its visitors, it was a curiosity. I think there was only ever one official Nazi directive, a complaint, really: that the museum was too nice.'

'There was no plan?'

'By the Nazis, no. It is a romantic ideal, this symbol of Nazi arrogance, of what could have been. But it never existed. There was never a plan by the Nazis to make a Museum of the Extinct Race. The term wasn't even coined until after the war.'

'Then why agree? Why allow a community you intend to exterminate to set up and operate a museum?'

'Free labour. Nothing more, nothing less. The Nazis saw it as part of the confiscation program. It also served as a balm of sorts—if they allowed a Jewish museum to be run by the community, maybe their intentions weren't quite so wicked. Maybe the Jews would be more willing to believe their promises of resettlement.'

'And my grandfather?'

'Had nothing to do with it. He never worked here, not during the war and not after. We became aware of him when this article was published. He wrote to us and included it along with a short biographical note, pointing out the obvious exaggerations. He said he had worked in Terezín sorting through books and promised to send a full report on the *Talmudkommando*. It never came. It is a shame, really, but we have learned not to hope for such things. Those who don't wish to be seen will always find new places to hide.'

'But he kept reaching out,' I insisted. 'To Yad Vashem, Beit Terezín. Only once did he get anywhere, much later on. One of his letters ended up with Alisah Shek. She was among the few who knew about the *Talmudkommando* and the only one to really care. For her it was personal. Her husband had been its youngest member.'

'Ze'ev?'

'Yes.'

'But he wasn't. He only worked in the Central Library in Terezín. Shek was a youth leader, a very promising young man. Murmelstein took a liking to him and, to protect the boy from transportation, assigned him to the library. But not the *Talmudkommando*.'

'They weren't related?' I was starting to feel dizzy. All these names, these institutions, blurring into one. Further obscuring my grandfather from view.

'Most who look back see the Holocaust as some great monolith. We've lost the ability to make out the contours, the cracks, the individual shapes. Who still cares about a bunch of books in any one camp? What difference does it make that there was a Central Library in Terezín, a Central Jewish Museum in Prague and, quite separately, a dedicated group, all sorting obscure Jewish books? Distinctions like this no longer matter. The horror has outgrown them.'

'When my grandfather wrote to you, did you know?'

'Unfortunately, no. Of course, we knew of the group from Murmelstein and the others but, aside from Otto Muneles, there was no survivor testimony. So far as we could gather they had all been killed. Muneles was a taciturn fellow. Dour. He struggled with survival, lost himself in the running of our new museum. He didn't speak of the others. When he died, so did our first-hand knowledge of the *Talmudkommando*.'

'So that's it, then? These few letters, cries for help, awkward posturing?'

'No. And here's what I find most troubling. As it turns out, your grandfather isn't unknown to us. His name appears on several documents, Nazi records from Theresienstadt. Only now do we have ready access to them. It's been our big project, digitising our archives, resurrecting them from their paper tombs. We couldn't have known it then, when he contacted us. We just didn't have the resources. And, anyway, we were too busy wrestling with the other Holocaust institutions for ownership of these memories. Each one was sitting on its own stash from the camp, guarding it like a nervous mother.'

She reaches into a drawer, pulls out a thick envelope and places it on the desk.

A ration card. *Rand, Jakob. Ck572. Category II. Eligible for premium margarine and sugar rations.*

An die Arbeitszentrale
VERZEICHNIS DER
BEZUGSBERECHTIGTEN
auf Prämien von Margarine und Zucker

für Unterabteilung: [illegible]

DEKADE [illegible]
MONAT [illegible]
Blatt Nr.
Glied. Nr.

Lfd. Nr.	Name u. Vorname	Trp. Nr.	Kateg.	Anmer.	Lfd. Nr.	Name u. Vorname	Trp. Nr.	Kateg.	Anmer.
1	[illegible]	[illegible]	II		21	[illegible]	[illegible]	II	
2	[illegible]	[illegible]	II		22	[illegible]	[illegible]	II	
3	[illegible]	[illegible]	II		23	[illegible]	[illegible]	II	
4	[illegible]	[illegible]	II		24	[illegible]	[illegible]	II	[illegible]
5	[illegible]	[illegible]	II		25				
6	[illegible]	[illegible]	II		26	[illegible]	[illegible]	[illegible]	
7	[illegible]	[illegible]	II		7				
8	[illegible]	[illegible]	II		8				
9	[illegible]	[illegible]	II		9				
10	[illegible]	[illegible]	II		0				
11	[illegible]	[illegible]	II	[illegible]	1				
12	[illegible]	[illegible]	II	[illegible]	2				
13	Meyer, [illegible]	[illegible]	II		3				
14	[illegible]	[illegible]	II		4				
15	Nathan, Nathan	[illegible]	II		5				
16	[illegible]	[illegible]	II		6				
17	[illegible]	[illegible]	II		7				
18	[illegible]	[illegible]	II		8				
19	Rand, Jakob	CK 572	II		9				
20	[illegible]	[illegible]	II		0				

eingereicht: | Kontrolle: | Zugeteilt: | angewiesen am | Anweisung Nr.

Arbeitsberichtführer
Trp. Nr. I/424-2558
Unterschrift [illegible]

A time sheet. *Rand, Jakob. Eight hours every day throughout October 1943 except for two absences: on the sixteenth and twenty-fourth.*

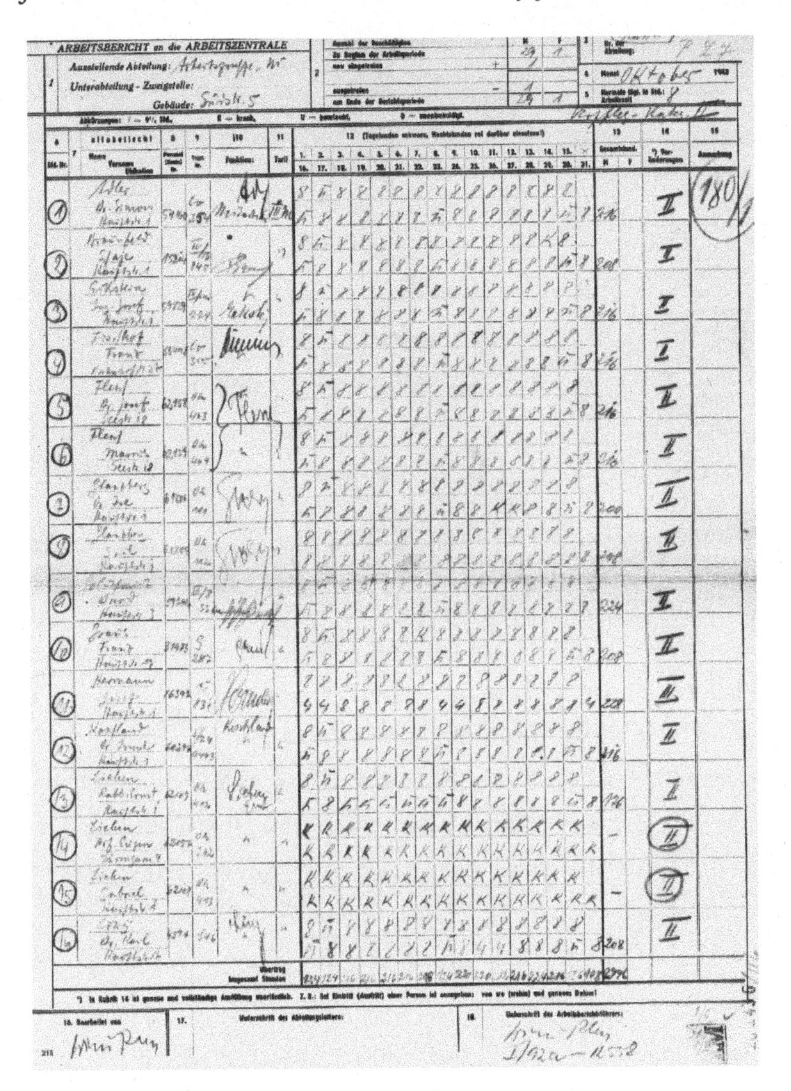
ARBEITSBERICHT an die ARBEITSZENTRALE

Ausstellende Abteilung:

Unterabteilung - Zweigstelle:

Gebäude:

A single notation in some medical records. *Rand, Jakob. 6 April 1944. Requiring medical transportation for an inflammation of the throat.*

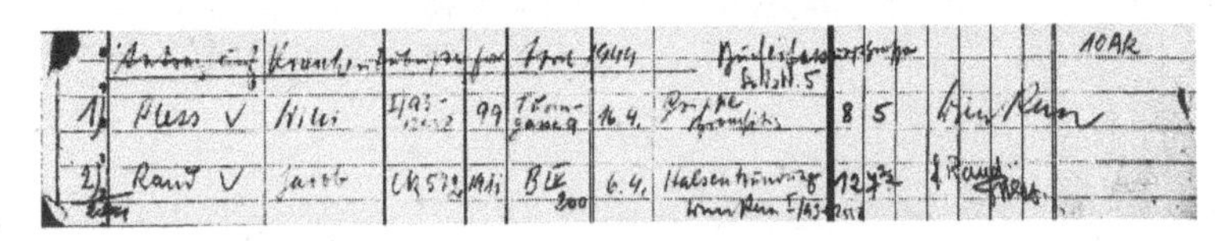

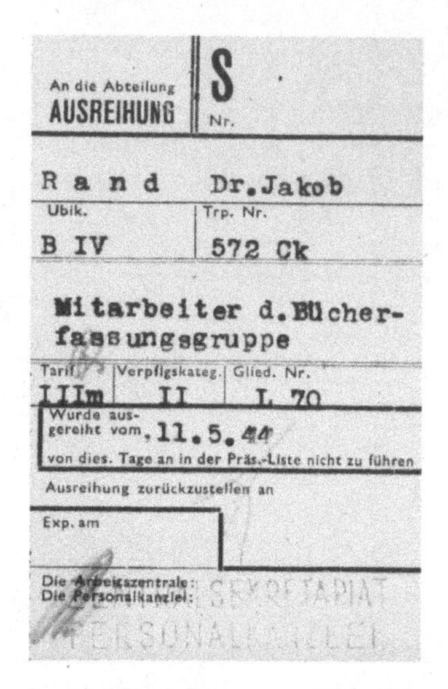

An die Abteilung
AUSREIHUNG
S
Nr.

Rand Dr.Jakob

Ubik. B IV
Trp. Nr. 572 Ck

Mitarbeiter d.Bücherfassungsgruppe

Tarif	Verpflgskateg.	Glied. Nr.
IIIm	II	L 70

Wurde ausgereiht vom 11.5.44
von dies. Tage an in der Präs.-Liste nicht zu führen

Ausreihung zurückzustellen an

Exp. am

Die Arbeitszentrale:
Die Personalkanzlei:

A pink docket, terminating his employment, preparing him for transport to the east.

There are other people, too, similarly listed, similarly marked. They are bound together on ration cards and time sheets, on exemption lists and pink dockets, this constellation of names under a common but shifting title: at first *Arbeitsgruppe 'M'* then, later, *Bücherfassungsgruppe*, the book sorting group.

At any one time there are around thirty of them; sometimes a name will disappear and be replaced by another. They are dispensable, interchangeable. That is what it meant to be privileged. I have come to know them like family. Georg Glanzberg, master violinist, lover of chess, Doctor of Oriental Languages, my grandfather's best friend. Isaac Leo Seeligmann, son of the eminent Dutch bibliophile Sigmund Seeligmann, whose fate was to sort through his father's beloved collection. His story will be remembered even if his name is not. It will live on in Yiddish, recast in the name of another, a man who will cry over his father-in-law's candelabra. That man will be Dr Eppstein. Much like the museum itself: a name misheard, misconstrued. There was no Eppstein. But there was a Josef Eckstein. And, of course, there is Otto Muneles, former head of the Prague Jewish Burial Society, future chief archivist of the Jewish Museum of Prague. They are all here, one way or another.

I have found the *Talmudkommando* and, with it, my grandfather.

In 1987, Dr Jan Randa picked up his copy of the *Australian Jewish News* and found himself the main character in a story that resembled his life. How could he tell them, all those who had read it too, that it was not him, this man with the same name, the same face? How could he say that, yes, like this man, he had been taken outside the camp but not to the Prague Museum, not to some great gothic structure, but to a converted barn, a modest little house at number 5 Südstrasse, within walking distance of the main gates, separated from that hell by a couple of chapels where, day by day, the steady moan of funeral dirges rang out? And, yes, he too knew a Murmelstein, a Muneles and an Eckstein. For God's sake, the name was Eckstein. Not Eppstein. They all featured in his life, but not as this story would have it.

To have trusted a journalist with his memory and have it end up like this. That was the greatest wound.

It would take him two years to recover.

Otto Muneles survived.

Isaac Leo Seeligmann survived.

Rabbi František Gottschall survived.

My grandfather survived.

None of them spoke in any detail of the *Talmudkommando*. Nor did they speak to one another. Each guarded his silence alone.

'We have scanned the catalogue too,' says the director. 'The entire work of the *Talmudkommando* is available online.'

'And the cards themselves?' I ask.

'We keep them in a warehouse on the outskirts of Prague.'

'Would it be possible—'

She cuts me off before I can finish. 'I'm afraid it's not allowed.' She scribbles down a web address. 'Here,' she says. 'I'm sorry. They are too fragile. We have a responsibility. I hope you understand.'

That night I sit at my computer and begin to click through the scanned index cards, hoping to recognise my grandfather's handwriting. Countless times I think I find it but I know only the script of an old man, his hand shaking, his letters ill-formed. He is everywhere in the catalogue. And nowhere.

It is after midnight when I go to bed. I cannot sleep. Next morning, once again, I will set off to find my grandparents.

~

I arrive at Bohušovice, the small outpost station that once serviced Theresienstadt. The building is abandoned. Bolts of tawny cement show beneath the cracked paint. Rusted pipes that once used to drain water from the roof now brace the corners like crutches. Bored teens have tagged the walls. I am struck by how small the station is, not much bigger than a cemetery chapel, here, where they all passed through on their way to the fortress town. There are no tourists, no other seekers of the lost. In its dilapidation, Bohušovice begs to be forgotten.

Outside, near the road, a corridor of grass cuts off the vast plain of dust and gravel that was once a parking lot and, before that, a gathering place for the damned. They were never in the station. Of that I am sure. When they arrived from Prague, when they stepped from the train, this field of dirt is where they came; it is where they stood and waited and wondered what was in store. From inside the station, the stares of those made accomplice. It was forbidden to look on, to bear witness. Often, the locals were ordered to stay home, close their blinds. And yet there are pictures of the endless procession through the main road, obscured by the flutter of curtains.

I cross the dirt towards the grass and find the tracks. What remains of the Theresienstadt rail spur—built by the inmates and opened in June 1943

to ease the constant flow of arrivals and departures—now lies buried in the overgrown brush. Bohušovice is lost to time. The station, the field, the tracks: they are not part of memory's theatre.

I drive on through the valley to the fortress town.

Terezín has filled again, people have made it their home. In the streets, there is an unsettling mix of tourists and townsfolk. Mostly, those who live here are poor. They curse under their breaths as they pass groups of well-dressed foreigners. There is a psychiatric hospital nearby. Its patients roam the square, begging for money. A strange schism between present-day Terezín and the camp called Theresienstadt. But I am not here to see what all the other visitors are here to see. I do not stop at the exhibits. I am here to search the forgotten spaces.

I walk the deserted road to the south, gravel crunching underfoot. Dogs are barking from the next hill, their snouts against the fence, their discoloured teeth catching the afternoon sun. They run back and leap at the knotted wire. I hear children laughing nearby. The dogs lose interest. To my right, the hill drops to reveal a wall of uneven bricks. A brown gate runs the length of this bunker. Flashes of colour between the pickets, and more laughter. At last I am here: number 5 Südstrasse. The *Klärenstalt*.

'Please,' says the woman, opening the gate. 'I've never had a visitor before. My husband apologises. He cannot make it back from work. He very much wanted to meet you.'

We stand in the courtyard while two young boys chase each other around with hockey sticks. Maria is in her early sixties, too young to have known Terezín as it once was, but old enough to remember it as an army barracks for the post-war Communist guard.

'I have been here all my life, in Terezín. My mother was a prisoner here, not Jewish. When it was over she chose to stay. It was all she knew. You have been there, seen inside. We are all victims. There is no escape, so why even try?'

My eyes are drawn to the house. It looks new, made from plasterboard. Only the window frames betray its age, chipped wood painted brown, peeling and cracked. It is as if the house has been built around them.

'I'm afraid you're too late,' Maria says. 'The house was destroyed in the floods back in 2002. We were evacuated and when we could finally return, when the water had subsided, it was gone. We lost everything, had to start again.' She looks to the bulwark built into the hill. 'See there,' she says, pointing to a series of deep cavities in the brickwork. 'It was a barn, to begin with. Those holes, they held the beams in place. Where we are now standing was once part of the house. When...' she pauses. 'Well, you get what I'm saying.'

Maria takes my arm, leads me towards the door. The boys stop playing and watch, suspicious, protective. 'After the flood, the insurance company wanted to demolish the whole place. They said it would be safer to start again. But there was something in the back of my head, a voice. I couldn't do it. We argued for months. My husband too. He thought the same as me. This house, our home, it had a history.'

Still grasping my arm, Maria pushes open the door and leads me inside to a cluttered kitchenette. A marionette hangs from the ceiling, its oversized lips stretched into a vulgar smile. 'My husband,' she says by way of excuse, 'he collects things. He likes to repair. It's his hobby.' She shuffles across the room to a yellow door with a smashed leadlight window. 'We couldn't allow it. So we came to an agreement with the insurance people. We could keep one room. You must forgive us, we have put up partition walls. It was no use to us, such a large space.' She opens the yellow door. I peer inside. The room is crammed with junk: electronics, toys, spare parts. 'Come,' she says. 'This is what's left of where your grandfather worked.'

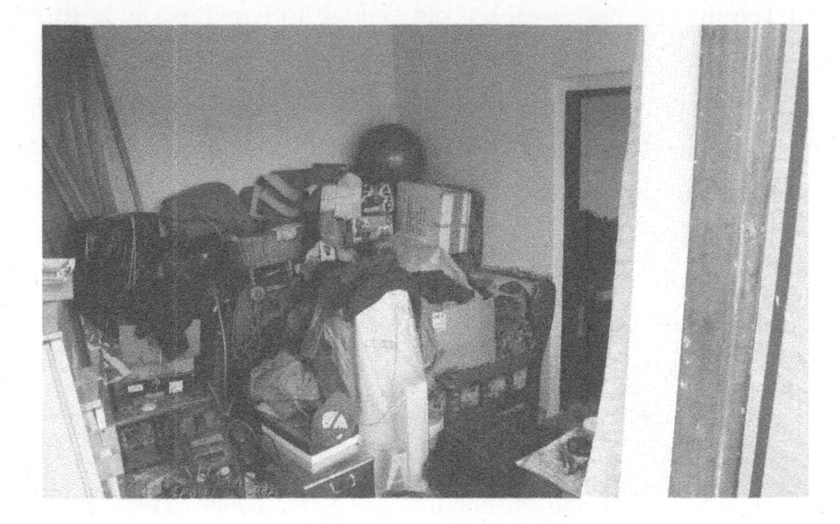

When I step back outside, Maria is waiting. She says nothing. The boys have disappeared and there is a soft cooing in the trees as the sun sinks on the horizon. Maria reaches out, takes my hand, holds it in hers. I must leave now, drive back to Prague. Tomorrow I begin my final journey.

Ludvík has already packed the car by the time I walk around the corner. I am late. We should have left by midday, made it through the main cities before peak hour. Ludvík is leaning against the door, cigarette hanging from his mouth. He looks up and waves.

'It's okay,' he says. 'I drive faster.'

In the car we don't speak. The radio squawks out old rock songs, interrupted only by the bleating of station IDs. This was his idea, to drive from Prague to Auschwitz. When I told him I planned to go he said, yes, he'd come too. It was something he'd been thinking about since his mother died. She had regressed in the end, returned to the Prague of her youth. There were moments when Ludvík saw it flash in her eyes: that place, the one his mother had never been to. It could still reach out and take her. It was part of him.

An hour out of Prague and the road bears the scars of Communist neglect. Hamlets appear by the highway and then, just as quickly, they are gone. Giant billboards, the garish flags of capitalist expansion, stake their claim on the hills. Soft drinks, fast food chains. The old Škoda rattles along the cracked surface. 'Soon we stop,' Ludvík says. 'You like McDonald's? Is better than Czech cooking on road. There you get sick.'

At the table he checks his phone. 'I book us hotel in Oświęcim. Is okay?' It doesn't seem possible. There is a hotel in Terezín, the old SS quarters. That is tasteless enough. But Auschwitz? I shrug.

Half an hour after we pass the city of Brno, Ludvík stops on the side of the road. He unwinds his window and points to the field outside. 'You see here,' he says. 'Is famous battle. Austerlitz. Maybe this interests you.'

I look at the vast green emptiness and try to picture the carnage.

We continue east.

'Do you judge her?' he asks me.

'Babička?'

'Yes. I am reading the letters. Try to imagine for her, for my mother and sisters. I think about grandfather. What he did. But you know she loved him. I think even after divorce they keep up relationship. Secret. He was very difficult man. Not only she says it, also neighbours.'

'And the times were difficult too.'

'She never married again. Maybe this interests you. Before Babička dead I ask her: *You know now he sacrificed for you, for daughters. Maybe do you forgive him for gambling, for destroying happy family?*'

'And?'

'She not even stop to think. Just look at me and say: *No.*'

The highway detours north as we pass the city of Ostrava and soon we are in Poland.

'Look,' Ludvík says, tilting his head towards the road's edge. Train tracks, clearly visible. Further along we pass the first sign: *Oświęcim 52.*

I turn to Ludvík. 'About the letters, the smuggling…'

'It is Marcela. She is one who went to country. She gets from uncles and aunts to send to sisters in camp. For Babička is not safe. Only for little girl. She learn from Daša and Irena before. How to go. How to bribe police at train station.'

'And Mr B?' I ask. 'Did your mother ever speak of him?'

'I have not heard it. I know about letters only afterwards.'

'Uncle Pavel said Mr B was a friend, someone who knew the family. They called him Bohuš. I have gone through the list. He isn't there. But maybe it's not his real name, just something they called him. Maybe it's short for Bohumil. Or Boruslav...Bedřich?'

'Bohuš?'

'Yes.'

'No. This is not Czech name. It means nothing.'

Night has fallen. We have arrived in Oświęcim.

The stillness unsettles me. I lie on the bed and stare at the ceiling. Over my shoulder there is a small window without curtains. There is only darkness outside. We should have stayed in Kraków. It is not right to be sleeping here.

I wake to a shaft of light creeping up the far wall and the sounds of a suburban morning. I am in a town, Oświęcim, Auschwitz, where people live, work, talk and breathe. Most of all, they hear. They see. I look out the window to the cobbled courtyard and, just beyond, to the grey, slatted concrete wall with its crown of barbed wire.

Its name was a cancer that spread in the soil, sprouting new tumours in the surrounding towns. Budy, Gleiwitz, Sosnowitz, Hubertschütte. With every kick, every shot, every bite, every cry, the poison grew stronger, extended further. In all, forty-three subcamps would bear its name before they sank back into the Polish countryside. But only one metastasised so aggressively that it came to consume its host. Birkenau. Two and a half kilometres away. That is what we mean when we say Auschwitz.

I walk the rail line through the gaping brick maw that once hungered for human flesh. I could turn around, walk away, but I continue. They are waiting.

It is the vastness that strikes me. The ruins stretch on to the distant forest. One hundred and forty-seven acres. An entire city. To imagine it full, pulsating—I simply cannot. And yet I have seen the mounds of shoes,

of glasses, of hair, of dolls. I have searched for familiar names on suitcases. I have witnessed what little remains of their lives. The last gasps of hope. But for me, my generation, it can only be this: an eleventh plague, emptiness.

Along the northern fence there is a dirt road that few bother to walk. Every hundred and fifty metres, a wooden guard tower looms overhead. I had asked a guide where I could find the Czech Family Camp. 'Go past the quarantine barracks and the Kommandant's house until you reach the main camp road,' he said. 'The *Familienlager* is the second subcamp on the left.' I thanked him and set off. 'It is not open for tourists,' he called out. 'But the chain on the gate is loose. You can probably squeeze through.'

When I reach it I am taken aback by how ordinary it looks. There are no grand promises here, no *Arbeit Macht Frei*—Work Makes You Free. That feted symbol of Auschwitz, with its mocking rejoinder to their suffering, belongs elsewhere. Those who found themselves in this place never saw it, were never given cause to hope. The wind is picking up and the two halves of the gate jerk wildly against the chain. I stare at the mountings, thick cement pylons braced to tall iron posts, studded with tarnished knobs that once pulsed electricity through the surrounding wires. Now, it is all oxidised, coated in rust. I lean forward, my eye almost touching a single black-crusted barb, and look through to the ruins, to a boulevard of bloodied fingers.

They jut out from the earth at unnatural angles, rough and flaked. When all went to ash only they remained, pointing accusingly at the sky, *how could you have let this happen?* But their question went unanswered and so they were left to point for eternity at a God that was deaf, dumb and blind.

Five thousand people arrived in the Czech Family Camp in September 1943. Set apart from the routinised slaughter that was the very essence of the industrial complex, they were given this land as their own, to administer as they saw fit, answerable only to the savage criminal, Camp Elder Arno Böhm, and his Kapo cronies. Thirty-two wooden barracks in which to build a world. Men and women. Children too. Within weeks there was a school, a hospital, but also disease and hunger. The inmates began to die. In December, another five thousand came. The barracks overflowed but those inside made do. It was better than beyond the wire, where bald, emaciated *Muselmänner*—those who had given up on life—floated by in filthy striped rags.

It didn't last. One night in early March 1944, all four thousand surviving inmates from the September transport were gathered together, forced to write postcards to their friends and family in Theresienstadt and moved to the nearby quarantine barracks. They were told that they would be sent to Heydebreck, a work camp in Germany. But there was no Heydebreck for them. It was another Nazi lie. Some inmates sensed what was to come; they encoded their cards with messages of impending doom. Others chose, in their desperation, to believe in the promise of Heydebreck. The following day, they were all loaded into trucks, driven along the main camp road, and delivered to the gas chambers. Among them was my grandfather's brother, Shmuel Rand.

And so the December arrivals came to learn the meaning of '6SB', the vague cipher that had been scrawled next to their names upon registration. *Sonderbehandlung*—special treatment—after six months. If their calculations were correct, they'd be ash before July. And yet they persisted with their makeshift society, stretching out the days with familiar routines, watching the sun set with dismay, wondering how they might have made the hours last longer.

Three hundred kilometres away, in the converted barn just outside Theresienstadt, my grandfather was still scribbling bibliographic notes on stiff white index cards, oblivious to the cynical act of theatre in which he was about to play a minor part. The Nazis were preparing the camp for a visit by representatives from the International Red Cross. Beautification of the streets was underway. Inmates were rehearsing plays and operas to perform for their guests. Two transports—some ten thousand people—had already been sent east in an attempt to ease the overcrowding. But it wasn't enough. By April, plans were afoot for one last transport to the Czech Family Camp in Birkenau. This would be my grandfather's role: to leave Theresienstadt, to help clear its stage.

How my grandfather came to be included on the May transport is difficult to explain. If his initial letter to Beit Terezín is any indication, he seems to have believed that the work of the *Talmudkommando* was done. After almost two years of privilege and protection he had suddenly become expendable. Yet the *Talmudkommando* continued its work until the liberation of Theresienstadt. There were still books to catalogue. Why then summarily dismiss and deport almost half of the workers, including my grandfather and Georg Glanzberg?

I am here in the Czech Family Camp, by coincidence, on the anniversary of his arrival, May 19. Sixty-eight years ago my grandfather stumbled off the train, clutching Georg Glanzberg's arm. They were met by a squad of prisoners, some of whom they knew. *Walk with us,* they were told over the tumult of barking dogs and soldiers. The train track through the main gate had not yet been built. They climbed into the back of a truck and were driven the short distance to the place where I now stand.

I slip sideways through the gate and walk down the cracked road that divides the camp in two. In the distance, the train track swarms with movement, a steady procession of tourists heading towards the crematoria. Some branch off, along the path of the living, into the two banks of sturdy brick barracks.

They know nothing of this subcamp.

Sonderbehandlung. Special Treatment.

Death.

That is what it meant to be privileged.

There was no roll call in June, no liquidation. Another seven and a half thousand inmates had arrived in May and filled the Czech Family Camp with stories of the model ghetto: its streets swept clean, the factory tents in the town square dismantled and replaced with trees and flowers. A new currency had begun to circulate, the Terezín Crown, to be spent at the café and shops that had popped up on certain streets. There was even a stage where jazz bands played on Sundays. Only the barracks put paid to the lie. They still coursed with squalor and disease. Inmates scratched angrily at their skin, picking off bedbugs and lice, eating them.

This place swallows names, lives, memories. *Familienlager BIIb.* Thirty-two wooden barracks, four latrine blocks, two kitchen halls. A shit-soaked shrine to cynicism, to arrogance, in this wasteland of the damned. Yet, viewed from the heavens, it is a small tract of dirt. Here, where reason left the world, the impossible flourished.

I am back where I started:

And so he taught Jewish children. He taught them in Prague. He taught them in Theresienstadt. And he taught them in Auschwitz.

I nestle into the crook of the chimney where Block 31 once stood. The Children's Block. A school. My fingers trace circles across the ground.

The Red Cross visit to Theresienstadt on 23 June 1944 was a success. The delegates wrote a glowing report: rumours of the harsh treatment of Jews were unfounded and the planned visit to a labour camp would not be necessary. Eichmann was delighted. He no longer required a backup plan. On 11 July 1944, the liquidation of the Czech Family Camp began. Only a few inmates—my grandfather and Georg Glanzberg among them—were selected as fit for work and transported to slave labour camps in Germany. The rest were sent to the gas chambers. By nightfall of 12 July, the camp had been cleared. Of the 17,500 people who had been imprisoned there, fewer than 1300 survived the war.

I look through the fence towards the forest over a kilometre away. There are three destroyed subcamps just like this one. *BIIc. BIId. BIIe.* Beyond them, I can just make out the ruins of the Kanada Barracks, where inmates sorted the belongings of all who arrived at Birkenau. Then, trees. I count the camps again, stopping when I am sure which is the third—*BIIe*—where my grandmother was imprisoned after arriving from Terezín on Transport EO on 6 October 1944, almost four months after the Czech Family Camp had been liquidated.

Hers was a most unusual welcome. On the morning of 7 October the *Sonderkommando* rose up and destroyed one of the gas chambers and crematoria, Krema IV. It was the only major act of rebellion in the history of Auschwitz-Birkenau. From their quarters in *BIIe*, my grandmother and her fellow deportees would have been closer to the battle than any other prisoners.

The rebellion was quickly put down and, for three weeks, my grandmother waited in the shadow of the chimneys, holding on to her last possession, a gold ring her mother had smuggled into the model ghetto. As it was for my grandfather, Birkenau would come to define her. Every story will be said to have happened here. To us, she will not have left in an undocumented transport on 28 October along with one hundred other women. To us, there will be no Upper Silesia, no Merzdorf, no textile factory where Jewish women were forced to process flax. Not until it is too late to ask.

I reach into my backpack, pull out the crumbling orange paperback and begin to read. I know these words by heart, an entire universe foreseen. For years I have pictured him in its pages but now I can see he is not here. This is not his story. Rather, he is both author and reader, both giver and keeper of lives. This book is the guide to his deepest grief, his enduring shame, to lives swept away by unknowable forces and cast aside. Between its covers lie his friend, Georg Glanzberg, and his mother, Gusta Randová.

There is a patch of grass growing on a mound of earth behind the foundations of Block 31. I crouch down and pick at the blades, dig my fingers into the mud. It is here their story ends, here where I must find peace in not knowing. There will be names—Schwarzheide, Sachsenhausen, Merzdorf—but nothing more. It is too late. What's left to fill the silence is no longer theirs. This is my story, woven from the threads of rumour and legend, post-memory.

I lie down in the dirt and stare at the crooked red fingers. I try to see the horror but it grows distant, blurring into the autumn sky. A cool drizzle begins to fall. My eyes have grown heavy. The stillness is broken by birds: a great flock, circling the chimneys.

The scene recedes into the background, leaving only the dirt and its blanket of white flowers.

REF. I-ARCH-I/1121-22/12

Dear Bram Presser,

In reply to your enquiry, the Auschwitz-Birkenau State Museum in Oświęcim would like to inform you that we have searched partially saved documentation which is kept in our archives. Unfortunately there is no information about RAND Jakub and ROUBÍČKOVÁ Daša. Prisoner number A-1821 was received by a man who was deported to KL Auschwitz-Birkenau in May, 1944 from Ghetto Theresienstadt. The State Museum would like to explain that during the evacuation and liquidation of the KL Auschwitz by order of camp authorities almost all important documents of KL Auschwitz including prisoners' personal files were destroyed. On the basis of the partially saved documents it is impossible to impart complete information about all people who were imprisoned in the camp.

We suggest you contact in your further search the International Tracing Service, Bad Arolsen...

Yours sincerely,
Piotr Supiński
Biuro Informacji o Byłych Więźniach
Office for Information on Former Prisoners

~

21 APRIL 2014

TO: ARCHIV@GEDENKSTAETTE-SACHSENHAUSEN.DE
SUBJECT: SEARCHING FOR DR JAKUB RAND

Dear Sir/Madam,

I am currently researching a book about my late grandfather, Jakub Rand, who was one of the 1000 prisoners sent from the Birkenau Czech Family Camp to the BRABAG gasoline plant at Schwarzheide on 3 July 1944 and then, a day or so before the death march, to Sachsenhausen. I was hoping there might be some documentation of his internment in your archives. His birth date was 25.12.1911, his Auschwitz prisoner number was A-1821.

Any assistance or information you could provide will be greatly appreciated.

Kind regards,
Bram Presser

TO: BRAM PRESSER
AW: SEARCHING FOR DR JAKUB RAND

Dear Mr Presser,

In reply to your inquiry concerning Jakub Rand, born 25/12/1911, I inform you that unfortunately no documents have been found in our archives.

Almost all the documents of the headquarters of Sachsenhausen including the card index of the detainees and nearly all the files of the detainees were destroyed by the SS in spring 1945 before the liberation of the concentration camp. The little, incompletely preserved files are for the most part in the archives of the Russian Federation. As far as these contain information on individual persons, they have been incorporated in a database.

In this database I could not find information relating to Jakub Rand.

Yours sincerely
Archiv
Gedenkstätte und Museum Sachsenhausen
Straße der Nationen 22
D-16515 Oranienburg

Numbers

I
THERESIENSTADT

Dusk.

A silken frost settled across the fields beyond the town's northern ramparts. Here, beneath the volcanic peaks, where grey cones threatened unspeakable violence, a great fortress had risen from the earth, its ravelins, escarpments and redoubts arranged like cascading stars, holding strong against malevolent winds. On top of the third bastion, Jakub R stood gazing out at the Elbe River and, on its furthest shore, the lone spire of Lidomerice's oldest church.

It was almost a year since he had arrived, since he had trudged through the slush in the streets of Bohušovice, hurrying his mother along on the final leg of their journey to the town once called Terezín. There they waited a week in the sluice yard, lying on straw, filling out forms, eating potatoes, before being shown to their separate barracks. Gusta quickly made a home of it—to her, Theresienstadt was just another exile, no better or worse than the city. With her knitted doilies and pinned pictures, she made her bunk comfortable enough. What little she ate satisfied her meagre appetite. Work in the central laundry was demanding but bearable. And, when the day was done, she had two of her sons, Jakub and Shmuel. She waited for them to come and, at the sound of the curfew siren, as they hurried off back to their barracks, she lay down and closed her eyes.

From the moment he stepped through the camp's sluice gate, Jakub, however, felt only the chill of confinement. He felt it in his back and in his knees as he crouched down to scrape ice from the pavements. He felt it in his arms and his neck as he hammered wooden boards to the crumbling barriers that separated the inmates from their captors. He felt it as the tepid brown liquid they called ersatz coffee sloshed around in his empty stomach. And he felt it on his cheek as he lay against the frozen straw pillow at night, breathing in the stench of his bunkmates.

Midway through January, Jakub was transferred to the Youth Welfare Department. 'Formal classes are forbidden,' said Gonda Redlich, when Jakub reported for duty at the boys' rooming house on Hauptstrasse. Jakub knew of Redlich from his student days in Prague. A few years his junior, Redlich had been a popular leader in the Zionist youth group movement. His distinct light curls, button nose and thick, round spectacles were instantly recognisable and lent him an unlikely, bookish authority. He had been transported to Theresienstadt early, in 1941, and following a brief tussle with Fredy Hirsch was appointed department head. 'Teach them songs, play games,' Redlich continued. 'And should the lyrics contain some educational elements, or the game include passing through the cities of Palestine, we cannot be blamed for what knowledge the children might absorb.'

Jakub stood before the class that morning and tried to sing but his voice shook and the children laughed. 'You shouldn't think about it too much,' said Redlich. 'The children get decent food. They have their own barracks with clean sheets and pillows. They do not experience this place like we do. You'll learn to play and sing and lie. That is your role. And for your efforts you will get extra bread, extra butter, sugar...sometimes even sausage.' Redlich shook Jakub's hand. 'I have put in a request that you be exempted from transport. There's talk in the Council of Elders of an amnesty, but until then we need to look after our own. Tell your mother you're safe. All of you.'

~

The bread was mostly stale, the butter often mouldy or rancid. The sugar was laced with grains of dirt and dead insects. Jakub tasted the sausage only once. It made him double over with cramps as he waited for the latrine. Still, he thanked Gonda Redlich and took his allotted rations so that he could provide for his family. Gusta made of them what she could, glad not to stand in line for the thin broth ladled out in the ground floor dining hall. She made stews and cakes in the warm-up kitchen and brought them back to her room. She divided them into portions, always sure to give herself the smallest one, and watched her sons eat—Shmuel quickly, ravenous from a day in the labour detail, and Jakub slowly. She could not see that he struggled to swallow, his throat clenched as he counted down to curfew.

Gonda Redlich was right. A transport amnesty was declared, but not before six transports had left the camp, taking more than seven thousand people east to a place called Auschwitz. It was, according to the Council, a labour camp. Jakub could see the change in the streets and in the barracks, but most of all he could see it in the classroom: children disappearing overnight, others turning to him when their parents were taken. Many knew him from their time at the school in Jáchymova Street. He sang them songs plundered from a childhood he had tried to escape. He invented stories, stringing them out until he could see the children smile. When Fredy Hirsch came to take the children for exercises in the yard, Jakub sank to the floor and folded his arms over his head. With eyes closed, he imagined himself under his father's *tallis*, and willed more stories, more songs to come back to him.

'Jakub?'

He righted himself against the wall. Gonda Redlich was standing at the door, bemused. Jakub brushed himself down and nodded for Gonda to come in. 'Sir?' It still felt strange to address the younger man like that.

'I'm glad you haven't left for the day,' said Redlich. 'The classes are going well?'

'Thank you, yes,' said Jakub. 'For the children, at least.'

Redlich fumbled in his pocket and pulled out a folded piece of paper.

'This came from the Council. Murmelstein asked me to give it to you.' He handed the paper to Jakub. 'You are to report outside the post office tomorrow morning. Murmelstein was cagey on the details but I know there's some new register of scholars. You've all been summoned.' Redlich pulled off his spectacles and rubbed them on his shirt. 'There's more to you than we knew.'

'Next. Yes, this way...Number?'

'CK-572.'

'Name?'

'R, Jakub.'

'Jakub *Israel* R?'

'*Doctor* Jakub Israel R.'

'Yes, yes. Here you are. Your qualification?'

'Law. Charles University.'

'I see. And you are working in—'

'*Jugendfürsorge*, sir.'

'Teaching the children?'

'It is not permitted. Mostly we play, sing, the like.'

'You take us for fools, Doctor Israel. Thankfully that is not my concern. Family?'

'My mother and brother. He has stayed on in the mobile labour detail. She was assigned to the laundry.'

'And your position affords them some...some privilege?'

'For now they are exempted from transport, yes.'

'But still you are here.'

'On Murmelstein's instruction. I am told this is important.'

'And with importance comes greater privilege.'

'I suppose it does.'

'What is it your sage says? *The son must sustain his father and mother according to his capacity.*'

'Maimonides, yes. Almost ten years my father has been in his grave. I am the eldest son.'

'And so here?'

'Here the currency is bread. Extra rations, exemptions—'

'Bread, yes. But also...how do you people call it? Vitamins C and P. Connection and pull. Essential for long-term health. I might add another vitamin: L, luck. That we seem to have in common.'

'Luck?'

'Your people have always fascinated me, Doctor Israel. My colleagues jeered when I set about studying you. Still, a passion is a passion. There is no escaping it. Five years ago I was in a small office surrounded by your books, praying for tenure, waiting on the next dinner invitation to remind me I was still alive. Then this...this all began. Those who had mocked me found themselves at the front lines while I am here, where my learning is valued. Such was the tide of history. Luck. Do you believe in the soothsayers, Herr Doctor?'

'Our sages warn against it. *Superstitions can harm only those who heed them.*'

'*The Book of the Pious*. Indeed. Still, they intrigue me. Those you credit as sages, those you fail to recognise. Take Maimonides, for example. Behind the misplaced devotion, he saw it exactly as it has come to be.'

'This? Here? With all respect—'

'But the meaning is undeniable. This war of Gog and Magog. You have already lost. God has moved on, chosen someone else. We of the Aryan bloodline have our Messiah, one who rules from Berlin. Yet here, in this town, in all the lands we control, your people continue to pray for miracles. You cling to folktales, blasphemies. I don't know what you expect. Soon the war will be over, just as Maimonides said, and when it is, the prophecy will have been fulfilled. The Book of Judges, chapter twelve. You are familiar with the first verse, Doctor Israel?'

'Not as you interpret it, but yes.'

'Very good. Then let us begin...'

For weeks after the strange interview Jakub waited but there was no news. He watched the children draw, helped prepare issues of the student paper,

Vedem. He tried to speak with Gonda Redlich but he was always busy.

Georg arrived at the start of July. Somehow word reached Jakub the following day; his friend was in the Bodenbach Barracks awaiting registration. Jakub hoped he would be assigned to the Youth Welfare Department. He asked Fredy Hirsch to pass on his request. *Back in Prague the children loved him*, he said. *He shares your views, is passionate about them. He will bring credit to the work. I'd ask myself but...*Fredy pulled him aside a while later. *No luck. Gonda says he has been promised elsewhere.*

Jakub's disappointment lasted only a few days. One evening, as he trudged back from his mother's barracks, trailing behind Shmuel, he thought of his friend and how it would feel to have a brother for whom he did not have to care, an equal. He went to the washroom where he splashed his face with water and rinsed his mouth of the foul lentil broth that had crept back up into his throat. Outside, the siren sounded, a call to fitful sleep. The main lights of the barracks flickered then went out, leaving only the dim bulbs that hung from the corridor ceilings. When he reached his bunk, he could see the outline of a man. It had happened before. Lost, confused souls. Souls who had ceased to care. Sometimes a stray from the madhouse in the Kavalier Barracks. The ghetto guard would come soon to collect him. But no, this outline was familiar. The rakish figure. The staccato finger-twitching.

'Georg?'

'It is hardly how you described.'

For six months they had merely acknowledged to each other that they were alive: one or two carefully crafted sentences on official card. Jakub had wanted to explain, but this place could not be described. For his part Georg, too, held back. Prague was desolate, every building a reminder of what once had been. He went from his apartment to the museum and back again until the inevitable summons, when he was herded onto a train. Just another transport of Jews.

'They've scattered us around the barracks,' Georg continued. 'Father is in Magdeberg, my brothers in Sudeten. Mother is in Dresden, at the other end.'

'You'll get used to it. It's a nightly waltz.'

'Father will be glad to see you.'

'He is with the Council of Elders?'

'Not really, but they keep him close. Light work, tending to the halls mostly.'

'And you?'

'Three more weeks in the labour detail then we'll see what happens.'

'It says only *Arbeitsgruppe M.* I'm to be at the gate on Südstrasse by eight.' Georg turned the narrow slip over as if there might be a clue on the back.

The following night Jakub waited for Georg in their room.

'Sorry, I was with Father. He sends his best.'

Georg said little about his work, only that it involved books, ones they had not even known existed. Jakub didn't press the matter. Georg was still adjusting to life in the ghetto.

'I mentioned you to Otto Muneles,' Georg said a few days later. 'Murmelstein has put him in charge of the group.' Georg sat down on his bunk and began to unbutton his shirt. 'He is giving a lecture tomorrow. Go and speak with him.'

Otto Muneles had lost little of his gruffness in the months since Jakub last saw him. He was stooped, as if still tending to the dead. He did not move while he spoke, his arms thrust downwards, his hands balled into fists. His voice was a whisper, a seesaw of pitch and punctuation. Jakub found it unsettling that Muneles spoke in public at all, even in the dusky greyness of a barrack loft; listening to someone who communed with the dead tore away the scab of civility.

A polite smattering of applause and it was over. The small audience dispersed, climbing over beams, ducking, tripping, until they reached the stairs. Jakub made his way into the light.

'Ah, Jakub! Good. Come closer.' Muneles leaned over the lectern. 'This group I have...I have gone over the original lists. Your name jumped out immediately. The officer who interviewed you was impressed. He was not certain you had the discipline required, but was confident you had the knowledge. In the end, he approved. It was the Youth Welfare Department that reclaimed you. Maybe Gonda thought he was doing you a favour. They have a healthy supply of Vitamin P. When it comes to drawing up the transport lists, the Commission immediately removes all their cards from the central registry. You can't be put on a train.'

Muneles gathered his notes and tucked them under his arm. 'Go back to your room. I just wanted to say that I've put in a request to have you transferred. Eichmann is unhappy with our progress. Like everyone else, we work slowly, make the job last as long as we can, but it is the attrition that troubles him. Murmelstein needs this to curry favour. He has installed me as a buffer, I know. He can't be seen to fail and will sacrifice me if he must. In return he allows me to speak in his name. Now we wait and see where the real power lies.'

Each night, as those around them drifted off to sleep, Georg spoke of paper wonders, the treasures of a mighty kingdom far from the dirt and noise. He guided Jakub's dreams to a world balanced on a spire of knowledge. The titles alone drew Jakub forward, called his heart to where the rest of him could not follow. Then, in the late summer, he received a yellow ticket.

He was to report to the gate at Südstrasse the next morning.

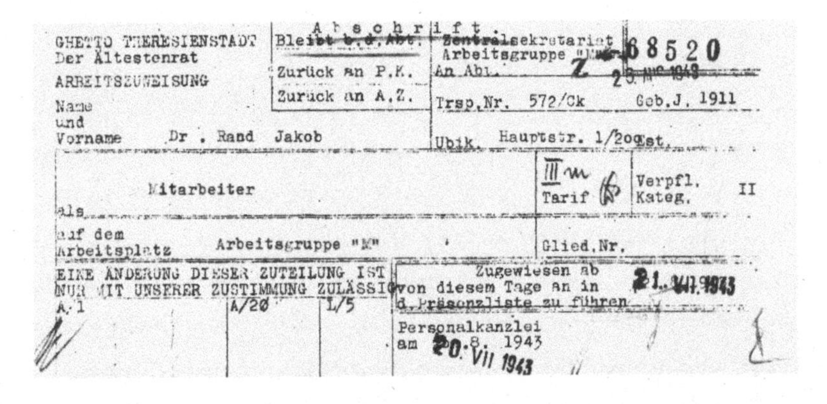

Abschrift.

GHETTO THERESIENSTADT
Der Ältestenrat
ARBEITSZUWEISUNG

Bleibt b.d. Abt.
Zurück an P.K.
Zurück an A.Z.

Zentralsekretariat
Arbeitsgruppe "M"
An Abt.

68520
Z 25. VIII 1943

Trsp.Nr. 572/Ck Geb.J. 1911

Name und Vorname Dr. Rand Jakob

Ubik. Hauptstr. 1/20 gst.

als Mitarbeiter

Tarif III m

Verpfl. Kateg. II

auf dem Arbeitsplatz Arbeitsgruppe "M"

Glied.Nr.

EINE ÄNDERUNG DIESER ZUTEILUNG IST NUR MIT UNSERER ZUSTIMMUNG ZULÄSSIG

A. 1 A/20 L/5

Zugewiesen ab von diesem Tage an in d. Präsenzliste zu führen 21. VIII. 1943

Personalkanzlei am 20.8. 1943
20. VII 1943

The *Klärenstalt* was a short walk from the gate, back in the direction of Bohušovice, tucked beneath the town's southern rampart. Three rooms sectioned off from the gardener's hut in what was once a barn. They gave themselves a name too. Not what was printed on their time sheets. Not *Arbeitsgruppe 'M'* or *Bücherfassungsgruppe.* No, they called themselves the *Talmudkommando.* These men, who sat on wooden benches, their knees aching, were the custodians of wisdom, of the divine inspiration that had found its way onto the reconstituted pulp of a felled tree. Together they would compress the knowledge into a catalogue that would itself be a library to be plundered, devoured, rewritten.

Their names had once reverberated through the streets of Josefov. Jakub had sat in lecture halls and felt his soul ascend on a chariot of their words. He had read their commentaries on the sacred texts. Mojžíš Woskin-Nahartabi, Rabbi Šimon Adler, Rabbi František Gottschall, Dr Isaac Leo Seeligmann, Josef Eckstein. Jakub saw in them the wise men of his youth, who had huddled around cluttered tables in the *shtibl* with his father, and argued with an intellectual ferocity Jakub could not fathom. He longed to tell his mother, to say that the spirit of her beloved sat with him while he worked, and guided her son's pen. But he would not add to her suffering.

In time, Jakub came to know the books by touch alone: the texture of their jackets on his fingertips, the deckled serrations on his knuckles, the pressure on his wrist as he lifted each one from the pile.

Transports resumed in September.

At first it had only been rumour, frantic whispers that cut across New Year's prayers. Then came the paper slips, left on bunks for the occupants to find at the end of the day. Shmuel was among the first. He ran to Jakub. *There must be a mistake. They...they promised. You have the letter.* Gusta, too, misunderstood the nature of Jakub's privilege. 'Go to the Council,' she pleaded. 'We are only three left. It is not right.' He joined the line of supplicants at the Transport Department, only to be summarily dismissed. 'This time we have no choice,' the man said. 'The Kommandant himself selected the names. Nobody is exempt.' His mother would not hear it. 'You should not have left the children,' she sobbed. 'With them we were all safe. What good are your books?' He tried to calm her. 'Don't listen to the *bonkes.* It is just another labour detail. And he will be free of this place.' He handed her what was left of his rations so she could make Shmuel something for the journey. For three days he made do with ersatz coffee. Six weeks later they received the first postcard. It said only that Shmuel was well and hard at work. Jakub stared at the postmark: *Arbeitslager Birkenau bei Neu-Berun.*

2
THERESIENSTADT

Gusta rocked the pot over the stove in the warm-up kitchen on the ground floor of the Hamburg Barracks. The aroma was not unpleasant. She knew that most nights they ate better than the others in their room. What was left she would share, a spoonful here, a spoonful there. She had stitched together a family as best she could. Two hours was not enough to be a mother, even before Shmuel was taken. The boys would come straight from work every few days at six and be gone by curfew at eight. Otherwise she was alone. Then the *mischlinge* arrived: a large transport in early March, dumping an entire community of confused children in their midst. The youngest among them found homes with adoptive mothers but the older ones were forced to fend for themselves.

Two sisters were assigned to the bunks beside her. The older one was surly, protective. She came from Prague. She didn't need any help, thank you. In a way Gusta found comfort in her brashness; the girl sounded much the same as her own daughter, Růženka, had at that age. The younger sister was different in both looks and manner. She spoke softly, politely, but seemed to feel safe only in her sister's presence. Gusta tried approaching when the girl was alone, but she shied away and scuttled to her bed, the bathroom or the corridor.

The sisters spoke hurriedly between themselves. Gusta gleaned that their father was also in the camp, a metalworker and roustabout, by the sounds of it. He seemed to arrange to see them but would be late or not show up at all. She heard them lament the nights they had sat on his bunk, picking at the straw, pressing their faces to his dirty sheets, breathing him in, waiting in vain. They spoke of his apologies and his promise of gifts that, they said, never came. They depended instead on their mother. Parcels would arrive regularly, some by the camp postal service, others through less sanctioned means—Gusta heard talk of a gendarme, a Sudeten man who was known to the family. For the first weeks the girls seemed impervious to the resentful stares from those around them. They refused to speak, not even to her. They showed no interest in her sons when they came to visit. And yet, when the lights hissed and went out, they joined in the chorus of sniffs and whimpers. Gusta edged towards them and cooed them to sleep.

Their manner thawed with the summer sun. One evening, when Shmuel arrived, the girls stopped talking and turned to watch. The young man handed Gusta a shirt and a button. Soon Jakub appeared. He hurried across to his mother, kissed her forehead and unloaded food from his jacket pocket—bread, jam, butter, flour, a jar of the acrid Terezín spread made from mustard powder and vinegar. Shmuel rubbed his hands together. 'Tonight another feast,' said Gusta. The brothers waited while Gusta rushed off to prepare their meal. When she returned the three of them ate on the bunk as if it were a banquet table.

Before leaving, Jakub and Shmuel kissed their mother, then touched their lips to a grey square of paper nailed to the inside column of her bunk. The next morning the older girl leaned across while Gusta was tucking in her sheet. 'What is that?' she asked, pointing to the paper. 'That is my husband, the father of my children.' The girl held out a small bonbon. It was all that remained of her most recent package. 'Please,' she said. 'My name is Daša.'

'And I'm Gusta. Please…call me Auntie.'

'Your mother…' Jakub bit the corner of the schnitzel and sucked on the oily crumb. 'I'll be at your house every night, I think.'

Daša laughed and cut into her potato. 'She knows it is my favourite. I'm just worried they'll spoil.'

'No. Keep them coming, please.' Jakub took another bite. He didn't wait to swallow. 'We promise they won't go to waste.'

Gusta put her arm around Irena's shoulder. 'It's good?' The girl smiled and leaned into her. Gusta held her for a moment, savouring the warmth. Then, to Daša: 'I'll come too. If it's not too much, of course. To think, we're almost neighbours and we've never met.'

'You don't leave the house,' said Jakub.

'I didn't know such charming girls existed. I must meet their mother. We have a lot to discuss.'

'Well,' Jakub said as he stood up, 'thank you both. And your mother.' He leaned over and kissed Gusta on the cheek. She prodded him, nodded towards Daša. 'Go on,' she said. Jakub began to crouch but caught himself and smiled awkwardly. 'Yes,' he said. 'Thanks again.' He knew not to turn around. Gusta would be shaking her head.

December.

Gusta's room had changed since Jakub's last visit. A maintenance crew had lopped the top tier from each bunk in the name of *beautification*. Some of the remaining inmates were packing cases while others bartered with what they would leave behind. Only the *mischlinge* were sitting casually on their bunks, indifferent to the bustle around them.

'What's the news?' Daša asked Jakub.

'They're saying another five thousand people will go. Half on Wednesday then the rest on Sabbath. The lines outside the Magdeberg Barracks stretch past the gate. Those who aren't seeking rescission are at the Labour Department begging for transfers.'

'Auntie Gusta is safe?'

'For now, yes. She longs to be with Shmuel in Birkenau. What do you hear from your father?'

'Not much. He promises a visit to the new café soon, maybe for Irena's birthday. His job pays, not enough for an entry ticket, but something. He has found a new circle. They play *skat* in their barracks after curfew. He's confident he'll be here for Irena's celebration but I don't hold him to his word. Mama wrote. She is making plans.'

'And you?'

'Yes. Me too. One way or another we'll celebrate.'

The transports left as scheduled. In the streets and the barracks, there was a sense of relief. Of space. Of guilt.

On the morning of Irena's birthday, Gusta reported sick to the Labour Department. A quick visit to the infirmary confirmed a mild case of *Terezínka*, the camp illness, diagnosed without examination by a harried nurse. The dormitory was empty by the time she returned but, as promised, each woman had left half a day's bread ration under her pillow. Jakub, too, had saved his extra rations and Daša had arranged for dried fruit to be brought in from Prague. *See you soon*, the accompanying note from her mother had said. Gusta crumbled the stale bread into her pot, tipped lukewarm coffee over it and waited for the mixture to thicken. She then stirred in the margarine, jam, sugar, fruit and some extra flour she had traded with a baker for more regular access to the laundry.

They waited until after curfew to celebrate. The women gathered in the centre of the room as Gusta carried in the cake. Together they sang the 'Terezín March' while Irena merrily clapped along.

Hey! Tomorrow life starts over,
And with it the time is approaching
When we'll fold our knapsacks
And return home again.
Where there is a will there is a way,
Let us join hands
And one day on the ruins of the ghetto
We shall laugh.

Irena closed her eyes and blew out an imaginary candle.

3
PRAGUE

At first, the postcards were enough. They came every few weeks, a couple of lines here and there: 'Just to say we have arrived and all is as it can be. Daddy sends his love too.' Then: 'I have found work in the kitchen. Irča and Daddy are also working.' And: 'Try as I do to mend them, our socks and underwear are wearing thin.' Františka Roubíčková sent long letters back, detailed stories of her work in the factory, of their sisters, and of their family in Miličín. But there was no warmth in words alone and, in time, she began to despair. How could she hope to help them when they were so far away? How could she hope to be a mother? That she still had Marcela and Hana was, she knew, only temporary. They, too, would be called for when they reached the requisite age.

She lay awake at night, afraid of what dreams might come. And what of Ludvík? Was there not, in the blood that had brought about their captivity, an obligation to protect, to make good on his sacred oath? She might even find it within herself to forgive if now, when they needed him most, he could finally be a father. As Marcela and Hana slept beside her, Františka buried her face in the pillow, stifling the litany of curses that she spat into the feathers. The hours passed and her rage turned inwards, a caustic mix of exhaustion, fear and loneliness. Most of all, guilt. She was, at last, living well. While most had been sent to munitions factories, she had been conscripted to a small textile firm in Nové Město, sewing garments that would be sent to the Eastern Front. It provided a steady wage, enough to feed three mouths. And that wasn't even allowing for the visits to Miličín. She had been spending much of her spare time navigating the bureaucracy of obtaining admission stamps for the packages, and the rest stockpiling the twenty kilograms she was permitted to send in each one: boxes with flour, salt, lentils, vegetables, with sweets and dresses. Most of all she sent a mother's unguarded heart and then waited

anxiously for the official postcards of receipt. But that was no longer enough. If she was to hold them again, she would have to go to Theresienstadt.

At dawn she kissed the two sleeping girls and rushed to the factory. She sat at her machine, forcing the material across its dimpled plane. The needle pecked at the seams, snatching them together. When a piece was done, Františka tossed it in the basket at her feet. Before lunch, she rose from her bench and approached the supervisor. 'I must go for a while.' The man was not unsympathetic; he had grown fond of Františka. She was skilled, able to patch together a jacket in half the time it took many of the other women. She was also known to slip him the odd cigarette, offer to join him outside for a smoke. He, too, had lost family. His wife's brother had married a Jewess. For months they tried to obtain an exit visa, bribed everyone they thought might have influence. The supervisor himself had given them money against his better judgment, money that he now wished he had kept. When the borders closed he found himself trapped in a hopeless cycle of charity until the letter came from the Jewish Council summoning the woman and their three children to the fairgrounds. Then he sighed with relief. 'Certainty, Roubíčková,' he said. 'That is what the family needed. Better just to know.' His wife now spent all her days with the brother, comforting him with lies. She hardly ever came home to see her husband. 'It has ruined us. But I dare not ask her to choose. Afterwards, we will see.' He wished Františka luck and sent her on her way.

Františka waited across the road, beneath a canopy of summer blossoms. She lit a cigarette, her third, and studied the uniformed men streaming through the main gate of Peček Palace. The building had grown into its reputation. If she was not mistaken, it had blackened during the occupation. Its very presence was oppressive, this greystone Goliath that stomped on the skulls of her neighbours. Even in the heat of the day, almost all the windows were sealed. Františka puffed one last time on the cigarette then dropped the smoking butt on the ground. She was ready.

'I wish to see my daughters.'

The man behind the desk had not even looked up when he called her from the queue. She was one of many and had waited for over an hour. Most before her turned around in tears. One man fell to his knees, pleading, crying. His howls echoed through the great hall as he was dragged away. Or perhaps Františka had confused them with the screams from the basement.

'If they are here, there is reason. Go home and wait. You will be notified soon enough.'

'No, you misunderstand. They are in Terezín.'

The clerk flinched, lifted his head. 'They are Communists? Criminals? Jews?'

'*Mischlinge*.' Františka forced the word through clenched teeth.

'It is not possible.'

'Everything is possible. I have means—'

'No favours. It is simply not possible.' The clerk looked over her shoulder. 'Next!'

'I am not leaving. I demand to see my children, to know they don't suffer.'

'We all suffer during war, Paní...'

'Roubíčková. I...sorry...Vrtišová.'

'Even the Reichsprotektor eats gruel, Paní Vrtišová. Your girls are no worse off than you or I.'

'I wish to apply for a permit.'

'I'm afraid such a thing does not exist. The town is closed to visitors.'

'Four months! Do you hear me? Four months I've had to survive on scraps of paper from my girls. Enough.'

The clerk looked nervously towards the approaching guards, shaking his head to ward them away. 'Paní Vrtišová, I wish I could help. The town is closed. That's a fact. Then there is the issue of travel within the Protectorate, registration and other such administrative burdens. First you must get...'

'Give me the papers. I will apply now.'

The clerk flicked through the wad of forms and pulled out two sheets. He slid the glasses from his face, squeezed the bridge of his nose. 'Do as you wish. What's a piece of paper if it will calm your nerves? Maintain order. That's what they tell me. But understand this: nothing will come of it.'

Františka returned every few weeks to renew the application. They all came to know her, this pitiful Aryan woman, her good sense turned septic with Jewish dreams. She took the forms without a word and filled them in at the bench in the corner before defiantly returning to have them stamped and filed.

When the plain enevelope arrived in late November, Františka Roubíčková tore it open and pulled out the paper. It took a moment to sink in: her name, a date, a heavy blue stamp. And beneath it a single word: *Bohušovice.*

Františka Roubíčková tilted the coat rack against her shoulder and dragged it through the hallway into the lounge. Scarves and coats drooped from its arms, brushing against the doorframe before coming to rest in wilted repose.

This will have to do, she thought as she stepped away from her makeshift tree. It could not stand in the usual corner, to do so would make a mockery of Christmas. Let it remain there awkwardly, in the middle of the room. She grabbed the coats from the rack and threw them against the window bench.

The gurgle of bubbling sour sauce drifted from the kitchen. Františka rushed back to stir the pot. The sauce was thick; specks of flour had congealed into tiny pebbles. In the oven below, orange light glowed over a fat fillet of beef. It was already blue by the time Marcela returned from Miličín, and had the whiff of decay, but Františka salted and scrubbed it before throwing it to the back of her icebox. To have beef at all was a luxury when the ration provided only for the discarded flank of a horse. She lowered the flame and left the sauce to simmer.

Marcela and Hana played in the back courtyard, diving into snowy dunes, squealing with delight. Most of the neighbourhood children had disappeared with their parents and so the building and its surrounds had become their private playground. Each day they invented new games based on the rumours that echoed through the stairwell, games like Razor Blade Man, where they took turns playing Prague's most feared phantom, hunting each other down with a sharpened twig. Or Gestapo Raid, which was much the same. Františka watched on from the window, proud that she had raised such resilient girls, but more so that Marcela had kept the worst of the occupation from Hana. More than once she had seen the two of them marching together with gusto or singing or sharing parcels of food she had packed for them. She asked them what they were playing, though she knew the answer. It was always the same. 'Daša and Irča.'

She opened the door and called to them. 'Come inside and wash. Aunt Emí will be here soon and there is *svíčková* for lunch. Then a surprise.' The girls looked up, uncertain. 'Marcela, watch over the pot while I'm gone.'

Františka headed towards the tram stop in Mladoňovicova Street. As she neared the corner, she glanced at her watch, Ludvík's watch; she was early. Emílie's train was not due for a while. A few steps away, the chimes above Žofie Sláviková's grocery door jingled. Františka ducked inside. Neither woman acknowledged the other. Žofie was eyeing her only other customer with suspicion, notebook in hand, pretending to write orders. Františka stopped to examine each item on the sparsely stocked shelves. She waited for the stranger to leave then picked up a few potatoes and a bushel of sugar before heading to the counter. Žofie Slávikova stamped the cards and handed them to Františka as the chimes went into a jangled frenzy. The two women watched Štěpánka Tičková scurry through the door, muttering to herself, arms wrapped around her hessian satchel.

'I have it on good authority—' she spat through cracked lips. It had been like this ever since her co-conspirator Jáchym Nemec was sent to the fortress town: Štěpánka Tičková wandered the streets of Žižkov, searching for a sympathetic ear. Turned away by all, starved of attention, she grew thin and mangy, her voice hoarse.

'Roubíčková,' the tattletale snarled.

'Good afternoon, Štěpánka.'

'Your daughters—' Her index finger unfurled with arthritic effort. 'I have noticed they grow fat.'

Žofie Slávikova slammed her fist on the counter. 'Štěpánka Tičková! Take what you've come for and be quiet about it.' Františka tucked the paper bag under her arm and rushed out the door to meet her sister.

~

Emílie sucked the sauce from her bread dumpling before dipping it back in. It was something she'd done since childhood, a habit that had infuriated their mother. 'So,' she said as a rising brown tide consumed the spongy dough. 'What time do you leave?'

'The train is at eight. I should arrive at Bohušovice around ten. Terezín is not far. And I will return on the last train.'

'If you don't mind, I brought gifts.' Emílie reached into her bag and pulled out a damp cloth sack tied with red ribbon. 'It's Christmas cake. Irena's favourite. For her birthday. Also, these.' She placed two wooden angels on the table. 'One for you. One for them. To watch over you all.'

Františka picked up one of the angels and ran her finger along the crest of its wings, up its neck, to the halo. From the lounge she could hear Marcela and Hana searching through Emílie's case for Christmas presents. 'Come,' Františka said.

So this was the surprise, a chance to chase away the storm outside. They plundered the drawers in Františka's studio and tore at the fabrics they found with scissors, with knives, by hand. They threw the strips in the air and watched them catch on the coat rack's outstretched arms. In each leaf on their makeshift tree was a forgotten dream, reclaimed and repurposed for merry hearts.

Long after Emílie had nestled into the forgotten recess of Ludvík's mattress, after Marcela and Hana fell asleep under quilted down, after the angel had been placed on top of the coat rack to bring peace on this refuge of tranquillity and hope, Františka Roubíčková tiptoed over to the dresser and pulled open the bottom drawer. There it was, Daša's old jewellery box, its hinges broken, the felt worn down to the chipped wood. It was all she could think to grab when Ottla B had tapped frantically at her door that night, almost a lifetime ago, hours after she kissed her eldest daughters goodbye. 'Please,' her neighbour had said, dropping a folded piece of paper in Františka's hand. 'Take this. For Bohuš.' Františka was lost for words. In her most desperate hour Ottla had found the courage to run, to escape Žižkov. 'When this is over, when he comes home, give it to him. Tell him his mother is coming. Promise me you will—' Ottla's voice faded on the wind. She looked around, saw two figures turn in from Mladoňovicova. 'Thank you,' Ottla said as she ran into the night. It was the last Františka saw of her.

Františka pushed aside the paper, pulled out a small felt pouch and tipped its contents onto the kitchen table. She picked up each ring in turn, testing them on her fingers, under her tongue, beneath the folds of her clothes. Her eyelids grew heavy and she settled on one Ludvík had given her soon after they first made love. A simple gold band. So this was the value of her heart, a currency greater than cigarettes, greater than coffee. Almost weightless, the infinite rounding of life. She pushed it into the moist Christmas cake and waited for dawn.

4
THERESIENSTADT

She danced between the lines in the kingdom of paper. It started with the slightest glimpse, a blonde curl behind a slanting *lamed*, a flash of skin—perhaps a wrist, a shoulder or even a thigh—through the crook of a *beit*. By some mistake of gravity he had ascended to the heavens where only gods and angels dwelled. He looked at Georg, at Muneles, at Gottschall, at Seeligmann, but they were lost between pillars of pulp, blinded to this shimmering sprite. She grew more brazen with the days, revealing more of herself on each new page. There was nothing suggestive in her moves, just the sheer delight of freedom. She cared little for his startled gaze. At times she swirled the ink around her in a frantic pirouette until the words blurred like a shroud across her shoulders.

Jakub sat back and wiped his brow. No, it was pointless. It was like leering at a sister, a child. And was he not just seeing her with his mother's eyes? He knew how Gusta looked on when they talked, imagining what might have been, what still could be. But theirs was nothing more than a convenient alliance: her packages, his privileges, pooled to create a semblance of plenty. Outside the barracks, away from these books, she danced for others.

He had seen her in the park on his way back from the bastion, huddled close to a young man under a tree. And what to make of the other times when she would loiter near the gate at day's end and run the moment she caught sight of Jakub coming up Südstrasse? Jakub was certain he saw the gendarme right himself before hurrying over to unfasten the lock.

Jakub looked at the SS man by the door. He rarely moved, as if asleep. Only once had he stood to attention, when Eichmann himself came to visit, to compliment these shackled scholars, to show that he, too, could speak in their tongue. *It is very important work you are doing, gentlemen*, Eichmann had said. That was before September, before the Council announced the resumption of transports. Before they took Shmuel away. He should have known. Eichmann's presence boded ill for them all.

Jakub pressed down on the calfskin jacket of his next book and hoped that when he opened it she would not be there. He read the words: *Sefer Darchei No'am*, The Ways of the *Torah*. A book of responsa by Mordechai Halevi, published in 1697. Now item number Jc 10008b. He jotted down the details and a short commentary, first on a blank sheet and then, when he was satisfied with what he wrote, on a standard index card. This time Daša was nowhere to be seen.

Jc 10008b
Signatur
Nr.
Verfasser (Vor-u. Zuname) Mordekhaj Hal-lewi
Titel (einschl. Verfasser)
Band
Verlagsort bezw. Druckort
Verleger, Jahr, Drucker (falls kein Verleger)
Druckort (falls vom Verlagsort verschieden)
Ausgabe (Auflage)
Nebentitel
Seitenzahl
Format

5
PRAGUE

II. I. 44

My dearest Emí,

I send you kisses and, of course, Marcela, who I hope remembers to pass on this letter.

Everywhere the winter's sun plays tricks with the light, making rainbows on the frost, but inside me there is only black. It is two weeks since I saw them, two weeks since I felt the warmth of their fingertips through the wire. Yes, a wire fence. Oh, Emí, forgive me. There was so much I couldn't tell you when I returned. I was tired but also ashamed, as much for them as for myself. I don't know what I expected, how I hoped it would be. Perhaps you will understand why I held it inside that night, why the following morning I walked you to the station without a word, why now I must tell you like this.

The train arrived at Bohušovice before eleven. Two men in different uniforms sat on the platform, smoking and playing checkers. One rested a rifle across his lap, the other had a whistle hanging from his neck. When I asked them for directions their faces darkened. The rifleman signalled for the other to deal with me.

The whistle jangled against his buttons as he stood. He looked me over from head to toe before his eyes came to rest on the box under my arm. I pretended not to notice but then the rifleman shook his head and mumbled something. Yes, *the other man said.* An inspection is in order. Can't be too cautious. *I held open the box and he looked inside. At last he took out the Christmas cake wrapped in its cloth sack.* My wife will like this, *he said.* Anything, *I thought.* Anything but that. *I thrust my hand into the box and—oh God, Emí, I am sorry—I pulled out the carved wooden angel. I held it out to him and for a moment he hesitated. Then the rifleman jumped in.* Yes, yes, *he said.* For my daughter. *The other placed the Christmas cake back in the box and escorted me outside.*

Bohušovice was a quiet town. The man with the whistle pointed to a road that cut through the centre. Just keep walking, *he said.* Do not branch off. *In the end I would reach the fortress. The people of Bohušovice are no longer accustomed to seeing strangers. I could read it in their puzzled faces. They have closed their minds to what festers beyond. I am told this is the same path they all walked, Ludvík and the girls, but they have since built a railway line so the townsfolk do not feel like accomplices to it all. I walked for half an hour, past the town and through the valley. Emí, it is strange to say but in many ways it reminded me of Sudoměřice. Even in the cold, with snow underfoot, there was a sense of serenity, of beauty. I wondered whether perhaps the girls might feel at home.*

Then I saw it. A heavy wire fence with razor wire curled across its top, stretching across the sunken brick walls of an immense fortress. The road led to a gate where a guard stood warming his hands over a fire pit. I greeted him. He responded in Czech; he was a gendarme, not a soldier. We spoke for a while; he seemed uncertain about my presence. One arm rested on his truncheon throughout. I asked him about the daily funeral procession. It would be here soon, he said. Just like Daša told me. I asked if he knew many of the people who lived here and he said he did. I took two cigarettes from my pocket and offered him one. We stood there smoking, taking in the strangeness of our encounter. There was something about him that bothered me. I asked whether he knew my Daša. It was an innocent question, just a way to pass the time, but his face, Emí, his face changed. You know what it's like to see a pleasant smile contort into a lecherous grin? There was hunger in his eyes. Hunger and knowledge. My chest burned. Yes, *he said, letting out a great puff of smoke.* She comes here some days during the lunch break. She has been making arrangements for your visit. I am glad to oblige.

I'm sure he would have gone on but we were interrupted by the approaching wail of the funeral procession. The hearse—a horse's cart wheeled by four men—was heading towards us. In front walked a rabbi with a deep voice, chanting lamentations for those who trailed behind. I saw the awful cargo, a pile of bodies, ten or more, covered only by a sheet that kept lifting with the wind. The gendarme released the latch on the boom gate and allowed the hearse to pass. The rabbi motioned for the bearers to halt and, for a moment, these poor souls rested on the precipice between two worlds. The families set upon the tray, clutching at their loved ones' arms. They kissed their hands and faces, whispered blessings. Only when the hearse moved on did I see the girls, at the back, among the mourners. They played the part, as if they hadn't seen their mother waiting there.

The gendarme stood guard while the mourners squeezed against the fence, straining to see the hearse as it rolled off. When at last it was gone, they began the slow march back into the ghetto until only my girls remained. Daša ran over to the gendarme and whispered something in his ear. He shook his head. She whispered something else. Without a word, he took out a cigarette and crossed to a nearby hut, where he sat on the stoop, his face turned away.

How we rushed at each other, Emí. Even through the wire we smothered one another's faces with kisses, careful not to catch our lips on the freezing metal. It is less than a year but they have grown! Daša is a woman now and Irena no longer looks like a child. Ludvík was unable to come. He is employed in a workshop at the other end of town. I asked if he provides for them. They were reluctant to answer but Daša kissed me again on the cheek and said, as if in jest, He gives what he can. *I could not let the atmosphere spoil so I reached into the box and pulled out some socks and other things that I had packed. I threaded them all through the fence, told Irena they were for her birthday but that she should share them with her father and sister. Then we sang together, loudly, joyously, because she was growing up and, no matter what the current situation, it was still Christmas. The gendarme appeared entranced by our ways, as if for a moment he had forgotten himself.*

Too soon the lunch break came to an end. Daša said that she was returning to the kitchen and Irena to the sewing workshop. I laid the box at my feet and pulled out the last package. I had wanted Irena to unwrap it but it was too big to pass through the wire, so it was left to me to peel away the cloth. They clapped and cheered when they saw it: the moist Christmas cake. Irena began to laugh. What is it? *I asked.* What is so funny? Oh, Mama, *she said.* If only you could have been there to taste my birthday cake. You cannot imagine how we must make do. *I passed them both a small handful.* Eat carefully, *I said.* You never know what Saint Nicholas has hidden inside. We are not children, *said Daša.* Yes, *I said,* but your teeth can still break.

It was I who got the ring. I felt it the moment the cake hit my tongue. What a fool I must have looked digging into my mouth, catching hold of it while I sucked the dough from its surface! I looked at the gendarme but he was facing the ghetto. I pulled Daša close and dropped the ring into her palm. For Christmas, *I said.* Use it however you must. *I looked again to the gendarme.* Remember who you are, *I said.* Remember what you are. *And like that it was over. Daša and Irena gave me one last kiss and ran off back down the road. The gendarme resumed his position by the gate.*

Oh, Emí, can you forgive me like I have forgiven Daša? To have kept this secret when my whole life I have told you everything. Why is it that I thought the worst of Daša and that gendarme? Could it simply be that I no longer recognise myself? That my eyes have lost focus? It is true. This situation has dressed us all in fraying rags. Pray that we may stitch them back together.

Always your loving sister,
Františka

6
THERESIENSTADT

Draymen in ragged trousers, their chests bare in the morning light, hauled wooden hearses towards the delousing station. Gaunt faces stared up—elderly and infirm—wincing with discomfort, grey hair tumbling in matted clumps around protruding cheekbones. Soon they would be back, standing outside the kitchens, begging for scraps, but for now the promise of chemical clouds, relief. Jakub and Georg kept their distance; rather be late than infested. At the nearest crossroad they branched off onto Südstrasse. The gendarme tipped his hat, greeted them by name and unlocked the gate. They passed through and headed towards the *Klärenstalt.*

Spring had thickened the air inside. It was early, or late. Here there was no time. Weiss, the carpenter, scurried from table to table, picking up books, darting back to place them in the waiting crate. The others hunched over their stations. Jakub reached across and took the next book on the stack. *A simple* siddur, Jakub thought. *A prayer book looted from the* genizah *of a synagogue that was now ash. Worthless.* The leather was dry, worn, rubbed, with splits along the spine and edges. Only the clasp remained intact: a tarnished lion, its claws clutching at a small orb. The blackness hid the intricacy of the metalwork, clogging the grooves that fashioned the beast's fur.

Jakub eased his nail beneath the lion and gently pulled. The clasp strained before springing open with a muted pop. He slid the strap aside and lifted the cover. The first page was blank, mottled by specks of mould and the smudges of impatient fingers. He flipped the page over, then another and another. All blank. Running his hand along the paper, Jakub could feel the faint relief of letters that might have been. The page was uneven: taut around the edges but slack in the middle. He turned several more pages then stopped. He looked around quickly and leaned over the book, shielding it from view.

The handiwork was crude but effective. Slivers of wood had been pasted around a hollowed compartment. The walls were far enough from the fore edge and top square not to arouse suspicion; to the casual eye it was a *siddur* like any other. The compartment was packed with a clump of tawny dirt, little more than a handful, but enough to fill the space. Jakub pushed the dirt aside, spilling some onto the surrounding paper. There must be something buried inside, he thought, something to warrant such effort to conceal it, but he could find nothing. He pulled a spoon from the buttonhole in his lapel and began to scoop the dirt into his tin cup, watching it suck at the last droplets of water. Soon the compartment was empty, only a few dark streaks across the pastedown at its base. Jakub blew into the space to clear the remaining dust. The streaks held firm, curled, purposeful. Two letters. *Mem. Taf.* Together *Met.* Death. He blew again and they were gone.

'Pencils down, gentlemen.' It was Muneles. Jakub grabbed the cup, covered it with his palm and rushed out of the *Klärenstalt* into the late afternoon sun.

'A lion, you say?'

Professor Leopold Glanzberg had been transferred to the Ghetto Watch after the August purge of young and, in the Camp Kommandant's opinion, potentially rebellious men. The new Watch consisted exclusively of men over forty-five, men who could be easily subdued, whose only real authority rested in the esteem with which these elders were held by the other Jews. Professor Glanzberg was little more than a kindly face standing at the gate to greet those who had business in the Magdeberg Barracks.

'And you are quite certain about the orb?' The black cap with its thin beige cresting wave and scalloped clover insignia was too small for Glanzberg's head. When he spoke it shifted around, releasing sprigs of grey brush that disappeared into his unruly beard. It was said his mind had softened but his eyes still burned with the intensity of the learned.

'Yes, it was grasping at a ball,' said Jakub. 'The sun, perhaps?'

'A grape. Yes, a lion picking a grape from its vine. The symbol of Rabbi Judah Löew, the great Maharal of Prague. He had it etched above his door in Široká Street. Few know of this detail. Most only think of the lion. Still, it's the empty pages that interest me.'

Jakub followed as Professor Glanzberg set off along the street. The town pulsated with the activity of another day's end. Shoulders collided, dust kicked at worn heels. Gendarmes manned the corners, tried to direct the flow. Jakub tried to pick Glanzberg's voice from the crowd.

'And you still have the book?'

'It is not permitted,' Jakub said. 'Weiss will have taken it. I...just...no.'

Professor Glanzberg broke from the weary stream into a narrow alley between two houses. 'Here,' he said and turned another corner to reach a deserted cul-de-sac. 'Please,' he said and held out his hand. Jakub passed him the metal cup. Professor Glanzberg peered inside, shook the cup, nodded. For a few moments he stood there, as if unsure of how to start. Then:

(The Story of The Book of Dirt...with interruptions)

'It sounds preposterous, I know. There was a woman, impossibly old. Mad. We didn't know her name, hadn't seen her around the community. She started coming to the museum several months before the occupation. She would visit every few days, more so once the Nazis came. We didn't charge her admission, there was no point. It was obvious she couldn't pay. She greeted us all warmly, hung her coat near the entrance. Then she would begin her rounds.

'I was given the task of following her, working out her game. It was the great advantage of my role; I was invisible, just the man in the background tending to the exhibits. I don't think it would have mattered to her, though. She was blind to all who passed by. It was always the same route through the display halls; she never missed a single exhibit. She talked to herself as she walked, not the soft mutterings of the old and infirm, but full, animated conversations.

'It took me a few days but I came to understand that she was giving tours, talking to an audience only she could see. On closer inspection—I dared step as close to her as I am to you, pretending to dust a nearby plinth—I saw that she looked only to the gaps between our displays. Her babble seemed to unscramble as I drew near. When I was right beside her I could understand every word she said. Here was a fragment of stone from the Ten Commandments, there was the knife Abraham had intended to use to sacrifice Isaac. In this cabinet was a dried chunk of flesh from the fish that swallowed Jonah, on that wall a spoke from the chariot Elijah rode to heaven. I reported back to the directors. They decided to leave her be. There was a certain charm in her presence. After all, what harm is there in a woman who sees what isn't there? It is a quality we might all do well to develop.'

'The Kavalier Barracks are filled with such people.'

'*Pshah*...Listen. There was one exhibit towards the end of her tour...something clearly tacked on to appease her imaginary audience. Like all our visitors they hungered for local fare. So she told them of a book, an ordinary *siddur*, with no identifying marks other than a clasp made of silver, a lion facing the rising sun, its claws stretching outwards, holding a grape. The Maharal's own prayer book. Nobody dared open it, she said, so great was the respect for this holy man. Just as well. They would have been horrified. Its pages were rubbed clean. Before he died, she said, he gathered the words so that he could take them with him to heaven. But there was another more pious reason for the harvest: he didn't want to desecrate a holy book. You see, she said, he had one final task before he could depart this world, something that would ensure he could die in peace, and the *siddur* was to play an integral part. Using the blade with which he had performed countless circumcisions, he fashioned a storage compartment within its pages. Then, she continued, in the middle of the night, while his students and followers slept, he dragged himself up the stairs into the attic *genizah* of the Altneu Synagogue where, in the back corner, under the old discarded *Torah* scrolls and holy books, there lay a splintered pine coffin with the disintegrated remains of his beloved *golem*. Rabbi Löew shuffled over, reached into the area that would have been the corpse's chest and, whispering a solemn prayer, pulled out a fistful of dirt.'

'The clay man's heart?'

'Precisely. I could see from the glint in her eye that she knew her audience was, like you, feasting on her every word. She went on: For years the Maharal had ascended his pulpit, confident in the knowledge that the *golem* was resting peacefully above his head. But one day he noticed that it had become an effort to take those steps. He could no longer address his people in the same strong voice that, for so long, had filled them with awe. He was an old man. Soon God would call on him to return to the kingdom of souls. Naturally, his thoughts turned to his child. What would become of it when he was gone? He'd watched his congregation grow sick, watched saintly men turn devious and conniving. They spoke openly of finding the *golem*, bringing it back to life. With such a servant they would have no need of faith. He summoned his beloved disciples, Yitzchok ben Shimshon Ha-Cohen and Yaakov ben Chaim Sasson Halevi, to prepare them for what was to come. *When I am gone, take the dirt and bury it in the cemetery on the hill*, he said. *Mix it with the earth so it may rest undisturbed, free from the designs of man.*

'A few days later, on what would soon be his deathbed, she said, he was struck with a sudden bout of remorse. To think his beloved child would return to the earth like any other man, that he would be nothing more than a memory. He simply could not bear it. What father can contemplate the erasure of his child? And so he resolved to use what remained of his strength to save the most vital organ, the clay man's heart. It would live on forever in the known world, in a simple *siddur*, hidden within the shelves of the eternal library of life.'

'And you think this...' Jakub angled the cup towards the old man.

'Is dirt. By its very nature it is what you make of it. But now I must go. Come by my *kambal* tomorrow night. Bring the dirt. There is something else you must know.'

Cold water sputtered from the washroom tap. Hands pushed forward, scrubbing, stippling the trough with the muck of a day's toil. A steamy haze emanated from the stinking bodies crammed together. Some soaked their shirts, squeezed them out, applied the cool dampness to their skin. Others threw handfuls of water against their chests. Jakub held his spot, watching the earth swallow the murky liquid and congeal into a muddy sludge that would not be washed away.

Alone on his bunk he spooned the mud into his hand and rolled it between his palms. It took form, not quite a ball, more the uneven contours of a child's fist. He squeezed and waited for a response but none came. The clay was heavy, warm. It left no residue on his skin.

When he woke it was still beside him. Who would steal a lump of clay, anyway? Shoes, cups, spoons, yes. But not this. Not dirt. Jakub reached out, slid his finger along its smooth surface. It was still moist. Across the narrow gap between the bunks, he saw Georg beginning to stir. Soon there would be moans, movement, chaos. Jakub slid the clay under the corner of his straw mattress and hoisted himself from the bunk.

For the first time he made mistakes. The books felt foreign, otherworldly. He had to check each detail, double-check. The words would not come, there was nothing to say. Had he not fled the village and escaped the folk-tales of his ancestors? Was he not a man of reason? Of enlightenment? Why now, in this ghetto prison, must his mind retreat into fiction?

Jakub rested his pen on the desk and looked around. The work continued as normal. That night he would go to the Magdeberg Barracks and find the Professor's *kambal.* Jakub knew little of such places, only that they existed. Neither bunkrooms nor apartments, they were the requisi-tioned nooks under staircases, behind storage shelves, in disused spaces, closed off and decorated for personal use. It was in these *kambals* that contraband changed hands, that young lovers met for undisturbed trysts, that false kings held court. But it was also where composers filled pages with clefs and crotchets, artists created life with whatever substances they could find, great minds distilled their thoughts. Professor Glanzberg's *kambal* was at the back of the Hall of Souls, the central filing room in which every prisoner's details were kept in triplicate, one copy for this world, one for the next and one to hang precariously in *geheinem Terezín*, the purgatory of Theresienstadt.

The halls of Magdeberg's administrative wing were deserted when he arrived. For once the ghetto was at peace. Jakub made his way past the department offices to the door of the Hall of Souls. He held the cup firmly to his shirt. The ball of clay had dried during the day and crumbled. By the time he returned to his bunk it was as he had first found it, an unremarkable mound. Jakub was careful to scoop what he could back into the cup.

The door opened to a narrow staircase lit only by a dull glow from the corridor. Scraggy grey carpet lined the stairs, crushed by the recent passage of ten thousand feet. He removed his shoes and socks and stepped down into the dim passage. The door whined shut behind him, drawn back by a rusted spring. Blackness. Jakub steadied himself against the wall, picking up speed on the stairs as plaster turned to stone against his hand. He knew he had reached the subterranean maze, an arterial system of tunnels that ran beneath the fortress town, where soldiers once scrambled to defend their empress's name against invading hordes that never arrived and partisans now ferried whatever necessities they could carry on their crooked backs. The hollowed earth held the chill of winters past.

A sliver of light across the ground signalled a door. He searched for a handle but felt only wood and cold metal straps. The light caressed his toes, and with it a warm breeze that carried the drone of a chant. He pressed his shoulder to the door and nudged it open. It was exactly as the *bonkes* had it: a vast corridor of filing cabinets reaching to the ceiling, lit by bulbs, stretching into the distance. At the far end, Jakub could make out a curtain, behind which were the shadows of two figures sitting in stillness over a raised ledge. The drone grew louder, swirling from all around in the dead air—*AH, ẠH, A̲H, AV, ẠV, A̲V*—a diminuendo of sighs.

As he approached the curtain, Jakub saw the shadow figures stir. One slid back and rose, growing to a monstrous height then shrinking as it darkened against the fluttering fabric. The curtain was pulled aside to reveal a squinting face. 'Jakub!' It was Professor Glanzberg.

'Please, please,' the old man said. 'You'll have to excuse the state of the place. With every new trainload the filing room expands and I have to make the necessary adjustments. The clerks fuss over the files. Bureaucrats! The noise is unbearable—paper brushing against paper...I tell you, it toys with one's sphincter. Then they ship a trainload off and I'm back to where I started.' Professor Glanzberg held open the curtain to allow Jakub through.

It took a moment for Jakub's eyes to adjust to the harsh light of an unshaded floor lamp near the hanging divide. The *kambal* was sparsely appointed: a single mattress wedged into the corner, a plain bookshelf against one wall and a table near the centre with four chairs—short, like those found in a house of mourning—placed around it. The man sitting down did not turn around but Jakub recognised his shape.

'In Prague we were ten,' said Otto Muneles without waiting for Jakub to sit. 'Now we are two. The Council of Formations. Or what's left of it. For years we gathered in the attic of the Altneu where nobody dared tread, but here...Please, take a seat.' Jakub lowered himself onto a chair. 'We weren't sure that you'd come,' continued Muneles. 'You have enough to worry about without this. And old Leopold's tales...I know how it must sound.'

'Prague is a city of stories,' said Glanzberg. 'Words are in its very mortar. Mostly we dismiss what we hear as legend or gossip. But know this, young Jakub: much of it is true. Take us, for example.'

Muneles shifted in his chair. 'Five hundred years ago, Rabbi Löew had a private audience with Emperor Rudolf II. To this day what they discussed remains a closely guarded secret.'

'Rudolf was a kind, tolerant man,' said Glanzberg. 'But he was surrounded by advisers who wished only ill for the Jews, and who filled the emperor's head with false accusations: sorcery, witchcraft, all kinds of treachery. Naturally, he grew fearful of what he had been told, but he trusted the great rabbi. He trusted in his reputation for learning and wisdom and honesty. And so the emperor summoned Rabbi Löew to an apartment in the castle where they could speak in private, and laid out his offer: Rabbi Loew was to investigate the legends and report back to the emperor. *Bring them to me,* Rudolph said, *so that my mind will be at ease. Together we can banish your* sheds *and* mazziks *from these lands.* In return, the emperor vowed to revoke all expulsion orders that his father had made, and allow the Jews to live freely in his kingdom.

'Rabbi Löew rushed back and called together nine of his most trusted friends to form the Council of Formations, and appointed as its leader the one who dwelled with the spirits, the head of the *Chevra Kadisha*. On the first night, they met in the attic of the Altneu. *We will do as he asks,* Rabbi Löew said. *We will make the proper enquiries. Then we will report back that it is all rumour, the superstitions of country folk. Quell his fears, yes, but whatever we find we must save. Beware the king with good intentions.*'

'Since then,' said Muneles, 'it has fallen upon those in my position to continue the holy charge. Here we are. Still searching.'

'There are others,' said Glanzberg. 'All working with the burden of their titles. The librarian, the architect, the slaughterer, the keeper of youth. You'd be surprised by the evidence they've found. The brick thrown at King Wenceslas—for which, legend has it, the quiet Jew Shime Sheftels paid a martyr's price—uncovered by my predecessor in 1753. Then, at the turn of the last century, a lump of dripping coal, prised from the hand of a dead woman as her body was being prepared for the grave. It was brought before the Council and tested extensively. Wouldn't you know, it proved to be just as its finder suspected: a magical artefact from the underwater kingdom, one of the gold coins given by the water sprite of the Vltava River as a dowry for his beloved on condition that her family remain absolutely silent. Legend has it that when the girl's mother could keep the secret no more, the riches turned to ashen clumps that continued to cry freshwater tears...

'It is a complex charge,' continued Glanzberg. 'These legends have a way of growing into themselves, multiplying. In every one there is the seed of the next. Our job is to examine those seeds, but also to scatter others so that the Jews do not make idols of them.'

'And so we obfuscate,' said Muneles. 'We muddy the waters. In that way we, too, have grown into ourselves, into our names. And we have lost control.'

Professor Glanzberg rocked back and forth in his seat, as if praying. 'When the stories began to circulate about Rabbi Löew, the Council of Formations did what it could to cultivate them. Let him become a myth, a legend. Then the Germans came.'

'They came and it all changed,' said Muneles. 'We met as the Council of Formations always did, in the attic. Leopold here saw in the occupation a chance to gather whatever artefacts remained and test them for evidence of folk magic. We approached the Department of Rural Affairs to petition the authorities, and ask that everything from around the Protectorate be shipped to Prague.'

'We also sent out teams in the city,' said Glanzberg, 'under the strict watch of a particular Jewish brute, to search every house that had been left empty by deportation. Only the odd piece proved to be of any worth. There were, however, two things...two things that made us reconsider the legend of Rabbi Löew.'

Jakub felt his fingers tighten around the metal cup. He pulled it back along the table, towards him. It seemed somehow heavier, as if the dirt inside had grown dense with Glanzberg's words.

'The first,' said Muneles, 'was a simple wooden box. On its sides were unsophisticated carvings, symbols that might have been a forgotten language or just mindless doodles. We could find no opening, nothing to indicate its purpose. We'd have tossed it aside had it not started jingling every time our colleague Pavel Pařík picked it up. For two days we watched as it rang out or stayed mute according to his presence. It became something of a game. We would place it wherever we thought he'd be going next. We even joked about giving it as a gift to his wife. Then, on the third day, he didn't come to the museum. At ten o'clock we received the call. Pavel Pařík was dead. He'd suffered a stroke overnight. It was then that we remembered the story: Rabbi Löew, in an effort to cheat death, once made a box that would chime out whenever the dark angel was approaching. Leopold rushed with the box to the nearby hospital and, just as we feared, the moment he stepped inside, it began to ring out and shake uncontrollably.'

'The second thing,' said Glanzberg, 'was a great deal more confounding. You are no doubt aware that the whole fascination with Rabbi Löew and his man of clay is based mostly on the work of the Polish Rabbi, Yudl Rosenberg, and his book *Nifla'ot Maharal*. Rosenberg claims to have come across the manuscript about Rabbi Loëw and the *golem* in the Royal Library at Metz in Northern France. He claims it was written by Rabbi Löew's own son-in-law.'

'But neither the library nor the son-in-law ever existed.'

'In his introduction,' continued Glanzberg, 'Rosenberg wrote of a second manuscript, penned by Rabbi Löew himself, that Rosenberg was willing to sell for eight hundred kopeks. An exorbitant amount at the time. He could be certain that nobody would take him up on it.'

'Except,' said Muneles, 'it appears that somebody did. And it was sold on through the years until it fell into the hands of the industrialist Max Landsberger. We found it in his son's house. Actually, you and Georg found it. You just didn't know.'

'We were forced to review our position on Rabbi Löew.' Professor Glanzberg gestured towards the cup. 'We had to face the possibility that the tales about him were real, that his *golem* was real.

'Prague was all abuzz over the clay man. Books, movies, plays—a steady stream to fill their heads with wonder. We began to hear new stories: the Nazis had tried to burn down the Altneu Synagogue only to be thwarted by the raging *golem*; a senior Gestapo man was found dead on the stairs leading to the attic, his body battered and broken. The people had found in this *golem* a saviour more tangible than any messiah. The transports were already in full swing. If only the force of the *golem*'s fury could be released before the last Jew was taken away. Frightened fathers beseeched the chief rabbi to open the attic, to let the clay man out to save their children. The rabbi came to me one night. What could he do? We both knew there was nothing to be found up there. The *genizah* had been cleared out years ago and, other than ten wooden benches upon which we would sit to meet, the attic was empty. But what rabbi will take away hope when it is all that is left to his congregants? And who will admit to having broken Rabbi Löew's prohibition forbidding anyone from ever entering the attic again?'

'So we did the only thing we could do,' said Muneles. 'We returned to the sources, studied every permutation of the legend, scoured the notes of our predecessors, hoping to find sign of the creature. Perhaps they had been too quick to dismiss it.'

'Picture this if you will: ten of Prague's greatest minds, crawling along the banks of the Vltava River,' said Glanzberg, 'feeling for the spot where the clay had maintained its shape. We searched the cemeteries, dug up the graves where damaged books and *Torah* scrolls were buried, went to Rabbi Löew's old house in Široká Street and lifted the floorboards. But we found nothing.'

Jakub peered into the cup. The dirt rested loosely inside, a few clay pebbles on top. He wanted to tell the men about it, about how it had kept its form, how it had stayed moist and firm beside him for one night before drying and crumbling in his hands. But, all of a sudden, he was not so sure. Had that even happened? Could it be that his memory was being shaped by the stories they told, that they were building *golems* in his mind? He shook the cup and watched the dirt tumble from side to side.

'It shames me to say,' continued Glanzberg, 'that we even tried to create him anew. Only this year, just before Passover, Otto and I went down to the water's edge and fashioned a figure from the mud. We followed the formula, recited the two hundred and thirty-one gates in the *Sefer Yetzirah*, just as the great Rabbi Eleazar of Worms instructed. We stayed there until morning, chanting, praying, crying and pleading, dancing in circles until the water lapped at our inanimate lump and called it back to the river. We trudged home but there was no clay man to keep us company.'

'We had failed,' said Muneles. 'And God laughed from on high, thunder rumbling in the distance.' He rested his hands on the table and lowered his head. Jakub had not seen him so uncertain, so defeated. Then:

'I returned to the museum and kept an eye out for artefacts until, two months later, I received my summons and was brought here.'

'The work continues in the city,' said Glanzberg. 'We made sure to leave one of our own in charge of the museum.'

'Old Jakobovits.'

'Pieces of all kinds come before him and his team examines them, tests those that might be of any significance, squirrels them away in the piles of confiscated goods. Here we only have books. Until now we had found just one item: the list of names read by Rabbi Löew to the Angel of Death at the cemetery gates in defence of his congregation. And now this...'

'The most unlikely evidence of all.' Muneles looked at the cup in Jakub's hand. 'When Leo came to tell me, I thought the fortress had gone to his head. Nowhere has the story of the hollowed book been written down. Could it be that the mutterings of a senile woman hold the key to the greatest mystery our city has known? The Council had already dismissed it out of hand. Now, in our little *Klärenstalt*, a *siddur* matching her very description appears...It is too much.'

'There is no way to test it here,' said Glanzberg. 'And woe to us all if the administration gets hold of it. No, we must get it to the city, to Jakobovits. He must store it with the rest of the artefacts so that it might survive even if we do not. Who knows, when this is all over, perhaps it can be taken to the banks of the river and mixed with the mud so that the creature may rise again and avenge us.'

Otto Muneles pulled a crumpled paper sachet from his pocket and flattened it against the table. Jakub made out the word 'Sugar' stamped in faded ink. 'Put it here,' said Muneles.

Professor Leopold Glanzberg took the cup from Jakub and tipped the dirt into the bag, clapping his palm against the cup's base to be sure he'd emptied it all. 'There are boys,' said the professor, 'young men who know their way through the tunnels, who have contacts in the towns outside the fortress gates. I will take it on my daily rounds, see it gets to one I can trust. Dr Jakobovits will have it in days. And Jakub?' He placed the sachet on the table and took Jakub's hands between his. 'Not a word to Georg. In the past I've tried, but he does not listen. Now this...I'm afraid he will think—'

Muneles picked up the sachet and rolled the top closed. Holding it in his palms, he tilted back his head and began to chant quietly: 'A heart with no form, with no chambers, no vessels. A heart that does not beat, that cannot ache, cannot love. A heart that can be scattered to the wind just as easily as moulded with the ground. What good is a heart alone, with no body, no home? It can only stain those around it with blood. *AH, ẠH, A̱H, AV, ẠV, A̱V.*'

Jakub tried to push it from his mind. That night, a heaviness set in his chest, a soft wheeze that whistled when he slept. By morning it had worsened, a burning in his throat. He could not swallow. With the pain came the chance of escape. Jakub put in for a transfer to the hospital barracks, where he was misdiagnosed with the early stages of pneumonia. He coughed and choked his way through four uneasy nights before he was deemed well enough for light work and discharged.

As he made his way back along Neu Gasse towards the Hannover Barracks, Jakub saw Professor Glanzberg scurrying about near the entrance to the girls' home. Catching sight of him, Glanzberg stood to attention, clicked his heels and ran up the road to greet him. 'Jakub,' he said, trying to catch his breath. 'Have you heard? No? There are rumours. Nothing official yet but...transports. Any day now. And worse. Our boy. The tunnel. He was captured. They've taken him to prison in the Small Fortress. And they're searching the *kambals*, clearing them out. Here!' Professor Glanzberg stuffed something into Jakub's pocket. 'A sympathetic gendarme from the security detail. Take it. Keep it safe and wait for word from Otto. We will find another way. Now go.'

The Hannover Barracks were deserted. Beds made in haste, rags strewn across the lumpy covers. The distant clamour of a cleaning detail. Jakub opened the battered case at the foot of his bed, fished the paper sachet from his pocket and placed it inside. There were others: salt, flour, lentils. A small reserve of rations, should the need arise. Jakub locked the case and set off to find his mother in the Hamburg Barracks.

7
THERESIENSTADT

Daša Roubíčková twisted her hand from side to side, watching the light dance on the surface of her mother's ring. She scraped at the veins of starch that lined her palms—the remnants of a day peeling potatoes. She had so little time to ready herself after work, to change from the stinking rags into something more appropriate, something *he* might like. She had settled on a pale blue dress that would distinguish her from the other girls in their drab greys and browns. In the washroom she patted down her blonde curls and tied them with a piece of twine. She searched for her reflection in the steel trough and tugged at the hem of her dress to stretch out the creases. He would be waiting, she knew. Or maybe he was fussing with his shirt, trying to assume an air of casual indifference to mask his yearning.

She didn't yet understand the contours of their love, if that's what it was. And why shouldn't it be? Love, after all, is the dominion of the nourished. Empty stomachs swallow hearts, devour them without grace. Daša knew how the other girls spoke of him, how they spoke of anyone with privileges. She knew how they skittered through the halls of the Magdeberg Barracks, ready to profess their love for whoever clutched an extra crust. In every sweaty liaison there was an unspoken contract. A lecher's bed was better than chastity's eastbound train. But that, Daša thought, was not love. It was not even commerce. It was subsistence. Survival. Too many times she had watched them pull bloody rags from beneath their skirts and hold them tenderly, as if wondering what might have been had they not sought treatment at the hospital, had they not given themselves over to the plague of so-called 'endometriosis', the cure for which was guilt and loathing and longing. Not her, though. Since she had watched her mother disappear into the snowy folds of the valley, she had sworn herself to purity. She had chased away the desire that spread through her like butter sauce whenever he brushed up against her. *Remember who you are. Remember what you are.* Yes, true love was found in resistance, in control. Only when there is nothing to be gained can you ask yourself whether you are in love, whether you can be loved.

Daša dropped her hand to her lap and looked across at the freshly painted pavilion in the town square. Two months it had been standing and there had yet to be a concert. Word around the fortress was that the Ghetto Swingers would be the first to tread its boards. She had seen them only once, a random assortment of players thrown together by circumstance, the very friction of which had electrified their performance. In the barracks at night, starstruck girls whispered their names and hummed tunes, riding the disorderly waves of jazz to temporary freedom. Sometimes Daša joined them, but her heart was not in it. She loved opera, like her mother.

He was late. Two gendarmes ambled towards the square. Without thinking, Daša clasped her hands together, hiding the ring from view. The ring. What had possessed her? She always kept it on her, dangling from a string under her blouse, against her heart. In the washroom, she held it under her tongue and clinked it against the back of her teeth to check she hadn't swallowed it. But to wear it on her finger? Madness. Could it be that she had grown brazen in this place, her good sense lost to privilege? No, it must be something more: a way to reassure *him* that she needed nothing, expected nothing. Or maybe it was the whisper of a mother who understood what she tried not to see and was watching from afar.

'Daša.' She jumped at the touch of a hand on her shoulder. 'You're early.'

'Bohuš.'

Daša skipped through the gate of the Hamburg Barracks. All around, women clamoured in the vast courtyard, heaving their mattresses to the dusty field in the hope of escaping the bedbugs that had invaded again with the early heat. Clouds of Zyklon B had sent the vile creatures into the walls' deepest crevices, but it was a short-lived reprieve. In darkness, they continued to breed, feeding on the squalor between the cracks. When they dared venture back out, they found only the emaciated bodies of the overworked, their blood a turgid syrup, difficult to draw from the veins. And so the bugs bit harder and burrowed deeper, leaving angry pustules on papery skin.

'Watch your step,' cried one woman, her finger shaking in accusation.

'Stupid girl,' spat another.

They were all standing around Gusta's bunk when Daša burst through the door. For a moment her heart sank. She had seen the bodies laid out each morning, the ones who had not made it through the night. 'Dear God!' Daša cried and the others parted to reveal Gusta curled up on her mattress, clutching a card to her cheek. The woman's lips were twitching, whispered words addressed to the greyed paper on the nearby strut. As Daša knelt close, Gusta jerked forward, pressing the card into her hands. 'Please,' Gusta said.

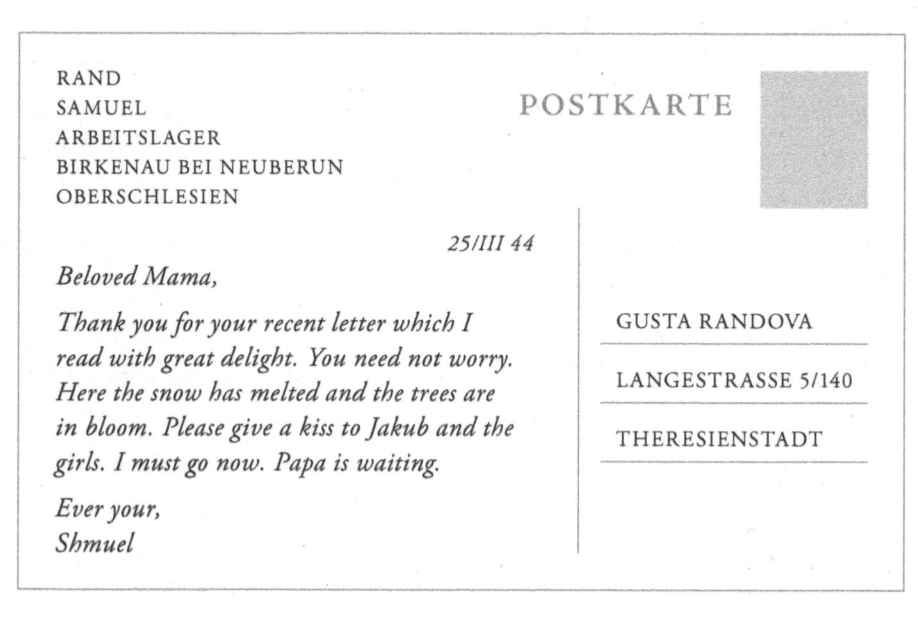
RAND
SAMUEL
ARBEITSLAGER
BIRKENAU BEI NEUBERUN
OBERSCHLESIEN

POSTKARTE

25/III 44

Beloved Mama,

Thank you for your recent letter which I read with great delight. You need not worry. Here the snow has melted and the trees are in bloom. Please give a kiss to Jakub and the girls. I must go now. Papa is waiting.

Ever your,
Shmuel

GUSTA RANDOVA
LANGESTRASSE 5/140
THERESIENSTADT

Daša read it aloud, as she did when each new card arrived, translating from the German. She paused at the last line: *Papa is waiting.* When she read out Shmuel's name, Gusta gasped and begged her to read it again. Daša read it over, Gusta's voice echoing hers. Only when the woman could say it by heart did she take back the card. The others had lost interest and were going about their nightly routines, readying themselves for bed. Daša climbed up to her bunk, where Irena was already asleep. Typhus had wracked the child's body in the winter and recovery was slow. Daša pulled the blanket over them both and turned to look down at Gusta. The woman was still whispering and kissing the card, her head nodding like a woodpecker.

~

Again she waited on the bench. It was over a month since she'd succumbed to folly and worn her mother's ring. Every week since that day, when she came and sat down in the square, waiting for him to arrive, she felt it hang from her neck, a millstone for her inattention.

Around the square, members of a cleaning detail scrubbed at the concrete. Swathes of colour radiated from the surface of the pavilion, as if the sun, tired of waiting for the Ghetto Swingers, had set about a performance of its own. In the surrounding plots, newly planted flowers watched on. They were all willing players in this process of beautification: Daša, the cleaners, the sun and the flowers. Behind her, on the main thoroughfare of Neu Gasse, couples strolled wearily towards the barracks, stopping to pick at the leaves of a tree or admire the fresh paint on an empty shopfront marked *Pharmacy* or *Perfumery*.

Daša refastened the bow on her collar. The blouse had arrived that morning, in a package from the city. Pink, frivolous. *For the new season*, her mother had written on the accompanying note. Daša hoped it would be enough to keep his interest. How long would he wait, she thought, when she could not see to his needs? Her body had jerked in fright when he took her hand. She was not ready for his touch, with its suggestion of shame and sacrifice. He had looked at her with kindness, with sadness. With pity. And they had talked, not of what had just happened, but of their memories of Biskupcova Street.

The next week he came but it was not the same. He appeared anxious. He spoke of strange men and tunnels and secrets that, for her own safety, he said, he dared not share. When she returned to the barracks she clung to Irena. The younger girl, exhausted from an evening's gymnastics, pushed her away. Daša rolled over and waited in the darkness for sleep. She woke with new resolve: she would promise herself to him, to the warmth of their own beds, to the disapproving stares of their mothers. It wouldn't be long, she knew. On every front the Germans were losing. The news swept through the streets with the gusts of spring. Italy had fallen. The Russians had pushed beyond the Polish border. Yes, their communion would be a celebration of freedom. If only he would wait. She readied herself to tell him. *Next week*, she said to herself.

Again, a hand on her shoulder, but this time heavy.

'Roubičkova.'

'Pan Durák!'

She had not recognised Ludvík's old employer when he first approached her near the entrance to the Hamburg Barracks. The gendarme's greatcoat, with its rows of gleaming buttons, added bulk to his frame while the rounded metal helmet hid the warmth in his eyes. His beard was gone. He was, in her mind, a stranger. To hear a gendarme call her name filled her with dread, not so much for herself as for her father. From the moment she had arrived in the fortress town she expected to hear that some calamity had befallen him; it was, after all, his way. He had not changed. Only when the gendarme began to speak of Prague's Old Town Square, and how the girls had played beneath the café awnings while Ludvík haggled, did it occur to her that she had nothing to fear. He fumbled in his pocket and pulled out three cigarettes and an envelope. It was from her mother in Prague.

Since then they had always met behind the kitchen. There he could tell her news from Žižkov, give her the gifts he had stashed in his case—money, cigarettes, coffee and tea—things forbidden in the ghetto mail. Otherwise, she hardly saw him. So why had he come now, while she waited for Bohuš? Daša felt the skin on her arm prickle.

'Look ahead,' said Pan Durák. 'I'm leaving for Prague tonight. No doubt your mother will be glad to hear you are well. Have you enough until I return?'

'Thank you, Pan Durák. Yes. For now.'

'And Irena?'

'The dizziness has gone. Tell mother she is in good health.'

'Daša…' His voice was soft, cautious. A snatch of music rang out behind them as the café door swung open to swallow a patron. 'I…I am here about your friend.' Daša went rigid against the bench. 'The boy.' How long had he known? What crude fantasies had he conjured in the things he saw? *Poor mother*, Daša thought. *To be met in her own home with such tales, such disappointment.*

She made to turn around but Pan Durák gripped her shoulders and held her fast. 'Straight ahead.' Daša felt the pressure ease. 'There has been an incident of sorts. Smuggling. Much of it is condoned, controlled even by the SS and gendarmes for profit, but this...this was different. Your friend was found under the fortress, in the tunnels that lead to a nearby village. There was a small group of them, I'm told, all arrested. They have been taken to the Small Fortress for questioning. It is not good, Daša.'

'Is he...?'

'I have not heard. Which means he is alive. He will likely be sent to the mines. When his body gives way he will be deported. That is, of course, if—' Daša stared towards the pavilion. The colour was gone. The flowers had drooped. 'There is another thing,' Pan Durák said. 'A car came today. With Eichmann.' He paused. 'Stay safe, Dašinku. I will report everything to your mother, have her keep making enquiries about your welfare with the Gestapo. It is your greatest privilege: to be loved, to be known, to be asked after. I return in a fortnight. God willing, I shall see you then.'

That night she did not sleep. She did not want to close her eyes, to abandon him to the damnation of her dreams. And so she listened to the sounds of the barracks, its creaks and hisses, moans and hacking coughs, until orange light leaked through the clouded glass. Daša climbed from her bed and crept into the corridor, towards the warm-up kitchen. On the wall, a fresh bulletin had been posted by the night sentries. She read only one word before spinning around and running back to her room:

Transport.

The word rang out like a morning bell. In the barracks, in the kitchens, in the streets, in the park, it was all they spoke about. The Kommandant had directed the Jewish Council to draw up a list of two and a half thousand people to be deported to Birkenau in three days' time. Another work detail.

The women reassured each other that they were safe. Daša sat on her bunk, her knees pulled up to her chest. She could think only of Bohuš, how he was now lost to this uncertain tide. She wanted to ask, to search, to beg, but what did they care? There were rules to be followed. He was not deserving of their pity, even if they had some left to give. Daša watched Irena tear into the loaf of bread that Magda, the block warden, had distributed the previous morning.

'Don't eat it all. Make it last.'

Irena stopped for a moment, sniffled, then stuffed another wad into her mouth.

The stillness of waiting.

All day they faced the Magdeberg Barracks and prayed.

Then: night. From the corridor came the crescendo of approaching footsteps. The solitary bulb sparked to life. The room filled with groans and muttered curses. A few soft mewls. One woman banged a cup against her bunk and began to laugh as if the night itself were a joke. Another sang an old folk song, shrill, out of tune. Dazed, Daša watched Magda weave from bunk to bunk, checking numbers, shaking those who had not woken, handing out the strips of paper. It pained Daša to bear witness, she who was still drenched in the lamb's blood of privilege. When Magda approached, she closed her eyes and waited to be passed over. *Gusta R*? The voice was firm. *CK-571. Gusta R*? Daša peeked out to see Magda lean over and shake Gusta's shoulder. Louder: *Gusta R.*

Gusta pitched upwards and snatched the paper slip. She held it close to her face and scanned the unfamiliar script, first from right to left and then the other way. What little she knew of the written word came from the pages of holy books. *Eshet chayil,* a woman of worth, whose value far exceeded rubies. Such a woman needed only learn to read God's language, and even then no more than was necessary for her to converse with Him at the proper time and in the proper manner. Beyond that, the world of letters was not her business. On the paper, Gusta knew, were the words of another god, a god that was fickle and malevolent, a human god, but a god who had at last listened to her deepest prayer: Gusta R had been summoned for transport to Birkenau.

Daša vaulted from her bunk the moment Magda left the room. She knelt beside Gusta in the dark, protesting, but Gusta shooed her away. 'Not now,' she said as she pulled the blanket over her head. 'Tomorrow. Maybe tomorrow.' Gusta was asleep in no time: a deep, dreamless slumber.

The suitcase lay open on her bed, its contents scattered across the mattress. Three times already Gusta had been made to distil her life like this, to strike the balance between the needs of her body and that of her soul. Each time she grew more compact. She found that value was, by nature, transient; it could depart one object and embed itself in another. That which remained—a threadbare blouse, a sturdy pot, a pair of leather shoes—held the accumulated worth of all that came before. And so it was again. She would share out what she could not take, let her presence linger in what was left behind, just as it had in the village, the city, Prague.

At first light, Daša ran to the Hannover Barracks with the paper balled in her fist. The ghetto had already lurched to life, set in motion by machine memory. Soon a train would roll through the southern gate, ready to ferry its load to the next world. *Birkenau.* All transports from Terezín went there. Depending on what the local engineer could spare, it might be a third-class carriage or freight or cattle carriages. For now though, the tracks lay bare, straps of wood and steel warming in the morning sun. Daša ran from them as fast as she could, up Badhausgasse, into Lange Strasse. Around her, a familiar routine: those unable to sleep, who had packed through the night, resigned to their fates, now filled the streets, dragging their suitcases, their backpacks, their bedrolls, circling the Hamburg drain.

She found Jakub outside the latrine on the second floor. He smiled and self-consciously patted at his damp hair. She could not speak, the breath rushing from her chest, her mouth hanging open as she gulped at the stale barrack air. She held up the paper strip for him to see. Jakub took in the details: his mother's name, a new number—*DZ-1211*—a time to report for transport. She had less than a day. 'It is possible she is in the reserve,' he said. 'They always call up more than they need.' From the latrine door they heard the crotchety snarl of the hygiene attendant. Jakub continued: 'Go back. Help with her preparations. I'll go to the Council and plead her case.' Daša took his hand and held it to her cheek. His lips twitched as if anxious to keep talking, but he pulled away and headed for the door.

A great bazaar fills the courtyard. They hawk their wares from tables and chairs; rags flutter in the wind, wooden spoons clang against steel pots. The ghetto town has contracted until it is just this: a tempest of beggars and thieves. A rumour: there are some who still have gold. Take only what you can carry. *Gold is light. Gold is small. Gold has lost its meaning. A case. A backpack. A hamper. Shoes. That is what they want. That is what they will pay for most of all. Gold. Gold for shoes. Bigger cases will be loaded as cargo.* Lighter bags can be carried by hand. *Shoes. Gold. Food.* Be sure to keep them with you at all times. *There is no security in cargo. No guarantee that you will see your cases again.* Take only what you need. *Take only what you can bear to lose.*

Jakub returned without news. The man had dismissed his plea before he'd even finished. The camp's Kommandant—its third, its most vicious—wanted too many this time and the Council could not supply them without reaching into the pool of the privileged. Compromises were made but it still wasn't enough. Jakub explained that those whose protection was only by association were no longer exempt. 'The train leaves tomorrow. I'm sorry.'

Gusta pulled the case from her bunk. It landed with a thud. From inside, the muffled clatter of metal. Gusta bent over and tested its weight. Jakub reached for it. 'Please,' he said.

They streamed into the western wing from the gate, from the courtyard, from the floors above. The train had not yet arrived. Hamburg was choking. Those who came in the afternoon could not get near the assembly hall and had to wait in the adjoining arcades. Members of the transport kommando worked their way through the crowd, checking names off lists, distributing labels, wading through the desperate horde. If only they could hold off until after curfew, when the numbers would thin, when husbands, wives, children and lovers would return to their barracks, not to sleep, but to listen, listen.

For the final time they ate as a family. Jakub stirred his spoon through the discoloured broth, watching potato peel and onion stems swirl up in its wake. The ghetto cooks had taken pity on the deportees and filled the vats with more scraps than usual. Those left behind would make do with a thinner broth for a day, if only to assuage their guilt. *They went with food in their bellies.* The kitchen hands, accustomed to skimming liquid from the top, plunged their ladles until they could feel solids collecting in the scoop. On that night, all who ate in the limbo of the Hamburg Barracks were favoured, all were privileged. Jakub plucked out the larger pieces with his fingers and dropped them into his mother's bowl. Daša surprised them with a heavy loaf she had baked from crushed chestnuts, salt and water. It softened in the steaming liquid and expanded like a bread dumpling. Irena, too, brought what she could: a stick of butter sent from Prague, sitting misshapen in the corner of a cardboard box. They slurped and licked, savouring the hints of flavour.

Daša woke in a pile of unfamiliar bodies. They had shifted in the night: those who would soon be gone and those who could not let them go. Only Gusta seemed at peace. Sitting on her case, she pulled out slices of dry sausage and stale crackers from her knapsack. The girls had packed it with enough for the journey—knots of black bread, jam, onions, turnips, crackers, a sausage and two tins of sardines from the Red Cross. She ate unhurriedly, from habit not hunger, her eyes fixed on the rear gate, the sluice through which Daša knew she was eager to pass. The train had still not come.

From across the room, Irena scrambled towards her, tripping on bedrolls and pillows. She must have woken early to get coffee from the warm-up kitchen. She clasped a metal cup in each hand, one for herself, one for Gusta. Nothing for Daša. Tepid liquid splashed over the rims, waking those who still slept.

Gusta's gaze did not shift. She reached out when the girl drew near, let the cup come to her hand and then brought it back to her lap. Irena crouched beside her, nestling against the woman's legs. They stayed like that, a single organism, mouths sipping the same murky swill, eyes staring off in different directions. Daša edged forward, stepping over an old man, asleep, his body wrapped around a beaten suitcase. As she passed, he kicked out and grunted. Daša skipped out of harm's way, landing softly by her sister. Still Gusta looked towards the gate. Daša cleared a small space with her foot and sat down.

'Maybe there's no train,' said Irena, her voice a whisper in the morning bustle.

'It will come.' Daša shuffled closer.

'Do you think we'll go?'

'Not today. No.'

'But later?'

'No.' A pause. Then: 'No.'

'I can work.'

'Of course.'

'I'm strong.'

'I know.'

'They...' Irena looked around the room. 'It's not fair. To make them work. It should be us.'

'It is not our place to say. The Council...they have their reasons.'

'And Auntie Gusta?'

'She will grow strong. With Shmuel she will find strength. Yes, with him she will grow tall and fat and strong.'

'And young?'

'Maybe.' Daša slid a hand through the crook of her sister's arm. 'Maybe.'

'You slept?' Jakub crouched beside his mother and kissed her on the forehead. Gusta flinched. Daša watched Jakub, sensing his despair, the knowledge of his own failing.

Whatever he might have said was drowned by a cacophonous shrieking from around the hall. Ghetto Watchmen and gendarmes had started filing through the sluice door, the signal for the transport kommando to reach for their metal whistles and call the waiting deportees to order. German soldiers also appeared, although they were careful not to step inside. Voices rose to a tumult then fell to a murmur. From the crackling speakers, a voice rattled out instructions nobody could understand. Outside, dogs were barking. And, in the background, the unmistakable chug of a train snaking its way through the southern gate towards the barrack siding that had, once again, become a platform.

Perched on top of an upturned crate, a gendarme raised a loudhailer to his mouth.

Attention, attention...

They are called in groups of one hundred. The first ones must push through the hall towards the men who wait by the gate with lists and pens and officious glares. This place is no longer their home. They are setting off for where it is said they are needed to fill the labour shortage brought about by a war that refuses to end. Men, women, children. The elderly, the sick, the infirm. Irena is right. It is not fair. But what is fair anymore? To stay or to go? It is for each passenger to create his destination. Why choose despair? Why not give yourself over to the conviction that the next place will be better? Birkenau. *A word of beauty, of hope. Where they could toil on wooded hills. Where mothers might once again hold their sons under the birch trees for which the land is named.* Birkenau. *Life.*

The slurry of syllables. Daša Roubíčková tried to pick out the sounds that would call Gusta away. An air of resignation had settled over the hall. Deportees waited patiently, stepping forward when their group was called, leaving orphaned cases for the transport kommando to load. Clutching their bedrolls and knapsacks, they assembled in line, flanked by friends and family, who would escort them as far as the rear gate. There, the Ghetto Watchmen would shout their transport number again and cross them from the list. One last kiss, one last embrace, and they disappeared behind the barrier.

In the far corner, the gendarme was calling through the loudhailer: *DZ-1000 to 1099, please step forward.* Daša looked at the tag on Gusta's case. Only two more groups before her.

'...for the journey!'

Daša turned around to see Jakub shaking Gusta's knapsack. Gusta snatched at it but he stepped out of her reach. They had been huddled together, spitting whispers in each other's ear. Daša dared not move closer. It was not for her, this squabble of departure. Gusta slumped back onto her case and crossed her arms. To her, the affair was over. Jakub held the knapsack out to Irena and then to Daša. 'She can't go like this,' he said. 'She has given the food away. We have enough here. She must take more.' The girls looked at Gusta, but said nothing. Jakub reached down, grabbed Irena by the arm and pulled her up. 'Here,' he said, shoving the knapsack into her chest. 'Take it. Go to your room and fill it. Whatever you can spare. And if that isn't enough, go to my room too. In my case there are supplies. Please. Just go.' He pushed her with a force that frightened Daša. 'Hurry.'

DZ-1100 to DZ-1199, please assemble now...

Irena disappeared behind the procession. Jakub, too, stormed off in the direction of the sluice gate where two members of the Transport Committee had just appeared with a sheath of rescission papers. They swatted away the encroaching throng as they made their way to the Ghetto Watchmen. For a moment the boarding stopped. All eyes were on the four men as they shuffled through the papers, looking at their clipboards then the sheath and back again. When they called out a series of numbers, great wails of relief resounded through the hall. Otherwise, curses. Daša moved herself behind Gusta and pulled the woman's head to her bosom. She could feel the warm, measured breaths, each one a sigh of surrender. A tug at her sleeve. Daša hunched until she could hear Gusta. 'Forgive him. Please, forgive him. It is against himself that he rages.'

DZ-1200 to DZ-1299, please assemble now...

Gusta readied herself, pushed her hands into her knees, and stood up.

'It's time,' she said. Daša checked the buckles on her case. 'Wait,' she said. 'Irena—' But Gusta had already moved to take her place in line. Daša held the bedroll under her arm; the worn horsehair prickled her skin. Jakub was at Gusta's side by the time Daša reached her. He held her in his arms, a protective shield. It was not how Daša had rehearsed it in her mind. Over a year the woman had found space in her heart for two more daughters. But here, in the assembly hall, Gusta had only one child, imperfect as he was in his parting. Daša saw how she looked at him: the inevitable realisation that, in the hope of reuniting with one son, whose only presence was an occasional, cryptic postcard, she was sacrificing the certainty of another. This man who had cared for her, protected her from the worst ravages of the fortress town, was once again just a boy, confused by a world over which he had lost the illusion of control. For the first time Daša saw Jakub cry, his face propped against his mother's shoulder as he muttered words of comfort. Lies. And Gusta, too, replied with the words a mother is supposed to use to calm a child. Daša could watch no more. She would not have the opportunity to say goodbye. She would merely place the bedroll at Jakub's feet and step away.

Daša Roubíčková leaned against the far wall. The deportees shuffled past, disappearing through the gate. In their wake, husbands and wives, children and friends, craned so as not to lose sight, then shrank back, collapsing into something less than they had been before. They filed out from the Hamburg Barracks, a single, continuous line, and disappeared into the dusty streets. Daša rested her head against the cold concrete. *Bohuš.* He was there, somewhere. In the Small Fortress, on the train. How was she to know? Prisoners do not pass through the sluice. Yes, Bohuš was there, but only when she thought of him: a memory.

Daša listened to the numbers. There was an oddly comforting randomness to it all. Whoever came was called. It slowed the process, the shuffling of pages, the search for each one. *DZ-1243. Hurry, hurry. Okay. DZ-1261.* Daša spotted Jakub in the crowd near the gate, his head jerking as he looked around for Irena. Gusta marched beside him in pixie steps. *DZ-1204.* Across the hall, Irena appeared and began pushing through the crowd. *DZ-1211.*

Jakub stepped up to the man, pleaded for time. *DZ-1211.* Jakub reached out and pulled Gusta to his chest. She stiffened then slumped into him. For a moment they were one, a child returned to his mother's womb. Then: a visible shudder. She reached up and held him. He crouched, whispering behind her ear. *DZ-1211, now.* The Watchman was insistent. He grabbed Gusta by the arm but she brushed him off and stood straight. She would leave when she was ready. She looked around, at the Watchman, at Daša, at Jakub and, lastly, at the large, open gate. A moment of freedom. Now she was ready. As Gusta stepped into the sluice, Irena crashed through the pack and thrust the bloated knapsack into Jakub's hands. 'Mama!' Jakub called, lunging forward, past the Watchman. The gendarme, still standing on the crate, scrambled for his whistle but Jakub was already backing away. She had taken the knapsack and pulled his head to her lips for one last kiss. Then she turned around and walked on. She did not look back.

Daša Roubíčková stabbed the paring knife into the potato's flesh, its blade sinking to the wooden hilt. Bubbles of creamy white dribbled through the fissure. Daša pulled at the handle, felt the potato split in her palm. She had come straight from the station, leaving Irena at the wooden partition that hid the platform from the street. Jakub, too, had rushed out when Gusta was gone. Daša chased after him but he was too fast. She watched him run up Badhausgasse, his hat bunched in his hand, and disappear in the direction of Südstrasse. Without Gusta they would be a burden for him. To stand by the bunk where his mother had slept would only remind him how his was a lesser privilege, a privilege that could, after all, be tossed away or forgotten. Around them, his power was diminished. Around them, he was less of a man.

What remained of the day passed like any other. The vats' deep gurgle erupted to a sputtering hiss, clouding the room with a heavy, earthen brume. The women wiped at their brows with their muddy forearms, peeling, scraping, potato skins falling at their feet. There were turnips too, and onions, all from the sunken garden beds on the shores of the fortress moat. Here there could be no waste. It all went in, the skins, the peels, the stalks, the roots. Pan Durák needn't have worried. There was little to steal anymore. Even the filth that collected on the ground was now scooped up and tossed into the slop. It seemed a formality that their pockets and socks were checked as they left. The kitchen supervisor looked bored by it all. At the end of the day, Daša held out her empty palms for inspection. She received a nod, and she was gone.

The other women stood clear of her bunk. Daša froze at the door, taking in the disarray. The sheets had been pulled from her mattress and were hanging from the wooden struts. Shredded stuffing spewed from the torn pillows. Her case was open, its contents strewn across the slats. Daša looked at the other women. Surely she would have heard had there been a raid. On Gusta's bed, an unfamiliar woman sat against the rear board, her legs crossed like a child, picking from a bag of lentils. Judging by her twitches and tremors, the woman must have just been discharged from the hospital in the Hohenelbe Barracks. Or worse, the Kavalier madhouse. Daša saw how the others looked at her, expecting the worst. This thief. This beast. Daša charged forward and jumped at the muttering witch. The woman scurried back but Daša was already upon her, clumps of hair clutched in her fist. The lentils fell from the bunk and scattered across the floor.

'Roubíčková!' Daša bucked at the hands on her shoulder. 'Roubíčková!' A searing pain across her cheek, the force of an open hand. Daša tumbled into the wall. Above her stood Magda, arm cocked, ready for another blow. 'I'll not have this in my room,' said the warden. 'I should report you. Now get off that bed. Leave the poor woman alone.' Daša slid from the bunk. Magda grabbed her by the shoulder and swung her across the narrow aisle. 'It was your friend,' Magda said. Daša scrunched her brow. 'The boy.' When she saw the hope in Daša's eyes, she shook her head. 'Jakub.' Daša clambered up the ladder and knelt on her bunk. She righted the case and began to sweep up her scattered belongings. Magda climbed the first rung and held on to the sideboard. 'He came here in a fit. Poor thing, his mother gone and all. We tried to stop him, but...' She pointed to the mess. 'Irena came in. He was screaming at her, angry words, hurtful words. He shook her. She ran away. I thought she'd run to find you.'

Daša dumped what she could in the case. 'I'll go,' she said. 'If Irena comes, tell her to wait here for me.'

She found the girl in the eastern wing, crouched at the top of the stairs to the attic. 'Irča?'

'I only did as he asked.' Irena shifted to the side, her eyes red and swollen.

'It's okay. Come.'

Irena paused, shook her head. 'He's been called.'

'For transport? It's not possible.'

'When he returned this afternoon. He's on the list. His friend too. They leave on Thursday.'

'He told you?'

'He was scared. I've never seen it before. He said it was my fault. That I'd ruined everything. That I shouldn't have taken the sugar from his case. But Daša…' Irena straightened herself, suddenly composed in her defiance. 'It was him. He told me to.'

'Come. Forget him.' They walked on along the corridor. From below they could hear the muffled bustle of another transport, shuffling towards the assembly hall. A second train would leave tomorrow, then another on Thursday. He would be gone, with his frustration and rage. Back to his mother's arms, to Shmuel. How fragile is family, Daša thought. How easily broken and stuck back together, its pieces never quite fitting like before. She had thought of him like that, and he, perhaps, thought something else. Not now. This creature he had become was no brother of hers. But she would remember Gusta, remember her kindness, the way she welcomed the girls into her family. Yes, she would remember Auntie Gusta with fondness. And damn it if he, too, would not creep into her thoughts, the way he cared for his mother when the silt of failure was all he had left to give.

Daša Roubíčková stood at the bunkroom window and looked out. The moon bathed the empty streets in deep purgatorial blue. The transformation was complete: beautification, with its park benches and flowerbeds, bandstand and sporting fields, shopfronts and children's pavilion. All off limits to the townspeople. The last train had gone, leaving her behind in this unfamiliar place: the Jewish Settlement of Theresienstadt. A model town. The jewel in a crooked crown. Soon the Red Cross would arrive. Rehearsals were already underway. *Oh no, Uncle Rahm,* the children would chime in unison. *Not chocolate again…*

8

BIRKENAU BIIb,
THE CZECH FAMILY CAMP

Thy magic power re-creates
All that custom has divided
All men become brothers
Under the sway of thy
Gentle wings.

A semitone sharp and several beats too late, the last voice faded out to a wave of childish titters. They all waited for the doctor, their eyes fixed on his pigskin gloves. Jakub stood uneasily to attention. Beside him, Georg fidgeted with a loose button, winding a wayward thread around its sagging base. 'Bravo, *kinder*,' the doctor said in his thin voice and brought his hands together once, twice; the damp slap of leather. They looked at each other—the children, the instructors—and when they were sure, they, too, began to clap. The doctor stepped forward, arms outstretched, to pat heads, caress cheeks. The children were eager to please. Perhaps he would take them from this place, across the dusty Styx to the Hospital Block where, it was said, there was more food, even beds with white sheets and pillows. They could not know for sure. None had returned. But the doctor was not like the others—not like the Camp Elder Arno Böhm, not like Büntrock, not like Tadeusz. The Kapos. The savages.

Jakub rubbed his temple, trying to relieve the pressure. He could not bear the children's shrill squawking. When he first heard them rehearse in the vast latrine block, their boisterous 'Ode to Joy' set to Beethoven's Ninth Symphony bouncing from the concrete walls, Jakub had cursed them to silence and then perched on the concrete slab waiting for the moan of his bowels. The music instructor, Felix Baum, took him aside that afternoon to apologise. It hadn't been this way when Imré was here. Poor Imré, the optimistic fool. Soon after Fredy Hirsch had talked the Nazis into allocating a barracks to the children, Imré offered his services as choirmaster. 'In music they will be free,' he said. Fredy took little convincing. He knew the power of song, not just to liberate but to teach. And so, while the other instructors recited books from memory and played games and pieced together performances to nourish these pitiable souls, Imré built up the greatest choir that Hell had ever seen. So great were they, so accomplished, that it was said they went to the gas singing the 'Internationale', the 'Hatikvah' and the Czech National Anthem in perfect harmony. Imré was last seen waving his arms with joy outside the large brick house from which he left as smoke.

With a polite bow and a wave, the doctor took his leave. Jakub watched him hurry along the central path to the front gate. His step was nimble, carefree. The children shuffled down from the makeshift stage, away from Snow White and her misshapen dwarf, away from the meadows and flowers, and broke into their groups, eager to resume their rehearsals. Having long ago forfeited their names, the children had once again found something of an identity in Block 31. They were not the numbers crudely carved into their arms. They were Swallows, Bears or Maccabees. And they fought for supremacy any way they could: scrubbing their stalls the hardest, chanting the loudest, picking the most dandelions from the patch by the perimeter fence. They fought with the ferocity only children can rally, the kind that knows no limitations, that is oblivious to danger. They fought as if their very lives depended on it. As if they didn't know they were already dead.

Jakub was scraping at the scab on his forearm, watching the numbers bleed black and red, when he learned that he, too, would die. 'My brother,' he said to Michal, his new bunkmate, on the first night in Birkenau. 'Shmuel

Rand. Please, I need to see him.' It had been his first thought as he stepped down from the train with Georg. Find Shmuel. Find Gusta. Then find the dirt. His heart sank when he heard the shouts: 'Leave everything on the train. All luggage is to remain in the carriage.' Those who did not hear, who would not listen, had the bags snatched from their hands. Michal's arm snaked from beneath his splayed greatcoat. 'They're all there,' he said, pointing to the ceiling. 'The chimneys, the fire. The smell. That is him. Next it will be me. Then you. Six months.'

Jakub turned to Georg but his friend was already asleep. On the train he had been quiet, sullen. Leaving his father tormented him. In Theresienstadt their roles had reversed. The ghetto policeman's uniform could not hide the old man's creeping confusion. He spoke in ever more peculiar fancies. More than once Georg had been called to the gate of Magdeberg to calm his nerves. There was even talk of sending Professor Glanzberg to the Kavalier madhouse but Georg pleaded with the Council on his behalf, for the sake of his father's dignity. 'He is harmless,' Georg had said. 'This place has undone him, it's true, but he carries on with his duties.' When Georg received his transport slip he pleaded again. 'You needn't worry,' said the clerk. 'Herr Professor Glanzberg is safe here. Go in peace.' On the train, Georg cursed himself. 'I've damned us both,' he cried as it began to heave along the track. Jakub sat beside him on the bench and held his hand. He longed to comfort his friend, to blow away the veils of pity and doubt. But to say something now, to speak of books and myths and secrets, would only confirm what Georg feared most about his father.

Jakub lifted the blanket from his chest and laid it across Georg's shoulders. Give him this moment of peace. Jakub lay back on their third-storey bunk and stared at the ceiling.

A storm of crashing wood snatched him from what he'd mistaken for a sleepless night. Shouts, like thunder, echoed through the barrack. Georg spun around, grasped at Jakub's leg. Michal, seemingly unfazed by the uproar, sat up and stretched, his bony arms pushing past his bedfellows' heads. 'Welcome to the first day of your death.'

Jakub and Georg climbed down and followed Michal outside to a large area near the gate between two kitchen blocks. Weary hordes streamed into the space. Jakub tried to spot his mother but it was no use; she was small and would be hidden in the crowd. In the distance he thought he caught sight of Shmuel. Then again. And again. All around him were faces that, for a moment, might have been the boy, but weren't. Beyond the fence, two towering chimneys loomed above the forest. From their black-tipped stacks, flames licked the grey dawn.

More shouting. Jakub looked back along the unfinished road that cut between the rows of barracks. Old men hobbled towards the assembly ground beneath a hail of blows. Their malevolent shepherds cursed them and laughed as they brought down the wooden cudgels. 'Green Triangles,' said Michal. 'Murderers. Rapists. Here they thrive.' And then, as if an afterthought: 'You'll learn.' Jakub turned his gaze to the ditch that ran alongside the cobbled path. All around it the ground was parched, but through this channel ran a constant flow of oily, effluent sludge. 'The big one is Böhm,' the bunkmate continued. 'He runs the place. Then there is Büntrock, the imbecile. But it is Tadeusz you should watch. Last month, for Passover, he threw the body of a poor boy who'd died in the night onto the camp flour supply. *Cut him,* he shouted. *Bleed him out. Make your bread.* And he waited until one of the bakers stabbed at the boy's chest. Never mind that blood would not flow. It was entertainment enough.' Michal spat on the ground and snorted. 'Do you have a wife? A sister?' Růženka. Jakub had not thought of her in months. Safe in America, thank God. He could not bear to imagine her in this prison. 'Here, no,' he said. Michal ran his fingers across his chin. 'Good. There is no end to his depravity. Even here, where we are already corpses.'

The muster began with a call for the fallen. Numbers sounded out from around the crowd. Family. Friends. Jakub lost count. After a pause, the roll master readied his list. Then: 'A-One-Zero-Three-Six.' Michal leaned over, whispered in his ear: 'Tadeusz. Bastard.' The one called Tadeusz was shorter than his comrades. Rags hung from his broad shoulders and over his paunch. Jakub could just make out the faded green triangle on his shirt. Tadeusz repeated the number: 'A-One-Zero-Three-Six.' From the crowd, a man's voice: '*Nein, nein.* Present.' Michal shook his head. 'Pervert,' he spat. '*Bitte, bitte, nein,*' the man was crying. Then a woman: 'My God. No. He is here. Can't you see?' Tadeusz fell back into line and the roll master called the first number.

The muster dragged on through the morning. The latest transport had filled the camp to overflow. When his own number was called Jakub shouted '*Jawohl!*' as he had heard those before him do. Then, he waited. The sun beat down, an early summer. At last: *Dismissed.* Jakub pushed through the bodies, to where he had seen a group of women. He found Gusta near the Registrar's office. 'Thank God,' she said. He held her against his chest. 'He is gone,' she said. There was relief in her voice, triumph even. 'Oh, Mama. He's—' She cut him short: 'In Heydebreck. I know. Don't listen to what they say. The worst kind of *bonkes.* A mother knows. A dead son does not send postcards.' Jakub chose not to argue. 'Your bag?' he said. She broke free, swatted the air. 'They wanted to take it but I thought Shmuel might…They took it from me, emptied it on the ground. I went to pick it up but I was pushed along—' She stopped, tilted her head. 'And Daša and Irena?' 'They send their love. When this is over we'll meet up in Prague.' He looked away. Then: 'I'd better go. They've assigned me to the Children's Block.' A quick kiss on her forehead and Jakub joined the procession back along the camp road.

Loss, he thought. *That, too, is a holy incantation.* To make something tangible out of loss is the soul of creation, of faith. And so Gusta had done what Muneles and Leopold Glanzberg could not: she had made real the man of clay in Jakub's heart. The dirt was mere fantasy until it was gone. Now Jakub crushed it underfoot, or breathed it in, or watched it swirl in the distance. Yes, the *golem* was here, in this place where stories ended. It was here and then it was not. Like Daša. Like Shmuel. Like all of them in time.

'Jakub!' A cluster of inmates huddled near the doorway between two barracks. Again: 'Jakub! Here!' It was Michal. Jakub veered from the path to where the men were gathered. They were peering down the shaded corridor that ran between the buildings. Michal stepped aside and pushed him into the group. '*Shhhh.*' He held his finger to his lips. At the far end Jakub could make out three heavy-set, bald figures standing over another, smaller man. The latter was lying on the ground, trying to shield his head. Even from a distance, Jakub could hear the thuds and cracks of wood and bone. 'There you go,' said Michal. 'A-One-Zero-Three-Six. Tadeusz is correcting the mistake in his reporting. Tomorrow this poor fellow's wife will be in the comfort block.' Jakub stumbled away, up the camp road as fast as he could go, swallowing frantically to keep down the bile. The paving ended halfway along the road and he tripped over the broken ground. From the barracks up ahead, a familiar song— 'Ode to Joy'—in pinched, uneven tones:

Joy, bright spark of Divinity
Daughter of Elysium
Fire-inspired we tread...

Again, a blur. The blinding fog of hunger. It was happening often since the rations had been cut back. Jakub steadied himself against a shelf. The children seemed distant, in another place. The haze gave way to a hundred tiny eyes, staring at him. Not children, puppets, seated in lines across the shelves, their feet dangling from the edge. Jakub reached out, picked one from the middle row. It was misshapen, ugly, like most things here. Still, he admired the crafting of its face, the droopy eyes, the smeared red on its cheeks. There was no mistaking the man after whom it was modelled: Tadeusz.

The performance had been planned for their final night. The night before they were scheduled to die. The doctor would be there. And the Green Triangles. Probably a guard or two. Most had seen the play before, when it was acted out by children, not puppets. *Heavenly Auschwitz, Earthly Auschwitz*. A comedy, really, written soon after the liquidation of the September transport. In it the children died and went to heaven, only to find that it was no different from what they had on earth. They were immortal, as souls are supposed to be, but stricken with lice and typhus and dysentery. They were beaten by guards and made to dig holes and fill them, senseless, purposeless labour, for all eternity. They begged for the release of death. God was confused. Had He not granted their wish once already? It was not possible to die again. And so the play ended with Him turning His back on the ungrateful brats like they thought He had done before to them.

The children, of course, were not fooled. If the message was supposed to appease, to make them thankful for what little they had here, it achieved quite the opposite. They knew of their classmates' fate. They heard the rumours. They knew of Fredy Hirsch, their fallen hero, who did not resist as they dreamed he would, but who took pills to avoid what was to come. No, they were not fooled at all. Still, any chance to mock their captors was seized upon with glee. They fought for the roles of the overseers and played them with spiteful exuberance. The instructors tried to temper the offence. They pulled green triangles from coats, mussed up slicked-back hair. Soon after the May transports, they announced that the play would no longer be performed. They would just sing. Or act out traditional Czech stories. Fairytales. They even danced for Snow White, who looked down on them from the back wall, while the choir sang: '*Hi ho. Hi ho. It's off to work we go.*' Another comedy for the Family Camp.

In early June, the children grew restless. They counted their time in days. Oskar Fischel, captain of the Swallows, proposed one last reprise of the play. 'This time,' he said, 'with puppets.' The instructors liked the idea. The children had stopped listening to their lessons. They had begun to bicker. A new production of *Heavenly Auschwitz* would keep them busy. Ten days to build a cast from whatever scraps they could gather. The children argued among themselves over who would craft which character and then retreated to their corners: it would be a competition between the three teams. Jakub recognised figures in the camp—Dr Mengele, the Green Triangles, but also the children's parents and friends and, of course, some of the children themselves. When the day was over, the instructors sat and ate their rations: soup and bread cooked in the nearby Gypsy Camp. 'Dredge for teeth,' Jakub had said to Georg the first time.

'To think this is what they leave behind,' said Erwin Glaser, the man who had taken Fredy's place after the March liquidation. 'They fashion their own faces, dust them with chalk to cover the dirt. Here, this puppet; once there was a boy just like him.'

Georg shifted to dangle his legs down the brick. 'And the villains,' he said. 'Have you noticed? Crafted with the greatest of care, as if to remember them is the most important thing. Each brushstroke is the finger of accusation.'

'Let them hang,' said Glaser.

'But it's a mistake,' said Georg, 'to put faith in creations. We cannot know God so we hope to stand in His place. We deign to know what will be. We're playing at idols. Nothing more.'

'Idols build strength too,' said Glaser. 'There is talk again of uprising. The locksmiths have come to deliver messages. The *Sonderkommando* are ready. They have been stockpiling weapons for months, hiding them among the cases in Kanada. Now they wait for our signal.'

'As they did in March,' said Felix Baum. 'Why trust us now?'

'We are under no illusion,' said Glaser. 'If we do not fight back we will die. And Georg and Jakub here will watch us spill from the chimney stacks.'

'And the puppets?' said Georg.

'These,' said Glaser, his hand sweeping over the benches strewn with half-finished figurines. 'These are their weapons. The children must fight too. To what end? It hardly matters.'

Jakub cradled the puppet of Tadeusz in his hands. Across the room, the children were still in their groups, talking excitedly among themselves. The doctor's visit was already a memory for them; they still clung to the hope of a performance and were practising their lines.

Jakub felt a tug at his sleeve. 'Sir?'

He looked up to see the familiar face of Arnošt Flusser. It had been two years since the boy first sat in his class in the Jewish school at 3 Jáchymova Street and, save for some facial stubble and a few inches of height, very little had changed about him. His eyes were filled with the same wonder and he often broke from his fellow Bears to float about on a mission none of the instructors could understand. When his father died, Flusser sat himself in the far corner of the Children's Block facing the wall for three days. The other children knew to leave him be. On the fourth day he did not come to classes.

Rumours began to spread that the boy was now in the company of the Green Triangles. He was seen running errands for Böhm. Whatever the case, it was short-lived. A few days after Jakub had given up on him returning, the barracks door swung open to reveal a bloodied Flusser, with his hair bunched in Tadeusz's fist. The Green Triangle dragged him halfway down the aisle, grunted, and threw him forward into a stack of benches. 'Heil Hitler,' Tadeusz said with a laugh and bounded from the barracks. The instructors rushed across to pick up the boy and whisk him into the cramped cubicle near the entrance. Arnošt Flusser remained silent while they tended to his wounds. He did not wince when they wiped at the cuts on his body, nor did he cry out as they tried to staunch the flow of pus and blood from his face. Only when they tried to help him from his clothes, loosening the string around his waist, did he flinch. Felix Baum took a damp cloth and dabbed at the spatter of dried blood and shit that streaked his inner thighs. The boy stayed silent.

Splotches of blue and purple on his body served to remind them all of what Arnošt Flusser had endured. The other children continued to ignore him as they had before. It was as though the strange boy absorbed their suffering. 'I will make Earthly Tadeusz,' he said, when the puppet show was announced. Erwin Glaser saw his lips move and hushed the others. The arguing stopped, freeing the air for his tiny voice. The children looked around anxiously. 'Master Flusser?' said Glaser. 'I will make Earthly Tadeusz,' Arnošt Flusser said again. 'There is no Tadeusz in heaven.'

'Oh,' said Jakub. 'I was just admiring…' He held out the puppet, tilting it so the boy would not have to look at its face. 'You have quite a talent.' Of all the instructors in the Children's Block, Arnošt Flusser had chosen him. Could he sense all Jakub had lost? It was said from the start that the boy had powers, that he could see beyond this world. Langer believed it. And Redlich. But they, too, were dreamers. Was it not simple familiarity that drew the boy to his old teacher when his faith in others had been so violently crushed? Jakub could not wipe the boy's blank stare from his memory, a look that gave nothing and pleaded for nothing, as if he had left his broken body while the instructors pieced it back together. At the time he thought the boy was looking straight through him, but the stare continued long after the wounds had healed. No, the boy was not looking through him. He was looking into him, piercing the corporeal divide. Jakub would not have it. Who was this child to preside? No, he would not submit to the court of the innocent.

From somewhere outside, a low moan of wind gusting between the barracks. 'Can I be excused.' A statement more than a question.

'You needn't ask, Master Flusser,' said Jakub. 'You are old enough.'

'There will be a storm. I must gather the dandelions.'

'I'm sure your friends will appreciate it.' *Your friends.* Jakub did not intend the offence in his words. Jakub often saw the boy sitting in the patch near the fence, gathering the weeds, when all the other children had run to meet their parents. What he picked he brought to Erwin Glaser for dandelion soup.

'They will blow away.'

'Yes, I understand.'

The boy rubbed his eyes. 'Doctor?'

'What is it, Master Flusser?'

'Nothing.'

That night Michal was restless. 'It's absurd,' he said. 'To live through your own death. I counted down the days, readied myself for what was to come. What a mockery, to make peace with it all for nothing. And you too. Were you not aching to be rid of me? It's okay. I don't take it personally. We'd all kill to make room, just to stretch out for one night. How do you think I felt when you came? God, I wished all manner of ills on you. I really didn't think you'd last a week.'

Outside, the wind howled, clattering against the barrack walls. Georg pulled off his shirt and wiped it across his forehead. 'You might still get your wish. For days I've dreamt of *stracheldraht*. Can you imagine?'

'But you live,' said Michal. 'I am the ghost who eats your bread. I no longer know how to sleep because I despair each passing moment. What is it your children say? Heavenly Auschwitz? I can tell you it's not the same. It's worse. Death is no release.' A great crash nearby. 'There,' Michal continued. 'The wind seeks to punish us. We have failed this world. We have refused its natural order.'

'And what of us?' said Jakub. 'We who remain in Earthly Auschwitz and are forced to resent the dead? Every day I meet my poor mother, I see how she withers away, and still I take the crust she has saved for me. Yes, it's true. I blame you. I blame you for staying here when you are supposed to be gone. I blame you that you share in what is supposed to only be ours. And most of all I blame you that my body aches, that my hunger plunges the dagger into my mother's chest. But I am grateful too. When I suck on the stale bread, feel it soften in my mouth, I thank you for absolving me of my crimes. That is the thing. Earthly Auschwitz cannot exist without Heavenly Auschwitz.'

'Well, I'm glad you are here,' said Michal. 'Dying is a lonely business. Your anger, your resentment. They are my anchors. I know it sounds strange, Jakub. But I don't think I'm ready to leave.'

Morning.

The whispers and moans of waking. Jakub turned restlessly and waited for the call to muster. Michal woke with a start. He looked at Jakub in fright and vaulted from the bunk. 'Today,' he said and ran off down the aisle. All around, a rising tide of voices. Jakub shuffled across and stretched into the new space. Georg was stirring, his eyes easing open then falling shut again. A single voice rose above the others: the block elder. An announcement. Jakub could not make out the words. He leaned across the side rail and looked towards the front. The barrack doors had not been opened. Georg sat up and crawled to the edge. 'What's happening?' said Jakub. 'Michal...I think it's begun.' As if conjured by the mention of his name, Michal appeared again beside the bunk, grinning like a madman. 'It's Tadeusz,' he said between breaths. 'Someone's killed the bastard.'

Jakub and Georg pulled Michal back up into the bed. 'Last night,' he continued. 'In the dust storm. An SS patrol found him this morning. The son of a bitch attacked a boy over near the fence. Poor kid was still alive, lying naked in the dirt, covered in blood. Someone must have seen it, come to save him.'

'After curfew?' It was Georg.

'I know. They can't make head or tail of it. Who'd have the strength to strangle that brute, anyway? We, who are starving?'

'Strangled?'

'Yes. Can you believe it? Big, muddy handprints around his neck. Crushed his throat.'

The barrack doors were opened at noon. The men spilled out onto the camp road, kicking up the dirt that had settled in the night, and hurried towards the assembly ground. The day would be spent at attention. The jubilation at Tadeusz's demise was tempered by the news that soon followed: the boy had died. In the barracks, some spoke of him as a martyr: the one who had given his life so that the world could be rid of a monster. Arnošt Flusser died picking flowers, they said, as if freeing him from the savagery of his death.

Jakub turned against the flow of bodies. He ran between the barracks towards the fence that separated the Family Camp from the quarantine blocks. When he came to the dandelion patch he fell to his knees. Around him, a scuffle of boot prints. The patch was bare. If there had been dandelions, the boy must have picked them. Jakub saw that the dirt was raised. In his head, a familiar chant. *AH, ẠH, A̲H, AV, ẠV, A̲V.*

He thrust his hand into the dirt.

9

BIRKENAU BIIe, THE FORMER GYPSY CAMP

Their bodies no longer radiated the warmth of the living and so they huddled together five, six, seven to a bunk to stave off the chill. Each night a new battle raged, to be the furthest from the wall, from the wind, to find the one who had eaten well, whose heart beat a little stronger, whose skin was not bursting with pustules, whose rags were not stained with brown dysenteric slop, who could be trusted not to try, when everyone else was asleep, to prise away a small soup tin or serviceable shoes, who might not, when the siren sounded before dawn, be found stiff against the straw.

They counted the days by the stubble on their flaking scalps and the angular shadows of their protruding bones. They knew it was an imperfect measure, that the body's regenerative ability slows as it starves, that there comes a time when the skin is just a paper sail across hardened calcium masts and it can retreat no further. Only those who had recently arrived still possessed a sense of real time. So it was that Daša Roubíčková knew she had been in Birkenau for three weeks. The bruises had almost healed, a swamp of yellowed puddles. She brushed her hand across the numbered cloth patch on her shirt then reached over to pull Irena close.

Tomorrow they would know if they had been selected.

When the door slid open at the platform, she could see nothing. For almost a day they had been locked inside, standing, pitching to and fro with every jerk of the train. It had been dark, the tiny window slats obscured by heads craning upwards for air. Her eyes adjusted with the dawn, drawing faces on the shadows around her. They were all the same, exhausted, desperate for this journey to end. She looked to the back wall. Irena was sitting on her case, her face buried in her palms.

A blast of icy wind threw her backwards into heaving flesh. From outside, a savage explosion of dogs and, behind it, the barking of men. And the air: heavy, sweet, rancid.

'Out! Out! Leave everything where it is. Out! *Raus! Raus*!'

Batons clanged against the sidings. Sobs, screams. The noise spilled over them as a thousand prisoners tumbled onto the platform. At the door, men in filthy striped suits and caps reached out to help the straggling few. She felt a cold hand against hers, a violent pull. Then a voice, surprised, choking. 'Daša?'

She looked into the man's face, his darkened cheeks, his wild eyes. 'Can it be—' the man exclaimed.

'Bohuš?' said Daša.

'Listen...' A swarm of SS pushed through the crowd, snarling, hitting bags from hands. 'You are twenty. Irena is eighteen. You are both hard workers. Remember, Daša, please.'

From a loudhailer nearby: 'Attention. Form two lines on the platform, men on one side, women on the other. If you are ill or do not have the strength to walk, identify yourselves and you shall be taken by ambulance...'

'Daša,' continued Bohuš. 'Be smart. You must appear strong, whatever it takes.' A guard drew closer. Bohuš pinched Daša's cheeks, first one, then the other. Traces of pink appeared in her face. 'Your father is here. I will tell him you've come. Look out for me near the trains, I will find you.' He pushed past her, began to climb up. 'Daša,' he whispered, eyes locked on her finger. 'The ring. Swallow it.' And with that he disappeared into the carriage.

The line moved forward at a slow, steady pace. At the front, a thin man in a deep green uniform glanced at the arrivals, pointing left or right. Occasionally, he stopped one, asked a question, considered the answer, looked them over again, then pointed. He was, she could see, deaf to their pleas. Couples who arrived holding hands were sent in opposite directions. Parents and children too. They would cry, scream, but he ignored them. All around, SS men watched on, talking to one another, joking, laughing.

'Age?' The man stared through her. His black hair was slicked down on his scalp, the widow's peak pointing at her in accusation. Bolts of lightning flashed on his collar.

'Twenty. I come from the country, a hard worker.' She spoke slowly, to make sure he could understand, but more so for the pain of metal in her parched throat. The rumbling splutter of an engine, a momentary distraction. The man turned away then back to her. He pointed to the right. 'My sister—' she began but a guard shoved her aside. Daša walked towards the huddled mass, checking over her shoulder. Irena skipped up to the man. Daša could see that she was pointing, nodding in earnest. The man pointed. Right. Daša felt the ring dislodge, slip down her gullet.

Neither one could remember the last time she'd seen the other naked. Daša did her best to shield Irena from the lurid gazes of those who came to leer. It was enough that the girl was still at the age of misplaced shame and bodily confusion. But to be stripped, to have all her hair shaved—it was too much. They stood in the vast chamber and waited. When it was full, the door slammed shut. All around, silence, then frantic whispers. Someone began to cry, then another. Low moans. The *shema*, sung in a soft, rising undertone, trapped in concrete.

From above: creaks and pops, then a long, steady hiss. Daša looked up to the network of copper pipes and held her breath.

Water. Scalding, blessed water.

The block supervisor, a surly Slovak with charcoal teeth, took an instant dislike to her.

'That's the problem with you *mischlinge*,' the woman said on the first night. 'Part of you believes in their nonsense. You think yourself above us, that your Aryan blood somehow makes you superior. And goddamn it, you're right. Look at you: plump, proud, strong. But stay here long enough and I swear…' And with that, the Slovak slapped the soup tin from Daša's hand, splattering her feet in brown muck. Daša scraped out the dregs and pushed them between her lips.

The breakfast ration stabbed at her gut and Daša hurried to the latrine block at the end of the camp. She shoved open the door, the odour of burning flesh overwhelmed by the stench of shit. The fumes of quicklime scorched her eyes and through her tears she could just make out the rows of figures crouched over holes along a concrete plinth. Daša found a place and squatted over the putrid hollow, clenching her anus until she could reach underneath and make a net with her fingers. Watery slop dribbled through. She closed her eyes and pushed. A terrible cramp gave way to an explosion of sludge. And then, something hard on her palm. Daša snatched her hand away, rubbed the ring against her shirt then slid it under her tongue.

The morning passed in a daze. They were unable to make sense of this place that was not Theresienstadt. Daša kept watch over her sister. 'I thought maybe it would be over when I woke up,' the younger girl had said when they first woke, her hand rubbing her naked scalp. Daša had no words to comfort her. She thought instead of Bohuš and wondered if he had merely been a spectre. Would it be the same with the others? Ludvík? Auntie Gusta? Jakub? Shmuel? As she was led back from the shower, Daša had been overcome by the vastness of the camp. Buildings, fences, soldiers as far as the eye could see. Through it all, a procession of phantoms.

She climbed onto the bunk and nestled in beside Irena. 'Daša?' said Irena, but Daša lifted her finger to her lips. 'Today we rest,' she said. They drifted off to the hum of muffled chatter and the fluttering of the coarse sheets that hung from each bunk. Before sleep claimed her, Daša thought of Žižkov and how Marcela and Hana might also be asleep behind the gauze. Her mind conjured the smell of *svíčková*, and then nothing.

Panicked shrieks jolted them awake. Outside, the howl of a siren then an almighty explosion. The bunk rattled, throwing the two girls against the wall. The barrack lights dimmed and brightened with a buzz. Nearby, the mutterings of prayer. Daša pulled aside the sheet and swung her legs over the bunk's edge. 'Come,' she said to Irena, and jumped to the ground. Another blast followed by volleys of gunfire. The earth shook. She joined the stampede towards the barrack door, pulling Irena behind her.

They spilled into the afternoon light, their hopes hitched to the sound of fearsome battle. 'Liberation!' shouted one as if the word itself would set her free. 'The Red Army!' cried another. A loud cheer went up. *Hurrah!* The forest beyond the barbed wire was aflame, grey smoke billowing to the sky. Along the road outside the camp, a convoy of flatbed trucks roared by, German soldiers poised with pointed guns. The women rushed at the wire, stopping only at the last moment, when reason returned to temper their frenzy. Daša pushed her way through the scrum. 'The chimney,' said the women next to her. Daša looked out at the forest and saw the chimney was gone. The earthen spire that had only yesterday spouted ash was now itself consumed by flame. A crescendo of gunfire, another blast, some lone shots and then silence. Only the crackle of burning birch. The women looked around, waited. Then: trucks rumbling slowly back along the road.

By nightfall it was quiet. Whatever had happened, it was over. Better to forget.

Days of filth and boredom, the unforgiving monotony of suspended existence. They were not here to work, nor were they here to die. They were here only to wait.

Twice a day they left the barracks to be counted. An hour, two, they stood, stripped to the waist, the rain like daggers on their skin. The SS men counted with deliberation. They had sickened of the starving female form, but these new arrivals were different. There was still enough of a shape on them to bring to mind their women back home. Some they made jump or skip or dance or run or just fall to their knees in the mud. The skinny ones, the sickly, the damned—those who had become one with the place—they simply marked off in their folders and moved on. Occasionally there was a selection: for reassignment, for transport, for death. When it was over most of the women returned to their bunks.

Waiting, they sewed, scrubbed and scraped. They talked of home and family, averting their eyes from the smokestacks beyond the forest that, once again, were breathing fire. They talked of war, of shifting fronts, approaching freedom. From it they learned a new language, more useful than any other. Even here it was possible to gain privilege if you knew how, who. This Kapo, that guard. They listened out for voices at the fence, the barking of dogs, the approaching ruckus of another transport. Together, they rushed to the edge, called out to those who had arrived, for food, for water, for clothes, for anything that could be thrown over the wire.

Long after the latest train had been emptied, after most of the women had given up and turned back, Daša lingered at the fence, the hum of electric current charming the hairs on her arm, and waited for Bohuš. The men from the Kanada kommando stood on the ramp with mountains of bags, hauling them onto carts and trucks. She spotted him, watched as he ducked away under the guise of collecting more bags. He came close, tossed a small package wrapped in cloth over the fence. 'Your father sends his love.'

'And Auntie Gusta?' she said. 'Still no word?'

'Look.' He pointed beyond the wire to the far end of the camp. 'For a while everyone sent from the fortress was there. Now they are gone. I didn't want to tell you before. I'm sorry.'

After the first week, Daša thought about home. She must write to her mother. For days she had been composing the letter in her head. *My dearest golden Mummy...*

Paper: three bread rations.

Pencil: a stick of mouldy butter.

Delivery: she had yet to consider her options.

Daša sat on the furthest hole in the latrines, facing the wall, scribbling furiously. When the lead grew blunt, she bit at the surrounding wood, refashioned the point. Her life, here, on two small pages. In each word, her own mortality, that of Irena, their father. She omitted nothing, just to be sure.

She read it over, pictured her mother holding it. It was not goodbye, but if it was, it would be enough. She folded the paper, stood and headed back to the barracks. A figure loomed at the door, blocking the way.

'*Mischlinge!*' The Slovak stood with her hand out. 'The paper.'

At the evening roll call, she was ordered to step forward. An officer stood, rigid, shielding the letter from the rain. Daša dared not look around. Twelve hundred eyes bored into her back.

'Who here can translate this? Step forward now or nobody eats.'

The Slovak waded into the group, pushed one of the girls to the front. Daša did not recognise her.

'Czech?'

'*Jawohl.*'

'Read it.'

The girl scanned the letter, drew a breath. 'It say...' she began in stilted German. 'It say: My dearest gold Mother. I am moved away from Terezín, off east.' The girl looked up at Daša. 'We have long train ride together. Here I am...healthy. Sister too. It is big place with many of...' A pause. 'Many of friends. Do not be fear for me. We are treating us well. We have big food and warm bed. I am waiting for chance to work again and I write you soon to tell about it. I miss you very much, dearest Mother, and also family. But I know'—the girl was barely looking at the page—'soon we be together again. Please give to everyone big kisses that I love them and always am thinking of them. Your biggest daughter, Daša.'

'That's it?'

'Yes, sir.'

Crawling, crawling. Hands sinking into the mud. So close. If only...

Daša woke from dreams of electric wire. Her ears were throbbing. The taste of metal on her engorged tongue. It was coming back to her, the beating, the horsewhip, black, polished boots. Her head filled with Irena's desperate howls. For a moment she caught the Slovak, arms around her sister, holding Irena back. A jolt—the ring was gone—but Daša could not break free of her delirium, could not sit up. Through puffy slits she could just make out a figure standing above her, observing. The face was warm, caring. It did not belong in this place. 'Try to drink,' it said. She looked at the glass, at the liquid they called coffee, and closed her eyes. Not yet. It still hurt to breathe.

The infirmary block was like all the others. Long, wooden, hollow. A home for dysentery, for typhoid. There was little medicine to speak of, only rest and the promise of a less disturbed sleep. The orderlies fussed over Daša, daubed at her wounds with dirty rags, scraped away the crusted blood. When her sister came, they busied themselves elsewhere, ignored the precious bounty she carried. *There is a man who gives it to them*, they whispered over soiled linen. Irena waited for them to move away, then leaned in close. 'It's okay,' she said and lifted her tongue to reveal the golden band. 'I have it.'

Another week had passed.

For three days she slept, oblivious to the bodies that climbed over her, the one that clung to her at night. She recognised her sister's breath, the even flow of whispered stories of the lake at Sudoměřice. She was woken only for roll calls, when she stood in a trance while she was counted. Twice a day Irena held a metal rim to her mouth and she sipped. Small clumps of bread passed her lips on pinched fingers and she waited for them to dissolve.

On the fourth day she stood up and headed to the cubicle near the front of the barrack. Her knuckles smarted against the flimsy wood. She did not wait for a reply, just turned the handle and stepped inside. The Slovak sat on a low bench, tearing at crusts of bread. A grunt.

'The letter. You knew…'

'Of course.'

'But you…'

'Tell me, *mischlinge*, to whom would you have given it? Your boyfriend in Kanada? It was a fool's errand. You would have been killed for sure. The guards, they'd have taken your letter, taken your ring'—she registered the surprise in Daša's face—'and seen you shot for sabotage. As it was, you wrote a dream. You are a young girl. There is no harm in that. I knew you'd be punished, but not death. Not now. Things here have changed.'

'And the girl?'

'She has been transferred to the main camp to work as a nurse. Now she eats, she has warm quarters. I don't expect to hear from her again.' The Slovak held out a piece of bread. Daša sat on the woman's bunk and pocketed the crust.

'Why me?'

'In this place, why anything? To protect myself. To save your friend. To help the little nurse. Because I, too, was a mother, a sister. Because I am hungry, bored. Because when this is over I want someone to remember that I was here, in this world. Listen up, *mischlinge*. Tomorrow there will be a special selection. A flax mill in Silesia has purchased two hundred of you to replace the boys they've sent to the front, and for some reason they want only Czechs. They are sending a foreman to interview possible workers. When they call for volunteers at the roll call, be sure to step forward. Take your sister. Remember, you are weavers. Your family are weavers. All you have ever known is weaving.'

~

The next morning, Daša was ready. She had stood before the man, told him of their mother, her millinery. He asked about fabrics, material, machinery. Yes, she said, she was familiar with them. Her sister even more so. Her head filled with the voice of Pan Durák, the way he spoke of clothes as living beings, and his words became hers. The man tested her with numbers, seemed satisfied with the answers. When it was over he jotted something in his notebook and thanked her for her time. The kindness in his words was jarring.

She waited to hear their numbers at the next roll call, but there was no selection and her heart grew heavy. Snow tumbled from the blackened clouds, the colour of midnight. Irena looked at her, anxious. 'Maybe they haven't decided,' she said. They lined up again in the evening. When the counting was done a different man stepped forward. 'If you are called, approach.' He read the list with indifference and she watched the women step forward. More than fifty, sixty, seventy. Then her number. And Irena's. Daša looked for the Slovak but she had returned to the barracks.

In rows of five, one hundred women march along the road in the direction of the forest. They follow the path between the ruins of Krema IV and the belching stack of Krema V until they reach the Sauna block. They recognise it in the fading light, see in it hope for what is to come: the water scalds, a welcome fire. As they file out, dripping, naked, they are thrown new dresses and shoes, ill-fitting but clean. Wind whips through the trees, lashing the fabric to their skin. They march onwards, past the Kanada Barracks and come to a stop beside Krema III. There they stand throughout the night, until the dawn comes, and with it, the shape of a third-class train.

Behind the wire, inmates stumble from barracks for the morning roll call. She watches them flock into the muddy fields, gather in rows as she makes her way down the ramp towards the train. She is leaving this world, will never speak of it. As she nears the carriage door, her eye catches a lonely figure standing by the fence. In his face she sees her own, her sisters'. She pulls at Irena's arm, points in the man's direction. He brings his fingertips to his lips. They do not see his tears, of joy, of relief, of farewell.

10
SACHSENHAUSEN

She watched him leave the Family Camp from behind the wire. He marched in step, turning to catch one last glimpse. Then another. *Take it,* she had said, holding out the stale crust. He snatched it greedily from her fingers, felt his hand brush against hers. Little more than bone. She cried while he ate and he began to mutter, *Sorry...sorry.* She wiped away a tear and ran her tongue along the shimmering trail it left on her wrist. *No,* she said. *Eat. Just eat.* He felt it crumble in his dry mouth. He sucked on the crumbs and waited for the flow of saliva. It isn't true, that the body cannot forget. It had been like this for weeks, since the day they were scheduled to die. He could feel his throat tense, a memory of swallowing. The bread stung as it tumbled through him. *Sorry,* he said again. His voice, hoarse.

It had come at last, the day they'd been expecting. Dawn. The camp filled with soldiers. He was told to report to the schoolroom. Block 31. He stood in line, stripped to the waist, as the doctor made his way across the room. A pinch. A prod. The thin skin on his arm puckered, unable to settle outwards. He flattened it back with his palm. By the afternoon he had received new orders. *Prepare yourself,* the man had said. *You are moving on.* He ran to her with the news, but she was not coming. She was old, weak, a woman. She had not even been examined. *Please,* she had said. *Don't remember me like this.* He marched away in the early light. How could he leave her? Outside the gate a truck was waiting. Georg marched beside him, almost unrecognisable but for the rhythm in his step.

She stood against the wire, still. As he stared at her, in a flash, her skin dried out and cracked, her body atrophied, and creeping wisps of earth sprouted from the ground to fill the spaces. The sky was empty above them. An engine turned and sprang to life. Puffs of black smoke. He stepped up onto the truck. It was the last he would see of his mother: a pillar of dirt.

From afar: *Jakub. Jakub, please...They're evacuating the camp.*

He lay in a shroud that might have been his father's *tallis*, drifting in the darkness. The sounds of purgatory, uncertain yet reassuring, floated past his sinking grave. His eyes were glued shut, his skin torn open. He had come apart but was somehow whole again. He remembered the skies filling with the shriek of impending hellfire while he staggered forward. Sirens, growing louder, pushing him into the field. He turned towards shelter but was chased away with barks and snarls and the tips of bayonets. Metallic fists fell around him like hail. He watched the others, his comrades, disappearing in clouds of pink mist, their loads crashing to the ground and sinking into the dirt. For a moment he was flying. Then nothing.

He woke to a stiff cocoon of hospital linen, surrounded by panes of shifting light, a constellation of swooping angels. *Here.* A hand slipped behind his head and pulled him forward. A lukewarm liquid splashed across his lips. *Drink.* The faint whistling continued inside his head from… from…It came back in fragments. Every day it was the same: sent into the fields to clear the rubble. The bombing was relentless and still the Schwarzheide plant churned on, synthesising fuel, fabricating hope.

'Jakub! For God's sake, listen. You have to get up. They're moving us.'

'Georg?'

'Yes.'

'How long have I…?'

'Two days. The wound in your leg…'

Jakub drew his arm up from under the sheet and rubbed at his eyes. Georg's haggard face emerged. 'The front is moving closer. They are evacuating the camp. At least if we walk there's a chance…Here.' Georg grabbed Jakub's arm and slung it across his shoulder. 'I'll help you up.' He braced his knee against the wooden bedframe.

'Save your strength. I'm not coming.' Jakub went limp, a dead weight. Georg heaved, twice, a third time, but grew tired from the effort. 'There's no point. I can't walk.'

'It is just an infection. Rest on my shoulders if you need. I'm not leaving you here.'

'I'm not moving. This is the last place.'

'Please Jakub...'

'Don't be an ox.'

Jakub reached into his shirt pocket and pulled out the small clay pellet that had been digging into his breast. 'Do you remember Tadeusz?'

Georg felt Jakub press the hardened dirt into his hand.

'Take this, Georg. It will keep you safe on your march. And when you get home, when this is all over, take it to the bank of the Vltava, the one closest to where the Maharal rests, and bury it in the mud. Next time the creature wakes, let him rise with the force of our murdered souls.'

'Come,' Georg said with a smirk. 'Your head we can fix later.'

'Your father...This dirt, I couldn't tell you...He swore me to...'

'Jakub, I know. The book of dirt. I've heard it too. And many more. They made a fortress within a fortress, he and his friends, its ramparts built of legend. Those poor men, great sages one and all, cut down by circumstance. Any other time and it might have been different. But in that prison? What did they have but each other and the comfort of dreams?'

'So I thought too. Until Tadeusz...'

'Killed in a cloak of dust. It's tempting, of course. To ascribe it to a clay man. But I'm afraid whoever killed that brute was all too human. Who didn't want him dead? And coming upon him in the act with that poor Flusser boy. Some horrors even the devil won't abide.'

Still, Georg closed his hand around the clay. After the bomb had fallen, after he had watched Jakub hurtling through the air in a spray of dirt like a discarded doll, after the silence had passed, Georg rushed across to mourn his friend, to stand over his broken body and utter the words he wished he could have said for his parents, his brothers, all his people: *Blessed is the true judge.* He had crouched to kiss Jakub's forehead, a final goodbye, but instead felt the warm rush of air from between his friend's lips. The soil had turned to peat in the blast, wrapping around Jakub and cushioning his fall. Georg reached down and helped Jakub to his feet. They stood at the bomb crater's edge and he brushed the dirt from Jakub's clothes. The blast had ripped a hole in the fabric at his calf, a gorge of open flesh filled with bloody loam. 'I'll get you to the hospital.'

The doctor cleaned it, poured in alcohol and sewed the wound together. 'You're lucky,' he said. 'The mud staunched the flow.' The following day, Georg helped Jakub hobble back to the site and watched as his friend sifted through the earth until he found a single hardened piece of clay unlike all the rest. They returned to news of liquidation: Schwarzheide was to be emptied. They would have to walk. Those willing to work would be exempted and transported by truck to Sachsenhausen, the main camp in the north. Jakub stepped forward, careful to look steady on his feet. Georg stayed back a moment, then joined him. But there was no work to be done at the other camp. Jakub and Georg waited in their new barracks, lost among the sea of unfamiliar faces. Jakub scratched at the wound, felt the molten lava of sepsis throb beneath his skin. Three days after they arrived, Jakub collapsed outside the barracks.

'Georg?'

'Yes.'

'Go. Please.'

Jakub turned to the wall and rested his face against the straw pillow. His eyes grew heavy.

A shock of blonde hair and the girl was gone. He chased her through a paper city, the ground tearing beneath his feet. All around him towers of books lurched in the storm. In the distance, he could make out the roar of an open furnace. She was leading him on towards the darkness. He ran blindly, panicked. He stopped to catch his breath, bent over. When he looked up he saw that the street had changed. The smell of smoke, ash, stripped of the sickly sweetness of burnt flesh, drifted from the city's glowing edge. The street shrank as the towers staggered inwards to consume him. At their foundations he saw the bent forms of old friends—Langer, Muneles, Jakobovits—a band of crumpled Atlases, their faces twisting under the weight. He jerked forward, tried to push his way through as they closed in around him, but it was too late. He was in the room again, in the old converted barn, at a desk sifting through the dirt he had found inside a weathered prayer book. They sat in their assigned spots, soldiers of clay, going about their duties. A blizzard of white cards blew around the room, each one streaked with crusted filth. He looked down to the pile before him and could see it pulsing to an irregular beat. From within, laughter, the forgotten sound of carelessness, of freedom. Then, the sound of his name. He thrust his hand into the dirt and sent it spilling onto the floor. He kept digging, throwing aside muddy clumps, filling the room around him. The laughter grew louder with each fistful. Soon the hole was deep enough for him to reach inside with his arm. He felt around, surprised at the warmth, until his finger caught on something: a delicate tripwire. He tugged at it. Nothing. Again. Propping his other arm against the desk's flat surface for leverage, he grasped at the thread and pulled it out of the hole. It was shorter than he had expected and coated in earth. He ran the thread between his lips and wiped it clean. It hung limply between his fingers: a single, delicate strand of blonde hair.

Jakub R held it to his breast and waited for death.

II

PRAGUE

25/XII.44

Our golden beloved mother

I have just had lunch and got up to write to my dears. I am writing this in such a lovely room, that is the toilet. Today is Christmas Day and I remember how you visited us last year. At the time, of course, we indeed did not think that we would still not be home this year. However, already next year we will certainly be home and make up then for the whole of the three years.

The last strain of the air-raid siren echoed down the deserted street. From above, silence—no hum of engines, no piercing whistle, no shaking thunder. Piles of garbage clustered like barricades on the kerb, spilling onto the snow-covered road. A low wind licked at the corner of a hastily pasted sign—*Closed for the Victory of the Reich*—on the door to Žofie Sláviková's grocery. Žižkov was at peace.

In the coal cellar of 13 Biskupcova Street, Františka Roubíčková flicked through an old copy of *Kinorevue* and waited for her neighbours to leave. Yet again they had crouched together in the shadows, in the chill of the bluestone crypt, those few who had not been taken, those not blighted by the yellow star, and braced for tremors that did not come. Liberation was near, if only they could live to see it. Františka was tired of this paranoid waltz, the way it insinuated itself into her anticipation. She resented the way it struck fear in her daughters' eyes, how it set back her quotas at the factory and forced her to work late, how it chased her tired legs from the tram to the nearest shelter, how it turned her fingers to matchsticks as she scoured her purse to find her papers lest the warden turn her away or, worse, report her. It was a farce, another way to shackle them inside this national prison. But after the November attack, when Allied bombs had rained down on a suburban electricity station and killed four people, one could never be certain. And so she had no choice but to relent, to cower, to wait for whatever might drop from the sky.

Why, though, must it always be such a bother? When the siren bellowed across the network of loudspeakers, Františka had been frying schnitzels. Christmas was approaching and Marcela had just returned from the country, her case full of treats. The southern rail was safe from strafing aircraft and so they could feast, both here and in Silesia. The fillets sizzled in the oil, hissing as the crust browned around them. It was an art: knowing the precise time to rescue them before the meat had dried or the crumbs had burnt. That the alarm should sound then, at the very moment she had put a new batch in the pan...Františka struck the bench with her spatula and cursed the clouds.

She had wept the moment she saw Daša's handwriting. Only a fortnight before, Pan Durák had appeared at her door in a panic—the girls had been transported east from the fortress town—and they cried in each other's arms. Then this. The envelope gave nothing away, her name and address in a stiff masculine scrawl. On the back a man's name, unfamiliar, and an address in Germany. She held it to the light, anxiety creeping through her at the thought of all Daša had risked, all she had come through. *My dearest*

Mummy...The note was short. Again they had been moved, this time to a garment factory in Silesia. *Write back, dear Mummy. Let me know you have received my news.* And, if it was not too much trouble, send some underwear.

Now, Františka looked across at her two other daughters crouched in the cellar. She had not yet mustered the courage to tell them of the other letter, the one on official Gestapo paper. The age restriction had been lifted. Marcela and Hana were to report in the New Year, to be taken and resettled in one of the camps for *mischlinge*.

Františka could not bear the thought of being alone.

> *You ask how is the postal service. Parcels arrive perfectly. We hugely enjoy the taste of everything. The parcel with the schnitzels was unfortunately delayed somewhere and, I hear, arrived all mouldy. It arrived at the same time as the last one. Mr B had to throw out all the bread, all the schnitzels and some cakes. The rest he saved. He is very nice and very busy with it. You ask whether you are doing it right with the contents. It is absolutely correct...*

The tram clattered unsteadily through the snow towards the city's black heart—the Gestapo office in Peček Palace. Around it, the road was empty, only the snaking trails of bicycle tyres. Prague had fallen into disrepair, its trams a fleet of moving wrecks. Františka braced herself for each shrieking halt. Litter filled the wooden slats at her feet.

'Madame?' The girl was no older than Marcela, her long dress a bright field of flowers, a premonition of spring. Františka wondered if they'd met, shared a class, played in the courtyard, this girl and her own. The New Year brought only the prospect of better tidings for such a child. In a perverse way, it helped to know that there were still those who could frequent the cinema, dine at restaurants, scrape finely chopped offal from snail shells in feigned elegance, rifle through racks of fashionable dresses at the emporia; those afforded the luxury of boredom, of searching out ways to fill their day. Františka tucked her foot back under the seat and let the girl sit next to the tram window.

She got off near the museum and hurried across the thoroughfare to the park. Below her, the great stretch of Wenceslas Square. From above, the stony eyes of gargoyles perched on top of the Prague Museum followed Františka as she walked towards the great columns and disappeared into Peček Palace.

'Come in, please. Sit down. I am surprised to see you again.'

Františka looked around at the sparse chamber. 'I've had other concerns. Time has its way. This—'

'Is what happens if you're not sent to the front.' The clerk shifted in his chair. 'Paper warfare,' he continued. 'I had hoped for a more active role in the organisation but in winter it is some mercy. Perhaps there is glory in shelter. My wife certainly thinks so.'

'I should have thanked you.'

'It wasn't my doing. I was pleased for you nonetheless. When you stopped coming I knew. You weren't the type to give up. A few of us had a wager. I have you to thank for six cigarettes. Tell me something Paní—'

'Roubíčková. It is my husband's name.'

'Yes, of course. So tell me, do you watch the planes?'

'I run to the cellar like everyone else. But yes, I have seen the odd one.'

'I've seen them all. I suspect they use the square as a waypoint. We are forbidden from taking shelter so we run to the windows. This place is safe enough. If the bombs should drop, assuming there isn't a direct hit, we won't come to any harm so long as we move to the middle. But this city is charmed. The planes have no appetite for its beauty. So we just watch them pass over in waves, stalking their way to the Fatherland while we play a fanfare of sirens in the streets below. You know, my parents are still in Berlin. I fear for Mother's heart. The years have weakened it.'

'I've come about my daughters.'

'I'm afraid it's no longer possible.'

'No. The others. Last week I received this.'

'Oh—' The man looked at the paper. 'Yes, sorry.'

'They don't know. What little they have of Christmas I wasn't going to take away. But it's almost the New Year and—' She pulled the little purse from her pocket and emptied it on the table.

The man leaned forward and inspected the jewellery.

'There is cash too. I have managed to save. Just take them from your list. Find a way.'

'You've never asked about my family. You know, all the times you came and begged to see your daughters you never once thought to ask.'

'I...'

'Three daughters. All under ten. My wife still promises me a son but we've finished. The thought that he might be conscripted, sent to the front. Not in this war, but there's always the next. I would worry from the moment he was born.' He scooped up the rings and carefully dropped them back into the purse. 'Take it. You will want to wear them again. Italy and France have fallen. Greece too. Stalingrad is a memory. The Reich is collapsing. The Protectorate...he will hold on until his dying breath but eventually...' The man pushed back in his chair and stood up. 'I ask only one thing in return. When the time comes, find me. Wherever I am, with the Russians, the Americans. Speak for me, for what I've done.' He scribbled his name on a sheet of notepaper and handed it to her. 'Tear up the letter, forget it ever came. Nobody will come for them.' He ushered her to the door. 'Take care of your girls, but also spare a thought for mine.'

The afternoon sun had turned the ground to a dirty grey mush. Františka Roubíčková stepped out onto Bredovská Street, pulled the sheet from her pocket and dropped it to the ground. With each step she cast him further from her mind until, when she climbed aboard the tram back towards Žižkov, he was lost to her, to history, forever. There will only be this: once there was a Gestapo man who sought in her an absolution she could not give.

So Mummy dearest, this is all for today, since I must still write to Marcelka and Hanička so that they are not angry with me that I never write to them. I wish you all a happy and merry New Year. Let it be happier than the last.

With many memories I say goodbye to you and send my kisses,
Your only Daša

12
THE MARCH FROM SACHSENHAUSEN

They did not stop to rest. Throughout the night they had walked along the road. The sun rose soon after they passed the second village, where roosters crowed to wake the locals, who stumbled from their shanties and stood at the roadside so they could spit and curse at the ragtag parade. Georg threw his clogs away before morning; the wood had sliced purple arches into his swollen skin. As he trudged on, he tore the blanket on his shoulders into strips. He asked one of the guards if he could stop to relieve himself. He squatted on a nearby knoll, his pants strung across his calves as sludgy droplets fell beneath him. The guard watched on, his bulky frame perched on an old bicycle, as Georg wrapped his feet in the blanket.

To a volley of threats and blows, they marched until sunset, when they began to slow. Georg lurched to the centre of his column and let the miserable stream of bodies push him forward. He looked at the ground, at the stumbling feet of the man in front of him. He did not look up when the shots rang out, or when the barks and screams and sounds of ripping flesh shattered the country air. Only the cheerful trill of a bicycle bell pulled him from the monotony of the march. The guards laughed like children and roared like beasts.

Another village. They were diverted from the road to an open field. Some fell to the ground, kissing the earth like it might open up and swallow them, steal them away from this glacial hell. Others plucked at the grass, hungrily snatching it to their mouths, chewing the blades. Nearby, a commotion. One man had found a snail. He chomped on it, shell and all, while those around him watched with envy. At the field's edge the guards had gathered to eat and drink: sausages, bread, canned meat, cheese and schnapps. They sang and laughed and shot indiscriminately into the horde of prisoners. They threw the leftover food into the mud, crushed it beneath their boots, then stood around to drench it in streams of their own piss. Then they gathered their columns and sorted the thousands of prisoners into groups of five hundred, to continue the march to Wittstock. The prisoners close by set upon the discarded slop, clawing at the mud with their bony fingers, digging out what morsels they could salvage. They swallowed them without chewing, the bread softened by urine, only to vomit them back up with a force long forgotten by their bodies. Those who did not scrabble to pick up the slurry were pushed aside by others who did not hesitate to see if they might fare better. Men who, for a moment, had glimpsed hope, life, were now doubled over in agony, on their knees, shivering in the field. When the guards were ready to move on, they sauntered over to those men and shot them one after the other so the march would not be delayed.

At night, while the stars hid behind a fleece of clouds, they were guided only by the sting of bitumen under their feet. The blackness spared them the sight of blood and pus and sloughed skin that streaked the road in their wake. In the early morning, they passed another town, larger than the others. Not a soul stirred as they trudged through its main street. Even the animals slept in their pens. Suddenly, Georg began to laugh. Had he not once said to Jakub that one must walk humbly before the Lord? That one ought not make a spectacle of oneself? Well, here it was, the paradox of observance. If only Jakub could have been with him to see it. For was there ever a more humble walk than this? Or a greater spectacle?

Not that it mattered anymore. Jakub was dead. Of that Georg was certain. Sachsenhausen was already in flames when Georg had begun to march. The SS were burning everything they could in the rush to flee. Georg could not look back, could not bear to see the inferno consume his friend. He walked on, hand in his pocket, his fingers playing their melodies around the hardened clay. It did, he had to admit, have a music of its own. He would fulfil Jakub's dying wish and bury it on the banks of the river. It was in this act that he would honour his friend's memory.

On the third day they reached Wittstock. Georg thought they might stop. He had heard the guards talking, heard them say they would wait for other columns to join before continuing. All the camps around Berlin had been evacuated. Most of the prisoners were marching north to the port of Lübeck, where they were to board ships, destination undecided. Wittstock was to be their point of convergence, the town that would remove the last vestige of their individuality, their camp identities. The people of Wittstock came out to watch them, left buckets of water and stale bread along the way for those who dared break from the columns. By the great gothic cathedral, women turned away so that the prisoners would not see them cry. Onwards they marched, five hundred after five hundred, thousands of men and women, flanked by SS guards and the German prisoners enlisted from among their own ranks to accompany the procession, through the streets and past the north-western boundary. The pavement gave way to gravel and the houses to trees: a canopy of spring foliage, teeming with birds and forest creatures that peeked out with curiosity and horror.

Without warning they came to a stop. The guards blew their whistles, told the prisoners to rest. They would wait for further instructions. Until that time, anyone caught trying to escape would be shot. They scavenged like voles, picking at the grass and leaves, searching for hidden veins of water. Georg slumped against an immense trunk. The bark scraped at his back. He tried to pick at the crusted green barnacles but his nails could not withstand the pressure and tore from his fingertips. He had not eaten in three days.

He woke to the sound of engines. Around him, a swell of excitement. He could catch only phrases. They were calling it the camp in the Below Forest. Sachsenhausen's final outpost. Then familiar words: Red Cross. They arrived in convoy, trucks laden with boxes of supplies. They kept the engines running as they jumped from the cabins to unload the cargo. Georg watched from a distance as Red Cross men negotiated with the guards, had them sign off on the load. The cluster of heaving bodies untangled to form long lines, winding through the trees. When the Red Cross boxes were torn open, a great cheer resounded through the forest. Georg pressed his hands firmly to the tree roots and pushed, willing himself up to join the line, but he could not lift even what little was left of his body. They had been right, those around him: this was a camp like any other. There was no need for gas chambers or crematoria; here nature would play the executioner. Georg let the air fill his chest, then closed his eyes. Beside him, a crouching woman was nibbling at a sausage and some chocolate. Georg reached out to her but the woman stumbled backwards, clutched the food to her chest. Georg began to speak, pleading for a bite. The woman looked at him, confused by the strange words. From her muttering, he understood that she was, like many of those on the march, a simple woman from rural Hungary, recently evacuated from Ravensbrück and brought to join the great procession from Sachsenhausen. What did she know beyond simple survival? Georg slid his hand into his pocket and pulled out the clump of dirt. He held it out to the woman, pounded at his ribs with his free hand and tried to explain, but the woman staggered away. The first stars appeared through the tree canopy. Georg closed his eyes.

The next morning the guards blew their whistles and told the prisoners to reassemble in their columns. The march to Schwerin would commence before midday. Georg tried again to stand. He straightened his back against the trunk, pulled his knees to his chest and pushed with his legs. For a moment he lifted from the mossy earth but his strength deserted him and he landed back with a thud. He could see the columns begin to move. He could see the march had begun. He didn't, however, see the SS man approach from the side. He didn't see the guard unclip his holster. He didn't see the gun raised to his head. And he most certainly didn't see the flash that watered the old tree with his blood.

Many years later, it might have come to pass that an old Hungarian woman would, on her deathbed, remember the slight man with the wavy hair who struck at his chest and cried out with that strange word: *golem, golem, golem.* But she, too, perished, shot in the neck only two days later, when she collapsed on the roadside not far from the town of Zapel-Ausbar. And so nobody will ever know.

13

MERZDORF/RETURN TO PRAGUE

She no longer knows silence. For almost three years there has only been noise. The hubbub of an overcrowded street. Gasps, whimpers, sobs. The steady hum of electricity pulsing across deadly filaments. Dogs: panting, barking, scratching at wood. The swish of buckets filled with human waste. Screams, coughs. An orchestra of motors. The crunch of heavy boots. The screeching needle of the loom. The thud of falling sacks. No birds. Never any birds.

She no longer knows freedom. And so she stays: a day, another. She ventures outside the factory only to find him, the one who saved her. But they have gone, deserted the town. She watched them flee on bicycles. Now she sits in the attic watching over the pile of rags that is her sister. Of all that she has endured, this is the hardest. She counts the breaths, uneven, quick, and waits for the thick fluid to break up. It is a relief, the cough. It means the girl is alive. From the corner window she sees them swarm in, their uniforms like the spring. Their voices drift upwards; they speak in tongues and she is relieved at last not to understand. Their guns are slung loosely on their backs. In their hands, bottles held aloft to toast the day. They crash into the surrounding houses, disappear. She hears them laugh, sing, cheer. But beneath their sound, there are others, yelps, grunts. Their conquest is all consuming.

'You must leave.' She recognises the man's voice, is surprised he is still here. For months he had sat in the corner, watched over them. She had not considered that he would have nowhere to go. 'It is worse than I feared,' another voice says, a fellow worker. 'The Russians. They are telling us to take what we want. Follow their example.' She points at the rags. 'Nothing is too much, too weak.'

The plague of consumption had swept the garment factory in the spring, striking them down where they slept. Those who stayed strong kept vigil, watched the rash expand outwards on their bunkmates, waited for the cramps, the vomit, the hacking cough. She checked Irena every morning, was relieved to find no marks. She paid little attention to the fatigue, the weight loss—everyday symptoms of factory life. Then a cough, not like the others, with blood. The girl clutched at her chest with every shudder. Each day Daša went out to the station, unloaded the sacks, waited for his visit. A kind-faced station orderly, the villager who asked only for cigarettes. When she returned, her clothes stuffed with parcels, food wedged between the burlap, she would check on the girl and feel the feverish skin shrink from her touch.

She knows what she must do. She puts Irena on her shoulders and walks to the stairs. Down, past the looms, another floor, the same. Then the bottom, where the soldiers once camped, and out the door. On the western road she finds a house, its door open, food still on the table. She lays her sister on the bed, props her up with pillows. She pulls a couch across the door so it cannot be opened. She opens the window, climbs out onto the grass and closes the window behind her. They are everywhere, shouting down the streets, knocking on doors. She doesn't understand what they are saying but picks up the word for freedom; it is close to her own: *osvobozhdenny*. One of the men approaches her, grasps her wrist and talks as if she might speak his language. He strokes her hair and tries to pull her towards him. She wrenches herself free, slaps his face. He stumbles back then falls to his knees in peals of laughter. His bottle spills over and he grabs it and takes another swig. She stands her ground, doesn't flee: no more running. The soldier stands, composes himself and grabs her again, this time with both hands. His breath is warm against her face. He kisses her on the cheek, a chaste gesture, and lets go. The last she sees, he is laughing again.

She hurries on, unsure of what she is after. Only when she sees it does she know. A wheelbarrow, left upturned in the front yard of a cottage. She runs her finger along its wheel, checking for punctures. It holds firm to her touch. She turns it over like it is a precious chariot. The handles are worn, digging into her hands. She wheels it back towards the house careful to avoid any looters who might want to use it for their load. At last she arrives. The door does not budge; the window is still closed. Her sister is safe. She lays the barrow on its side and pushes up the windowpane. A jump. Another. On the third she catches the ledge and heaves herself onto the sill. From the bed, a familiar soft wheeze. She pulls the couch away from the door and brings her sister to the porch.

The barrow is gone. She expected it. She runs to the corner and looks down the street. It is being pushed by an older woman she knows from the factory. It is already full with food, blankets, silverware. From the surrounding houses she hears laughter and grunts, the shattering of glass. She runs towards the woman, sees that she can hardly stand up. The barrow is her crutch. In the distance, the grumble of approaching engines. She grabs the woman's shoulders, shoves her to the side. The woman falls to the ground and looks up at her with hollow eyes. There is no time. She empties the barrow beside the road and runs back to the house. Scooping up the pile of rags, she barely registers the weight of her sister. She begins to walk west.

'Come on, Irča,' she says. 'Let's go home.'

Františka Roubíčková unfolded Daša's letter again. The paper had already begun to age. The war was over. But where were her girls? In March she had answered a knock on her door and been met with a face she had never seen. His name, he said, was Josef. He had been in Birkenau with Ludvík. For several months they had shared a bunk. He had come, he said, to fulfil a promise to his friend. They had survived together until January, when the camp was evacuated. For days they marched in step, clutching at each other's shoulders for support. They huddled against one another at night in barns and open fields. They were, Josef said, like brothers. Ludvík had spoken of Františka and his girls. He spoke of love, of sacrifice. The rest of his life, Josef said, he had committed to making amends. On the fifth day, for no particular reason, he was shot in the head by one of their escorts. His body was dragged to the side of the road and the group marched on. 'I'm sorry,' Josef said, 'but I've no idea where it was.' Josef offered his hand in consolation; Františka was too stunned to take it. He tipped his hat and left. Františka returned to her chair and looked up at the last remaining picture of her husband.

That word: widow. She could grow into it no more than she had the others:

wife, divorcée. But what do you call a mother who has lost her children? No. She wouldn't accept it. She made enquiries. She owed it to Marcela, to Hana. They still harboured hope. Every day she went to the authorities to ask if there was any word about Daša and Irena Roubíčková. Always 'and', never 'or'. She could not leave one behind. The men who received her were sympathetic and counselled patience. Be comforted by the lack of news, they said. Most news, they said, was bad. And so she would return to 13 Biskupcova Street and take the letters from the Baťa shoebox and read them beneath Ludvík's watchful gaze. For those few moments they were together again. Her family.

A knock. Františka jerked, her thumb crumpling the page's edge. She cursed and tried to straighten the tissue paper. Time was already stealing her daughters' words away. Again, a knock. Františka turned the page over to protect the faint pencil marks from the light and stood up. Outside the window she noticed the unlikely shape of a wheelbarrow. She shrugged. War drags all kinds of flotsam in its wake. Františka bustled down the hallway and opened the door.

'*Ahoj*, Frantishku.' It was Radka Fialová from apartment four. 'I...I bring news.' Radka was the quietest of the neighbours. A kindly woman with no children, she had lost her husband in the first war and mourned him ever since. Františka would often make a point of speaking to her on the stairwell or in the street. 'It's the girls,' Radka continued. Františka felt a thump in her chest. She steadied herself against the doorframe. Perhaps it was the younger ones that Radka meant. Maybe they had got themselves into mischief. They were of that age now. But then...Oh God. *Most news that comes is bad.* Radka didn't wait for a reply. 'They are with me. Daša and Irena. They came just now. It...they wanted to warn you. They look... it is possible you won't recognise them. They asked I come first.' Františka Roubíčková could not move, could not breathe. Her knees grew weak. A single tear fell from her eye. Radka fumbled in her apron pocket, muttering to herself. She was not good at these things. She knew only how to be consoled, not to console. Her hand stopped suddenly and she pulled it out in a fist. 'Here,' she said. 'They said to give you this.'

And her fingers unfurled to reveal a simple gold ring.
The infinite rounding of life.

14

A man comes to a door in an ordinary apartment block, at 13 Biskupcova Street, in the city that is once again his home. He has come almost every day for over a month. In his hand, as always, is a gift: bigger, more precious every time he comes. The door is ajar; he hopes to recognise voices in the apartment.

He has come here, this man from the country, directly from the Old Town Square, where he stood before an idol, his idol—its fur coat, its large, pointed nose, and its long, thin, black beard resplendent in the sun—and prayed for those he has lost. His suit does not fit; it is too big. It was given to him when he returned to the city. He is sure there are fleas under the lining. Sometimes he talks to them, asks them for the courage that seems always to elude him. He tugs at his cuffs to make sure they cover his wretched mark. *A-1821.* All his experiences over these long years gather themselves in his head to one point: he must keep his word. He must see her. This time he will not run away. He goes back onto the street and double-checks the names on the list of residents, his gaze resting on the one he wants: *Roubíček.*

Jakub R walks inside, approaches the door and knocks.

Epilogue

I too have returned.

I sit at the table in the kitchen of 13 Biskupcova Street, where I smoked my first cigarette, where I picked at undercooked chicken, where I tore the wrapping paper from around a handcrafted marionette. Ludvík sits opposite me, beneath the portrait of his grandfather that has hung in place for over seventy years. Old Ludvík did not return and yet, from this story, only he remains. Here, where once they all gathered. Where we all have gathered.

'Do you still look?' Ludvík asks me.

'No,' I say.

'There are stories,' he says. 'More stories. Is time Babička…'

'It's enough,' I say. He nods and runs his hand along the table, sweeping crumbs onto the floor. I watch him bring his foot down, crushing them. He looks up. 'You hungry?'

I take in the room for the last time. I will be flying home tomorrow. I will try to make sense of all this, begin to write it down. *Within a few generations almost all of us will have been forgotten.*

I follow Ludvík into the sun. As I step onto the pavement, I breathe in a gust of spring. Out of the corner of my eye I catch a glint on the concrete and look down.

To know them as more than just names on brass stones/

that is enough.

Františka Roubíčková and the author, 1984.

A GUIDE TO CZECH PRONUNCIATION

Czech spelling and grammar are used throughout *The Book of Dirt.*

A, Á 'ah' as in *art.*

E, 'e' as in *bed.*

É 'eh' elongated 'e' as in *there.*

Ě 'yeh' as in *yesterday.*

I 'i' as in *hip.*

Í 'ee' elongated 'i' as in *marine.*

O 'oh' short 'aw' as in *water.*

Ó elongated 'aw' as in *poor.*

U 'u' as in *put.*

Ú, Ů 'oo' as in *root.*

Y 'ih' as in *syntax.*

Pl 'pul' as in *pulse.*

B 'bir' as in *birthday.*

C 'ts' as in *cats.*

Č 'ch' as in *church.*

Ch 'Kh', guttural Germanic sound as in *Bach.*

Ň 'ny', palatalised as in the Italian *Bolognese.*

R rolled *R* sound, as in Italian.

Ř 'rzh' where the sounds are pronounced almost simultaneously, the *R* rolling into a sound like the *S* in *measure.* Sometimes, such as with the composer Dvořák, there is more of a space between the syllables (*dvor-zhak*).

Š 'sh' as in *ship.*

T' 'ch' as in *tube.*

Ž 'zh' as in the *S* in *measure.*

Consecutive vowels in a word are pronounced separately.

The stress on almost every word falls on the first syllable. Accents might change pronunciation of the letters themselves but do not imply a change in the stress of the word as a whole.

Czech has three grammatical genders: masculine, feminine and neuter. In *The Book of Dirt*, female characters are named using their feminine forms (*-ová, -á*).

Ahoj—(Czech) Hello

Babička—(Czech) Grandmother.

Bar mitzvah—(Hebrew) Thirteen, the age at which a Jewish boy is considered a man.

Bat mitzvah—(Hebrew) Twelve, the age at which a Jewish girl is considered a woman.

Beit—(Hebrew) The second letter of the Hebrew alphabet. Has the consonant sound 'B'.

Beth Din—(Hebrew) Jewish religious court.

Bonkes—(Yiddish) Fanciful rumours.

Bris—(Hebrew) Colloquial for circumcision.

Cheder—(Hebrew) Religious study class.

Chevra Kadisha—(Hebrew) The Jewish Burial Society.

Dikduk—(Hebrew) Grammar.

Dybbuk—(Hebrew) 'The clinging of an evil spirit.' A ghost that possesses the body of a living person.

Elul—(Hebrew) The last month of the Jewish calendar, a time of repentence.

Genizah—(Hebrew) A room set aside for the storage of torn or damaged religious books and items.

Golem—(Hebrew) 'Shapeless man.' Humanoid created from dirt and animated through the mystical power of Hebrew letters.

Irgun—(Hebrew) Jewish paramilitary group in Palestine during the British Mandate.

Kambal—Camp slang for a nook in which inmates made private living spaces.

Kippah—(Hebrew) Head covering worn by Jewish men. Also known as a *yarmulke.*

Lamed—(Hebrew) The twelfth letter of the Hebrew alphabet. Has the consonant sound 'L'.

Lashon hara—(Hebrew) Malicious gossip against which there is a Jewish religious prohibition.

Mazal—(Hebrew) Luck.

Mazal tov—(Hebrew) 'Good luck' but used as a congratulatory cheer.

Mem—(Hebrew) The thirteenth letter of the Hebrew alphabet. Has the consonant sound 'M'.

Mezuzah—(Hebrew) A small parchment scroll containing religious verses that is affixed, usually in a protective case, to the door of a Jewish home.

Mikveh—(Hebrew) Ritual bath used for purification.

Mitzvah—(Hebrew) A good deed.

Neshamah—(Hebrew) Soul.

Pan—(Czech) Mr.

Paní—(Czech) Mrs. Also used to address an older single or divorced woman.

Payes—(Yiddish) Sidelocks. It is custom not to cut the hair that grows from near the temple.

Purim—(Hebrew) A joyous Jewish festival that commemorates the salvation of the Jewish people in Persia from a plot by the king's adviser to kill them all. Purim is celebrated by dressing in colourful costume, drinking and feasting.

Rebbetzin—(Hebrew) The wife of a rabbi.

Rosh Hashanah—Jewish New Year.

Sefer Yetzirah—(Hebrew) The Book of Formations, a classic Jewish mystical text.

Shacharit—(Hebrew) The Morning Prayer Service.

Shalom Zacher—(Hebrew) Celebratory gathering to welcome a baby boy. Usually held on the first Sabbath evening following the birth.

Shammas—(Hebrew) Synagogue beadle.

Sheds and *Mazziks*—(Hebrew) Types of demons in Jewish mythology.

Shema—(Hebrew) One of the holiest Jewish prayers: 'Hear O Israel, the Lord is our God, the Lord is one.' It is often said when anticipating death.

Shikse—(Yiddish) Derogatory term for a non-Jewish woman.

Shiva—(Hebrew) Seven days of mourning following a death.

Shloshim—(Hebrew) The service to mark the thirtieth day since a person's death.

Shtibl—(Yiddish) 'Little room.' A small Hasidic synagogue.

Siddur—(Hebrew) Prayer book.

SOKOL—(Czech) Youth movement dedicated to a 'strong mind in a strong body'. Much of the youth resistance during the occupation was centred around and coordinated through SOKOL clubs.

Stracheldraht—(German) 'Barbed wire.' The dried vegetable leaves that did not soften when thrown into the watery soup.

Svíčková—(Czech) Beef stewed in cream sauce.

Taf—(Hebrew) The last letter of the Hebrew alphabet. Has the consonant sound 'T'.

Tallis—(Hebrew) A traditional prayer shawl.

Tashlich—(Hebrew) Service after Jewish New Year where 'sins' are cast into flowing water.

Techelet Lauan—(Hebrew) 'Blue white.' Czech Zionist youth group.

Tefillin—(Hebrew) Leather phylacteries worn on the head and arm during morning prayer.

Tishrei—(Hebrew) The first month of the Jewish calendar.

Torah—(Hebrew) The Old Testament, Five Books of Moses.

Tzitzis—(Hebrew) Tassles that hang from a prayer shawl.

V Boj—(Czech) *The Struggle*. The main newspaper of the Czech underground during the occupation.

Yom Kippur—(Hebrew) Day of Atonement, the holiest day of the Jewish year.

Zeli—(Czech) Sauerkraut.

A NOTE ON HISTORICAL SOURCES

Although *The Book of Dirt* is a novel, it makes use of a number of original historical images and documents. The family photographs, photographs taken at significant locations, and scans of official documents speak for themselves. In the interests of transparency and historical fidelity, however, I should comment on the newspaper article and various letters and emails that appear in the book.

The article 'Dr Jacob Randa and the Books of the Extinct Race' is a greatly condensed rewrite of 'A Strange Scholarship' by Sam (Shmuel) Bennett that appeared in the *Australian Jewish News* on Friday, 19 March 1999 (although in the novel I have made it 2005). Bennett's article was a reworking of a chapter in his book of collected journalism, *Chronicles of a Life*, which was itself an expansion of a piece he had written in Yiddish for *Di Oystralische Yidishe Nayes* (the Yiddish supplement of the *Australian Jewish News*) in 1987 that was syndicated in Yiddish newspapers around the world. I have tried my best not to alter the substance of the article. There was, however, one exception: I changed the third museum worker from Rabbi Šimon Adler to Otto Muneles in order to contain the book to the characters already introduced. As both Adler and Muneles were members of the *Talmudkommando* I felt comfortable taking that liberty.

The extracts of correspondence between Jan Randa and Beit Terezín and Yad Vashem in Part Two appear in the novel exactly as they were written but for one word. In his initial letters, my grandfather referred to the *Talmudkommando* as '*Talmudhundertschaft*'. This accords with the German grammatical naming structure of many work groups in Theresienstadt. For the sake of consistency (and given that I refer to it by its two other official names), I thought it best to just use *Talmudkommando*, the term by which it is most commonly known.

The 'Merzdorf Letters' in Part Three (including the letter around which Chapter 11 of Numbers is structured) were written by Daša and Irena in pencil on brittle, grainy paper. That they survived is thanks only to Hana

Košťálová (née Roubíčková) who hid them in a shoebox at the back of a cupboard for sixty years. The translated extracts in the book are transcribed almost verbatim. I did make a couple of minor edits, removing the names of several people whom the girls asked after in Prague. There were also a couple of references to people from the neighbourhood who had been in the various camps with Daša and Irena. For example, the line I wrote as *We were where all transports from T go...* reads, in the original letter, 'We were where Hugo is (all transports from T go there)...' In making these slight edits, I have endeavoured not to change the meaning in any substantial way.

The various emails are extracted verbatim from the originals, edited only for style. One change was made—the name of the museum director.

All other letters, including those between Františka and Emílie, the postcards sent from Daša to Františka in Chapter 3 of Numbers, correspondence between Jakub and Georg, and the postcard from Shmuel in Birkenau, were written by me. I hope that I've been true to their voices.

Maps

MAP OF THERESIENSTADT (TEREZÍN)

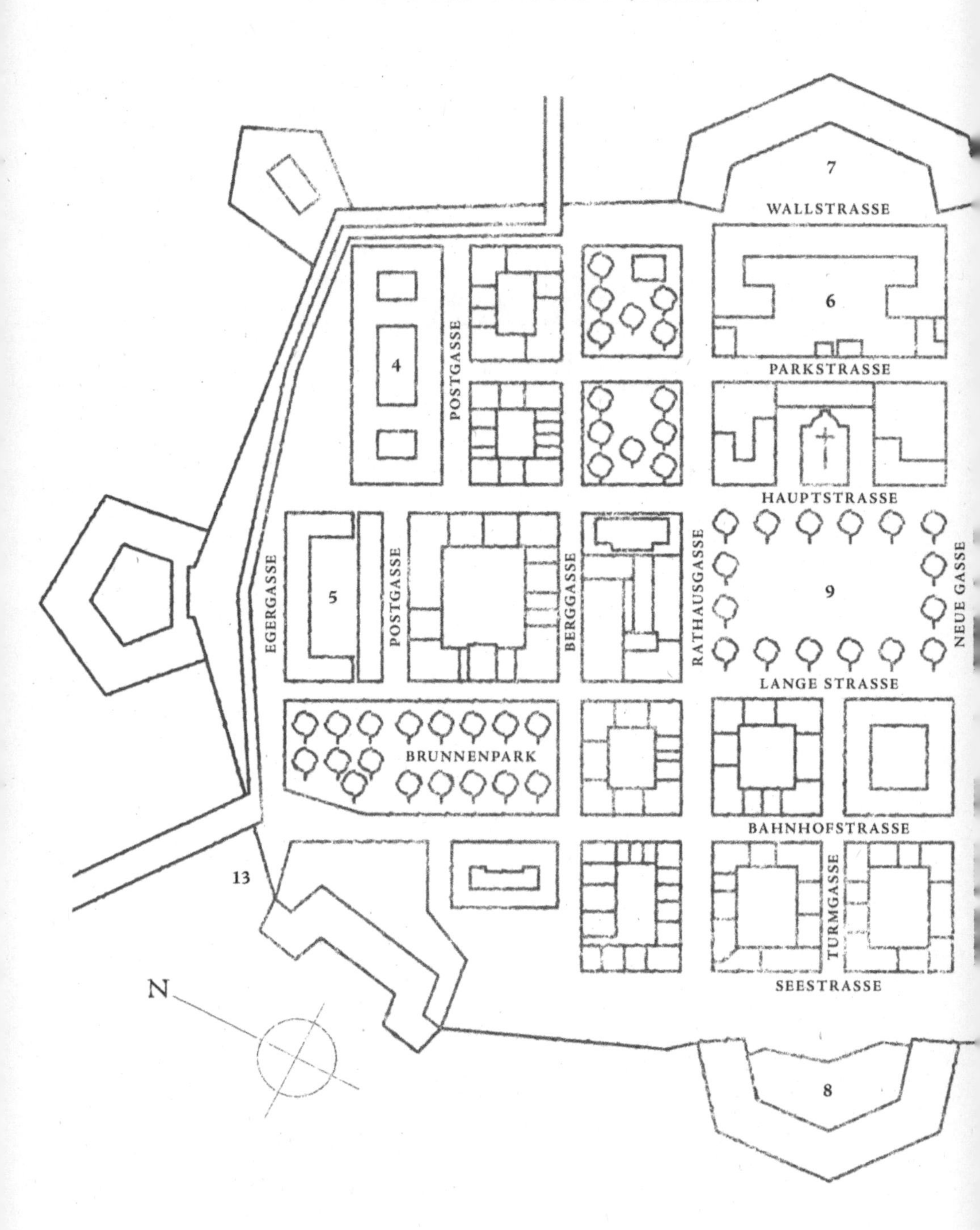

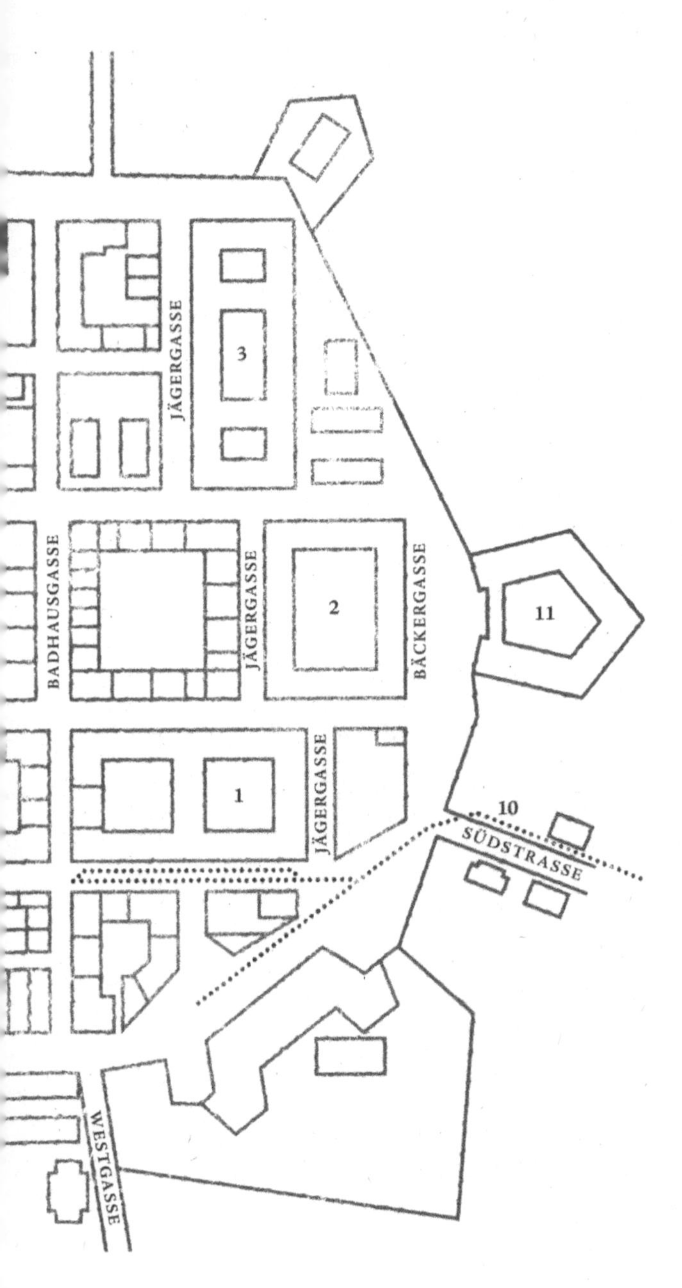

1 Hamburg Barracks

2 Hannover Barracks

3 Magdeberg Barracks

4 Dresden Barracks

5 Bodenbach Barracks (The arrival sluice)

6 Hohenelbe Barracks (The hospital)

7 Kavalier Barracks (The mental hospital)

8 Sudeten Barracks

9 Town Square

10 Südstrasse (The road to the *Klärenstalt* and Bohušovice)

11 Bakery and foodstore

12 The café (during beautification period)

13 Third Bastion

MAP OF BIRKENAU (AUSCHWITZ II)

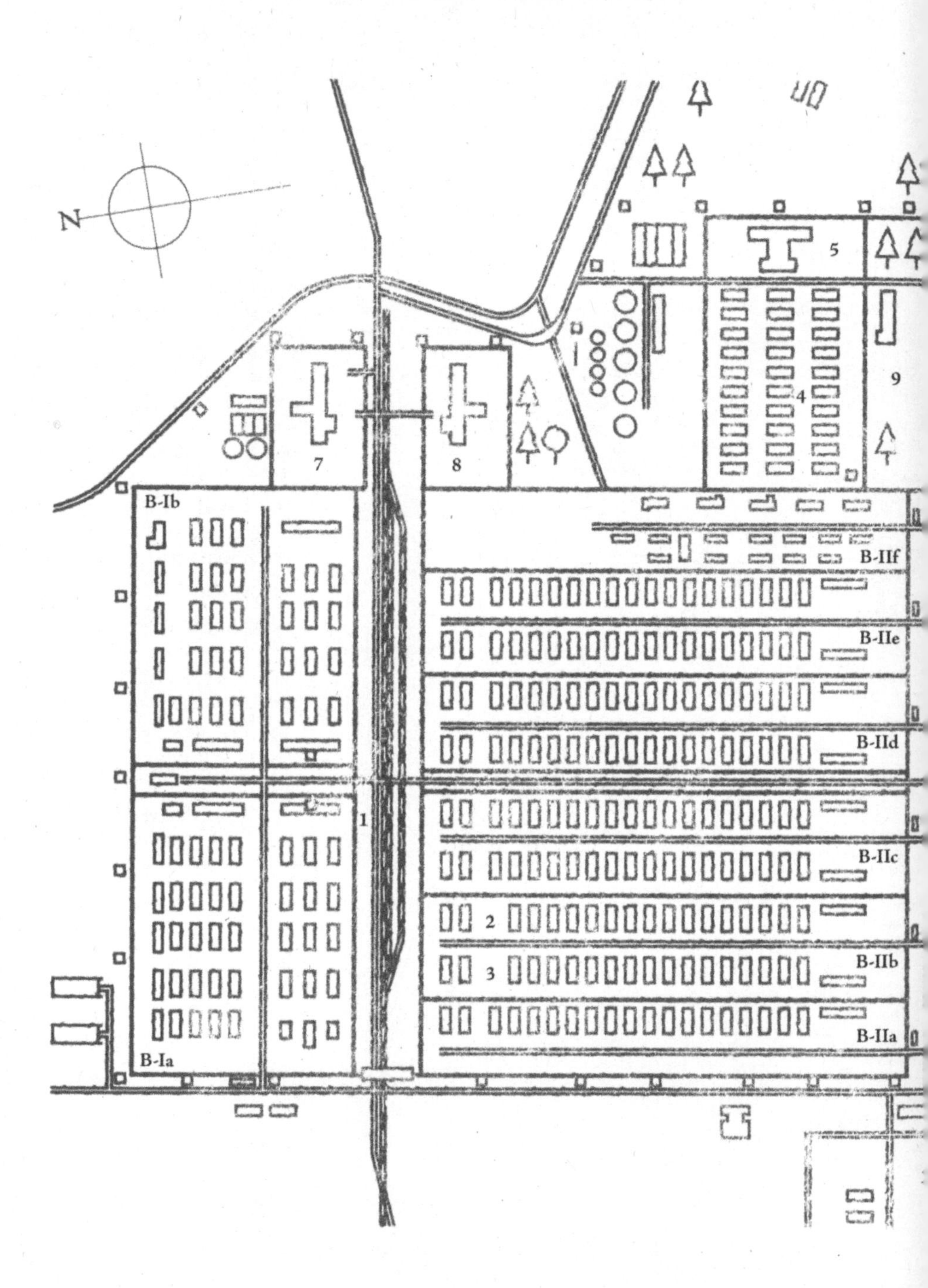

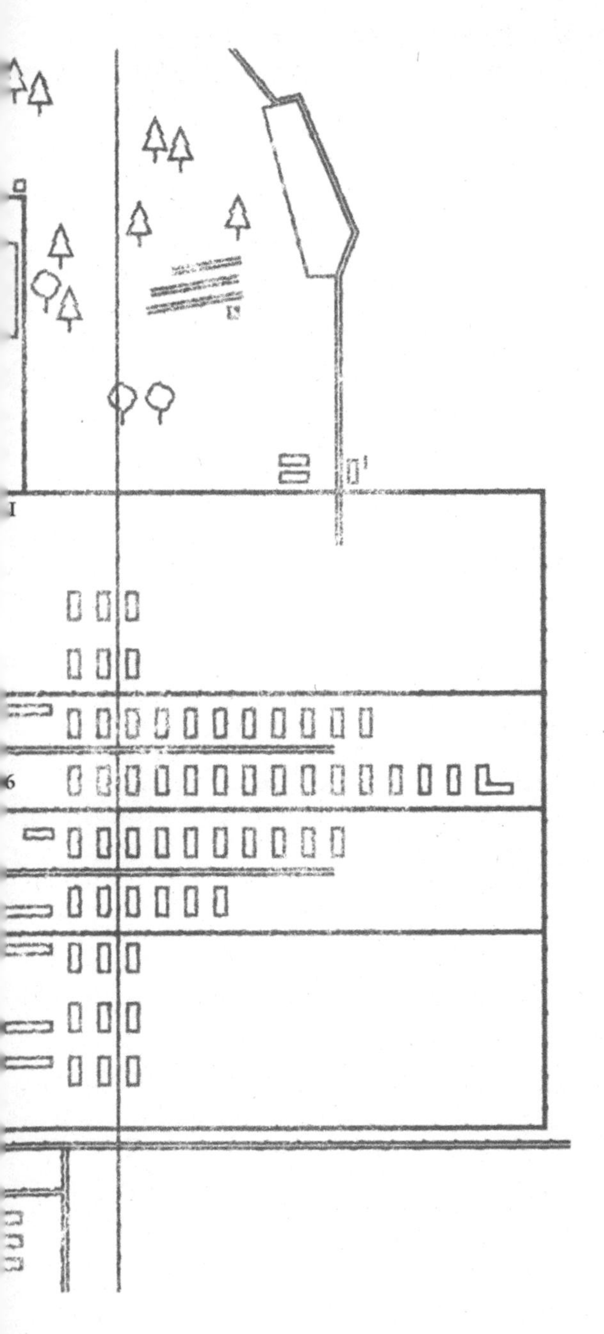

BIa	Men's Camp (until 1943), later Women's Camp
BIb	Women's Camp
BIIb	Czech Family Camp (until July 1944)
BIId	Men's Camp (after 1943)
BIIe	Gypsy Camp (until August 1944), thereafter miscellaneous use as holding/transit camp

1 Selection Ramp (as of 1944)

2 The Medical Block (Block 32 of BIIb)

3 The Children's Block (Block 31 of BIIb)

4 The Kanada Barracks

5 The Sauna

6 The Incomplete 'Mexico' Camp

7 Krema II (gas chamber and crematorium)

8 Krema III (gas chamber and crematorium)

9 Krema IV (gas chamber and crematorium, destroyed in *Sonderkommando* revolt, 7 October 1944)

10 Krema V (gas chamber and crematorium)

LIST OF IMAGES

ACKNOWLEDGMENTS

First and foremost, I wish to thank my grandparents, Dr Jan and Daša Randa, and my great grandmother, Františka Roubíčková. I hope that I have done justice to your stories.

To Frank Bright and Ludvík Košťál: without your help this book would never have been written. Thanks for opening doors I didn't know existed. Thanks also to Jarka and Petra Košťálová, who were very much a part of this adventure even if they didn't make it into the book itself.

Many thanks to Louise Swinn and Zoe Dattner at Sleepers (RIP), Jason Steger at the *Age*, the *Australian Jewish News*, the Australian Society of Authors, Magda Veselská and Michal Bušek at the Jewish Museum of Prague, Piotr Supiński at the Auschwitz Museum Archives, Alfons Adam, Andrea Jelínková, Julia Reichstein and the Jewish Holocaust Centre, Martina Stolbova, Michele Nayman (my feet and eyes in Prague after I'd left), Shira Nayman, Will Heyward, Mieke Chew, Emma Schwarcz, Daniel Kovacs, Adrian Elton, Zev and Marg at Sunflower Bookshop (RIP), Oliver Driscoll and the Slow Canoe team, Janine, Noè, Esther and my partners in crime at Melbourne Jewish Book Week, Justine and Michael at Sydney Jewish Writers Festival, Myki and Briony at *Vice Magazine*, Arnold Zable, Alec Patrić, Kristin Otto, Leah Kaminsky, Lee Koffman, Alex Skovron, Elliot Perlman, Kevin Rabalais, Miles Allinson, Gerard Elson, Howard Goldenberg, Raphael Brous, Steven Amsterdam, Eli Glasman, Daša Drndić, Nir Baram, Mireille Juchau, Antoni Jach and Team Shred (Rocket, Flix, Mads, Marion, Josh, Lachy and Rachel), Tali Lavi, Mark Baker, Dr Leo Kretzenbacher, Dr Timo Lorenz, Vera Hasen, Stens Silavecky, Paul Bartrop, Mark Rubbo, Chris Redfern, Clifford Posner, Josh Gurgiel, Idan Dershowitz, Matthue Roth, Ron and Brett Tait, Rabbi Yaakov Glasman, the always fine Debbie Miller, Tim Byrne, Luke Turbutt, Amy Vuleta, Daniel Carroll, Suze Stein, Kate McFadyen, James Ley and Peter Haskin.

Much of *The Book of Dirt* was written in the creative hub that is Glenfern. Thanks to Adriane Howell and the team at Writers Victoria for giving me the space and, particularly, for awarding me the Grace Marion

Wilson Fellowship so that I could shut the world out and finally finish the thing! And to Iola and my Glenfern crew (Jim, Janine, Fiona, Bel, Jacinta, Andrew, Erin, Caroline and Amelia). I can think of no one with whom I'd rather share a haunted house.

Finally, thanks to my families both new and old: Penny, Michael, Alice, Chong, Jess and everyone at Text, my parents, Dan and Eva, my brother Justin, Grandma Ruby and Pop (in loving memory), Randi, Dari, Louie, the Cohens and Bernstein-Cohens, and Tim Hulse. And, of course, Debbie: I wish I could dedicate this book to you a thousand times over but even that would not be enough to express my love and gratitude. So I hope you'll make do with one at the beginning and one at the end.